"Coughlin and Davis hit the action-adventure 10-ring again." —*Kirkus Reviews*

"Former Marine sniper Coughlin stretches but does not strain credulity in this intricate story that aptly illustrates the maxim 'no plan survives contact with the enemy.'" —*Publishers Weekly*

## CLEAN KILL

"The pages fly by as Swanson must face his most personal mission yet. The military tactics take a backseat to the characters, creating a strong and compelling narrative. Coughlin and Davis have concocted another winner that should only encourage a growing readership." —*Booklist*

"Former Marine Coughlin and bestseller Davis combine a well-paced, credible plot with a realistic portrayal of modern combat . . . The climax . . . will leave readers cheering." —*Publishers Weekly*

## DEAD SHOT

"Compelling." —*Publishers Weekly*

"The [plot] propels the pages forward, but this one isn't all about action: Swanson proves a surprisingly complex character . . . *Dead Shot* suggest[s] a hardware-heavy story that only an armed-services veteran could love.

Surprisingly, it's completely the opposite. Readers will be compelled . . . and will look forward to another Swanson adventure." —*Booklist*

## KILL ZONE

"Stunning action, excellent tradecraft, insider politics, and the ring of truth. Just about perfect." —Lee Child

"Tight, suspenseful . . . Here's hoping this is the first of many Swanson novels." —*Booklist*

"The action reaches a furious pitch."

—*Publishers Weekly*

## SHOOTER
The Autobiography of the Top-Ranked Marine Sniper

"One of the best snipers in the Marine Corps, perhaps the very best. When I asked one of his commanders about his skills, the commander smiled and said, 'I'm just glad he's on our side.'"

—Peter Maass, war-correspondent and
bestselling author of *Love Thy Neighbor*

"The combat narratives here recount battlefield action with considerable energy . . . A renowned sniper, Coughlin is less concerned with his tally than with the human values of comradeship and love."

—*The Washington Post*

# LONG SHOT

A S N I P E R
N O V E L

GUNNERY SGT. **JACK COUGHLIN,**
USMC (RET.)

WITH **DONALD A. DAVIS**

St. Martin's Paperbacks

LONG SHOT

Copyright © 2016 by Jack Coughlin with Donald A. Davis.
Excerpt from *In the Crosshairs* Copyright © 2017 by Jack Coughlin with Donald A. Davis.

For information address St. Martin's Press, 175 Fifth Avenue, New York, NY 10010.

ISBN: 978-1-250-13023-5

Printed in the United States of America

St. Martin's Press hardcover edition / August 2016
St. Martin's Paperbacks edition / May 2017

St. Martin's Paperbacks are published by St. Martin's Press, 175 Fifth Avenue, New York, NY 10010.

10  9  8  7  6  5  4  3  2  1

# LONG
# SHOT

ROME, ITALY

**THIS HAD TO** be a head shot. Under normal circumstances, a sniper goes for the chest, which not only provides a larger area and is thus an easier target, but the chest also is the gateway to the vital organs of the body. A big bullet in there goes spinning and bouncing around, breaking bones and shearing veins and pulping muscles, and collapsing the frail human machine that made life possible. Kyle Swanson knew that as he ignored the easy shot and instead dialed in on the head of Roland Lewis Martin from Bellwood, Indiana. The CIA sniper knew a lot of other things, the total of which meant that young Mister Martin had richly earned the .50-caliber bullet that would soon tear off his entire skull and leave his quivering body with a bloody stump of a neck.

Martin was a nice-looking young man, at least as seen through the powerful scope mounted on the Excalibur sniper rifle. Only twenty-nine years old, he still had the muscular build of his days being an offensive tackle on the Bellwood High Blue Jackets football team. The continued physical conditioning was a testament to the exercise he had received in his years of fighting for ISIS, the murderous Islamic State jihadists. His hair was black and cut short, and his cheeks wore a stubble of beard. The broad nose had been broken twice, healed a bit crookedly, and his teeth gleamed plastic and bright after so many caps and root canals. His white cotton shirt was open at the neck, showing the deep tan. The sleeves were rolled up, exposing the blue tattoo of a snake that coiled from his wrist to his elbow on the right arm. Martin had picked that up in Yokohama during his short career in the U.S. Navy, which had taught him computer science. The black slacks were clean and pressed, with matching socks and leather loafers. A tiny earring twinkled on the left lobe. The tip of his left little finger was missing due to a childhood tractor accident. In all, he looked pretty good; a capable poster boy for ISIS, a former cold-blooded killer turned recruiter.

Swanson had decided to use the new clear polymer-encased M33 ball ammunition for the job instead of the standard brass, primarily for the lighter weight. The 687-grain bullet was a shade under five and a half inches in length, would leave the muzzle at a velocity of 11,091 foot-pounds of energy to cover the 200 yards to the head of young Mister Martin in only two-tenths of a second, actually .231 seconds. It would strike with enough power to take down a tree. The plastic covering on the bullet interested Swanson. Trying out new things was part of his day job.

Rain was on the way and the air seemed heavy, even apprehensive, as if the weather knew something was going to happen and wanted to serve up an appropriate background of thunder and lightning. The skies would burst and the dark clouds would empty and the Eternal City of Rome would be cleansed once again. So far, not a drop. That was a good thing. The three young people at the table of the sidewalk café could remain outside, talking, as the ISIS recruiter slowly reeled in his catches in the sunlight. The sniper watched as a girl with long brown hair leaned close to Martin. She appeared to be in her midteens. Her friend, a brunette only a couple of years older, snapped their smiling picture on her cell phone, then showed it to them. They all laughed. Martin topped off the wineglasses of his American visitors. An unfolded street map of Rome lay on the table.

From his prone position on the third floor of a rather common yellow neoclassical villa on Quirinal Hill, Kyle Swanson could see an edge of the elegant Trevi Fountain, into which the girls and Martin had tossed a few coins and wishes before they all settled in at the corner café a few blocks away. It was hard to find a place from where you could not see any monuments or splendid ruins in Rome, for they were everywhere, old stones with stories to tell. The three million people in the city passed through the historic paths with a leisurely pace that was bred into them. Nothing ever happened fast in Italy. The brothers Romulus and Remus probably took their time while being suckled by the she-wolf in the founding legend. The dolce vita was the city's charm, and it was practiced from the Vatican to the Coliseum. Of course, Romulus murdered his brother later on. Brutus assassinated his good buddy Julius Caesar. Various Popes were poisoned, strangled, stabbed and one was thrown into the sea with an anchor tied around his neck. Life was not the most expensive thing in Italy.

"One minute," said the spotter beside Kyle. A dark-haired Oklahoman with the lean build of a marathon runner, Dan Laird had been with the CIA Directorate of Clandestine Operations for almost five years after leaving Delta Force, and was no stranger to pressure. He was busy handling the spotting scope, the cameras and the communications. "Everything in the green."

"Umm," Swanson hummed in reply. He breathed with his mouth open slightly, feeding measurable amounts of oxygen into lungs that had been conditioned by years of aerobic training. His heart rate was under control, with his pulse steady at forty-five beats per minute. His mind was clear, focused as much as his eyes. A lot of things could go wrong in a minute, or even in a second. The fleshy tip of his right index finger rested lightly on the trigger of the long rifle, and the world before him was in slow motion. The target was right where he was supposed to be, his back to the street, unmoving in his chair, nothing beyond him but a meticulously parked truck that would eat the big bullet. The wanted terrorist filled his scope, but Swanson ignored that fact, for to dwell on the madness of this evil man might have stirred the sniper's emotion, and that might alter the target picture; this was no time for buck fever.

Young Mister Martin had been dug out by the intelligence analysts of the Central Intelligence Agency some months ago, and at first they did not realize who they had found. He had been posting in chat rooms and using American idioms to woo impressionable girls in the United States into coming to visit him. *Don't believe all of that crap in the media. All Muslims aren't evil just because there are a few crazies. Look at me! Do I look crazy or scary? Come on over for a visit and we'll have some fun in Rome.* His accompanying picture showed a handsome guy leaning against a white Mercedes convertible beside a beautiful beach. The man was a hashtag Romeo, and several American girls who had bought his Twitter act never returned home again. Once ensnared abroad, it was simple enough to drug them and smuggle them straight across the Tyrrhenian Sea to Tunisia and into lost lives they would never have imagined in their most horrible nightmares.

But as the ISIS trolls reached out for new brides and potential agents in the United States, the terrorist group was itself being trolled by even better hackers who were on the payrolls of many governments, and those were the bleary-eyed wizards who had hooked Roland Lewis Martin. When his picture beside the luxury car was studied, it was determined to be a Photoshop digital stage set. That aroused enough suspicion to wash it through multiple facial-recognition and other identification databases, which pointed up the blue snake tattoo, the missing fingertip and the pierced ear, matched his height, erased the beard, fixed the proper eye color by erasing the contact lenses, chalked in personality traits, and discovered that this target was really Abdul Ansari Mohammad, the jihadi American who had decapitated a captured U.S. journalist in Iraq on live video.

Washington moved to set the trap, and tagged Swanson to do the hit. For many years, he had been the deadliest sniper in the U.S. Marine Corps, where he was the trigger-puller for a top-secret special ops team known as Task Force Trident, and won the Congressional Medal of Honor and a salad of other decorations. That was all in the past, and while his current day job was vice president of the multinational defense industrial company called Excalibur Enterprises, he had another job, too. Like Laird, he performed special missions for the CIA.

With the cover of being a businessman, it was easy for him to arrange a business trip to Rome without arousing suspicion. The rest of the team was waiting for him there, including the two women operatives who would act as the bait. They were made up to appear to be in their late teens, although both were college graduates.

The girls rendezvoused with Martin at the famous Trevi, a magnet for tourists, and guided him to the nearby sidewalk café. He planned to take them out later for dinner and a sightseeing trip around Rome by night. It had worked before, and he had a confident swagger as they reached the table, which had been set aside by the cooperating Italian police, the Agenzia Informazioni e Sicurezza Interna, or AISI, one of whom had become their waiter. Martin took the chair beside the street so his guests could watch the passing throng. The opening chit-chat was friendly.

"Thirty seconds." Dan Laird pressed a button on his cell phone, and the phone in the back pocket of one of the girls vibrated silently. Swanson watched the agent casually dab her lips with a white napkin, then say something to her girlfriend. She never looked up to locate the sniper. Her friend asked Martin where the bathrooms were located. He pointed inside, the two women smiled, promised to be right back, and pushed out of their chairs. The waiter also vanished. There were no other customers, and police a block away were quietly detouring tourists around the site. Martin, confident of his quarry and very pleased with himself, did not realize that he was alone on the street. He took a drink, fished his own phone from a pocket to send a coded message that once again, the kidnap operation was going very well.

"Area is clear. He's all yours." Laird's words were businesslike, but Kyle could sense the tension and his peripheral vision caught the agent's hands moving to cover his ears. Kyle preferred not to wear ear coverings, balancing the need to hear what was going on around him against the unconscious anticipation of a loud explosion.

Swanson had no further adjustments to make. The head was as big as a Halloween pumpkin in the scope, and steady. He slowly brought the trigger straight back with no lateral pressure, felt the slack disappear, and then came the explosion as the sniper rifle boomed. A .50-cal shot in the tight confines of an urban center sounded like a cannon blast, and the first thought of unaware people who heard it was that a terrorist bomb had been detonated. Pedestrians and tourists scattered, and pigeons soared away in flapping panic. Sirens began to whoop. Kyle soaked up the mighty recoil and brought the glass back on target.

The body of Roland Martin had been jerked almost out of the chair, but was still in it, canted sideways over the strong metal arm. The head was gone and the debris of the skull and brains had spewed in a long trail toward the parked truck.

"Done," he said.

"Done," agreed his spotter. Laird kept the camera recording as police vehicles wailed up to the curb, uniformed cops set up a perimeter and as soon as the two women came out, they were roughly arrested and cuffed and put into a marked van. That was part of the show in case ISIS had a watcher. The pair of agents was released as soon as they were out of sight.

"Strange," said Dan Laird, looking at his cell phone as Kyle packed away the rifle. A police car was waiting for them downstairs.

"The boss is in town."

"Marty?" Martin Atkins, the deputy director of clandestine operations, was long past his days as a field officer, but ran the secretive clandestine operations department with meticulous planning, including the care and protection of agents at the sharp end of the dark CIA spear. From the Agency headquarters in Langley, Virginia, Atkins was like a spider in his web, controlling everything, and he seldom left it.

"Yeah. Probably wants a firsthand briefing on this op."

Swanson had the Excalibur safely in its case and was straightening his clothes as Laird finished packing. "Maybe he wants to post that video on the Net. The op was symbolic and intended to remind those ISIS crazies that we can and will reach out and touch them whenever we please."

Laird gave a deep laugh. "It would go viral in ten minutes. Let the social media pass the word for us."

They took their time getting downstairs. Nobody was hunting them because the cops were in on the action, although they had not been told any more than they needed to know. The small unmarked car that met them had another agent at the wheel, and Swanson and Laird climbed into the rear seat. Kyle started thinking about dinner tonight, wanting something special before he and Laird left tomorrow to take out another ISIS recruiter, a British predator operating out of Cairo whose game was convincing gullible American kids to come visit the pyramids in Egypt.

The Agency safe house was west of the Tiber River in the working-class neighborhood of Trastevere, far from the grandeur of the Vatican but equally a part of Rome, a city that was saddled with a Madonna-whore complex. The people who served the upper-crust Italians and rich tourists had to live somewhere, too, and the squalid apartments along the tangled medieval streets of Trastevere had housed them for generations. The CIA had a multistory building with a middle-aged Italian couple living on the street level, where the stew was always warm in the little kitchen and the floor tiles were always chilly. Marty Atkins was waiting on the upper floor in a soundproofed room that had bulletproof glass in the window and was examined for electronic eavesdropping equipment daily.

His gray hair had grown out since the last time Kyle had met with him several months ago, and the new style gave him a more distinguished look, an obvious loss of some weight had sharpened his features. Laser surgery on his brown eyes meant he no longer wore steel-rimmed glasses. Atkins had figured out that further advancement in government required that he moderate his former hell-for-leather lifestyle and look like a gentleman when meeting politicians. His temper still needed work.

He was reading briefing papers when they entered, and put them aside to greet his visitors warmly. There was a tenseness about him, and a sense of apprehension. "Dan, hate to seem rude here, but I need some private time with Kyle. If you go on over to the hotel, I'll spring for drinks for everybody in about thirty minutes."

Laird shrugged. "Free drinks sounds good. Can I ask if this concerns tomorrow's mission?"

Atkins exhaled and shook his head. "Yes. That job is not going to happen."

Dan Laird had been around the Agency long enough to know when he was a supernumerary. Only two people were to be part of this conversation, and Laird made three. Counterintelligence was a fluid, ever-changing game. Nothing personal. Just part of the job. He winked and left without another word. They would tell him what he needed, when necessary.

Atkins motioned Swanson to an awkward overstuffed chair beside the table near the window, and picked up one of the briefing papers he had been reading. He studied the sniper. "Do you know a Russian by the name of Strakov? Ivan Strakov?"

Swanson did not recall the name immediately, but slowly an image swam into shape. Long ago, there was an intense, skinny enlisted man on an exchange training program between Russian naval infantry and the U.S. Marines. He wanted to be an elite sniper. Kyle, as the instructor, washed him out of the program because of poor shooting scores and had ordered him to undergo a thorough medical examination. The Russian had been hiding the fact that his vision was failing, but the scores spoke for themselves. He was a lousy shot. Strakov could no longer hack it, which meant the end of his career in the Russian marines.

"Yeah. I remember him, vaguely. Very intelligent and great with numbers, but so bad with a long gun that we called him Ivan the Terrible."

"This is beyond top secret, Kyle," Marty Atkins said

as he handed over the one-page memo of a few short paragraphs.

Kyle read it, then slid the paper back onto the table. "When do I leave?"

"Go back to the hotel and shit, shine, shower and shave, then you're outta here."

"Where am I going?"

"You don't need to know that yet. Call me when you get there."

**S**WANSON FONDLY REMEMBERED the days when he traveled so lightly that a duffel bag and a ValPak could hold everything he owned, from shaving cream to shoes, and how he had gotten along quite well. The U.S. Marine Corps furnished almost everything he needed, all the way up to formal dress blues. That, however, was a long-ago yesterday, before he switched over to the Central Intelligence Agency. Now it felt as though he required not only a hotel cart and a bellhop, but a mule train and a couple of Sherpas to carry his luggage. The handcrafted small suitcase, the medium suitcase and the large suitcase were accompanied by a matching suit bag, all made of tough leather with brass trim. The set cost more than most people earned in a month. It was the stamp of success. It was part of his cover.

Kyle had changed into a pin-striped gray suit with a deep gold tie imbedded with subdued green dots, brushed his styled sandy brown hair into place and transformed into somebody who did not at all resemble the sharpshooter who had just blown off the head of a terrorist. Instead, he was back to his day job of being the executive vice president of Excalibur Enterprises, a globe-trotting salesman with cold gray-green eyes and an intolerance for business screwups. He could go almost anywhere in the world, hidden in plain view as just another American millionaire with attitude. A stranger's first impression was that Swanson was to be avoided, if for no other reason than he was an unpleasant jerk. The bankroll was provided by the company, his own salary and private holdings, plus a CIA slush fund.

"I still think you look goofy when you get all dolled up like a Eurotrash gigolo," Dan Laird said, chewing a toothpick while driving Kyle to the Ciapino airport. Cars and trucks and motorbikes passed in an unending river, and the eyes of the two agents snapped through the throng, always looking for potential trouble. In Rome, they mostly saw only Italian men in suits puttering along on scooters with pretty girls clinging to their waists.

"Still feels strange, too. I can still kick your butt, though."

"Never happen. And I would not want to get blood on your pretty shirt. Where you going, or can I ask?"

"You can ask, but I'm not supposed to tell you, which is easy because I don't know myself." The car radio was droning some anonymous instrumental and Kyle punched the audio system to scan for an all-news station off the satellite. He found one, but there was nothing out of the ordinary; not even a report yet about their hit in Rome. No mention of Ivan Strakov.

A Gulfstream V jet, a bland bluish-gray machine almost invisible in the ground clutter of any airport, had its engines humming when they arrived at the combination civilian and military facility, where a pair of uniformed enlisted men placed the expensive luggage in the bird's cargo hold with a great deal more care than they would have shown ordinary bags. Swanson stepped aboard, hung up his coat, picked out a comfortable seat, stuffed his laptop overhead and strapped himself in; the hull was sealed and the plane began to taxi. Dan Laird, with a placid, almost bored, look on his face, peeled the plastic wrap from another toothpick and watched the little jet climb into the sky and disappear.

When it finally reached altitude and steadied into a course, Kyle knew they were headed north. That was not very helpful, since most of the entire boot of Italy lay north of Rome, and then Europe, and eventually, the North Pole. The flight could be going anywhere. He got his laptop down and plugged it into a charger in the arm-rest, opened the word processing program, found the folder containing information on the new company's polymer-encased bullet experiment.

Excalibur Enterprises was on the cutting edge of weapons development, and any possible reduction of weight was always an attractive element for a soldier. The average American infantryman, when all geared up with comms, ammo, batteries, pack, water, rifle and other necessary items, carried about as much weight as a me-dieval knight's suit of armor. Having lugged more than his share of tonnage around a battle zone, Kyle knew how those loads seemed to increase at every step. Trim-ming fractions was important, and plastic cartridges were not only lighter than brass, but cheaper, too. Excali-bur could reap another fortune if it could get the bugs worked out and the patents approved.

His challenge was to report back to his boss-mentor and surrogate father, Sir Geoffrey Cornwell, the CEO of Excalibur, without leaving a word trail that might connect the company to today's murder. Having questions asked in Parliament or by a congressional investigating committee was to be avoided.

The locked door to the pilot's compartment clicked open, and Swanson looked up casually as a pilot in a U.S. Air Force flight suit stepped through, turned and locked it again. The major, on loan to the Central Intelligence Agency, wore no name tag. Kyle closed the laptop lid.

"Welcome aboard, sir," the flier said, leaning on the seatback in front of Kyle. "Take off your tie and make yourself comfortable. Drinks are in the aft refrigerator, including some of the harder stuff. Blankets are stowed in the overhead. We're going to be flying for several hours, so I am required to run through the emergency procedures for all passengers: If we crash at six hundred miles per hour, we're all going to die. It would be appreciated if you wouldn't scream a lot on the way down, because we will be busy up front with the parachutes."

"Thanks for that information, Major. You filed a flight plan, correct?" Swanson cocked an eyebrow.

"Yes, we did." The pilot walked back and grabbed a soda. "Want one of these?"

"Not right now. So it's not really a secret about where the plane is going, right? I know we are heading north, but that course could change at any time."

The pilot laughed, then took a pull of the cold drink. "No longer a secret, sir. We will continue on this heading all the way to Helsinki, tracked by the radars of about a half-dozen countries en route. There is no mystery to a straight line. Anyway, that's where you will get off. Other than that, I don't know nothing."

"Finland."

"An unusual destination, if I may say so."

"Yes. It is."

"Lots of blond young ladies and saunas. That could be a nice combination."

"Do pilots ever think of anything other than airplanes and sex?"

"What else is there?" The pilot grinned, turned and went back to steering his sleek contraption through the sky.

Kyle thought: *Finland?* He turned his attention back to the computer keypad and resumed drafting his carefully-worded report.

He did not remember drifting into the dreamless sleep, because he was exhausted after the long day that had started before sunrise in Rome. It was about midnight, local time, according to a clock on the bulkhead, when the pilot woke him up by announcing on a speaker in the main cabin, "Prepare for landing." Kyle went to the bathroom and washed his face and straightened his clothes, then he buckled back into the seat as the Gulfstream slid gracefully down over the dark Baltic Sea and touched down at the Helsinki-Vantaa International Airport. The aircraft rolled for a while to reach the military sector, which gave him time to pack away the computer, and check for his cell phone, wallet and cred pack.

The hatch opened to become a short stairway, and waiting at the bottom was a giant in an unbuttoned overcoat. He stood at least six-six and with the fur hat, he was about a foot taller than normal people, had a square jaw and a big chest. The man asked in a gravelly voice that came from a mouth that might break if he smiled, "Are you Swanson?"

"Yes." He knew the open coat would provide the man with easier access to a sidearm. Kyle wondered why that was necessary. Swanson was without a weapon of his own, and he considered that the man was a trained professional who had to weigh north of 260. "Who are you?"

"This way." The question was ignored as the escort stalked away toward a row of buildings. Most of the windows were dark, although the city lights lit the sky behind. To one side, a ground crew was working on an F/A-18 Hornet fighter outside a hangar and the pungent smell of jet fuel hung in the night air. Spring had not yet come to Finland in the first week of April, and Swanson felt the penetrating bite of wind freshly chilled from crossing the Arctic Ocean. By the time they reached the door, he was ready to go inside to just escape the weather. The big man allowed him through first. Swanson heard the metal *snick* of the lock.

At a small table in the middle of a windowless room sat a man with jowls of a bulldog, eyes of a basset hound and a burr of steel-gray hair like a terrier. A manila folder was open and Kyle recognized an old picture of himself in uniform clipped to the front. "You're Swanson," the man said.

"I am. Who are you?"

"Sit." It was a command, not an invitation.

Kyle was in no mood to be bullied. "No. I think I'll leave now. I'm tired after the long trip."

"You are not going anywhere," the man at the table

brusquely commanded, and the big escort stepped to block the locked door. "Not until you answer some questions."

"I need to make a call first." Swanson lifted his cell phone from his pocket, wrapping it in his hand so the bottom edge was visible.

"No calls until we're done. Hand over your cell."

"No."

"Take it away from him, James."

The large man reached forward. Swanson did not hesitate, for he knew that if that grizzly ever laid one of those big paws on him, the fight would be over. Kyle stepped inside as quickly as a snake, lashed out with his right fist, using the hard corner point of the phone like a set of brass knuckles. He whipped it hard into the man's mouth, gouged the bottom of the nose and then skidded it up to the right eye. When Swanson's right arm reached its full length, he hammered the phone point hard against the stunned man's temple, jerked him forward, kicked the right knee, and rode him down as he collapsed on his face. Swanson jerked the collar of the overcoat down over the shoulders to impede the arms, but the fight had already gone out of the man, who was woozy and semiconscious by the surprise attack. A quick search turned up a snubby Sig Sauer P229R in a belt holster and the gold and blue badge of a U.S. Diplomatic Security Service special agent.

The man behind the table had jumped to his feet during the two-second fight, his hands waving, and surprise written large on his face. "Whoa! Whoa-up. Easy, there. No need for that."

"Hell there isn't." Swanson held the 9mm pistol

loosely. "Put your weapon and your identification on the table. Go slow. Left hand only. Do it!"

"You just assaulted a federal agent. I should arrest you." The older man awkwardly spread out a worn leather cred case that contained the same kind of badge, and dropped another SIG on it.

"You're both DSS? I might have shot you." Swanson tossed the 9 mil pistol onto the table, reached over, grabbed the bleeding agent's elbow and pulled up. "Come on, big guy. Go to the bathroom and stuff a towel on your face. It's just a busted nose and a black eye, and maybe a torn ACL. You'll live."

The man stumbled to his feet, holding a hand to his bleeding nose. Instead of throwing another punch, he grinned. Special Agent Lem James did not lose many fights, had never given up his gun or his badge, and admired the quick, sure moves of the man who had just laid him out without breaking a sweat. "Thanks," he said. "Good idea with that phone thing." He limped away.

Kyle sat down, and the older agent did the same. The fire had been doused. "Why didn't you identify yourselves?" he asked.

"That was my call. A mistake, as it turns out." He adjusted his clothing, as if he had been interrupted at dinner. "I'm Bob Carver, the RSO at the Helsinki embassy. That is Special Agent Lem James in the bathroom."

"You knew I was on that plane, so you know I'm CIA."

"Yeah, Swanson." The DSS regional security officer patted the folder. "I know all about you, at least according to your personnel file, which has been filled with empty pages and scrubbed until it is virtually useless. I know only that you were born in Boston, spent a lot of years as a Marine, won a Congressional Medal of Honor, are a stone killer and think that rules don't apply to you. I do not know whether to trust you."

Swanson grunted. "That street goes both ways. Why didn't somebody from the CIA meet me?"

"I called in a personal favor to get a look at you before letting you step into my embassy. Since I work for the state department, that's my turf, and you spooks are all just visitors who come and go."

The big man came back into the room, a drenched towel held against the right side of his face, and took the third chair at the table. "Going to have to send my overcoat to the cleaners because of the bloodstains. Think you chipped my tooth, too, you fuckin' little monster. I saw stars." The words came in a friendly tone, professional muscle acknowledging another professional.

"Sorry," Kyle said. The man waved it off, refolded the towel and placed it back against the bruised and swelling cheek. To the RSO: "What do I need to do to make you believe that I can be trusted?"

"You passed that mark when you didn't blow my ass away a minute ago. Anyway, my core problem is that I already have a very strange character, a total walk-in, cooling his heels at the U.S. Embassy right now. He is a smooth bastard who says his name is Ivan Strakov, and that he is a Russian intelligence operative. He won't say anything else, and claims he will only talk to Kyle Swanson. I sure as hell don't know or trust him, and putting the two of you together wasn't going to happen until I was satisfied that it all isn't some setup. Understand?"

Swanson nodded as his memory pulled up Ivan Strakov. It was so long ago that the picture was fuzzy. "OK. That makes sense. I haven't seen or heard from this guy in about twenty years, back when I was in the Marines and he was an enlisted man in the Russian naval infantry. I have no idea what he has been doing since then, or why he picked my name out of the hat. Let me ask: Is he in a rush, or nervous, or acting urgent?"

Carver put his hands behind his head and looked up at the ceiling briefly. "No. Like I said, he is cool. Just waiting to see if you turn up. We have him in a private little facility within the embassy right now and are treating him well."

Kyle nodded again, coming to a decision. "I don't want to deal with the Russian tonight. I started early today way down in Italy and have ended it brawling with Shrek here, and I'm bushed. Let me get some sleep before starting the game tomorrow morning."

Bob Carver agreed. "Just watch your six while you're in town, Swanson. The place is crawling with Russian intel people. Tensions are high."

"I'll drive you to the hotel," said Lem James, throwing aside the bloody towel. "You need to buy me a drink to make amends."

## HELSINKI

**A** **MESSAGE WAS** waiting when Swanson checked into the Hotel Kämp on the Norra Esplanaden. He signed the registration, directed that his luggage be placed in his suite and went to join Lem James at a back table in the bar that overlooked the sweep of a park reaching down to the waterfront. The place did not close until one in the morning, so they had about an hour. James had already downed his first Mannerheim's shot and had one of the icy vodka blends waiting for Kyle. The glass was filled to the very brim, a local custom that made sure everyone received an equal pour. It packed a kick.

> *Colonel Max Piikkilä will be delighted to meet with Mister Swanson of Excalibur Enterprises at 1400 hours at the Ministry of Defence—Janna.*

Kyle let James also read the note, then put it back in the envelope. "Now I have an official reason for being here.

I'm just a salesman peddling product to the country's director of procurement of defense matériel."

"You may not be through at the embassy by then," James commented, then ordered another round of Mannerheims.

"No choice, Lem. I'm no spy. I'm a specialist, like an independent contractor, on call when needed. Otherwise, I am a businessman. The Agency and my office manager, Janna, apparently set up this meeting on the fly to give me at least a bit of legitimate cover. I will take a break from the embassy thing if necessary, go over there, do a dance and sing my song about why Finland needs to spend a bunch of money on our latest techno-gear. Then I can go back to the embassy."

James ticked at his sore tooth with a fingernail. He had a gauze patch taped to his nose, and the cheek bruise was getting blue. It didn't seem to bother him. "The colonel may be in the market for more upgrades than you realize. The Russians are doing unwelcome flyovers, and the bastards live almost right across the street. St. Petersburg is less than two hundred miles from where we are sitting."

"I saw a Hornet parked out at the airport," said Kyle.

"The Finns are repositioning a lot of military assets, although they won't go to war against Russia. No way." He drank off the second vodka shot, ordered a third. "Who is Janna?"

"Janna Ecklund, who runs our Excalibur office in Washington. She is a former FBI agent who keeps a Glock 19 strapped beneath her desk. She's also with the Agency." The thought gave him an idea. Janna was from this neck of the northern woods and might be a good backup if this thing dragged out. She also spoke Swedish and looked like an ice princess. Might fit right in.

"So what were you doing down in Rome?"

"Same thing. Trying to convince the Italians to buy more Excalibur product. We're working on a nice polymer-encased .50-caliber bullet and some new software. They seemed interested."

The DSS agent's eyes narrowed. "We got word last night that an ISIS terrorist, an American, was whacked in Rome by a sniper. No suspects."

"Is that right? Good. The asshole probably needed dying." Kyle emptied his shot glass, flipped it upside down and pinned it hard on the napkin. "I'm going to bed, Lem."

"I'll pick you up out front at nine o'clock. Then I go see the dentist."

Ivan the Terrible. *Why is Ivan Strakov asking for me?* Kyle barely knew the guy except for that brief, inconclusive time at the Scout/Sniper School so many years ago. Swanson puttered around with the question after hitting the cushy bed in a room in which the floorboards squeaked from the grandeur of the really old days.

Back when he gave Ivan the bad news that he was never going to make it as a sniper, Kyle had taken the young Russian sergeant out for a night to drown his sorrows. Russia was a pioneer in the sniper game; their sharpshooters had turned the German siege of Stalingrad into a nightmare for the Nazis and laid the groundwork for snipers in urban combat. A lot of those lessons were still being taught today, and Swanson had praised that long history for the disappointed Russian. Kyle explained, over about the sixth beer, that back in the rubble of that bloody, freezing siege, Strakov probably would have been hailed as a hero. He was that good, but "that good" was no longer good enough.

Ivan's accent that night had drawn the attention of a couple of girls in the country-and-western bar. Kyle bought him a cowboy hat, which Ivan jauntily tilted forward, and the ladies taught him the Texas two-step while a pair of fiddles fueled the music. Swanson explained that being an elite sniper in the next century, which was fast approaching, meant being able to do precision fire from extremely long ranges, not just across the bombed-out tractor factory. Shots of more than a mile were going to be commonplace, and so many things could bugger up the target picture at those distances that only the best eyes and steadiest nerves need apply. Even then, computers that had not yet been invented would be needed.

"We are like the pilots who pursued the speed of sound with early jet planes back after World War Two," Swanson explained.

"The Great Patriotic War," Ivan corrected, pouring another mug of beer.

"Yeah. Whatever. Anyway, the sound barrier was out there somewhere and most experts believed that nothing could break that invisible wall. Bullshit, of course, because bullets were supersonic all the time. Eventually, an American pilot named Chuck Yeager broke Mach 1, and the so-called barrier vanished."

"We Russians did it first. Yuri Pobedonostsev!" Ivan hoisted his beer mug in salute.

"Point is, my friend, that there was no barrier. Same thing applies to modern shooting. We don't know the outer limit, but we snipers keep searching for it through the mud and the sand and the jungles. That unknown fact can get a man killed."

"Or a woman could get killed, too. Some of our greatest snipers were women." The Russian's dark eyes were growing misty and emotional, and he burst out in verse, with a sweep of his bottle in salute to his lost military future:

> *"Hell and damnation,*
> *life is such fun*
> *with a ragged greatcoat*
> *and a Jerry gun!"*

"That was by Alexandr Blok," he explained, and settled into a pout.

Kyle drained his own beer. "Stop that. Stay on the topic." Get a Russian drunk and they were as bad as the Irish for mixing mournful poetry with booze. "Look across the room, up at the stage, Ivan. You see that guy playing the acoustic guitar in the band?"

"I do, most certainly. My eyes are perfect. Fucking doctors."

"How many strings are on it?"

The Russian stared, with his hat tilted. Their table was better than fifty feet away, there was smoke streaming in the air and distracting movement everywhere. "He has six strings, of course."

"Twelve, pal. It's a twelve-string guitar. You couldn't tell the difference."

Ivan stood up, angry. "You play tricks with me. You say I am good enough for Stalingrad, but you fail me because of guitar strings? My superiors in the exchange program will insist that you give me a passing mark!"

Kyle shrugged. "Sit back down, Ivan. I'm probably saving your life. You don't want to be out in the bush and give such an edge to an enemy sniper. I know you're a smart guy, a brave man and a good soldier, but I have to protect the brand of 'Sniper.' If I pass you, then I open the door to having to pass others who do not even have your level of professionalism. I cannot bend for political correctness."

"I have spent my life defending my Motherland, Gunnery Sergeant Swanson." He plopped down heavily, his disappointment alleviated once again as he watched a sturdy blonde in denim and boots at the bar, who was watching him right back.

"Then find a way to do that in another field, Ivan. Every sniper has to stop at some point, and this is the end of the line for you. Mine eventually will come, too."

"What will I do, then?"

Kyle scratched an ear and shrugged his shoulders. "You are really good at computers, and could probably move into private industry and double or triple your salary. I can't even suggest that I know all of your skills. Right now, I think you need to go ask that girl at the bar to dance and have another beer."

Ivan Strakov lurched wobbly to his feet. "That is the best thing you have said all night, Gunnery Sergeant. You are my friend, eh? My good friend!"

"You bet," said Kyle. And they had not seen each other since.

Swanson was out of the hotel door at 6:30 a.m. for a morning run. He had never been to Helsinki before and looked forward to watching the city come awake. It was a good way to get to know a new place, he thought, and although it might not work in cities like Mosul or Kabul, a civilized place would reveal a lot about itself to a visitor who just bothered to look.

A few minutes later, while he was stretching out in the Esplanadi Park that sloped down to the water, Swanson realized he was already too late. It was the fourth day of April, and although spring had not arrived, the snow was gone from the city and was being replaced by patches of green. The grass was coming alive. The Finns were already out in force—joggers, runners, walkers, cyclists and convoys of men, women, boys and girls who zoomed along the pavement on rubber-tired skis to stay in shape for next winter's cross-country treks out in the deep forests. Fitness was a priority. He loped off, staying in the slow lane along the sidewalks and boulevards so as not to be run over by some Flying Finn.

Senate Square, the cathedrals, Parliament House, monuments, government buildings, the libraries and government buildings, and boats in the harbor all spun quietly by, and all of them seemed extraordinarily clean and scrubbed. Early-bird workers in fashionable clothes were arriving on trams to get their offices open by eight, and vendors and customers were already busy in the Hietalahti flea market. Four miles later he was back where he started, bent over, hands on knees, catching deep breaths of cool air, and he understood that what he had witnessed were outward manifestations of contentment in the capital city of Finland.

He found a newsstand and bought a copy of the *International New York Times*, then found a sidewalk café and sat outside beneath an umbrella. A young woman with thick golden hair that fell over her shoulders appeared as soon as he was seated. "May I suggest a light breakfast, sir?" The English was perfect.

Kyle looked at her. Tall and athletic. "How did you know I spoke English?"

"You look like an American and you're reading an English-language newspaper. Almost everyone here speaks it, and Swedish, which is really our national language." Her smile was as bright as the morning. "Finnish, too, obviously. It can be confusing. Since you are apparently a tourist, let me suggest a warm bowl of rolled oat porridge with butter, cheese and fruit, and a large mug of light-roast coffee."

"I like my coffee strong," he countered.

"Try this first. The water from the mountains makes it a local favorite. We should know. We drink more coffee than anybody on the planet."

"Seattle might challenge that."

"Seattle would lose."

"OK. I'll give it a try." She went away and Kyle leafed through the big pages of the newspaper. It seemed almost archaic in the world of technology, but there was just something about handling the paper, reading long stories without having to jump around through a lot of Web sites, and even getting smudges of ink on his fingertips that gave a newspaper the familiar feeling that Swanson enjoyed.

Nothing on the front page interested him, since it was mostly about politics. Another bomb in Baghdad. Inside, there was a five-paragraph wire story about a terrorist being killed in Rome. Front-to-back, no mention of Ivan the Terrible. The breakfast came and the waitress had been right about the coffee. The porridge tasted like grits and berries. She had pink sunshine on her cheeks, edging away the winter paleness.

A scan of his cell phone gave him no more fresh

information than he had gotten from the newspaper. Janna Ecklund had e-mailed the day's schedule for the Washington office of Excalibur, and she wanted to know how long he would be in Finland. He answered with a brief response that he would know more after the meeting at the Defence Ministry. In other words, he had no idea. The business-related chatter was needed to keep the cover tight.

Then he still had some spare time before meeting Big Lem, so he had another coffee and thought about Finland some more. *Why is he here?* The nation was more complex than it appeared on the surface. The lessons of history had been very hard, but the people had put together a country that reflected who they were. Although they were not warlike, they were fierce fighters. The Nazis had found that out the hard way in World War II when they ran into the Finns in the mountains, as had the invading Swedes hundreds of years earlier, and the Russians later on. Even today, there was mandatory conscription of two years for every Finnish man, but peace had worked better than war in this isolated part of the world. There was a social democracy with a cradle-to-grave welfare structure that was uniquely Finnish. The citizenry was protected, educated, safe and secure. Laziness was not rewarded, however, and the country had a thriving economy. Camelot in the snow.

So, Swanson thought, it seemed to have been sort of silly of him to carry a concealed weapon and his credentials on his sunny morning outing, but that was who he was. And just because no bunch of terrorists was running around throwing bombs, and there was no noticeable street crime, did not mean that danger was on holiday. In fact, Swanson had the sense that everyone in this city was intent on wringing every drop of happiness they could get out of this warm new season, before it was too late.

He paid the breakfast bill, left the newspaper folded for some other reader, and headed back to the hotel, where he halted on the first step, turned and waited for the two people who had been following him to catch up.

**T**HEY HAD NOT been cautious with their movements, which indicated they had nothing to conceal nor anything to fear, which further indicated that they were a pair of cops.

An attractive middle-aged woman wearing a plain-knit white crewneck sweater and jeans stepped forward. A mane of blond hair parted in the middle swept to her shoulders. Her partner was a solid, straw-haired man with sharp blue eyes set in an otherwise blank face that had been leathered by the winter sun. An outdoorsman, and in good shape, Kyle thought. The man edged off to one side, opening space to triangulate Swanson, who recognized the tactical shift. It was the move of a professional and meant that if Kyle chose to resist, he could only deal with them as individuals.

"Mister Swanson, I am Inspector Rikka Aura, and this is Sergeant Alan Kiuru. We are with the Security Intelligence Service and would appreciate a few minutes of your time." She flashed a badge. She was not really asking; she was telling. Inspector Aura was with Supo, the Suojelupoliisi, federal police, and had the power of her government at her back.

"I'm right here in front of you, Inspector. What do you want?"

"In private, if you please."

He grinned. "I prefer that we stay in public view. I feel more comfortable out here."

"I must insist," Aura answered politely. "We prefer not to discuss national security issues in front of big hotels."

With the preliminary fencing complete, Kyle nodded. "Let's go up to my suite. I'll order some coffee," he said. He had forty-five minutes before the American DSS escort agent was to arrive. The CIA was expecting him. People at the U.S. Embassy knew he was coming. The Finnish Defence Ministry had him scheduled for after lunch. Ivan the Terrible, the Russian who had started the dominoes falling, was aware that Kyle was probably on the way. Now a pair of Supo agents had shown up, and it wasn't yet nine o'clock. For a mission that had begun in the utmost surprise and secrecy less than twenty-four hours earlier, a lot of people knew that Kyle Swanson was in Helsinki.

The inspector got comfortable by taking the largest chair in the room while the sergeant stayed alert near the door. The room maid had not yet been around, but the place was still tidy because Kyle's military training had ingrained in him the need for being shipshape in his personal space. Her eyes vacuumed the place while he ordered room service, coffee for three.

"So. What is this about, Inspector?" Kyle asked.

Like all cops, she answered with a question of her own. "Why are you here, Mister Swanson?"

He came back with, "Do I need a lawyer?"

Aura shook her head. "This is a courtesy visit. No, you are not in any trouble. Why are you in Finland?"

Swanson sighed with resignation and found a straight chair off to one side. "A combination of business and pleasure."

The sergeant by the door had pulled a small notebook computer from his jacket and read from it. "Executive vice president of Excalibur Enterprises, Limited, based in London and Washington, D.C."

"Yes." Best to keep the answers simple.

"And you have a meeting at one o'clock today with Colonel Max Piikkilä at our Defence Ministry." A bit of acting.

"No. It's at two o'clock."

Inspector Aura spoke. "That is your only business appointment, and it was only requested late yesterday afternoon. Why was that?"

"I hope to get the colonel's advice and permission for a tour of some Finnish industrial plants during the next few days so as to introduce our product line around. That sort of thing, Inspector. Normal outreach procedures, scratching for new customers and suppliers. You know how it is."

She kept the pleasant look on her face. "You arrived very late at this hotel. Why was that?"

"I flew in from Italy after a business trip there, and it was a long flight."

Sergeant Kiuru pulled up more information and spoke. "Yet you did not arrive on any commercial flight.

You cleared customs on the military side of the airport. That is peculiar."

Kyle answered, "Not in my world. We frequently fly on private aircraft, and, in fact, own one. Waiting in airports is a waste of time, and time is money."

Now the inspector's eyes grew flinty as she took over. "The plane's tail number shows that it is an aircraft that we know is owned by a front company controlled by the U.S. Central Intelligence Agency. So I am wondering why this wandering important business executive with only one appointment in Finland flies in on a CIA plane."

Swanson waved off the question as also being unimportant. "There is nothing mysterious about it at all, Inspector Aura. My company deals in advanced military technology and maintains very good relations with various government agencies. My office discovered the plane was available in Rome, while our company jet was in England. It was a simple lease arrangement and it happens all the time."

"A man with your incredible military record flies all the way from Rome to Helsinki on a CIA jet for a business appointment that had not yet been made?"

"You spent a long time in the U.S. Marines," read the sergeant. "Exceptional sniper."

Kyle did not respond other than nodding in the affirmative.

"What of the pleasure side, Mister Swanson? You mentioned business and pleasure."

"Now you are getting personal, Ms. Aura." He intentionally dropped her official title. "Who I want to see in my personal life is none of your business."

She rolled her eyes, as if enjoying the verbal fencing.

"Ah. An affair of the heart. Perhaps you have a secret lover in our country. How touching. What's her name?"

"Again, none of your business."

"It is all my business. Sergeant? What does your computer say about all of this?"

"There was nothing romantic at all. He was brought to the hotel by Special Agent Lem James of the U.S. Department of State Security Service, and they had drinks. The bartender and registration desk confirm."

"So Lem James is the friend that you came to see? I've known him for several years. Very nice man. Very professional and quite large. Do you know where he was born? I do. How many children does he have?"

"You can ask him about his life story in about thirty minutes. He's meeting me here."

"Where are you going?"

"Lem is taking me over to the embassy to introduce me around to the trade and military people there. Then we have some lunch and I go to see Colonel Piikkilä . . . "

"And then you go tour some plants and maybe take a reindeer sleigh ride and watch the northern lights with your secret lover. Before you do any of that, can you tell me why the U.S. Embassy has tightened its security so much? The Marine guards have even requested extra local police patrols. What's going on, Mister Swanson?"

"Since I have never been there, I don't know what they do." Kyle thought Inspector Aura's grandmother may have been a great white shark.

The woman got up and brushed down her jeans, as if she had just eaten crumbly toast. "No. Of course you would not know. I mean, how could you? Before we leave, however, you need to understand a bit of important Finnish history."

"Fine. I'm listening. Anything to get rid of you."

She smirked. "Our country is a proud member of the European Union. We have never joined NATO, not only because we think that it is merely a front for American policy in the region, but also because we signed a neutrality treaty in 1948 with our trading partner and good next-door neighbor, Russia. Our government has no intention of antagonizing Russia more than we do already on almost a daily basis."

"May I reply to that nonsense?"

"No. I came here to inform you, Mister Swanson, that whatever is going on with you and the American embassy will not be allowed to spill beyond those gates and put our country at risk." Her words were sharp and then, from her purse, she withdrew a U.S. passport. "This is yours, sir. It will be returned to you tomorrow morning when you leave. You can make your own arrangements, but you are no longer welcome in Finland. Meanwhile, our people will follow you . . . for your own protection, of course. We wouldn't want anything to happen to an important business executive."

"Wait a minute. You are kicking me out of the country?"

She and the sergeant were at the door, ready to leave. "Yes," she said. "And don't come back."

There was a small traffic jam in the hotel hallway as the Supo officers almost collided with the coffee trolley being pushed by a room service boy, and Lem James stepped from the elevator.

"Hello, Lem," Inspector Rikka Aura said with a genuine smile. Old friends.

"Morning there, Rikka. And Alan, too." James was

puzzled, but showed no surprise at coming so unexpect-edly upon Aura and Kiuru. He saw there was a coffee service for three on the little cart that pushed through as they stepped back against the hallway walls to let it pass. Kyle Swanson was leaning against the open door of his room, grimly watching. James wanted to ask, *"What the fuck is going on here?"* but instead said, "You guys are up bright and early."

"Yes," confirmed Alan Kiuru, with a satisfied look. "Early birds out catching worms. What happened to your face?"

The DSS agent's right eye socket and cheek was a pattern of yellow, black and purple, and his lip had been cut. "My son and I were doing mixed martial arts last night," he explained.

The inspector laughed. "Your son is four years old." She flicked her eyes back to Swanson. *I know the family.*

"He got lucky. I'll get him next time."

"I would like to stand here and learn more of that as-sault, but we are in a hurry right now. We will see you later today, I'm sure. Please say hello to all of my friends over at the embassy." They stepped aboard the elevator, which had not yet closed its doors. She waved. He waved back.

The trolley was now in the room, and Swanson signed the chit and the bellman left. James asked what the hell was going on.

Swanson poured two cups of the hot liquid and took his own over to the bed, where he sat down. "That bitch just dropped by to throw me out of their damned country."

James picked up his cup, and the dainty china looked

tiny is his hand. He remained standing, his eyes and brain busy absorbing the events of the past few minutes. "Watch your mouth, and don't call Rikka a bitch, Swanson. She's a friend. And she is also the best counter-terrorism investigator in Supo, and Kiuru is a rising star. If those two came by, the expulsion order came from the top."

Kyle fluffed a pillow, lay back and sipped the dark coffee as he thought. "Yeah. She's no dumb flatfoot. I got that. She ripped through my cover like a paper shredder. Fuck Finland."

Lem James picked his cell phone from a pocket. "You get ready to go while I alert our powers-that-be over at the embassy that our Finny friends are acting weird. You know that in one town over here, they have an annual Carry-Your-Wife Contest?"

Swanson went to the bathroom and turned on the shower. Before closing the door, he called out, "And I think their light-roast coffee sucks!"


"Of all the embassies in all the towns in all the world, he walks into mine." Bob Carver, the State Department's regional security officer at the American legation, massaged his temples with his fingertips. His poor Humphrey Bogart impression from *Casablanca* came from being saddled with a Russian defector who was creating storm waves in the normally placid Helsinki diplomatic pond. The guy hadn't said anything yet and people were already asking questions.

Swanson was beside Carver, looking through a one-way glass into an interview room where a man was sitting alone, at ease, and looking back at what was only a reflection. He was about six-feet-tall, slim, clean-shaven and with neatly styled, soft, coal-black hair. The blue eyes were amplified a bit by modern no-rim glasses that perched on a knife of a nose, accentuating the high cheekbones. The mouth was narrow, but not in bitterness. He carried an air of both confidence and competence. He was in a gray crewneck sweater over jeans, with nice shoes, not boots.

"Tell me again about how he came in," Swanson instructed. "Step by step."

"We had opened the doors of the consular section, which is separate from the embassy itself, as usual on Monday morning. There is a local law security post outside, but they do not interact with visitors unless there is some problem. In this case, there wasn't. This guy looks just like a lot of others, and he blended in without a problem."

"How far did he get?" Kyle knew the drill, since he had worked at several embassies while he was in the Corps.

"As I was saying, he went through the outer door and got to the public area, which has a few chairs. He didn't sit down, but went straight into the hard line. At that point, we have regulation private security behind bulletproof glass, with a Marine in a booth, like a teller at a bank drive-through."

Kyle understood without being told that that was where things began to get strange. Had the visitor been seeking a simple visa or some other routine piece of business, he would have been buzzed through the barrier, walked through a metal detector and allowed into the secure area to wait in line with others. Not this one.

"So this dude asks the guard, 'Can I speak to you privately?' and the Marine shoos away the civilian security man. When they are alone, he announces, 'I wish to speak to someone in your intelligence section. I wish to defect,' and he slides over his ID card." Carter folded his arms and rocked on his heels, glowering at the man in the other room.

"The Marine takes one look at the credentials and almost has a heart attack. The cards said that he is a colonel in the GRU."

Kyle agreed that would be enough to give pause to anyone having duty at the barrier. GRU was the acronym for the Glavnoye Razedyvatel'noye Upravleniye, which was Russian military intelligence. It was only good training that kept the Marine corporal from betraying his surprise or soiling his pants. Instead, the guard politely asked our unusual visitor to have a chair while he made a quick call up the stovepipe and asked a CIA type in the consular office to come down. That guy almost had a bowel problem himself when he met Ivan Strakov.

"They took him through the hard line and the rover Marine handcuffed and searched him and put him in that very room we are looking at right now. The higher-ups were notified. Strakov remained cool all the way, obviously familiar with the routine. He identified exactly who he was, who he worked for, who his boss was and a taste of what he has in his head."

"Which is?" Kyle asked.

"The organizational chart and layout of a Russian army artillery regiment that moved into the Crimea last week. His recitation was amazing, right down to food- and fuel-consumption estimates for the next three months."

"Interesting information, then, and not just bullshit?" Kyle wanted a professional judgment.

"It is more than interesting, Swanson. It is an intelligence diamond because Moscow denies the regiment is there at all. We got busy with the physical proof and recognition factors, and he even volunteered some DNA. The conclusion was that he is the real deal."

Carver huffed and glanced over at Kyle. "When we told him we were satisfied with his identity, that's when he bombed us with the demand that he would talk only with you; the only American he really trusted. Can you make a physical identification to back up the numbers?"

Swanson had recognized the Russian on sight. He was some years older than the last time they had been together drinking longneck beers in a cowboy bar, but Ivan was no longer a kid in any way. More than a soldier, too, he looked like a successful hedge fund manager on a day off, and there was obvious arrogance running in his veins. He was fully aware of his importance, and would not sell his goods cheaply.

"And he wants to defect."

"Yes. That's what he said."

Swanson paused. "What's the plan from here?"

"He goes out tonight to Washington as part of the diplomatic pouch, aboard the same Gulfstream that brought you in." Carver spread his hands on his wide hips. "I'll be glad to be rid of him."

"That works for me, since I'm being expelled tomorrow morning anyway. I'll get what I can in the meantime, then we both wash our hands of him. Also, the sooner the better for our Helsinki pals, eh?"

"Swanson, I am no genius, but I've been in this game a very long time, and I think this guy is going to be big. He has nothing to do with Finland, nothing at all, other than turning up on our doorstep like a baby in a basket.

He had to start somewhere, and he chose us, and maybe you will find out why. Do not trust him. Don't trust any defector."

"Of course not."

"All of that personal data, you know? The DNA and the fingerprints and the background that proves he is absolutely who he says he is? There is one thing that still puzzles me." Carver shoved his hands into his back pockets, a movement that made his belly bulge against his belt. The basset-hound eyes turned fully to Kyle.

"And that is?"

"That same sort of foolproof material was also used a few weeks ago, and delivered results that were just as positive. It proved that, without a doubt, Colonel Ivan Strakov sitting over there in the next room is dead."

**T**HE METAL DOOR set in a metal frame was the color of milk and had an electric lock. It opened only when a five-digit code was punched into a numeric pad on the outside. There was no knob inside the square fifteen-by-fifteen room. Kyle pushed through after a DSS agent tapped his security number, and the door opened with a dull *thunk*.

The Russian was on his feet, facing the door, as if some vibe had alerted him. The room was soundproof and the mirrored window was unbreakable. Audio and visual recorders were monitoring every sound and movement. Recessed fluorescent lights were behind metal grates in the white ceiling, while the floor was concrete, layered with a thick epoxy that would not chip. The walls were as thick as those of a castle.

"Hello, Gunny." The voice was controlled and revealed no discomfort, despite what had to be a mental storm raging inside the defector's brain.

"Hello, Ivan. Or should it be 'Hello, Colonel Strakov'?" Then, in a calculated bit of tradecraft to break

the ice, Swanson extended his hand and the GRU officer shook it. The grip was warm and dry, and the gaze
was steady, giving no sign of nervousness. "It has been
awhile, hasn't it?"

The Russian officer's face surrendered a bit of a smile
that was more amusement than sincerity, for he knew
how the game was played. He had interrogated many
men and women, at times using what the Americans
quaintly called enhanced techniques. Feigned friendship
was also an effective ploy. Nevertheless, he was truly
glad to see Swanson again. Not only did it mean the
Americans had caved in to his first demand, but he really
did hold a reluctant personal admiration for the sniper.
"I am very pleased to see you again, Gunny."

"Word has it that you are dead, Ivan." Swanson moved
to a chair and sat down. "A plane crashed in Lake Baikal,
way the hell up in Siberia. Two people were aboard, you
being one of them. That seems a little peculiar to me."

Ivan replied with a line from a Robert Service poem
about strange things being done in the land of the midnight sun.

"We have been here less than a minute, and already
you're spouting poetry. Screw that. Explain the crash."

The Russian crossed his legs. "Yes, I had been scheduled to fly to Irkutsk for an inspection aboard a small
military aircraft that most unfortunately crashed in Lake
Baikal. At the last moment, I could not make the flight
and therefore sent the plane on without me, telling the
pilot I would catch up with him later. My name remained
on the flight manifest, my schedule stated I was to be
aboard, and there was a substantial amount of additional
evidence to prove that I was going to that barren place.
The trip had been a month in the planning. As you know,

Baikal is the deepest freshwater lake in the world, more like an ocean, and when the plane went down, the wreckage sank without a trace. It was most unfortunate."

"In other words, you set it up."

"I required a bit of misdirection, Kyle. You appreciate that in evasion and escape. Without my GRU colleagues hunting me, it would be less difficult to travel in the opposite direction, say, for instance, to the American embassy in Helsinki."

"You murdered the pilot."

"That is merely a technical term. I needed it to serve the greater good. So what? What is your point, Sniper?"

Swanson looked steadily at the Russian. There was no need to get into the morality of killing, or arguing the finer points of death, on orders versus deliberate and personal. The colonel was in custody, across the table from him in a locked room and the only real question was: *Why?* Not the moment yet to ask that outright, Kyle decided, and changed the topic.

"Last time we were together, Ivan, you were just a punk sergeant in the naval infantry. Now you are a colonel. Tell me about that magic carpet of promotions."

"That is thanks to you, Kyle. When you flunked me out of the program, you ended my career as a sniper and advised me to find some other way to serve my country. Within a few months, I had put down my rifle and volunteered for military intelligence. I did not have a college, but knew that I was pretty smart, Kyle, always good with numbers and computers and techie stuff. After a lot of testing, they discovered not only that I had an off-the-charts IQ, but that I also was an *eidetiker,* which means that my memory is almost photographic. They were so happy that they started me as a captain."

Swanson was quiet for a moment, trying to reconcile the scatterbrained young Russian he had known with the certified genius he was interviewing. "Still, your age does not fit your rank, Ivan. That makes us think that there is something else going on with this so-called defection." Strakov was a sergeant in his late twenties when they were on the range, but the official record had him graduating a few years later from the Moscow Military Institute of the Federal Security Service, coming out as a lieutenant colonel. Then the blank, dark years of his work within the GRU and back to school at the Academy of the General Staff, graduating as a full colonel. A general's star was surely on the horizon. It reminded Kyle Swanson somewhat of his own recorded history, which painted a picture with a lot of parts missing.

The colonel shook his head. "There are official records and then there are nonofficial records; just as there are riflemen, so must there be fighters in higher ranks." Ivan dodged the question with a stanza from *The Scythians*:

> *We shall ourselves no longer be your shield,*
> *no longer launch our battlecries;*
> *but study the convulsive battlefield*
> *from far off through our narrow eyes!*

"So you became a spy. One more damned poem and I walk out."

"No. I ran the spies." Strakov shifted his position again. "Look, Kyle, all of this is unnecessary. The CIA is going to wring me dry, and I will spill my guts willingly.

I hate what is happening to Russia, and it's up to people like me to stop the slide in any way possible—including defecting to you guys."

"You are still arrogant, Ivan. What makes you think you have anything that we don't already know?"

"Now we're getting somewhere. There are two names with which everyone in the modern intelligence world is familiar—Wikileaks founder Julian Assange and your renegade NSA computer whiz Edward Snowden." Strakov rose and took a few slow steps to face the big mirror, knowing that more Americans were watching from behind the glass. "That is the level on which I have come to play. I have spent several years planning this personal exodus, Kyle. You and your people should consider me a Snowden from the other side." He smiled genially into the mirror and said, "I'm going to rock their world."

Swanson got up and stretched, then took his time finding a place to lean against the thick wall. He was really happy that all of this was being recorded on video and audio. "Why me?"

The Moscow spymaster turned to face him, falling smoothly into a professorial mode. "The first step was to make my escape. That has been accomplished. Next I have to prove that I have information that is worthwhile."

"You already gave up some material about some artillery regiment in the Ukraine, right? More of that kind of thing?"

The Russian began to slowly pace, with his hands in his pockets, his blue eyes sparkling with excitement. "Not at all. That was nothing. Your satellites would have caught most of that anyway, eventually. No, I wanted Kyle Swanson because I need to send you out on a mission. That's what I really trust; your ability to get the job done."

Kyle barked a laugh. "You want to send me on a mission? No way."

Strakov was unruffled and continued. "Oh, you will go. The people in the next room will make that a priority. Right now you are all convinced that I am real and alive, although listed as being dead. Now you will determine if my information has value."

"And how are we going to do that?"

"You take a quick trip, Kyle. Go south, into Finland's little neighbor of Estonia, and conduct a surveillance of a certain place through your sniper eyes. Be as thorough as possible. Then you return and I will explain to you and a committee of experts what you saw. It will only take a few days and there should be no hostile opposition."

"Well, Ivan, that won't work."

"Why not? It is a simple in-and-out."

"I can't return to Helsinki, even if I wanted to. I'm being expelled."

"No matter. You Americans were going to ship me somewhere else anyway, right? Where?"

"A safe house, I would guess." Swanson avoided a direct answer. "I don't know any of the details."

"Right now, they are thinking of putting me somewhere in Maryland or Virginia, a place that is handy to your intel agencies. They can forget that. I will need to be around Belgium or France."

"You don't get to pick and choose, Ivan. It may just be a dark hole on the hard side of Detroit."

Strakov continued, as if Kyle had said nothing. "When you return from this mission in Estonia, I predict with great certainty that your people and a lot of others are going to want me close to NATO headquarters in Brussels. Nobody knows where Estonia is right now, Kyle, but in about six months, it will be on everyone's map. There is a whisper of war in the air."

"That's not another poem, is it?"

"No," replied Colonel Strakov. "It's a promise. Take a powerful scope or binos up to the highest point you can reach in the big castle in the eastern border city of Narva in Estonia, and have a good hard look across the river into Russia. Then come back."

"A castle in Estonia?" Kyle cocked an eyebrow.

"Yes. It was built in the thirteenth century. Now go up in the castle." Then Ivan clammed up again.

Everyone agreed. This had all the ingredients of a terrific video game: A council of elders would decide whether to send a brave warrior on a quest to a spooky old castle in a faraway medieval land to find a magic sword held by a fearsome enemy and save the world. All that was needed was a princess and a dragon.

The elders, in real life, were the hierarchy of the U.S. Embassy staff in Helsinki, and an hour after Swanson spoke with Strakov they were gathered in a conference room. At the head of the oval table was Ambassador Extraordinary and Plenipotentiary Mary Line, who had compiled an illustrious career as an academic and an athlete, and had even flown in space before becoming a political appointee. Her husband was chairman of a giant computer company and they were generous donors to the political party of the incumbent president. The previous year, she had ridden her bicycle some eight hundred miles around Finland.

"I don't like this one little bit," Mary Line said forcefully. "Sending a secret agent on a mission only on the word of a Russian spy will certainly antagonize Moscow!"

On her right was Jack Loran, the quiet career State Department Foreign Service officer who was deputy chief of mission, which made him the power behind the throne in times of crisis. He was the manager and the ambassador was the figurehead. "It is unusual," he agreed.

Bob Carver, chief of the Diplomatic Security Service, was at the other end and feeling an ulcer bubbling in his belly. "Our first priority is to relocate Colonel Strakov before the Finns uncover what is going on. We have air transport available tonight, but need to decide where to send him. I vote for Washington."

"He wants Brussels." The ambassador reminded everyone.

"Screw what he wants, ma'am," Carver shot back when she gave him a stare. "Sorry."

Jack Loran looked over to CIA Station Chief Sandra Bentley, who said, "The people back in Langley have already made that decision, Madam Ambassador. The plane will leave for Paris tonight. Further arrangements will be made from there."

Kyle Swanson liked the response. Sandi Bentley had been around the CIA for years and had earned her stripes in the field; she had run the stations in both Spain and New Zealand before coming to Helsinki. She guarded secrets carefully. She was courteous, but the ambassador did not need to know where Ivan was headed after he left Finland. Nor did she need to know where Kyle was going. He had nothing to add on that subject.

"And Agent Swanson will be leaving as soon as possible, too?" Ambassador Line was unhappy about all of these outsiders coming in and disturbing her orderly domain.

"Yes. He leaves tomorrow, too." Bentley hardly looked up from her papers. The ambassador thought Swanson would fly straight back to Washington. The CIA station chief did not correct that erroneous conclusion.

"What do you recommend on the Russian's request for Swanson to visit Narva, Sandi?" asked Loran.

"We'll take care of that, too," she replied. "You and the ambassador will have to officially log what has happened here, minute-by-minute, in case there is some future congressional investigation, Jack. Therefore, the State Department's diplomatic involvement ends here, with the handover of the defector, and the CIA is putting a top-secret lid on all of it. Is that OK by you folks?"

"But . . . " the ambassador started to speak. She wanted to know more, but she looked over to her deputy chief of mission. Jack Loran gave a negative headshake and closed his folder. "That's good."

Swanson liked the decision. The CIA lied to the ambassador without actually doing so, and officially cut the State Department out of the loop.

The temperature rocketed down and the beautiful weather of Tuesday collapsed into a leftover winter day on Wednesday. The frozen air out of the north, a dump of overnight snow and the following gloomy gray sky beyond the hotel window matched Swanson's mood even before he was intercepted in the lobby by Inspector Aura and Sergeant Kiuru from the Finland Security Intelligence Service. She was tapping his American passport on a forearm, burning restless energy, waiting for him.

"You were supposed to leave this morning, Mister Swanson. Surely you remember that?" She snapped the question.

"I am leaving, Inspector, even as we speak. If you step aside I will check out and be on my way." He squared off to face her, tired of the pushiness.

"You did not make an airplane reservation."

"That's because I am not flying anywhere. If you would be so kind as to let me have my passport now, I will do the paperwork at the front desk and depart your lovely country. The ferry over to Estonia leaves in about an hour and I don't have any more time to waste with you, as much as you enjoy jerking around a legitimate businessman."

The eyes narrowed. "Why are you going to Estonia?"

"Because you are throwing me out of Finland."

"No." She held the passport like a lifeline and glared. "What is the reason?"

Swanson offered his palm for it. "I had a sudden urge to visit the old family farm and some distant relatives, and maybe do some business that I had considered doing in Finland. Estonia is a forward-leaning country. That's where Skype was invented, you know, and Excalibur Enterprises is heavy into technology."

She puffed out her lips in exasperation. "Do you even speak Estonian, Mister Swanson?"

"Of course. It is a beautiful tongue."

"You are such a terrible liar."

"And you are boring me. Arrest me or give me my

passport and get out of my way. Good-bye, Inspector Aura."

DSS Special Agent Lem James was waiting behind the wheel of his personal car, the motor running to keep the heater going. Kyle climbed into the front while a bellman packed his luggage into the trunk. "Did you have another pleasant meeting in there with my pal Rikka?"

"You didn't tell her about my taking the ferry over to Tallinn, did you?"

James laughed so hard that his body quaked. "No, of course not. Make her work a little bit, you know?"

"She is arrogant and stubborn."

"She says the same about you." James handed Kyle his boat tickets and other paperwork, slipped the car into gear, and they drove away along the freshly plowed streets to Tyynenmerenkatu 8, the sprawling West Terminal used by the boats of the Tallink & Silja Line. Swanson noticed that although it was freezing outside, the Finns were going about their business pretty much as they had done the previous day in the sunshine. They knew how to live with weather.

"You take care of yourself over there, Swanson. One of your people, a trade attaché at the American embassy, will meet you on the other side."

"Couldn't I just rent a car and drive to this castle?"

"Trust me, pal. You need a guide in this strange territory. You don't speak Estonian, do you?"

"Not a word."

"It sounds a lot like gargling mouthwash while yodeling. Your best bet is to remember this one phrase: *ma ei räägi eesti keelt*—it means 'I don't speak Estonian.'"

"Oh, boy." Kyle muttered the strange words. Not a chance that he could remember that.

"Yeah," said James. He scribbled a private telephone number on a business card and gave it to Kyle. "Good luck. I'm off this case officially as of yesterday, so I'm just acting as a friend. Call me if I can help. Otherwise, I'll see you when I see you."

**6**

**T**HE BIG WHITE ferry trimmed in lime green stripes rode ten decks tall and loaded more than two thousand passengers for the two-hour journey out of Helsinki, across the Baltic Sea to Tallinn, the capital of Estonia. Unmelted blocks of ice still bobbed in the cold water. A helicopter would have been much quicker, but the chopper service did not awaken from its winter season until May, more than three weeks away. Swanson went up to the plush business lounge on the sixth deck, and from the windows, looked down at the terminal and saw Lem James standing beside Inspector Aura and her sergeant, all of them waiting for the boat to shove off and take Kyle away from Finland.

He opened his laptop PC and logged in, surfing the Net for nothing in particular. He e-mailed Janna Ecklund back in Washington to say he was taking a ferry to Estonia and would be available by e-mail or cell phone. Messaged that he would be back in the States in a few days, anything to keep the surfing going and the Wi-Fi connection alive. There was no doubt that he was being

electronically tracked, so he wanted to make it easy
for the snoopers to confirm his exact position. The boat
finished filling with passengers, cargo and vehicles, the
powerful engines began to turn and the crew tossed
the ropes. It headed away from the pier right on time.
Kyle put on his heavy black wool coat and went outside
on the rear deck to give Inspector Aura one last confirmation sighting. It was very cold, and he pulled up his
collar. He saw Lem James and waved. The agent pointed
and the inspector took a picture. He stayed out there until the vessel was on open water and the cold wind increased in velocity.

Back inside, he drank hot chocolate for warmth, shut
down the laptop and read a few newspapers to help the
minutes pass. The vibration of the ship was felt in his
bones. He watched for faces, for followers, but spotted
no one on his tail. As everybody involved now knew,
and the GPS coordinates confirmed, Kyle Swanson was
exactly where he was supposed to be, right on schedule,
and responsible people were waiting at the other end of
the short voyage to put a new leash on his collar. They
would be comforted by that certainty. Excellent, Swanson thought. It was time to change the rules.

There were one hundred eighty-five private cabins on
the ship, and he had a ticket for one of the ninety-two
rooms that had views of the water from large, curtained
portholes. He hurried up one flight to Deck Seven. The
room was large, by ferry standards, had a private shower
and could handle up to four people with ease, or one rich
American like himself. The luggage was lined neatly in
one corner. He opened a medium bag that contained
neat partitions for pairs of shoes, and one space for the
bag of used underwear. He removed the footwear and

the dirty clothes, disarmed the security device and popped the false bottom.

Everything he needed was in there, including cellophane-wrapped bricks of $10,000 in U.S. currency. He took one, closed the case, set the alarm and returned to the business lounge. A foreign money exchange sign showed that one European Euro was worth about one and one-quarter American dollars, so he exchanged $5,000 for €3,996 plus change, minus a small transaction fee. The clerk at the banking facility in the elite Business Class section did not bat an eye at the amount. On the way back to his cabin, Kyle made another trip outside and, once on the frigid deck, he pulled the memory card from his cell phone and dropped both devices overboard. They splashed into the ferry's turbulent wake and sank.

Back inside, Swanson descended all the way down to the bottom, where hundreds of vehicles were solidly chained into long rows, orderly and tight, bumper to bumper, side by side. The vehicles rocked on their springs in rhythm with the waves pounding the steel hull. Passengers were not allowed on this deck during the voyage, but from a catwalk above, Kyle examined the space, uninterested in the colorful lines of over-the-road trucks, sedans and sports utility vehicles. On the port side near the bow, a section was given over to about a half-dozen motorcycles, packed in tightly and also secured. From there, as soon as the ramp was lowered, the bikes would be allowed to buzz off first to get them out of the way of the larger traffic. He gave his silent approval. He could do business there.

Back in his cabin, he called for the steward, who was

an English-speaking youngster named Matias, wearing a uniform tunic with the ship's logo. A deal was made for when the boat docked in Estonia. The kid was to personally load the luggage into a taxi and deliver it to the Radisson Blu Sky Hotel and leave it with the concierge there, on hold for the arrival of Kyle Swanson of Excalibur Enterprises, who had a reservation. A bonus if Matias could track down the owner of the sleek black BMW R nineT motorcycle that was presently tied down on the vehicle deck. The boy agreed.

Kyle shucked out of his business suit and put it on a hangar in the folding bag. He would dress for a ride in cold weather, and no cotton garments would be able to wick away the sweat. The resulting sheen of moisture on the skin would pull away body warmth. He had to layer up. First came the soft, synthetic boxers and T-shirt and socks, and over that he slid a set of long thermal underwear. He finished with old jeans and a black T-shirt, and a pair of good boots. That was not nearly good enough for a long ride on a cold road, but it formed a good building block.

Digging in the hidden stash again, Swanson removed a set of fake hair additions and, using a bit of spirit gum as adhesive, affixed a thick brown mustache above his lip, smoothing it straight with his fingertips. His hair would not require a wig. Unfolding a backpack, he put in most of the cash, a notepad and pens, several fake press passes that showed he was Canadian journalist Simon Brown and a Visa card. Neatly arranged at the bottom of the case was a blanket, a rain suit, the monocular and a pencil-thin flashlight. Finally, he shook out a loose gray hoodie that covered a clip holster containing a Beretta Px4 Storm Compact handgun along with a spare clip of 9mm ammo. He closed up the suitcases again, leaving the laptop inside one of them.

Kyle breathed easier. In a few minutes, he would be off the grid.

Bikers hang together like leathery birds on a wire. No matter what type of machine they ride, they speak in the code of the road about how it is to ride through a world that is unknown to normal motorists; a magical path of wind in the hair and bugs on the teeth and death just a patch of loose gravel away. Matias, the steward, had furnished a name for the BMW owner and Swanson prowled the lounges until he found a group dressed mostly in black leather, with a scattering of helmets on the tables.

"Excuse me. I'm looking for Andre Parl," he said. The conversation stopped as the riders gave him a once-over. With the boots, jeans and hoodie, he was deemed acceptable.

"Why do you want Andre?" asked a man whose belly pushed at his belt. He had a thick, unkempt beard.

"I want to talk about his bike," Swanson replied, and took a seat in their circle without waiting for an invitation.

"What? That Beemer? It's an expensive pile of junk."

"Hey. My bike is just fine. I can run that candy-ass Harley of yours into a ditch." He looked at Kyle. "I'm Andre Parl, and my R-ninety is not for sale."

Swanson looked him over. Black leather bib overalls were unhooked at the chest and folded down, and unzipped at the ankles to show thick socks and long underwear. The jacket hung over the back of his chair and the scratched helmet was underneath. His fingernails were crescents of dirt and grease.

"Let's talk in private," Swanson replied, motioning to a corner table. They made the move.

"My motorcycle is not for sale," Parl said again. "I bought it new, and it cost me more than fourteen thousand dollars U.S. I'm still paying it off! I maintain it myself and I know every screw in it. It is my baby."

"How much?" Swanson had an easy smile, because he knew that everything had a price and for him, today, money was no object. The maintenance comment by the owner meant the kid knew his machine, and the bike was probably as good as it looked.

"Why do you want my bike? Why not get that fancy-pants Gold Wing? Old man like you needs comfort." His English had a strong accent that Kyle pegged as being some sort of Scandinavian.

"Ten thousand cash, right now."

The young wrench-banger scoffed. "You are not even in the right range, Mister. Who are you, anyway?"

"My name is Kyle Swanson and I am a business-man with a very generous expense account. I need those wheels because I may need to take it off road. The Gold Wing can't do that. How much?"

Andre Parl cocked his head to one side. The man was serious, but the bike was valuable. "Twenty thousand dollars," he said.

Swanson did not even wince. Instead, he countered with an offer to lease it. "Thirty-five hundred for three days, and you throw in your leathers and helmet."

When Parl hesitated, Kyle added, "Plus, you get your bike back in three days and keep the money."

"You want to *rent* my bike for a thousand a day?"

"Yes, and with a written agreement that gives me legal possession in case I'm stopped. Three days from now, you will find it parked in the Radisson Blu Sky Hotel garage here in Tallinn, and the key will be waiting in your name at the front desk. If not, my company will pay your twenty-thousand asking price." He handed over an Excalibur Enterprises business card.

The biker exhaled. Money was falling on him. The business card looked legitimate and Kyle took him back up to the business center so he could call London and verify the identity. Parl was impressed. The stranger really was a vice president. "Deal," he said. "You can have the helmet, but not the leathers; I'm not wearing pants beneath."

"Good enough," said Kyle. He pulled out a paper he had printed up earlier in the business center, filled in the numbers, counted out the cash and both he and Parl signed.

They returned to the biker bunch with fresh cups of coffee. "I've got to take a long ride when we dock and this shit will freeze me to death," Kyle said, slapping the denim jeans. "So I'm in the market. Top prices, no questions, for heavy outer and warming gear; anything you can spare." The roads would still have a few patches of snow, and icy bridges, but hypothermia would be his greatest enemy.

Swanson did a brisk business after the others learned that he had persuaded Parl to lease out his beloved machine, for that made him part of the two-wheeled brotherhood. When he asked them to forget that they had ever seen him, because of a police situation, they all smiled. No problem.

The ship's announcement came for drivers to return to their cars and prepare to dock in Tallinn and the bikers trooped down together, popped open their saddlebags and outfitted their new friend with everything he needed, including sealed heat packs. An insulated sleeping bag was lashed behind the seat. He paid their outrageous prices without question. Andre Parl gave him five minutes of instruction on the tendencies and peculiarities of the R nineT.

Finally, Kyle slid a black neoprene neck-protecting gaiter into place over his neck, chin and mouth, pulled on the scraped black helmet and lowered the goggles, tightened the backpack straps, then fitted his hands into gauntlet-style gloves. He was ready.

The bow door opened and the ramp went down.

Swanson was fifth in the line of motorcycles that moved carefully down the ramp, and he was also going slowly to get the feel of the bike between his knees. The big 1170 cc engine, tuned to perfection, ejected a deep mumble from the short exhaust pipes.

When his wheels touched the solid pier, the BMW steadied, and he took a moment to glance around, confident that he could not be recognized under the layers of garments that covered him from head to toe. In a group of greeters at one side stood a woman in a long black coat, probably his CIA escort, holding a white sign that read: SWANSON. At her side was a bird colonel of the U.S. Army. Kyle twisted the handle throttle and rode away rumbling, thinking: *Why didn't they just put it up in neon? Let everybody know that the American special agent was coming in.* The pair kept their eyes on the gangway, searching among the disembarking passengers for a single man in a dark suit and overcoat. They knew he had no car.

One of Swanson's biker friends led him through the labyrinth of port streets, then around a few corners and pointed to the entrance for a multilane highway, the E-20, which would take him from the red roofs of Tallinn's Old Town for 122 miles, all the way over to Narva, on the Russian border. Kyle waved a casual good-bye, then sped up with a twist of the throttle, merged into the traffic heading east out of the capital city and was immediately cruising at the speed limit of 110 kilometers per hour. The motorcycle strained at the slow pace, for BMW's brilliant engineers had not crafted this machine to go only 70 miles per hour. When traffic thinned, and the roads were totally dry, Kyle cranked it up to 90, and settled in for a few minutes before cutting back to 75. That speed would not attract the attention of police, since he would not be slicing through traffic at high velocity. Drawing the attention of a traffic cop was the last thing he wanted.

Swanson was alone now, trusting only his instincts and training. The unusual mission that started in Rome had been off-kilter from the start. He didn't know why. The Italian hit had been meticulously planned far in advance and in total secrecy, with the corresponding successful result. The follow-up step was to take out another ISIS murderer, again behind hours of precise planning and backup. That operation was as black as a coal mine, the sort of consistent professionalism that he liked about the clandestine operations of the CIA. A blue Audi loomed in front of him, and Swanson swept around it, then returned to the slow lane.

But since Rome, the veil of secrecy had been traded for a gaudy tapestry of urgency, all on the word of a single person, Ivan Strakov, a Russian colonel who was defecting. Or was he? It was as if Ivan had lit a fuse that was burning fast, although no one really knew anything about him. The CIA cover hastily thrown up to protect Kyle had been demolished by the Finnish security cop, and now the Agency had shuttled him over to Estonia, where someone at the dock was holding up a sign with his name on it. And who the hell was the bird colonel?

As with the temptation to open the throttle wide, Swanson understood that some things could move too fast. Even at 70, the press of cold air was eating through the insulation of his suit and leaching away his body heat. He would have to slow down. Now that he was flying solo, he would slow everything down, and try to bring this wild mission under control.

On the roadside berm, a green sign with white letters read: Narva 10 km. Swanson kept going until he spotted a distance marker of three kilometers—less than two miles. He cut the speed and steered the motorcycle off the main highway. He would go into the city, as instructed, but very carefully.

NARVA, ESTONIA

**G** O UP IN the castle," Ivan had directed. Swanson had not spent much time in castles. He was more familiar with Cinderella's palace in Disneyland than those in the real world, where centuries had passed them by. They were anachronisms in modern warfare. After weaving lazily through the back streets of Narva on the R nineT, he looped around the big Route 1 traffic circle, and there it was, a big and brooding stone fortress that had been anchored beside the fast-flowing river for more than seven hundred years. On the far side of the river was another one. It was in Russia.

He parked the bike and just rested on it, studying the structure and imagining having to go against such a defensive bulwark with a spear or bow and arrow. *Good luck with that!* The Danes, Germans, Swedes and Russians all passed through those old stones at one time or another, and none had managed to stay. Finally, the bombs, tanks, artillery and sheer explosive power of World War II had ruptured the walls and ruined the cas-

tle. Restoration was still incomplete. Time and techno-
logical change might conquer such a place, but Kyle did
not have a lot of time on his side. Neither, however, was
he trying to conquer it. Swanson would go inside tomorrow as a tourist, for what was a castle good for these
days other than to serve tourists?

It was almost four o'clock, and the sky was thick with
black clouds, foretelling probable rain. Cruising the
downtown area, Kyle found a coffee shop near the river,
a small place with a picture of the Swedish Lion painted
on the street window and beneath it was taped a small
cardboard sign: *Speak English Here.* He nosed into the
curb, peeled away some of the heavy gear and went inside. It was small but neat, and he was the only customer. He chose the table at the rear, with his back to
the white wall and facing the street outside, an automatic
choice for a man who lived with danger. A young woman
at the counter glanced his way, shoved her cell phone in
a back pocket and ambled over, looking at him curiously.
"You are English or somewhere."

"Good guess. I'm Canadian. I saw your sign," he
replied pleasantly. "How did you know?"

"First, I have never seen you before, so this is probably your first time in Narva, yes? Also, you have no
beer belly and do not stink like a Cossack, so you are
not a Russian; you have neat hair, look healthy, but are
too dark to be Scandanavian and too pale to be a Slav.
I see all people. You are early in the season, too, are you
not? This is only April, and the *predapokaliptichesky*
is in July." She handed him a little menu that had thumb-
nail pictures of food and drink, and when he raised his
eyes at the long, strange word, she translated. "Our
Narva International Motorcycle Festival. Your expensive

European bike is outside." She crossed her arms and cocked a hip, waiting. "You want beer?"

"Sure," he said. "What do you have that is a local brew?"

"Saku is good, and is cheap." The girl was only about twenty, slender, with the long legs of youth, huge smoky eyes and long brown hair that tumbled to her shoulders. "If not for the motorcycles, why are you here? I would never come to Narva on a holiday."

"It is my work. As you say, the bike festival, your *predap*whatever. I am a freelance magazine writer and I'm doing some advance work."

Satisfied, she walked to the counter and called out the order. An old man with a drooping Kaiser Wilhelm mustache pulled a foamy beer into a glass, and the server brought it back and took a seat across the table. She lit a cigarette and checked her phone while Kyle tasted the beer. Not bad. "My name is Anneli Kallasti," she said, examining his face as if measuring it. "You are?"

Kyle took a second, deeper swallow of the amber liquid as he considered the answer. She was a cyber-type, obviously quick with her cell phone. She would immediately run it through Google, which would confirm the cover story, but also it would risk pinging the CIA net back home and give them his GPS numbers. In the age of computers, staying totally off the map was getting ever more difficult. "I am Simon Brown, from Toronto."

"Simon Brown, you should not be telling people that you are a writer. They may think you came to Narva to write about politics. Our municipal election is a very important thing this year."

Kyle laughed. "Politics? I saw a lot of leaflets tacked

to poles and posters on walls and guessed that it was about candidates. That stuff is beyond me, Anneli, and it is boring, at least to me. I just do motorcycles and tourism pieces. Tomorrow I will go see the castle."

"Politics can be dangerous here." Her eyes darted around the shop and the sidewalk beyond and her face grew serious. "I give you this. Leave your tourism and bikes and do Narva politics now. The world will be watching."

What the hell is she talking about? "Sorry, but no politics. Can I buy something to eat here?"

"Our politics are more interesting and important than bikes. Finish your beer," she said, rising and making a round trip to the counter. She came back with a tourist street map and wrote quickly on the back. "Go out and do some tourism reporting. See this memorial. It is the most important in our city." She leaned forward and rested on her elbows. "Then you return back here in two hours and take me to dinner. Meanwhile, I give you a few more places to go and see."

"There is a difference of about twenty years in our ages, Anneli. I'm not looking for a good time." He took a look at the map. She had placed an *X* on the location of the coffee shop, circled a few other points and traced a line from his current location to the memorial.

She tapped a few numbers on her phone, then settled back after reading the screen. "There are many hundreds of Simon Browns in Canada. So, yes, Mister Brown, although you are not totally unattractive for sex, this is not a romantic date, and I am not a prostitute. I will take you to meet my boyfriend. You will need to hire me as a translator because not many people in

Narva speak English. Also, he is in politics. He is going to be our new mayor!"

Narva bore concrete scars and more sour memories than charm. It was almost destroyed when the Red Army took it back from the Nazis during World War II, only to later designate it an off-limits industrial zone. Incredible pollution of the land and air, and poverty for the people, followed. When the Soviet Union disintegrated, the Russians pulled out, taking whatever valuable industry they could salvage along with them, while burying the radioactive waste from a failed nuclear facility. Communist apparatchiks who had run the city remained in control. The legacy of decades of Soviet rule was a uniform architecture of big, square and rectangular buildings, many of them still empty, concrete signatures of collective failure.

Swanson used the reference points marked on the map to take a slow, meandering tour of the city, and thought it looked worse than the bad side of Detroit. They reminded Swanson of big box stores in America, but here, the boxes were stacked high atop one another, with windows empty of glass, brickwork collapsed and weeds taking over. No wonder young Anneli would not choose to be a tourist in her hometown.

And while the black, blue and white flag of Estonia snapped in the wind, and St. Peter's Square promised to be a starting block for urban renewal, the city as a whole had remained stubbornly Russian, very reluctantly embracing its important new role as the third-largest city in an independent country. Now that he began to notice details, he saw campaign posters everywhere, in every color. He did not understand a word on them.

When Swanson felt he had absorbed enough sadness, he retreated to a forested area near the river south of the city, ventured deep into the trails and set up a cold camp. It would be uncomfortable to sleep outside, but he had the proper gear and had been in worse places. He wasn't planning on being around for more than one night at the most. Checking into a hotel was out of the question, for that would leave electronic traces. He walked to the riverbank and looked across at a mirroring forest in the Russian Federation and wondered what was buried back in there.

Swanson was thoroughly ready for a drink by the time Anneli Kallasti climbed onto the back of the motorcycle and guided him to the strangely named "German Pub." It was a cellar joint on Malmi that was sedate on the exterior but was rocking inside. She had pulled her hair into a ponytail and wore low-cut jeans with patterned silver spangles on the back pockets and a tight burnt-orange sweater beneath her jacket. The loud music smashing from overhead speakers brought an instant smile to her face. It was early, but people were already on the dance floor. She grabbed his hand and led him to a table, and called for three mugs of beer and a plate of bratwurst appetizers while checking her phone.

"Brokk, my guy, will be here in a minute," she said as her eyes roamed the gathering crowd. They were mostly twentysomethings, bursting with energy.

It reminded Swanson of the musical *Cabaret*, about a club that operated in Berlin during the early Nazi years, and customers left their problems outside the door to spend a few hours forgetting their troubles in wine and beer and music. Was this place part of the rebirth of Estonia, or was it a last gasp of freedom? He drank his beer and watched.

Anneli used a mirror to fix her pretty face, which lit up when Brokk Mihailovich came through the door and immediately started greeting friends. He was tall and slim, with onyx eyes that flashed over the crowd until he saw Anneli, who waved. Then, with the confidence of a veteran politician working a rope line, the man in the droopy white wool sweater and worn jeans moved with almost feline grace through the crowd, trolling for votes by sharing a handshake here, a whispered confidence there, or a pat on the shoulder or a quick hug, never losing the smile nor slowing down. Good cheer followed in his wake, adding to the loose atmosphere of the club. Like if Brokk was present, this was the place to be.

Anneli jumped up and gave him a public and proprietary kiss on the lips, as if establishing her territory, and Mihailovich lifted her off the floor with an effortless embrace. He turned her loose and extended his hand. "I am Brokk Mihailovich, Mister Brown. Welcome to Narva." The English was almost without accent.

"Good to meet you," Swanson said. Anneli had obviously briefed him.

Mihailovich and Anneli slid into the booth and spoke briefly in Estonian, shared a private laugh, then switched to English as they started on the brats and beer. Brokk paused now and again to wave or greet someone.

"Why are you so popular?" Kyle asked.

"I am running to become the mayor of Narva," the young man said. "The youngest candidate by far, so these people are my constituents, what your politicians would call my base. I work hard to keep them on my side."

"Ah. Anneli told me you were political."

"Everyone is political, including you, Simon . . . may I call you that?"

"Sure, but you're wrong. I'm about as political as a tree. I stay as far away from that stuff as I can get."

Anneli laughed. "We don't have that luxury, Simon. This city is ninety percent Russian, by heritage, language, age and preference. Brokk is a lawyer and is a leader in trying to create a true democracy, and a true national identity. That's why we all love him."

"Good. Best of luck." Swanson raised his mug in a toast. "The Old Guard giving you a lot of opposition?"

The lawyer moodily nodded. "Every day. We will win eventually, but progress is slow. Their time is over, and now we are all waiting around for that whole generation to die off. This election is important because my main opponent wants to resurrect legislation to make Narva autonomous, to officially split off from Estonia and take this city back to being officially Russian. I want you to interview me for your publications and help me win. Estonia must remain whole."

Kyle gave a guffaw of disbelief. "I write travel stories, Brokk. I'm not a political reporter or a news correspondent. I am not qualified to interview you on details of your platform, or whatever."

Mihailovich never lost his sense of humor. "You are a journalist, Simon, a voice to the outside world and we need you. *The New York Times* and the papers in London would buy this story on the spot. Everyone writes about the castle, so you would have the exclusive on what this town is really about."

"And maybe drop in a couple of quotes from you and an observation that Narva is changing and modernizing?"

"Exactly." Brokk was a convincing young man.

It sounded logical, but Swanson said, "Maybe. Do

you have some other stories that I can combine it with to help get it published?"

Anneli looked at her lover. "The Lenin statue. That would work."

Brokk agreed. "Like every other country in the USSR, Estonia was littered with statues of Vladimir Ilyich Lenin, standing proud and bestowing the blessings of communism on all the little people. We had a large one in St. Peter's Square, but when we became independent, we discovered that it was hard to attract foreign investment with old Lenin still dominating the middle of town."

"What did you do?"

"We moved the famous old Bolshevik into an obscure corner of the castle. Out of sight, out of mind," Anneli said. "Oh, you should have heard the old Cossacks howl in protest. That will be a good story, right? You can get photos of it and then post it all over the Net. And you can use it to push the current political angle and get Brokk's name out to millions of people around the world."

Mihailovich stretched a long arm around Anneli's shoulders and brought her close. "She is convinced that social media is going to get me elected. Twitter and Facebook and all the rest."

Kyle pursed his lips in thought, then asked, "On the city council, wouldn't you be dealing with routine things like construction permits and sewage arguments? I mean, what's the point? You would not set foreign policy."

The magnetism of Brokk Mihailovich was getting to Swanson. A man in a hurry, sure of his path and his future. "Sure, I will do that routine stuff. But I can also do a lot more, Simon. I will make life better for the people of Narva and get us out from under that Russian boot even more. Human rights. The Disappeared. Our staggering economy. Better care for our old, sick and homeless, less police brutality and civic corruption."

"Sounds like you may be running for president, not mayor. What are 'the Disappeared'?"

Both of the young people turned serious in a heartbeat. "We must tread carefully on this, Simon," Brokk said. "Proof is hard to come by, and the Russians are volatile about the subject."

Anneli slapped her hand on the table, leaned across and hissed in a softer tone, like a cute, poisonous viper. "Well, *fuck* the Russians. People like us—the opponents of the leftover commies—have begun to vanish in the past few months from towns all along the border. One day they are amongst us, and the next day they are gone without a trace. Nothing is ever heard from them again and the police say they probably just left town."

"Shhh," Brokk cautioned her. "Maybe we can discuss that later, after I get to know Simon better. After all, he may be a spy sent to entrap us."

"I have no secrets, Brokk. I'm a writer for tourists. If you want to know how much it costs to go up in the Eiffel Tower, then I'm your guy. The name of a good restaurant with low prices in London? Got you covered. Anything else is out of my league." He finished his beer and signaled for another. "I never discuss religion or politics while drinking, and frankly, I do not like the idea of being used by you two revolutionaries."

Both stared at him. Anneli finally called for another beer herself, and declared, "Then you are a useless human being."

"Yeah. That pretty much sums me up," Swanson said.

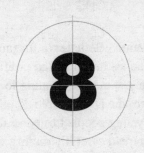

**T**HE RAIN GODS had been merciful and the little camp that Swanson had made in the forest remained dry throughout the night. Alone, shielded by the forest, he bagged out and slept well with the soothing rush of the wide Narva River at his side. On awakening in the gray dawn of Thursday morning, he stretched out and thought about building a fire and making coffee, but suppressed that urge. Fire and smoke drew attention. Instead, he washed at the edge of the river and the frigid water finished the wake-up. Some juice and an energy bar were his breakfast, then he climbed back into the sleeping bag and snoozed for a while longer. Both his pulse and heartbeat were low, and his mind was clear.

He had not carried much for the trip, but took his time to carefully roll, tie and stow everything, and to bury trash and unneeded items. When it was time for the trip out, he brushed over his tracks and started the big BMW. He had to keep the tourism writer charade going for just a little while longer. Tonight he would be sleeping in a hotel suite in Tallinn with hot showers, and eating steak on a plate. He did not dwell on the political and social aspirations of the energetic young couple he had met the previous day, for he did not have a dog in that particular fight. They were little-league protestors scrapping with a cub, while Swanson was dealing with the whole Russian bear. However, he would pass their names along to the CIA and perhaps the pair might be cultivated as on-the-ground information assets. Reliable human intelligence sources, HUMINT, were precious in the spy game. Still, it was hard not to like the emotional youngsters, and he wished them success.

Once parked at the castle, he used some time to walk around the sprawling grounds to familiarize and get oriented. The more than seven acres that were steeped in bloody history were an interlocking masterwork of defense. The grounds, studded with individual bastions, swept up from the west side of the river to the dominant crown of the Hermann Castle, which was the official name. Just across on the east side of the river was the imposing Ivangorod fortress, and the grounds of both had been modernized and improved over the centuries as arrows gave way to firearms. Together with the area's other waterways, dense forests and soupy swamps, it had been a military choke point in the old days and still was. Kyle stopped to make a note of that as he checked his map.

A ticket to the castle cost only a few Euros, and he actually played tourist, although he looked at things through military eyes. The Northern Yard had been rebuilt to showcase life as it had been in the seventeeth century, the colorful Linnaeus Garden was struggling into bloom, and he found the ten-foot bronze statue of

Lenin hidden away in a corner and caked with dirt, as if embarrassed. The inner museum was mildly interesting, as were the tight tunnels and the soaring ceiling in the refectory. Kyle made it obvious that he was taking notes, playing reporter. He sketched in his pad. He had lunch. He blended.

Finally, about one o'clock, he made his way into the Pikk Hermann Tower, a massive square edifice that soared up more than 160 feet, and the stairs tested anyone not used to exercise. There were a few tourists around the topmost gallery, but they came and went, and the single security guard strolled through once. When the guard was gone, the journey through ancient history was over for Kyle. Time to work. He brought out his Bushnell 7x50 binoculars, compact and powerful, with a built-in digital compass, and leaned on the waist-high safety railing to steady his view.

The Ivangorod castle, of course, dominated the close view. It was lower and flatter, with crenellated walls, a dreary piece of architecture that had not kept pace with the renovation of its counterpart in Estonia. From his high position, Kyle could see over and around it for a long way.

A long, solid bridge alongside the pair of castles connected the highway between the two nations. Swanson examined it. Cars and trucks were in line to get into Russia, but it was a long wait today due to the construction on the Russian side. Gangs of workers were shoring up, strengthening and expanding the roadway from behind the entry points on out of sight to the east. He made notes and drew it, using a fresh page.

The town of Ivangorod itself was not very large, with a population of only about eleven thousand people, and weathered old rooftops poked through thick belts of trees near the downtown area. To the south of the castle, he spotted more heavy construction in the distance that indicated the possibility that an airport was being laid out. He consulted his guidebook. The airport nearest to Ivangorod was about seventy-five miles away. Pretty logical that they might want a closer one, although he was seeing something a lot bigger than a single landing strip for small planes. His pencil raced over the paper, and he noted the compass bearing and turned the page, shifting his attention to a third point of interest.

What looked like an industrial area was busy. A lot of trucks were moving to the area, and he did not see any major buildings that would indicate some major foundry or manufacturing facility. There were no smokestacks, a normal part of Russian construction, where air quality was not high on the priority list. Instead, there were round tanks in which liquids could be stored, and a lacework of shiny new pipes to shift it around. He pinpointed the location and noted, *Chemicals?*

Then he realized that he had dismissed the Russian castle itself because it was such an obvious location and, drawing his binos in tighter, he spotted fresh rail lines snaking into the rear area. Not rusty steel, but shining in the midday sun. Behind the back stone wall he spotted a series of low and long buildings at precise positions, equidistant. Then, with the sun so high and at a slight angle, he saw the barbed concertina wire around one of the buildings. A few uniformed soldiers with weapons walked the perimeter. The people inside the courtyard of the castle were also soldiers, and not tourists. He had simply overlooked them as being too obvious. Swanson quickly drew it all, made his notes, but didn't commit his conclusion to paper. He needed to think about it before doing so. Swanson folded up the tablet, put away the binos and just stood still, taking it all in, pivoting his head left to right and back again.

A new airport, rail lines, a possible fuel farm, some military barracks, a prison and road construction that would support heavier weights. It could be a surge of economic investment, but he didn't think so. The kids last night told him that the inhabitants of the neighboring town had recently applied to Moscow to be allowed to join Estonia, which was not the act of people enjoying a surge of economic prosperity. That highway improvement, he thought, could just as well be used to handle tanks and armored vehicles. Forgotten little Ivangorod was being polished up with all the makings of a first-class FOB, a forward operating base, a military jump-off point. The only place for Russia to jump to from there was into Estonia. That was why Ivan had sent him here. Nothing else made sense.

"Simon! Simon!" The panicked screams of Anneli Kallasti were punctuated by the pounding of her feet on the stairway to the gallery. She was running as if from death itself. Swanson instantly jerked away from the world of vague thought back into the present and to a full mental alert. He moved away from the railing of the parapet and toward the stairway entrance, and heard heavier footsteps farther below.

"Simon!" came the cry again. "Are you up here?"

"Yeah, Anneli. I'm here. Come on up." He had no idea what was happening, but the fright in her voice was clear. He stepped into the middle of the walkway to maximize the amount of room to deal with whatever was coming up that tight staircase.

She burst into the gallery with her hair in disarray and clutching the rail as she forced herself up the final steps and saw him there. Swanson could still hear the feet down below, coming closer with each second, and she fell into his arms, gasping for breath. "They came and took Brokk this morning! Now they are after me!" Her eyes were wide as she coughed out the words and sank to her knees.

"Who? Who took Brokk?" He raised her back up, and guided her to a nearby corner.

Her breath was slowing to strong, openmouthed gulps for air. "THEM! Two Russians in a big car took him away. Two more are chasing me. I didn't know where to run, but I remembered that you were going to be in the castle today. Please help me, Simon. These are the people who make us disappear. They will take me away."

The footsteps on the stairs were closer, but slower. Whoever it was had been slowed by the climb, while the young girl had been fueled by fright. Kyle rose to his feet, leaving her sitting beside the wall. "I believe you, Anneli. Let me see if I can sort this out, quiet them down and get the whole story."

"No, Simon. They are killers! They will kill us both."

"That's not going to happen. You just stay right where you are while I talk with them." *Damn. The pistol in the clip holster beneath his sweatshirt could not be used—it was too noisy and there were too many civilians and guards were in the castle. It would have to go hand-to-hand.*

Anneli responded with a low moan of despair and

curled into a fetal position, with her face buried in her hands. Kyle turned from her just as the first man came up into the gallery, with a face that was flushed bright red from the exertion of the climb and etched in fury. He was a big, wide guy in an ill-fitting coat and his fists were balled up, ready to pound somebody. The black eyes glanced to the girl, then settled on Swanson.

So much for conversation. The silent equation was simply that to reach the woman, the attacker first had to go through the stranger standing before her. The big man charged.

Kyle slid his left foot forward as if taking a boxing stance, and the man flicked out a hard jab aimed at Swanson's cheek. Swanson grabbed the extended left wrist with his own left hand as the fist whizzed harmlessly past, pulled and immediately cupped his right hand beneath the big guy's armpit, which provided two points of contact on the outstretched arm. The man was immediately off balance and his momentum, combined with the sudden yank, carried him forward. Kyle squatted and pulled the guy onto his back, grabbed a leg, stood quickly as if he was lifting a sack of feed from a pickup truck, and hurled the attacker over the railing, releasing the hold as he went. The man was so surprised that he didn't start to scream until he was halfway through the fall onto the gigantic stones waiting below.

Swanson didn't watch him go. His mind was already busy with the tactical situation. That one was gone, but another one had cleared the top step and was moving into the fight. This one was more of a normal-sized human, about Kyle's own size, and he appeared more agile. Kyle wasted no time letting him think about what was happening, but swung around in a spinning side kick that planted his boot heel hard and deep into the liver, just below the rib cage, and returned to his original stance.

The attacker was backed up a couple of steps by the force of the blow, as the nerve package connected to the liver shivered beneath the power, but he showed no other immediate response. Swanson gave him the necessary room, knowing that the human body needs a few seconds to react to the agony of a full liver strike. Sure enough, the man suddenly winced in pain, his mouth fell open in a sickening grunt as he lost all of his air, then his legs went out, and he doubled over. Kyle finished flopping the guy to the deck, climbed aboard and put a rear naked choke on him, locking legs around the stomach in a figure-four hold. Squeezing with the vice of his legs kept the lungs from expanding while the choke hold cut off the airways. Then it was just a matter of holding on, like riding a wild horse, for the approximate thirty seconds needed until the thrashing thug was dead.

Anneli was crouched against the wall, her hair hanging over her face, and gripping her knees to her chest. She was sobbing, and her cheeks were wet with tears from wide and fearful eyes.

Swanson knelt before her and spoke softly. "Anneli, we have to go right now. You have to get on your feet and come with me. Now."

She mumbled something that sounded like, "Who are you?"

"We have to go, Anneli. I am going to take you someplace safe, but we have to get moving. People will be coming up here. I'm going to touch you, so don't be frightened." He rested his palm on her arm to establish a gentle physical contact. She did not shy away. Already from below came the sounds of people yelling. The falling man had created a surprise among the tourists.

She stared at the nearby dead body, then looked in horror at Kyle and said quietly, *"You're a monster!"*

"Perhaps. But I'm *your* monster, Anneli. Now get on your feet and stay with me. Don't bother looking at that guy. We're going down the stairs. Concentrate on only that. Follow me down the stairs." Kyle lifted her to her feet and she hugged her arms across her chest, but took a step forward. "Good. That's good. Let's go."

He stayed in front of her, keeping his ears open for her trailing steps, while his eyes ranged over the surroundings. The fallen body had attracted the guards and a small circle of workers and tourists. A few were craning their necks back to look up at the gallery. Guards would start coming up the stairs soon but, for the moment, they were occupied with the grisly remains on the ground. Kyle and Anneli picked up their pace and managed to reach the bottom before encountering anyone else.

He took her hand and stood close. "We are just a couple of tourists now. We walk slowly to the parking area. I'm going to put my arm around your shoulders like I am comforting you. You keep your head down. Let's move."

The black motorcycle was waiting on its kickstand and, without another word, he got on, then she boarded behind him and grabbed his waist tightly. She leaned her head against his back as the engine throbbed to life, and Swanson eased the BMW away from the parking ramp, accelerated into the street, turned a couple of corners and was headed south.

They stopped at his encampment from the night before just long enough to gather the gear. "Where can we go, Simon?" she asked while struggling into the weatherized protective clothing. "That's not your real name, is it?"

"No time for questions right now, Anneli. We're taking you back to Tallinn and some friends who will keep you safe."

"I need to stay and find Brokk!"

"You would only get arrested yourself. The best way for you to help Brokk is to come with me. We have to get out of here before whoever those guys were working for figures out what happened back at the castle. Narva is not where we want to be. Not a minute longer. Climb aboard."

They rolled out without further conversation. When he looked in the rearview mirror, he could see the towering castle tower looming against the sky, as if it were watching them run for their lives.

**T**HE HOTEL LOBBY was floored with rich limestone and thick carpets, while the vaulted ceiling and huge windows and tapestries bespoke richness and elegance. The uniformed doorman gave a quizzical look to the approaching man wearing dirty jeans and carrying a backpack, accompanied by a much younger woman. The *I belong here* attitude and the hard-set face were silent warnings for the attendant to tip his hat and say "Welcome, sir." The man offered no explanation for their rather shabby appearance.

Anneli was unsteady and shaken after the long ride, she was freezing and felt as though she might as well have just landed on the far side of the moon. Where Narva had been dank and threadbare, Tallinn was booming and vibrant and filled with colors that made her senses reel. She would have hidden behind Kyle had he not kept a firm hand on her elbow and gently marched her by his side straight across the carpet to the front desk.

He dropped his backpack at his feet with a loud *clunk*,

unapologetic for his sudden appearance. "I am Kyle Swanson. Excalibur Enterprises," he told the immaculate clerk in the starched white shirt and dark suit and tie. "I have a reservation for a suite." He turned and winked at Anneli.

The clerk kept a straight face and pecked at his computer, stifling a gulp when the reservation came up. The new guest who looked like a pub crawler was actually an important visitor: executive vice president, Excalibur Enterprises, London. "Yes, sir, Mister Swanson. Welcome. We have been expecting you." The clerk was now on familiar turf, dealing with a member of the high-powered clientele, many of whom were as eccentric as hell. He remembered the Saudi prince who carried a peregrine falcon on his wrist, an obese and cigar-smoking German industrialist who spat on the marble counter, and the countless older men escorted by younger females, beautiful ladies who were never introduced nor officially checked in. The hotel simply added an additional guest fee to the total, for the guest's firm had posted a ten-thousand-dollar line of credit, with overage protection guaranteed.

"A representative of your company checked you in two days ago and took your luggage to the suite. It is waiting for you."

Swanson nodded. "Very well. Are there any messages?"

"Your friend left this." The clerk handed over a small envelope along with a pair of electronic keys. "You are engaged in the Republic Suite, sir. The top floor. It has a splendid view."

Swanson gave him an envelope in return that contained the motorcycle key for the bike parked in the covered garage, plus a $500 bonus, and addressed to Andre Parl. "This gentleman will come by later today. Please give it to him."

"Of course. Anything else?"

Anneli had written down her clothing sizes and needs during one of their brief stops on the trip, and Kyle gave that to the clerk. "Please have the concierge have someone purchase these items and deliver them to my room as soon as possible. Add it to my bill."

The clerk did not flinch. It was a familiar instruction. To him, the list spelled: *mistress*. It called for a pair of jeans, a pair of slacks, two tops, heavy sweater and jacket, boots and trainers and socks, underwear, and a black pantsuit with matching low heels. There was no price range mentioned. "Of course, sir. A dinner reservation perhaps? Our own restaurant is excellent, or the concierge can recommend some specialty places."

Swanson hoisted his backpack. "No thank you. We will just have room service tonight." He walked to the elevator, steering Anneli alongside.

While waiting, she wrapped her hand around his bicep. Beneath the jacket and the calm exterior, he was also still shaking from the cold. In the garage, his teeth had been chattering. She asked quietly, *"Who are you?"*

When the door closed behind them in the suite, Swanson threw the dead bolt and slid a chair in front of it. "You take the big bedroom. I'll sleep in this one over here," he said. "Anneli, I understand that you are confused and frightened right now, but do not worry. You're safe with me. I have to take a hot shower right away to knock off this cold—goddam, I'm freezing. You order up room service. Steak and potatoes and a salad with oil and vinegar, and a platter of fruit, cheese and cold cuts. A large pot of coffee. Then I'll explain everything . . . and you do not have to be afraid, Anneli. We are out of danger."

Swanson made a brief tour of the room and closed the curtains, pleased that the unknown CIA team that checked him in had been so careful with his clothing and luggage, and had stowed it away neatly after no doubt searching every thread. He picked out some fresh clothes, and stopped at the little desk. On a piece of notepaper, he wrote, "Cameras and listening device in the room. Act normal." Leaving it in the open so she could read it, he disappeared into a large bathroom and she heard a shower begin running hard.

Anneli took a deep breath and lowered herself onto the king-size bed, feeling the silkiness of the linen duvet with her palms. Her emotions were a vortex of turmoil: fear for herself, fear for Brokk, and fear of the man in the next room who wasn't who she thought he was. Not at all. When she had found him in the coffee shop, he was supposed to be a harmless travel writer, then she watched him kill two men with his bare hands right in front of her in the castle tower, seemingly without effort. Now they end up in a top-floor suite in a five-star hotel, where he had changed identities and was receiving almost royal treatment from an obsequious staff. As comfortable as he had tried to make her, Anneli viewed him as some apex predator, like a friendly wild wolf. All that she really knew was that she was safe in his shadow. Except for the fact that the room was bugged and someone was watching. It was too much to process, so she rolled facedown into the soft pillows and wept.

Thirty minutes later, Swanson felt almost human again. The hot deluge and steam had boosted his body temperature back to normal after it had loitered south of iceberg range during the last leg of the motorcycle trip. He heard the shower going in the master bath, and assumed Anneli was also washing away the cold trip. Room service was on the way with food.

In comfortable gray sweatpants and a loose pullover, white socks and sneaks, he slowly roamed around the suite, disabling the eavesdropping and video devices as he went. It had to be the CIA, he thought, and he would be dealing with them tomorrow. They knew where he was, and that was all he was willing to allow for now. Meanwhile, all he wanted was a steak and a good night's sleep.

The knock on the door was a polite rap. Swanson tucked the little Beretta 9mm under his sweatshirt and peered out. Two men in suits were standing there. He opened the door.

"You're not room service, are you?" he said, curling his right palm around the pistol grip at his back. "If you don't have steaks, then I don't want to see you."

"Mister Swanson, I am Chief Warrant Officer Mickey LeCroix and this is Mister Harrelson. We are both with the U.S. Army Civil Investigation Division. May we step inside for a moment?" LeCroix had a pleasant face, and looked in shape. His eyes were blue and busy. Harrelson stood off to the right, scowling and with his jacket open.

"I don't care who you are, Mister LeCroix. I have had a long day and I'm getting ready to eat and go to bed. Go away."

LeCroix laughed that off. "Not quite yet, sir. We have

come to escort you to meet with Colonel Thomas Markey. It won't take long."

"Never heard of him."

"Well, sir, apparently he has heard of you. Let us in and I will explain."

Kyle stepped aside and the two army investigators entered the suite. "So explain."

LeCroix unbuttoned his coat and put his hands in his pockets to show no threat. "Colonel Markey is a senior fellow here in Tallinn at the NATO Cooperative Cyber Defence Centre of Excellence."

Swanson settled into a big chair, maintaining the cover of an arrogant businessman. As he adjusted the pillow behind him, he stuck his pistol between the cushion and the armrest. "Good for him, but I've never heard of that, either, and I'm not in the army."

With the good guy/bad guy routine, Harrelson finally spoke in a deep voice as he flipped his coat back to reveal a holstered weapon. "Fuck you, asshole. Enough games. Get on your feet and let's go."

LeCroix half-turned to his partner. "That's not needed, Ralph. Stay cool." Then he looked back at Kyle. "We are aware of your military background and your current status with a certain government agency, sir, so I'm afraid that we must insist that you come with us."

Swanson carefully withdrew the Beretta from the cushion and rested it on his knee. "And I insist right back that I'm not going anywhere. Keep your hands where I can see them, Ralphy-boy. Here is the only deal I'm willing to make. You go back and tell the colonel that I am a private citizen and a businessman with a major defense contractor. If he wants an appointment, I can give him twenty minutes tomorrow after breakfast. Then I leave town. He should be here at nine o'clock."

Harrelson snapped, "You can't talk that way to us, or dismiss an army colonel's order, you rich snot."

Swanson responded, "Leave now."

The two warrant officers exchanged looks, then at a motion from LeCroix, they went to the door. "The colonel is not going to be pleased with this noncooperation," he said. "After all, we are all on the same team, right?"

The room service cart arrived five minutes later, awash with delicious aromas. A luggage cart was also there, with the new clothes for Anneli. Kyle signed the chit, including a nice tip, and lifted one of the curved metal lids from the food tray. There was a T-bone steak, medium rare, with sautéed onions, mushrooms, and a silver cell phone on top of the sixteen-ounce cut. It bore a gravy-stained card that read: PRESS CALL BUTTON. Swanson dropped the card in a trash container, wiped the phone and made the call.

"We've been waiting for you to show up," said a male voice.

"Here I am. I cannot talk now. I will call you tomorrow morning and straighten everything out. Where is Ivan?"

He heard the man chuckle. "I will tell you tomorrow morning. What are you going to do with the girl?"

"Turn her over to you. She's wanted by the bad guys, and is a potentially very valuable HUMINT asset."

"I figured that. You have already bought her some clothes, so you are going to buy her a few more. Tomorrow morning at eight o'clock, take a taxi to the Kristiine Shopping Centre, a mall that specializes in fashion. Look for a store called Rags, and ask for the owner.

Her code name is 'Calico.' She will take the girl off your hands, and then we'll meet up."

"Safe house; the works. Trust me, she can help us."

"Yes. You leave at noon for Brussels for the debrief."

"Okay."

"One last thing. How did you get off the ferry without being seen?"

Kyle laughed. "I don't know what you're talking about. I just walked down the gangway like everybody else."

The caller repeated the instructions. "Rags. Calico. Brussels. Look forward to meeting you the next time through here." He hung up.

Kyle dropped the phone in his pocket, then called out, "Anneli! Come on out. Chow time."

She emerged from the master bedroom wrapped in a thick white hotel robe, using a rumpled towel to dry her hair. She warily walked to the table on which he had laid out the trays, and picked at the salad. "I'm not really hungry," she said.

"I am," Kyle said. "I turned off the electronic snoops so we can speak freely, Anneli. I will tell you what I can. Mostly, one more time, you are not in danger here. You have stumbled into some waters that are way over your head, but we are going to fix that."

She sniffed and dabbed her nose with the towel. "I need to save Brokk," she said. "I am worried sick about him."

"People will be working on that, too, but first things first. My real name is Kyle Swanson and I really am with a large business called Excalibur Enterprises, based in London. That is the truth, and all you need to know about me."

"I saw you kill two men. I think you are a soldier." She picked up a fork and knife and trimmed off a small piece of steak. The proximity of the food was calling to her.

Kyle kept eating, pausing now and then to push the narrative without giving her everything. "I was in the U.S. Marines for many, many years, Anneli. That is where I learned how to fight. I remember the training."

She curled her bare feet up beneath her and ate another piece of meat. Her hunger had replaced the initial reluctance. "So why did you pretend to be a tourist journalist in Narva?"

"Now, what I am about to tell you is secret. You will understand why. I also work once in a while for an American government agency. My trip over there to Narva was to gather some specific information, and that was why I kept my distance from you and Brokk. It was not that I did not want to help you, but I could not jeopardize my mission."

She just stared at him for a while with those dark eyes, chewing a small potato slice. "I was not part of the deal, huh?"

"No, you weren't. The coffee shop and the pub were no problem. However, once you ran onto the gallery, we had no choice. I wasn't going to let them take you away, and we couldn't stay in Narva, could we? So here we are. Questions?"

"I have a million questions and you probably will not answer any of them."

"Probably not. Tomorrow morning, we're going to meet a woman who will take you on the next step of this new journey. Your life is about to change, Anneli, but not in a bad way. My agency is going to give you a velvet-glove welcome and do everything possible to find Brokk, too."

"It is the Central Intelligence Agency?"

He handed her a small white pill. "You will be told everything at the right time. Right now, just enjoy the food and go get some sleep. You have been through a lot today, and this will help you rest if you need it. Be ready to leave at eight o'clock in the morning. Wear the black suit."

**10**

**THE SHOPPING CENTER** was a fashion rainbow. After decades of living in a drab communist world, where utilitarian clothes matched black and gray skies and hopeless faces, Tallinn had charged into the modern world. It had become a place where clothing mattered and it was permissible for a woman to be beautiful. The mall was lined with shops that featured the latest in women's wear, and business was brisk even at the early hour. Clothing was coming in and going out of the loading docks on wheeled racks that darted through the corridors. Despite her personal anxiety, Anneli Kallasti could not suppress a surge of excitement as she went inside with Swanson, beneath the painted gazes of mannequins dressed like strutting peacocks.

Rags occupied a lot of space in a far corner, from which it had access from several directions. The signs were modest, but the prices were not. Large brown easy chairs were scattered about, with magazines on tables, to help husbands wait while their ladies tried on different outfits and were tended with care by professional seamstresses and the sales staff.

Swanson told the woman at the cash register in front that he had an appointment with the owner, and Anneli repeated the request in Estonian. They were pointed to a hallway cluttered with racks of garments. The door at the end opened and a willowy blonde sailed out on a big smile, calling out loud enough for others to hear, "Kyle! You are a scoundrel for not calling me earlier! And Anneli, too! How delightful to see you again. Both of you get in here." She threw her arms around Kyle and leaned close enough to whisper, "I'm Calico."

She hustled them into the office and shut the door, then turned to Anneli, and her character changed. "Oh, you poor girl. You poor thing," Calico said as she wrapped the bewildered girl close to her in a hug. "You poor, poor thing. You are safe now. You are safe." The tight, protective wall that Anneli had built around her emotions since the previous afternoon burst at the outpouring of sympathy, and the two women clung together, crying. Calico stroked the girl as if comforting a kitten.

She was tall, even taller in her stylish heels, and wore a soft cotton dress of Spanish blue that touched two inches above the knees. A gold wedding band twinkled on her left hand. She let the weeping Anneli cry for two full minutes before releasing her and guiding her to a sofa. Calico sat beside her, still holding her hand, but turned to business.

"We don't have much time. I want to get Anneli under cover as fast as possible. A bit more advance warning would have been helpful."

"There was no time. It is what it is." He had skimmed

the office while the women were in consolation mode and noticed that beside the trappings of a busy business in the clothing trade, there were no personal mementoes, family pictures, diplomas or certificates on the walls or the shelves. "Who are you?"

"My name is Jan Hollings, and I was given only a short brief by our people here and from Helsinki last night. Your reputation is that you are a package of problems, Swanson. You like to work alone, even if it screws everybody else."

Kyle took another chair and leaned forward. "I get results. Plus, Anneli here was worth my trip to Narva. She is a brave and very intelligent kid who has already figured out that we are with the Central Intelligence Agency."

Anneli finished dabbing her eyes with a paper tissue. "Are you with the CIA, too, Mrs. Hollings?"

Calico gave her hand a reassuring squeeze. "Call me Jan, and yes, I am. Does that bother you, dear?"

The dark-haired girl's lips were in a tight line and her eyes were pools of determination. "No. Not at all. Will you help me find my boyfriend?"

"I cannot promise that we will be successful, but I can promise that we will try to find Brokk, and we have a lot of tools. Will you help us find him?"

"Yes! Anything you want, I will do! I must find him."

Swanson choked back a laugh. Calico was slick. She had signed up Anneli as a new recruit in less than five minutes, a catch who was going to pay large dividends with her language skills, intimate knowledge of the Estonian culture and the people, and a hatred for the Russians that flamed white hot.

He studied Anneli. She was ready to move on. "Okay, then. I'm going to leave you with Jan. I have to get back to the States."

The girl jumped to her feet with a look of alarm. "When will you come back? When will I see you again?" The thought of losing her security blanket was startling.

"In this business, who knows? I hope so. You take care of yourself, and I will keep tabs on how you're doing." That was a lie. He did not plan to ever return to Estonia. "Good luck."

She launched herself at him and began crying again. Calico watched the interplay between them and would include it in her report. The girl genuinely admired Swanson, who, although kind, did not return the affection. He just wanted out of there. Anneli gave him a kiss on the cheek, and disengaged. "Thank you," she said. "You saved my life."

"I hope we find Brokk. I liked him," Kyle said. He gave her hand a final squeeze and walked out. He had ten minutes to get back to the hotel and meet the shitbird colonel, Thomas Markey.

"Mister Swanson." The hotel concierge greeted him in the spacious lobby as Kyle was heading for the breakfast buffet restaurant. "Your guests have already arrived."

*Guests?* Kyle asked himself. *Probably the two CID bird-dogs are with the big guy.* The room was long and comfortable, and a few customers were eating and reading newspapers or fiddling with their portable computers through the hotel's free Wi-Fi. A steaming covered buffet table was along the near wall. At the very back, beside the kitchen's swinging doors, four men were at two tables. The CID types were in front, quiet and as inconspicuous as a pair of concrete gargoyles. Behind them were two other suits, and one waved to him. Kyle poured a cup of coffee at the buffet, went over and took a chair at their table. No one offered a handshake.

"I am Deke Cooper, the local chief of station. This is Colonel Tom Markey, U.S. Army." Cooper was a short, slim man with an old-style crew cut that was going gray.

"Why are we meeting in a public place right by the kitchen doors?" Swanson watched a waiter burst through the swinging portals carrying a tray for the hot table.

"Elite spook tradecraft, my boy. With all of the noise and pot-banging and shouts in that kitchen, eavesdropping is impossible. Anyway, it's good to finally meet you, Swanson. Everything go well with Calico? She's one of our best. Like you, she is a legitimate business executive who has established an incredible network. Trots all over Europe, even into Russia."

"We are talking about confidential matters in front of this colonel?" Kyle was puzzled. The man might be an army officer, but he was still an outsider.

Deke Cooper laughed. "Set your mind at ease, pal. We are the CIA, but we don't have any secrets left, thanks to Mister Snowden and other traitors over the years. Truth be told, we probably have not had a real secret since about 1956. The colonel has more than the necessary clearances, and Calico is his wife."

"Jesus Christ Almighty," Kyle muttered and drank some coffee. "I'm going to get something to eat." He needed to buy some time to think, so he went to the buffet and grew hungry as he went down the line. He loaded up and went back to the table. More coffee.

After a few bites, he said, "Colonel, she introduced herself as Jan Hollings. Not the same last name as you."

"For the sake of her job, she didn't take my last name."

"So how can I help the U.S. Army today?" he asked after tasting a warm slice of local bread.

"Ivan Strakov," replied ColonelMarkey. "My old enemy, Ivan Strakov." The voice was soft but filled with purpose. He had intelligent brown eyes, a militarily correct posture, and a thick wave of sandy hair. "You are going to debrief him during the coming weeks, and I want you to let me know what he says. Through back channels, of course."

Swanson ate some eggs that had been scrambled with cheese and a mild spice. He shot a glance at Cooper. "Sorry, Colonel, I can't do that. I don't know what you have been told about me, but it's wrong."

"You work for the CIA, Mister Swanson. Deke has cleared my request."

Kyle swallowed the food and chased it with coffee. Then he pushed back a bit from the table and checked the surroundings before speaking. The kitchen roar was continuing. "Now, guys, that is technically correct, but not exactly accurate. Things have gone off track. I do work with the CIA, but I am neither a spy nor an analyst, and Deke is not my boss. The only person to whom I answer is Martin Atkins, the deputy director for clandestine services, back at Langley. I do specific special assignments on rare occasions, and that is all. This whole thing of coming to visit Estonia was a surprise to me, and I don't like surprises. I will be going back to the States as soon as possible."

Cooper did not lose his good mood. "You are flying

to Brussels later today and will dance with Ivan. That's firm. After that, who knows?"

Kyle snorted and went back to the food. "I know what happens next, Deke. Brussels is the end of the line for me. After I corroborate Ivan's story, then he is all yours. Stick him full of truth serum or shove apples up his ass to make him talk. I don't care. I have to get back to work."

The colonel shot him a long look. "I know more about Ivan Strakov than you do, Swanson."

"No argument there, Colonel Markey. You probably do. I only knew him for a few weeks many years ago when he was just a sergeant, little more than a grunt with a rifle. I still am bewildered that he tabbed me to talk with when he defected."

The colonel finally showed some emotion. "What if I tell you that Strakov wasn't a sergeant at the time, Swanson. Young Ivan was already an intelligence officer on assignment to evaluate and report on your Scout/ Sniper program. I saw that you guys called him 'Ivan the Terrible.' The reason he could not shoot up to your standards is because he was never trained as a sniper at all. He was sent to join your course as a spy; he milked you like a cow."

Kyle Swanson stopped eating and listened with growing incredulity as Markey gave him unexpected information, with Deke Cooper offering occasional side comments. After ten minutes, the breakfast adjourned and they all trooped up to Kyle's suite for privacy. The two CID investigators stood guard in the hallway outside.

Markey said that he had been Strakov's "mirror." Their careers had roughly run in parallel, on opposite sides of the strategic aisle, and they had parried frequently in both official and social settings. Ivan and Tom knew each other, but were not friends.

"I never bought the story that he died in some little plane crash in Lake Baikal. Discarded that as soon as I heard about it. Ivan would never have taken such a chance. In that part of Russia, in this season, he would have been traveling aboard a transport with multiple engines. So I thought from the get-go that he was playing another one of his games." The American colonel was looking from the hotel window as he spoke, as if watching spring bloom in Estonia. He was a worried man.

"Swanson, you know now that I am posted here in Tallinn, right? The official title is as a senior fellow at the NATO Cooperative Cyber Defence Centre of Excellence?" The officer seemed to be growing nervous, talking to the window. "Have you wondered why that vital organization is located in this little burg of a country, right in the armpit of Russia?"

"No. I had other things on my mind. Tell me about it."

Deke Cooper of the CIA took over. "The short version is that after the collapse of communism, Estonia was left with nothing. It had one point two million people and still had to do more than ninety percent of its trade with Russia. It was little more than a beggar state at the time. Estonia had one foot still in the nineteenth century, and one in the twentieth and both feet stuck in the mud. So the country made the radical move of betting the farm on the twenty-first century, and has since become an economic Baltic Tiger."

Swanson said, "I couldn't tell that over in Narva. That place is Russian to the core."

Colonel Markey found a chair. "It is, but the country as a whole is leaving Narva behind. This is now one of the most wired places in Europe, and any kid who reaches high school without having developed his or her own app or start-up tech company is considered a slow learner, a social pariah and will probably never get laid. The Estonian government saw early on that computer science was the future. They built an infrastructure to support it, and now a lot of kids call their homeland 'e-Stonia.' Skype was not invented here by accident."

Swanson saw the pieces coming together. "And that makes the boys in Moscow uncomfortable?"

"Better believe it. Back in 2008, there was a monster cyber-war hacking attack against Estonia, one of the biggest ever. It was of Russian origin, of course, although the Kremlin never admitted guilt. Everything over here was infected, spammed, or was virused like a plague. All it really did was make the Estonians work harder and get better at the game."

"Was Ivan Strakov part of that attack?" Kyle asked.

The colonel nodded. "Yeah. It was his baby. He was deep in the background, but I recognized his shadow and fingerprints. He done it, Sherlock, which is another reason that I don't trust that sonofabitch as far as I can throw a piano."

"And where do I fit into this picture? Like I told you both, I am not a spy. I am not a trained interrogator. I do other things." Swanson was dizzy with this new information. "I plan to swing by Brussels, do the thing with Ivan, then go home and tend to my own business.

Nothing you have said, while surprising and interesting, indicates that I should do otherwise."

Deke Cooper moved around, stretched, then folded his arms across his broad chest and leaned against a wall. "Fact is, Swanson, that the secret called Ivan Strakov has already leaked. Maybe he left a trail of bread crumbs, or a note, or who the hell knows, but the lid is already off of his defection. Moscow knows he has gone over to the other side, and Europe, NATO and Washington will not be able to contain it. Social media will have it within forty-eight hours. Think *Snowden*, man. Old Ivan is about to become a global celebrity."

Now the colonel finally showed some emotion. "Even if everything he tells us is true, Kyle, somebody has to be willing to call bullshit. This is a chance for you to get some payback on him. Deke and the alphabet agencies will do all the donkey work of the interviews and follow-up, but you could be on the inside, because he wants you there. For some reason we cannot decipher, he needs you once again. The whole thing is much too hinky for me, because Ivan Strakov is not a cowboy; everything he does has a reason. What I want from you is gut feelings. Get me the right information, and I'll stop him."

"Or what?"

"Or we go to war, probably."

"Another cyber-war between Russia and Estonia?"

"No, Kyle." The colonel's face grew tense. "Real war. Russia against NATO, which includes the United States."

Swanson snapped a humorless laugh. "You guys want me to spy on the spy, then report straight to you instead of to my real boss at the CIA. Nothing wrong with that,

Colonel, except it is borderline treason and I could end up in some supermax prison. Thanks for the chance to help save the world, but Deke and his boys are much more qualified for that sort of thing, so I pass. Get somebody else to carry that water. I'm going home."

**S**WANSON TOOK AN evening Lufthansa flight out of Tallinn primarily because it was not Aeroflot. German efficiency and timeliness was to be trusted, while riding on a Russian commercial aircraft was never really a choice if there were alternatives. His arrival in Belgium was without incident, and the check-in at the downtown hotel was smooth. It was just another city, just another airport, just another hotel. Total routine.

He had been provided with a new laptop computer and cell phone by Deke Cooper and the electronic equipment had been loaded by CIA techs with everything he might need. Brussels was six hours ahead of Washington, so the business day was just wrapping up on the other side of the Atlantic when he checked in with the office.

"Things are kind of stacking up around here, boss. When are you coming back?" Those were the first words from Janna Ecklund, who was running the place in his absence. "You were supposed to be gone for just a few days."

"Hello to you, too. Anything urgent?" Swanson enjoyed bantering with Janna and knew she had everything under control. Her FBI career had trained her not to leave loose ends.

"Sir Jeff is concerned because you were expelled from Finland. How does anybody get expelled from Finland? He wants to see you soon. You should give him a call. I've got some documents for you to sign. The people at XenTek Research in California are getting antsy for you to get out to Twentynine Palms for some new tests on Project Hydra."

"Use the electronic signature, or just forge my name," he instructed. "Tell Jeff everything is good on our end. I will contact XenTek as soon as I get back to the office." Hydra, a laser-guided bullet for a .50-caliber sniper rifle, was the latest invention coming off the drawing board from the skilled researchers and engineers of Excalibur Enterprises and its partners, and had a potential upside of millions of dollars in contracts.

"So when will that be, going back to my original question?"

"I will be in Brussels all day tomorrow, Janna. Then I have a direct flight straight into Dulles the day after."

"You sound tired." She had no idea why he was in Belgium and knew better than ask to on an open line.

"I am."

She laughed. "Stop whining. You can sleep when they're dead, Jarhead."

"See you in forty-eight hours, Feeb." He hung up.

Janna was right. He was tired. Exhausted. It wasn't the travel, but the saddle of concern that he was lugging around since the meeting with Colonel Markey and

Deke Cooper. The colonel was a combat veteran with several tours in the Sandbox, so he was not one to panic in the face of a little adversity. The problems he laid out were bona fide, even without Kyle sharing his own observations from the trip over to Narva. He thought about Anneli, the girl he had rescued, and her Disappeared boyfriend, Brokk. He thought about the spy network being run by the colonel's fashion-plate wife, Calico. He dialed his memory back even more and thought about the two goons who had tried to kidnap Anneli and kill him in the castle. Even wild combat usually has some meaning or discernible pattern to help it all make sense. He saw nothing in this mess.

One more drink, some bourbon over ice cubes, and he peeled back the cool white sheets and crawled beneath the covers.

The nightmare assaulted him. He dreamed of grime and grit, hopeless desolation, the stench of oil coagulating on the water around the blackened hulks of ships, and the burned remains of vehicles and shattered human bodies. Gaunt and frightened columns of refugees, mangled soldiers with their guts spilled, and buildings in smoldering ruin beneath an evil sky full of choking smoke that blanketed the countryside. Television sets flashed scenes of carnage. Politicians in world capitals arguing about who started it, who would finish it and which flags would still be flying when the war was over. Timers counting off seconds to launch the nukes. Swanson tossed and turned in the big bed, and moaned aloud, as if his brain was in physical pain. He was dreaming of war.

Out of the chaos in his mind appeared a figure who came to him almost like clockwork when things began to flood out of control. The singularly ominous figure was draped in black scraps, and steered a battered skiff with a single oar. The Boatman, as Swanson had come to know him over many years of the hallucinatory visits, was a herald of death.

*Three corpses sat in the long boat and their blank eyes were fixed on a horizon of fire. Kyle recognized them as the ISIS fool from Rome and the pair of careless assassins in Narva. In these dreams, the Boatman collected the souls of Swanson's targets and ferried them off to hell. A sulfurous wind flapped the dark cloth as the bateaux coasted close and the Boatman stood there with his usual hideous grin.*

*"We did not have an appointment here, Sniper,"* came the hiss of a voice. *"It was to be one from Rome, and yes, there he is in the front. Then you were to collect another in Cairo. I planned my schedule accordingly, only to have to change it."*

*Swanson replied. "I know the feeling."*

*"Change is uncomfortable, but I adapt. I had to add this pair from Narva to my roster because no other boats were available to pick up your droppings on such short notice."*

*The skiff rocked gently on imaginary waters. Kyle asked, "Why are you here?"*

*The answer was quick. "I am here because you are my responsibility, and as I said, all of the other boats are busy. Ask me why they are all busy."*

*"Okay. Why are the other boats busy?"*

*"They are being made ready for the Big One."*

*"The war, you mean? Don't be so dramatic. There is not going to be a war."*

*The Boatman cackled. "No. That part is guaranteed. You will get it started. I have a lot of trust in your ability."*

*The stormy sky above the Boatman loosed forks of lightning that snapped and popped along the white-topped waves. Curtains of ash and rain followed. "Then you are wrong. I have one more quick assignment with no blood involved, and then I am safe and sound back home. No war."*

*Again the laughter seared. "Again, my gunnery-sergeant-turned-spy, you are not asking the right question."*

*Swanson's mind swirled and in his sleep he felt dizzy and nauseous. "Then what is the right question, you bag of rags?"*

*"Do not ask why I am here tonight. Ask instead what you are doing here."*

Kyle felt as if he had been struck by one of those ominous thunderbolts. He lurched from the bed and fell to the floor with his head spinning and his stomach in spasm. Crawling to the bathroom, he heard the final echoes of the Boatman's laughter as the nightmare released its hold. He made it to the toilet bowl and leaned over and vomited hard, and a foul smell rose from the water as the waste splashed in. He heaved again, then once more, and finally rolled to the chill tile floor. Reaching up, he managed to flush it away.

Why am I here? How did Inspector Rikka Aura in Finland know to track me down?

Swanson struggled to his feet, holding the sink to steady himself until the uneasiness faded. He wandered the room, turning the dream over in his mind, went to the window and looked out over the old city. Inspector Aura had said she had discovered he was aboard a CIA plane coming in from Rome because he went through Finnish customs on the military side of the Helsinki airport. That was a lie. Why did she check that in the first place? It was not an uncommon thing—diplomats and other officials wanting to remain out of public view did exactly the same thing on a daily basis. Picking up on his name could not have been accidental.

His eyes closed and he drank some more whiskey and slammed the tumbler down hard on the wooden windowsill: She knew that he was coming! She had been told in advance! There was a fucking leak!

He put the pieces together. Swanson went to Finland only because Ivan the Terrible had popped into the U.S. Embassy in Helsinki, and would only talk to Kyle. Inspector Aura from the Finland Security Intelligence Service had no previous idea of who he was, but she was expecting him that night. Then she expelled Swanson immediately, swooping down without so much as a protest from the U.S. Embassy. Her action had spurred Kyle to move quickly, and he had decided to follow Ivan's instruction to go to Estonia. Kyle had done so, as compliant as a puppet on a string. He remembered the colonel's warning about how Ivan always played games and always had a reason for everything he did.

Swanson went to the sink and washed his face and brushed his teeth, then staggered back to bed. He had been used and had not even noticed.

Kyle Swanson did not go to the massive central NATO headquarters complex in Brussels the next morning.

Instead, still another CIA type met him in the hotel lobby and drove him northwest into the lightly populated municipality of Koekelberg. The small, out-of-the-way part of the central region of the metropolis was ideal for the safe house that was an entire building only a few blocks from the huge Basilica of the Sacred Heart. Another anonymous company escort waiting at the elevator in an underground garage checked his creds and then took him past a guard with a submachine gun and up to the second floor. Nobody said a word.

He had not made up his mind on how to handle this meeting with Ivan Strakov and was still measuring the variables when he stepped into a neat little conference room. After having listened to Colonel Markey and being visited by the Boatman, Kyle was seething with anger at the Russian for having duped him back in the sniper school days. Balancing that personal affront was the fact that it was only Swanson's ego being bruised for that one. After all, Ivan was just doing his job as an intelligence officer, and he had not learned any secret material because he flunked out before getting very far along in sniper training. But after the strange, brief visit to Finland and the deadly trip to Narva, Kyle was certain something serious was going on, and the Russian was part of the mystery, so it was worth hearing what he had to say. Some day in the future, perhaps, he could get Strakov alone and beat the crap out of him just for old time's sake. For now, Swanson knew he should remain cool, listen to what the defector had to say, then dump the whole matter onto someone else's desk. He would prove the Boatman wrong this time.

THE BLACK TRAIN

Brokk Mihailovich writhed on the bucking and jerking floor of the freight car, searching for a bit of comfort. His bruised eyes and the broken nose and the cuts on his face gave him the look of a battered raccoon. The forsaken passengers aboard the train had lost one man during the first night, an elderly fellow with a bad head wound who had coughed blood from the moment he was thrown into the stinking car. So far today, the only death had been a frail child who had been hauled in along with her mother. Both had been cruelly brutalized. The child, about twelve, died with tears on her face, unable to comprehend what had happened. That left a cargo of nineteen people still alive and rolling northeast, unaware of any legal charges against them, unaware of where they were going, unaware of what the next mile might bring.

Mihailovich lay still so it didn't hurt so much as the train lurched onward. He had spent the previous night— *Two nights ago, was it now? He had missed some hours while unconscious*—in a warm bed with Anneli after drinking with that Canadian writer who could hold his liquor but who had proven to be of no use to them politically. Breakfast had been a bit of pastry and coffee, and she was still beneath the sheets when he left for the university. He was scheduled for a nine o'clock lecture on the strategic business skills necessary for working in this changing new day of progress in Estonia. A few students were still yawning during the early class, but they all made it through. It was a bright group, and he had hopes for them. They were the future of the nation.

By noon, Brokk was well into the stride of his work-day and had gathered his popular usual luncheon group on the greening lawn to discuss politics. He acted as an unofficial moderator so the kids could debate aspects of freedom and reform. It was stimulating and hopeful and inspired volunteers to help his campaign for mayor.

When Brokk went into the bathroom to empty his bladder of the strong coffee and tea he had been drinking throughout the morning, there was a large, lumbering man with wavy brown hair and a round face at the sink. He looked out of place on the campus in his lace-up boots with thick heels and heavy vest over blue work trousers; he smelled of cigarette smoke. The man did not even glance into the mirror, but concentrated on washing his hands, sluicing water around and around.

Brokk stepped to the urinal and pulled at his zipper and stared down, as men do in public bathrooms to create a polite zone of privacy. The man at the sink turned off the water, pulled a paper towel from a dispenser on the wall and slowly dried his hands. Brokk finished, straightened himself, adjusted his backpack and went to the now-vacant sink. The big man reached into a vest pocket as if he was taking out a cell phone, but suddenly spun back and plunged the twin prods of a stun gun into the side of Brokk's neck. The young lawyer arched back in pain as the electricity seized him and there was a sudden smell of burned flesh. He collapsed to the dirty floor with arms and legs thrashing in spasms, his mouth gaping open in surprise, then his body went limp. Brokk did not feel the prick of the needle that was thrust into his arm to administer a strong sedative.

That was when he lost track of time, for when he swam back to the surface of consciousness, he could not count how long he had been out. He awakened in a windowless room of sturdy stone walls. When he had groaned, someone sloshed water into his face and demanded, "Where is the girl?"

Brokk's confused brain could not shape who was yelling at him or what the loud voice was yelling about. The beating began. "Your slut, lawyer-boy! Where is your partner, Anneli Kallasti?" He realized that whoever this was did not have her in custody, a bit of knowledge that made him feel better. Knowing his own future had flown from being bright and limitless to being as bleak as a dirt grave no matter what he said or did, he would not give her up. They worked him hard. His lies made no difference.

Later, he was pulled from the room with his toes dragging along the stones because he could no longer stand on his own. In a cavernous terminal waited a diesel locomotive and a string of freight cars, all painted flat black and lined up in deep shadow. It seemed like a long, hungry snake. Soldiers with weapons guarded each car. Other prisoners shuffled forward on their own or were carried into the cars, then the guards slammed and locked the doors. Brokk passed out again. When he awoke, pain was squeezing his head and he rolled to his side and threw up, coughed and wiped his bloody mouth on a sleeve and wondered in a brief moment of clarity if he had said anything that might have helped them find Anneli. He hoped not.

The train was under speed, stopping periodically to load even more prisoners and remove the corpses. It was impossible to tell time or direction, but the stunned prisoners talked among themselves and decided it had to be going east and north, and out there lay the great Siberian wastelands.

Dying wasn't so hard, Brokk thought as blood hemorrhaged in his head. He had made a difference, had done all he could to help his country, and although the election would turn out badly now, he hoped the people would rise up to stop any attempt at reunification with Russia. Also, and just as important to him, he had enjoyed the love of a good woman; every moment with Anneli had been a treasure. Finally, tired and hurt and without hope of being saved, he gave up, smiled at the remembered image of her face and floated away. His final view was one that was conjured by his imagination; a black train far below him, snaking through the dark countryside.

ST. PETERSBURG, RUSSIA

**N**ATO, **THE NORTH** Atlantic Treaty Organization, had existed for more than half a century, a security alliance founded upon the pledge of mutual defense in the event of an armed attack on any member state by an external party. It achieved its original goal, which was to corral Soviet expansionism in Europe. The demolition of the Berlin Wall in 1989, the reunification of Germany, and the end of the Cold War meant that NATO had won. In a sudden rush, the countries of Hungary, the Czech Republic and Poland, free of Moscow's rule, joined the alliance. Since then, another seven former Soviet republics that had been members of the defunct rival Warsaw Pact came aboard. By 2009, NATO boasted twenty-eight member nations, from as large as the United States to as small as Estonia. Russia was reduced to being a second-rate power and a shattered empire. The Russian economy stagnated, so did the military budget, but eventually the big ship had righted itself. Now the Bear was stirring again, starting the long climb back into the game. It dealt first with the rebels in Chechnya, and then had tamed Georgia, and next took a big bite of the Ukraine. NATO did nothing. The time had come to pay attention to the northern front.

General of the Army Pavel Sergeyev, the chief of the general staff of the Russian Federation, could read that story just by looking at the huge map of Europe that dominated an entire wall of his magnificent office on Znamenka Street in Moscow. All of those upstart Warsaw Pact deserters were now having second thoughts: Moldavia, Romania, Slovenia, Lithuania, Latvia and Estonia were quaking in their boots. He laughed to himself. Tiny Lithuania had announced with great fanfare that it had formed a Rapid Reaction Force to confront any Russian aggression.

Sergeyev pressed the handset of a telephone close to his ear to better hear the cold voice of Colonel General Valery Ivanovich Levchenko, the commander of the Western Military District, who was headquartered in St. Petersburg. The colonel general was an active man, popular among his troops for his touch with the common soldier. Chief of Staff Sergeyev asked, "How was your run this morning, Valery Ivanovich?"

"Brisk and satisfying," came the reply over the encrypted line. The man had the lean body of a greyhound. Each day, the colonel general went for a run of ten kilometers with an enlisted man from one of his services. Today, a common soldier from the 20th Guards Army had been given the honor of galloping alongside the fifty-year-old general, and the younger man's fresh lungs were burning with effort by the time they finished the hard pace. The general did not jog; he *ran* and always finished with a hard, kicking sprint. It was all right for the enlisted man to finish first, and be rewarded with a week's liberty, for the general was no longer in the condition he was in back during his Olympic years, but woe be unto any who could not finish the workout. Break an ankle, pull a hamstring, rip a knee muscle or fall out of the run for any reason at all and that soldier, sailor or airman would be demoted one rank on the spot and transferred to what the general called his "Goon Squad" that pulled every dirty job he deemed fit. For Levchenko, there was no excuse to ever quit until the job was done.

"Are you prepared to launch the exercise?"

"At your command, sir." Colonel General Levchenko was not flustered by the implied criticism of his superior. Of course he was ready. "The needed infrastructure is in place along the border for Operation Hermitage, and we are shifting units forward as the fields dry out enough to support armored vehicles. More fuel and ammunition and air-assault units still need to be prepositioned. It will not take long."

Chief of Staff Sergeyev thought that through for a couple of moments, with his head down and his chin on his chest. He puffed on a cigarette. "And where do we stand with the resettlement program?"

"The voluntary relocation is, of necessity, going slowly, but progress is satisfactory. Elements of the Sixteenth Spetnaz Brigade, in civilian clothes, are furnishing manpower to help convince dissidents in the target areas that they might be happier living elsewhere."

"Nicely put, Valery. 'Voluntary relocation.' I like the sound of that," said the army's chief of staff. "I think that someday you may wish to take off that uniform and become a politician."

The business was done, and they were just fencing

now. "I have no interest in politics, Colonel General. I have served the Motherland for thirty years, and my only wish is to continue doing so as a commander. I understand that this operation is part of a larger and important political component and I gladly leave that to you and our other leaders in Moscow."

"I know, Valery. I know. You are the best field commander I have and your skills are needed where you are." There was a pause. "I told the men in the Kremlin that the only problem was that Valery Ivanovich would want to personally lead this from the front lines. They were shocked, and I agree with them. One reason for my call is to remind you, Colonel General, that you must remain within your headquarters."

"Ah. The problem with being a general is that I cannot be aboard the lead tank going into the fight. I work best when my boots are muddy." He poured a glass of good vodka and drank it down in one swift gulp.

"From where you sit in your St. Petersburg palace, Estonia is only ninety-two miles away. That is close enough for my valuable commander. Let our young soldiers do the fighting. That is why we train them."

"Whatever you say," replied Colonel General Levchenko, knowing it was a lie when he uttered the words. Things were in motion for the run-up to Phase One of Operation Hermitage and he did not have to be personally on the scene until it was time to spring the trap with Phase Two. Then he would be where he was really needed. The men within the redbrick Kremlin walls and generals in the military headquarters in the Arbat did not have to know that. Colonel General Levchenko did not believe in sharing his plans. The bureaucrats could order him to boil water, but building the fire was up to him.


BRUSSELS, BELGIUM

Kyle Swanson got his first surprise of the day when he met the case officer who had been assigned by the CIA to oversee the initial debrief of Colonel Ivan Strakov. He recognized the blond hair, slim figure, elegant bearing, fashionable clothes and open smile of Jan Hollings. Calico stood and extended her hand.

"You?"

"Don't worry, Mister Swanson. I left Anneli safely tucked away for a few days. The company brought me in last night because Ivan apparently operated partially on my turf. The theory is that I might be able to recognize flaws in his story." She sat down again, then introduced two other agents, a younger tech and an older analyst. "I will return to Tallinn as soon as you are through with him and things check out. Still, it is nice to see you again so soon."

The woman was full of surprises. At no point had she mentioned her husband, Colonel Thomas Markey. Agents were always changing their appearance with such little alterations. Beneath that cool outward appearance, Calico was a very complicated woman. Kyle had no problem with her running this show. Anybody, as long as it was not him, was acceptable.

"Fine by me. When you see Anneli, please tell her that I said hello. She's a good kid. No word on her boyfriend?"

Jan twitched her lips. "No. Too soon to hope for that. I honestly do not have high hopes, but she thinks you are Superman and can find him." She lifted her chin toward the tech, who switched on the video and audio equipment, and a black curtain slid away from the one-way mirror.

Ivan Strakov waited patiently in a chair at the usual table. He wore glaring orange coveralls, but was not in restraints. Instead, he was working a crossword puzzle, although he was not allowed a sharp object like a pen or pencil. Ivan was unraveling the tangle of words in his head.

The technician handed a clear earbud to Kyle, who stuffed it into the canal of his right ear and wiggled it to make it comfortable. It was invisible. "Testing. Can you hear me?"

Swanson said, "Perfectly. I'm ready."

The technician slid on a pair of earphones and turned to his electronic control panel. "Ready here, too," he said. The older analyst nodded, his pen poised over a legal pad.

Calico gave them all a final look, and said, "Then in you go, Swanson. Do this. I'm anxious to hear what he has to say." She opened the door and Kyle walked through, then she closed it behind him.

Ivan Strakov tossed the folded newspaper onto the table. "Took you long enough," he said.

Kyle placed his briefcase on the flat surface, opened it and removed some notes. "Narva is a dump," he said, spreading his papers. Sketches and written reminders with other notes such as laser ranges scribbled in open spaces.

"There are a couple of nice castles, though, right?" Ivan responded. "Good view from up in the gallery. So what did you see, Gunny?"

"Not much, actually. The only thing worse than being in Narva, apparently, is being across the bridge in Russia." Swanson peeled through the data, point by point, for thirty minutes, then called a break. He mentioned the upcoming election, but did not speak of the fight in the tower, nor the young couple he had encountered. He stuffed the material back into the briefcase and returned to the other room and handed it to the analyst. "For your files," he said, and the man took it without comment.

"That was a good general overview," said Calico. "I recall much of that myself, although without the ranges and tactical details. Narva is a bleak place and doesn't change much."

Swanson poured two cups of hot coffee and took a sip of one. To the tech, he said, "Ask Ivan if he prefers milk and sugar."

The youngster hesitated and looked at Jan Hollings, who looked at Kyle. "Come on," Swanson said. "The guy is a spy. He knows we are watching and listening, so let me break the ice a little better with a common courtesy."

"Milk or sugar in your coffee, Colonel?" The tech asked with a calm voice.

"Milk. Thank you," he responded.

Swanson went back in and gave Ivan the coffee. They sat silently for a while, just waiting. "So you directed that you would only talk to me, Strakov, and I came. Then you sent me off to chase this goose in Narva. I went. So it's your turn."

Ivan agreed that it was fair to give something back. He asked, "Did you see the monuments?"

Swanson nodded in agreement. "Even the bald guy, old Vladimer Ilyich Lenin himself, who is now hiding in a niche of the castle instead of standing in the square. I tried to catch most of them."

Strakov had a laugh, a genuine bit of humor. "Yes. Moving Lenin was quite a daring move by the Estonians. Then they also moved the war memorial, a statue of a Red Army soldier, and that really upset President Pushkin. What else? Think, Kyle. This is important."

"If it was important, why didn't you tell me to be sure to find it?"

"The process of discovery, Kyle. If I pointed you to it, my information would have been discounted. Tell me about the sad-looking cross that rises out of the stones down by the railroad tracks, with the big numbers nineteen forty-one through nineteen forty-nine."

"I've got to look at my notes again," Swanson said to buy some time. He left his coffee on the table when he went back outside and checked through the papers. "Aw, shit," he said softly, drawing a concerned look from Calico. "I should have caught that. So *fucking* obvious!" He went back in.

"That is the memorial to the Estonians who were deported to Siberia by the Russians during and after the war," he declared.

Ivan Strakov rubbed his right palm over his face briefly, pulling at his cheeks. "Right."

"The Disappeared."

"Right. They are doing it again, this time to silence the critics and the dissidents, the journalists and clergy, the students and labor leaders. With those people removed in secrecy aboard what is known as the Black Train, a new tone can arise behind them and clever propagandists will rally to return beneath Moscow's wing."

"You are preparing the battlefield." Kyle pushed back in his chair and crossed his legs. He realized with a clutch of his gut that Ivan's comment explained what had happened to Brokk Mihailovich and why those punks had come after Anneli. Had to be. With Brokk and his energetic adviser out of the way, the other candidate would win the municipal election in Narva and try to return it to Kremlin ownership. "Incredible. Moscow must know NATO will react to that."

"Of course, but it is not me. Moscow is doing it and fully realizes the risks and the rewards. The Black Train is the only free item on my menu today, Kyle. Now that I have crossed the line and left my job, I need money. I will want a lot of money for further information, with more to come as I yield more intelligence gold, and I want my new CIA friends to arrange a new and comfortable life for me."

Kyle grinned. "How about this instead: We throw your skinny ass into a prison if you don't tell us everything?"

Ivan did not change expression. "Ah. At last, we are bargaining. The best things in life aren't free." He finished his coffee in silence, then he spoke again. "That deportation tip is free because I wanted to establish a baseline that will prove my information is valid and important. I want a million dollars for the next big thing, which you obviously did not see during your visit. I admit being a bit surprised that you missed it."

Swanson gave a derisive grunt. "Hardly. It does not require a genius to figure out that the new road construction, the fuel facilities, the nice new airstrip and the buildup of troops in and around the Ivangorod Fortress are to increase tension along the border."

Now it was Strakov's turn to smirk. "You really *didn't* catch it, did you? I should be asking ten million."

"What? You want the cash, earn it."

"Go ask your masters, or put me back in my room, Swanson. You, of all people, know they could not break me in any interrogation." He glared over at the big mirror. "When the shit hits the fan, the world will ask why the CIA let this all happen for a lousy million bucks. Let me remind you that we are not even at the good stuff yet; the codes and the data banks."

Swanson walked out of the room. The analyst and the technician were sitting there dumbfounded and Calico was already on the telephone to Washington, describing the defector's revelation. She held a finger up to keep him quiet and listened for a minute, then said, "Yes. I consider that the first nugget he handed over is very important. It is confirmation of what we had heard about a Black Train taking away prisoners, but could not confirm. Russia is clearing out its critics in the Estonian border, probably shipping them to Siberia, just like in the bad old days."

Her golden hair picked up available light in flashes when she nodded in the direction of CIA Headquarters in Langley, Virginia. Her voice was soft, but firm. "Yes. That information about the Disappeareds alone is worth the price. God knows what else he's got. I recommend we do it."

A longer reply. Calico turned and stared at Kyle. "Yes. I recommend giving him the whole package: new identity, a secret account, the works. We can always take it back and shoot the son of a bitch if he's lying." Jan Hollings terminated the encrypted conversation and pointed at Kyle. "They are patched through on a live uplink, so they heard and saw it all. Go make the deal," she said.

Swanson returned to his seat, carrying two cups of fresh coffee. "Okay, Ivan. You're a rich man now. So impress me. What did I miss?"

Strakov said, "Excellent. Good decision. The Armata, Kyle. You did not mention the Armata!"

Kyle closed his eyes for a moment, and exhaled a long sigh, almost visualizing the panic in the adjoining room and back at Langley.

**13**

**SWANSON KEPT HIS** face like stone, but thought: Well, that was certainly worth a million. It was also the ticket that would allow him to leave the negotiation. People at big desks and wearing stars on their collars would soon notice they were suddenly having trouble breathing, and wondering about those chest-tightening squeezes around their hearts.

Kyle had not seen an Armata nor any evidence whatsoever that there was one around Narva. The last memo on Russian military preparedness had declared the weapons platforms were not even supposed to exist yet. The timetable for the first MBT Armata T-96 main battle tank to roll off the production line at the Uralvagonzavod factories was still more than a year away. At least that was according to the best data collected by the Western intelligence agencies over the past decade. If Ivan was right, then the analysts had seriously screwed up and the Russians had fielded a tank that could maul the best U.S. armor in a head-on fight.

"An Armata?" he finally said to the colonel. "I call

bullshit on that, Ivan. Russia has a hard time building a decent automobile, much less a Star Wars muscle tank way ahead of schedule. Even field testing has not yet begun on that toy."

Strakov stifled a chuckle, and a big smile lit his face. He knew he had their attention now. "Kyle, we don't care about building cars because we can buy Italian Ferraris or Japanese Hondas from dealerships in any of our big cities. Military development is an entirely different beast. There are at least one hundred operational Armata platforms in the immediate area around St. Petersburg, all of which could be vectored over to the Narva bridgehead within an hour. Black Eagle tanks, Boomerang armored vehicles, tracked artillery, mobile antiaircraft, and Kurganets infantry fighting armor. Quite a few are already around Narva. I was counting on you seeing at least one."

"Well, I didn't. So they are probably not there. You could be lying through your teeth about this just to get cash."

"But I am not. What this tells me is that our new electronic stealth-and-cover technology is also working, leaving your satellites blind. Otherwise, how could they miss a fifty-ton tank being hauled into position? That information is probably worth another million, and I have a lot more than hardware."

Swanson heard Calico's voice in his ear, soft but urgent, telling him to wrap it up. He stood away from the table and stretched. "Well, buddy, you've just graduated far beyond my pay grade, so our session is over. You obviously have good info, and I think you can stop worrying about the value of a Russian ruble."

Ivan Strakov was not ready to break off the talk. He held the upper hand and didn't want to stop. "Oh, we're not done yet, Kyle. I still want you as my intermediary."

Swanson shrugged. "You are out of my league, Strakov. I'm just a washed-up old sniper who now hustles for a living in the private sector, while you are a slick intelligence genius. The U.S. government and NATO have specialists who can understand what you have to say. I do not. I mean, apparently I could not even see the world's meanest tank when you pointed me straight at it. So, adios, compadre. See you around the campus."

Strakov said, "Don't think you can walk out on me, Kyle."

"That's exactly what I was thinking, Colonel Strakov. Good guess."

"You will be back soon."

"No. I'm heading back to Washington in a few hours. My personal opinion is that you were a liar twenty years ago and you are a better liar now. Send me an e-mail in about thirty years to let me know how this all turns out. I'm done with you."

Strakov's eyes turned hard as marbles and humorless and he walked over to face the mirror, looking through his reflection to those on the other side. "You people in there have a problem. Your negotiator here thinks he can call me a liar, then just up and leave whenever he wants. Change his mind. You are facing a madman and a major threat to NATO. You have no time to spare; absolutely none!"

The three CIA people had the looks of a small herd of deer caught in oncoming headlights when Kyle reentered their lair. "You're not seriously considering leaving now, are you?" Calico raised an eyebrow. "We're just getting started. This stuff is gold, Kyle!"

"I am totally serious. Ivan will talk to your experts for enough money, or if you put a hood on his head and let our pals in Guantánamo have a crack at him. You don't need me for either of those things." Swanson held his hands before him, palms up. "Worse, I don't like him, and I think he is blowing smoke. Do not think that a brick of cash will guarantee the truth."

Jan Hollings said, "Armata battlewagons being deployed is not smoke, Kyle. Quite the opposite."

"That hardware was going to be online sooner or later anyway, Jan. They have been on the trade-show circuit for so long that you can probably buy a detailed model at your local hobby store."

"But we are not ready for something like that! NATO isn't ready! It would be a disaster if those beasts start rolling."

"Then tell NATO to get ready. There is nothing I can do about that!" Swanson was exasperated. All he wanted to do was leave. "The value of Colonel Strakov is in an entirely different area. You really want what he may possess: cyberspace, black information and intent. The Armata dump is a sideshow, just to get your attention. I am no tank warfare genius, but neither is he. No tank, not even a super-tank, can fight a war all by itself. He dropped that pearl just to get your attention. He got it."

The analyst spoke in a low tone. "You are misreading the situation, Agent Swanson. The Armatas actually do represent a serious threat. If a hundred of those monsters descend along Estonia's border all at one time, it would be catastrophic. NATO would have to respond. A war would erupt."

Kyle blew out a breath. "That is not going to happen. You are the ones misreading the situation. The question is not about a new piece of hardware, but why is Ivan painting this nightmare. I am a trained scout, spent years doing it, and nothing that I saw over in Narva indicates any fight on a massive scale. For one thing, there were no huge ammunition dumps or major supply depots. Those things have to be as big as mountains to sustain a major attack. So possible trouble, yes. Escalating tension, yes. War, no."

"But suppose you are wrong, Kyle?" Calico reached for the encrypted phone. "We have to imagine the worst-case scenario."

"Whatever. I bid you all a fond farewell and wish you good luck, fair winds and following seas. I have a plane to catch." He straightened his jacket and walked away.

## ST. PETERSBURG, RUSSIA

Dirty weather came roaring down from the Arctic Circle early Sunday morning. Force-nine winds churned the Baltic Sea into a maelstrom, as towering rollers alternated with falling troughs and the winds skimmed away the foam on top in long streaks of spray. Captains of big ships buckled into their control-room seats. Overhead, the sky was the color of concrete and so turbulent that commercial airlines were rerouted rather than chance flying through the clouds. On the ground, trees and signs bent to the power of the storm, which threw debris at motorists. Animals huddled in shelters, away from the heavy snow-rain mix.

The ugly conditions did not darken the mood of Colonel General Valery Ivanovich Levchenko in his opulent headquarters. On some days, the commander of the Western Military District felt like a lone dray horse trudging along an endless road, pulling the heavy load of the entire Russian Federation in a sleigh behind him. It was tiring. Outside, the wind clawed at the windows of his office, teasing him.

Then came a ray of sunshine in the form of an urgent communique from Moscow. As he read it over word by word for a third time, he felt both anger and joy. The information only reconfirmed his belief that General of the Army Pavel Sergeyev, the chief of the general staff, was a timid old woman. This was the latest example of "Do Nothing Grams" from him. It stated that there was growing evidence that a certain Colonel Ivan Strakov of the GRU, who supposedly had perished recently in an airplane crash in Siberia, was not only still alive, but had defected to the Americans. Deep-cover intelligence sources reported that Strakov had shown up unexpectedly at the U.S. Embassy in Finland, and immediately had been swept into secrecy.

The Kremlin message warned that if the report was true, Strakov posed extreme harm to Russia because he had for years been given immense access to top-secret material. Therefore, General Sergeyev in Moscow was ordering all senior military commanders to temporarily halt all operations that might be interpreted as aggressive and just remain vigilant pending further developments. They were to undertake absolutely no provocative actions. That, thought Levchenko, was the same as doing nothing.

*Ivan, you slippery bastard! You did it!* Levchenko felt the heavy sled that he pulled advance a bit, and the load seemed a bit lighter as he plodded another step forward. Levchenko shouted, and his own chief of staff hurried into the office, snapping to attention. The chief knew the contents of the note, since he had been the one to decrypt and deliver it. He had been waiting for his boss to react.

The colonel general was at the desk and had pulled a legal pad toward him and was furiously writing an order in longhand. "Pyotr Ivanovich, my friend, do I recall that during a briefing yesterday, there was a report that two GRU agents were murdered in that little castle over in Narva? Is that correct?"

"Yes, sir," the chief confirmed. "They were part of a sweep of some dissidents."

"No doubt it was an ambush, then? They were lured into a trap and killed. I mean, how else could a pair of highly trained GRU operatives be overpowered?"

The chief could almost see the wheels turning within his boss's busy brain. In his own opinion, the two thugs just got careless and picked on the wrong dissident, and on the wrong side of the border. "Yes, sir. It was an ambush. Without a doubt," he agreed. "Two good, loyal police officers who were just doing their duties."

"At the request of local authorities in Narva, no doubt." He was looking for a loophole in the facts.

"Without question, sir. The locals would have asked for assistance in a dangerous mission against terrorists." The chief made a note. He would arrange paperwork to back that up.

With a grim smile, General Levchenko made the decision. "Then it was a deliberate provocation! We cannot sit by idly while those Estonian terrorists murder our people. Therefore, we are going to take advantage of this horrible weather to test combat preparedness under most adverse conditions. It will send them the message that we are prepared to act if these provocations continue, and we demand that justice be done. This storm is a blessing, Colonel. All divisional commanders will immediately begin preparations for Phase One of Operation Hermitage. Our troops are to respond to a simulated NATO attack on St. Petersburg."

"Sir? In this mad weather? We will surely lose valuable men." The chief of staff read the crisp two-sentence order to be sure he had everything straight in his mind before leaving. It would stir the Baltic and the Northern Fleets to life, launch elements of the 6th and 20th Guard Armies, Spetsnaz and air assault units, and then the 1st Air and Air Defense Forces planes would take to the skies. Almost everybody in the district was going to get wet on this miserable and dangerous day. His general was not angry at all. In fact, he seemed excited and pleased. In a matter of minutes, he had molded the bad weather, the terrible news about the defector and the deaths of a pair of careless GRU thugs into a singular reason to start the gigantic war game. Moscow would be unable to question the decision.

"Of course we will lose a few, Colonel Dolgov! Nature does not cooperate with military men, but we must be able to fight through it all. We will begin surveillance overflights of our entire border with Estonia to test NATO alertness as soon as possible," he said. "I don't care if this is the greatest storm in history, those pilots will scramble and take off or I will put my boot up their rear ends for being cowards."

"Yes, sir. As you order." The colonel saluted and headed back to his adjoining office, happy that he was not in the air force.

"And after you dispatch those orders to get Phase One under way, gather my Goon Squad. This is a great day for a run."


BRUSSELS, BELGIUM

The black pearl finish of the Audi A8 luxury sedan was beginning to spot with rain as Kyle Swanson sat comfortably in the rear compartment and let the driver do his job unmolested. He watched the turbulent sky for only a moment, knowing that his flight, a British Airways Airbus, would be moving away from the incoming storm that was battering northern Europe, and in the first-class cabin he would make the trip as smooth as possible. Money insulated him against many of the bumps in life as other people did the things necessary to accommodate him. The airline and limo reservations, everything from baggage handlers to concierge services, had been made by Janna Ecklund back in the States.

He found the VIP waiting lounge at the airport, where he was surrounded by even more helpful people who served him drinks and snacks, took care of the ticketing and escorted him to a small private office. Thousands of people were on the move throughout the airport, but that was an entirely different world. With the rails greased even more with his black diplomatic passport and CIA creds, Kyle Swanson hardly had to lift a finger. Polite customs and security people came to him for a private security check. He felt like a fraud. This was not who he was. He was from a place that smelled like gun oil, not eau de cologne.

Swanson checked the correct time as he opened his laptop. Belgium was only an hour ahead of London, so he would not be disturbing Sir Geoffrey Cornwell with a quick call. The old man probably wanted to know why Kyle was still hanging around Europe when he should be back in the Washington office of Excalibur Enterprises, milking cash out of the Pentagon budget. He selected the Skype icon at edge of the screen, the machine swam to life and seconds later a head-and-shoulders image of Sir Jeff appeared.

"Kyle, my boy!" Cornwell called out, and in the background, off-camera, Swanson heard his mom, Lady Pat, shout out, "Is that Kyle? He's still in Brussels, isn't he?" She angled onto the screen with a smile. "Come to London!"

"Hi, folks. How did you know where I am?"

Jeff gave a guffaw. "You have been causing trouble again. I have received several calls from Belgium and from Langley within the past hour."

"Jesus H. Christ." Belgium meant NATO, and the CIA was headquartered in Langley, Virginia. They had moved fast since he had walked away from the interview.

"Yes. Well, dear boy, what is your status?"

"I am finally about to board a plane and go back to the States. I am tired, and need to get back to the office. Also, I am more than a little pissed off at what has been happening around here, particularly those calls. We can't really talk about this over Skype."

"Then come to London!" Lady Pat repeated her invitation, tinting it with an edge of demand.

Jeff turned serious. "Let us talk about business for a moment, Kyle. As I understand it, you desire to return to the office as soon as possible, am I correct?"

"Yes. The original parameters of my trip to Europe were changed without my advance knowledge or approval."

"I see. I see." Cornwell was making a note. "I am afraid that a lot of things have changed. Some of the calls I received were thinly veiled reminders that European governments and our friends in Washington are the biggest and best customers for Excalibur products."

"The bastards. That's blackmail. I don't do what they want, we lose future contracts."

"My dear friend Freddie R. was most vocal about the situation," said Jeff. "You recall Freddie, of course."

Kyle did. Left unsaid was that General Sir Frederick Ravensdale was the deputy supreme allied commander in Europe. "He was somewhat threatening, to be precise."

"Blackmail," Kyle repeated.

"That's a very harsh term and should not be bandied about lightly where our friends are concerned. What I take away from all of this nattering is that they want you to stay involved. Insist on it, actually."

"What about Excalibur?"

"Janna is handling the Washington affairs quite adequately for the time being. I am more concerned with the company's future access to our friends and allies.

Those links must be maintained at all costs, Kyle. Do you understand?"

Swanson gritted his teeth in frustration. Here it was again; that feeling that he was being used by forces unknown. Sir Jeff and General Ravensdale, the Deputy SACEUR, were formidable men. In Kyle's view, they were also being used. By who and why, he had no clue.

"Okay, boss. I'll do whatever the hell you want me to do. That may be the quickest way out."

"Very well. I knew you would understand. And Pat is right. When this is all done, drop by and spend some time with us here before you head to Washington."

"Yea." Pat cheered off-screen.

"Still, I want some control over my own operations. How about lending me the boat for a couple of weeks? I can park it nearby and stage out of it." The company yacht, its private helicopter, solid communications suite and crew of military veterans would provide a comfort zone. If Swanson was being forced to play the game, at least he would attempt to play by his own rules.

"Consider it done. I'll get the *Vagabond* started. Be careful." The older man's face was now that of a concerned father and less of the former SAS colonel who knew more than he let on. "If you need anything, I am here."

"Love you both," Kyle said, and terminated the video call, then whispered to himself, "Damn."

**14**

ESTONIA

**S**TAFF **S**ERGEANT **B**RENDA Hutchinson of the U.S. Air Force was startled and cried out with both surprise and pain. She was strapped into a seat aboard an RC-135U reconnaissance plane that was flying a racetrack pattern over the Baltics to keep an eye on the Russians by monitoring the electronic cloud. The long flight from the spy plane's home base at RAF Mildenhall in the United Kingdom had so far been without incident, as they usually were. The four-engine plane with swept wings was calmly cruising in the sunlight above the Sunday storm that was pummeling the earth below, and it was over Estonia when she was blasted by a sudden eruption of signals that came out of nowhere, without warning and at a volume so loud the sergeant jerked her padded earphones from her head. The screen in front of her that charted aircraft and ships turned to green-and-white jibberish.

"What's wrong, Hutch?" She felt a hand grip her shoulder as Captain Stan Morris leaned over. He also saw the normally crisp screen fall into meaningless flashes and zigzags and looping swirls.

"We were just jammed with an electromagnetic pulse, sir," she said, quickly clamping her headset back on to begin working the knobs and switches and reading her dials. "Something fried us hard, all across the spectrum. We're almost blind."

The intercom was alive with similar reports from other stations on the aircraft and the big plane was jerking in the sky as automatic controls balked and the pilots fought to resume command. After about twenty seconds, the plane steadied and the electronics came back online through the emergency backups.

"Find them, Hutch," the captain said. The diminutive sergeant knew her business, and her fingers attacked the keyboard. "Find the bastard. Get the source."

On the intercom, they heard the aircraft commander tell everyone to hold on because they were breaking off from their pattern and retreating to the west, where a couple of NATO F-15C fighters could rendezvous and escort them safely home.

"Too late! They're right on top of us!" Hutchinson yelled. "There's an Ilyushin-20 coming up at two-sixty degrees, blasting and jamming." The powerful Russian electronic intelligence plane had hidden in the storm by flying low and cloaking itself with the lightning and bad weather, and had jumped up when the American plane was less than five miles away and closing.

"It's got company!" Sergeant Hutchinson shouted, discarding her normally measured, quiet tone.

Also rising like hungry sharks from the gray storm into the bright sunshine were a pair of giant Tupolev-22M2 Backfire bombers and four Sukhoi-27 Flanker fighter jets. They barreled forward to intersect with the American spy plane in the middle of its evasive curve, almost on a collision course, with the IL-20 electronics devil painting the path between them with overpowering strength.

The entire Russian formation continued to climb by them, intentionally giving the Americans a perfect view of full racks of rockets and antiaircraft missiles on the Flankers. Each Backfire bomber had a huge AS-4 cruise missile slung beneath its center line. The electronic jamming ceased abruptly and as Staff Sergeant Hutchinson watched her controls come back to normal limits, the Russian flight went majestically on its way, carving through the sky of Estonia in clear violation of designated border air space. They did not care.

BRUSSELS, BELGIUM

Swanson mulled over his new instructions and hoped that the airline could extricate his luggage from the plane before it took off. It was to be taken back to the hotel, and he would return to the same room he had left only a few hours earlier. That gave him plenty of time to wait in the VIP lounge and try to shuffle the pieces of the puzzle.

*Why me?* That was the question, not what he was doing in Belgium. Whoever was running this show wanted Kyle Swanson and no one else to be on hand, which made no sense at all to Kyle. He was not suited to the task and felt uncomfortable and inadequate trying to do it. Swanson did not buy the explanation that Ivan Strakov would speak only with him, for they barely knew each other. They had been on duty together only for a single bit of time back in the day, and even then, it was not a close friendship.

Strakov had crossed over from Russia with more than enough clout to set ideal conditions of his acceptance by the United States intelligence agencies and be treated like spy royalty. Instead of residing in some comfy CIA safe house in the fox country of northern Virginia, he had steered the decision to move to the stuffy confines of Koekelberg, a neighborhood of Brussels. Colonel Tom Markey had observed that Ivan was always devious and operated behind the scenes in the world of intelligence, and that he seldom made a move that he had not planned out thoroughly in advance. There was no reason to trust the Russian.

A hostess in a dark skirt, white blouse and a bright red scarf knotted around her neck approached Swanson and said the bags had been rescued, then she wanted to know his next step. Would the gentleman like for her to call a hire car for the trip back to the hotel, or perhaps just a taxi?

Kyle came out of his reverie. The one thing that the Russian defector really knew about Swanson was that he was a big-league sniper. They had met on the job, and Strakov, as a student in scout-sniper school, had watched Kyle fire with incredible precision. After they went their separate ways, perhaps Strakov the spy was able to keep tabs on his former mentor, although most of Kyle's record was intentionally blank because of the secretive nature of his missions. It was a long reach, but it made some sense, because it was the only strong link between them. For some reason Strakov had this strange determination to keep him so close at hand.

There was no reason at all that he should trust the Russian.

"No, miss, thank you," he said with a sunny smile to the hovering hostess. "Instead, I would like to board the next plane leaving here for Tallinn, Estonia. What time would that be?"

She turned and examined a screen discreetly set into the wall. It listed the departures and arrivals. "There is an Estonian Air flight leaving in about two hours, weather permitting. Would that do?"

Swanson nodded and fished out a corporate credit card. "Would you please get me a first-class ticket? Put the bags on it, and also please bring me a glass of beer. Thanks." While his wallet was opened, he pulled out a hundred-dollar bill and gave it to her as a tip. "Appreciate your trouble."

"It is not a problem, sir. I'll make the arrangements, and then I will fetch that beer." He watched her walk away, moving easily and confident in her abilities. The hostess, about thirty years old, her brown hair tucked neatly out of the way, was used to dealing with important executives and did not bat an eye at the unexpected request. Dealing with problems of elite passengers was her job and she was good at it and reflected her years of experience. In such a major airport, she had seen it all. Beneath her extremely personable act was an efficient machine.

Kyle, too, was a machine, only at another level. His skills were quite different from those of the hostess. One thing that he had learned over the years was that when all of the computations had been made, sometimes you still had to rely on your gut instinct and come up with what snipers called a SWAG—a scientific wild-ass guess. He rose and checked the screen himself, affirming his decision.

A call to Calico confirmed that he would be back to participate in Ivan's strange debrief, and that she could call off the dogs. In trade, he wanted a brief visit with Anneli Kallasti at the safe house. He said he needed to pick the girl's brain about something that happened in Narva before talking to the Russian again. Calico gave him the address.

Kyle then used his directory to call up the private number of Special Agent Lem James of the Diplomatic Security Service back in Helsinki. He dialed and the gruff voice answered immediately. Swanson made it quick, asking the big man to see if his pal Inspector Rikka Aura of the Finnish Security Intelligence Service would reveal the source of her tip that Swanson was to arrive on a specific diplomatic flight on that fateful night in Helsinki. James agreed that it was odd she knew the exact arrival time, and said he would try. Kyle promised a beer in return for the help, and hung up.

WASHINGTON, D.C.

President Christopher Thompson preferred casual clothes to suits and ties and formal wear, although some criticized him for not properly carrying the dignity of the office. He worked better in an old sweater and tan chinos and comfortable running shoes, but could change into the dark suit costume within minutes in the private bathroom just off the Oval Office in the White House. He had been elected because of his intelligence and political skill, not because of his tailors. Two years into the office, the public had grown to tolerate the personal quirks of the tough former U.S. senator from Missouri who campaigned in a pickup truck. "Truman-like" was the usual term for his decisive decision making, and his desk proudly displayed the little sign "The Buck Stops Here" that had been made famous by President Harry S. Truman.

"So is this Russian guy the real deal? He seems to me to be a pretty weird duck," Thompson asked. He had read the brief and was now walking around the Oval Office, a rangy figure with a full head of hair that was turning silver, and his hands in his pockets. Outside, the sky was blue and the rose garden was in riotous bloom, as were the Japanese cherry trees along the National Mall and the Tidal Basin. He was stuck indoors on a beautiful Sunday afternoon.

National Security Adviser Dean Thomas answered. "Right now, it appears that he is, sir. The first thing he gave us was a winner. He revealed the previously unknown information that Moscow had fielded their new Armata battle system, their biggest and newest tanks, in total secrecy. We knew nothing about that. Then the Russians began this giant military exercise in the area around St. Petersburg yesterday and those things suddenly popped up all over the place. Satellite pictures showed them clearly. NATO considers the machines to pose a serious threat."

"So score one for this Colonel Ivan Strakov," said the president. He recalled that the State Department was protesting the increasingly hostile Baltic overflights by Russian aircraft.

"Yes, sir. The tanks are one thing, but Strakov's real value is going to be in the cyber-warfare arena, once he starts talking."

"Tell me again why he is still over in Europe instead of being locked up tight and safe over here? That makes me uneasy. The Russians might try to retrieve him." The president stopped, leaned back against his desk and crossed his arms. He sounded accusatory.

Thomas replied, "Our allies want to keep him close at hand in Brussels. They have him well protected."

The president rounded the desk and picked up the morning's copy of *The Washington Post*. A front-page story had broken the news of Strakov's defection, carried an old photograph of him in uniform and was comparing him to the American spy Edward Snowden. Television news had jumped on the story and it was spreading on the Internet like a rising wave. "Leaks like this drive me crazy, Dean. What's next for him?"

"We are still weighing the options, Mr. President. The chief problem remains that he will only talk to one American: Kyle Swanson."

"Swanson is another weird duck," said the president, who knew the man's checkered history. "Why is that a problem? He's known for getting results."

"Well, sir, right now, we don't know where Swanson is."

NARVA, ESTONIA

The young man was about twenty years old, and beneath an unruly mop of yellow hair was the exuberant and handsome face of a boy who was in a hurry to become a man. Anneli Kallasti spotted him as soon as he entered the little club. "That one," she quietly told Kyle Swanson.

Kyle looked over. The kid wore an olive drab summer service uniform, with his garrison cap folded under the waist belt, and the single plain bar on the shoulder epaulets revealed that he was a corporal in the Russian army. It didn't matter what his specialty was because Swanson just wanted to snatch a low-ranking plodder, one of those nondescript soldiers who actually make up an army. This one would be just fine. "Good. Let's do it," he said.

Kyle had dashed from Belgium back to Estonia and went directly to the CIA safe house pinpointed by Calico, Jan Hollings. It was a small building divided into four apartments, with the ground floor designated for communications and logistics and minders. One of the upper apartments was vacant and Anneli was staying in the other, safe but bored. She was astonished to find Kyle at her door. He had her sit on the bed while he outlined his plan, betting on a positive reaction from her. With no word on what had happened to her boyfriend, Brokk Mihailovich, she had become nervous and unsure. Little had happened since Calico had put her in this secure but isolated location, because the problem of dealing with Ivan Strakov trumped the needs of a walk-in refugee. She jumped at the idea of returning to Narva for another brief expedition with Swanson, and changed into inconspicuous jeans and a dark sweater, and found a wig of shoulder-length auburn hair that instantly altered her looks.

They were out of the safe house within fifteen minutes and drove away without telling the CIA watcher where they were going, only that they would be back very soon and to keep that spare bedroom ready to receive another visitor.

This time, the road to the border city was busy with traffic, although the weather remained sour, and making the trip in an automobile was much easier than doubled up on a motorbike, battling through freezing wind. Anneli talked almost nonstop, emptying her soul of worry, until Kyle slowly exerted control and focused her on the night's mission.

They went to a different place this time, because she and Brokk were too well known at the German Club. It was more of a down-scale bar frequented by Russian soldiers who crossed the bridge on leave to enjoy a tiny taste of Western decadence. Heads had turned when Anneli walked in, following slightly behind Kyle in a subservient manner. The soldiers saw a beautiful woman and a tough, scowling man, and commented that the world was unfair to allow such an ugly gorilla to have a princess like that. Must be a gangster, they concluded. Kyle kept his manner silent and stern as the couple went to a table, where he let Anneli do the talking. They had a small dinner and beer and watched the soldiers, many of whom openly gaped at her. Just watching her was worth crossing the border for on this wicked night. None of them was acceptable.

Then about eight o'clock, the corporal came in with a few friends, and went directly to the bar for a drink. When he eventually turned his attention from his vodka to look over the crowd, he locked eyes with Anneli, who did not look away. The youngster blushed and turned back to his friends. The man who was with the beautiful girl suddenly slapped the table hard and jumped to his feet, leaned over and whispered something at her that made her start to cry. He stomped out of the club, leaving her alone, teary.

Three other soldiers made approaches but she waved them off, and finally, young Corporal Valentin Serov shyly came to her table, and was lost in those big, wet eyes. Other soldiers silently cursed him. In ten minutes, when he had gentled her emotions, she rather guiltily asked Val if he would see her home, she didn't want to be out in the street alone if that other man should attack her. Serov couldn't believe his luck. He escorted her to the door and waved good-bye to his hooting friends at the bar.

She guided them just around the corner, beside a row of parked cars, and as they passed by, Kyle Swanson stepped out from between two vehicles and slugged Val Serov behind his right ear. Anneli had the rear door open before the stunned boy hit the ground and then she helped Kyle shove the wobbly corporal into the back-seat. She drove while Swanson secured the soldier with duct tape and covered him with a blanket.

"Good job, girl. Back to the safe house," he said, climbing into the front seat as she turned onto the main highway, driving carefully and doing nothing to draw attention.

TALLINN, ESTONIA

**WAKE UP, CORPORAL."** Valentin Serov heard the persistent voice of a woman pulling him from a comfortable reverie of sleep. A cool cloth bathed his face. "Come on, now. You are fine. Everything is fine." The words were Russian, and he responded, coming smoothly out of a drug-induced stupor in which he had been suspended for the past six hours. He blinked, saw shadows and light, and gradually came to his senses. There she was.

Serov saw scraps of returning memory, fragments of everything from the moment he had worked up the courage to go and say hello to the beautiful girl in the bar. He had soothed her then, just as she was helping him now, and then they had stepped outside, with his hopes so high and his attention so totally on her that he had not detected any danger whatsoever. He could hardly believe his luck. Then he remembered being stunned by a painful slam on the head, being roughly handled into an automobile, being bound and gagged, and a sharp needle pinching into his arm. Beyond that, only a deep sleep.

"Wake up," she repeated as his eyes came into focus. Anneli Kallasti smiled down at him, and he smiled weakly back until he realized that he was secured to a bed. He jerked his wrists and tried to move his legs, but was too tightly bound, and when he opened his mouth to shout, she covered it gently with her hand. Her touch silenced him before he could scream, and he remained quiet.

The woman was even more beautiful than he had remembered from last night. Instead of the long red hair, she was now a dark brunette with gray eyes and pouting lips. She dabbed at his face with the wet cloth. "Hello, soldier. Welcome back. You're safe here, and you will not be harmed. I apologize for the rough treatment last night. I think you really are kind of cute."

As if to prove it, she unbuckled one of his wrists. "You will still be unsteady, but my friends are going to take you to the bathroom and help you shower and give you some pills to help with that headache. Then we will talk. Now don't try to fight, okay? No harm will come to you if you do not resist. I promise."

"Who are you?" His voice was a frog's croak from the dry mouth. "Where am I?"

Anneli gave a small laugh and leaned across to unbuckle the other wrist. In the process, she pressed her body lightly against him. The captive soldier almost sighed with pleasure. She pulled away and turned to a pair of men in the room, Kyle Swanson and a duty CIA field agent at the safe house. "He's all yours."

Serov was still weak and did not resist as the men

finished freeing his bonds and lifted him to his feet, then slowly shuffled him to a small but clean bathroom. His limbs were responding more by the minute, and he drank a glass of water, was able to urinate, was allowed a quick, warm shower and even brushed his teeth. The two escorts watched the entire time, but did not say a word, and soon he was back in the bed, lashed up but comfortable in a set of blue hospital scrubs. He saw his uniform hanging neatly on the back of a door.

"You probably have many questions, Corporal Valentin Serov. Your identification was in your wallet," the girl explained. "I won't tell you much, because my friends and I kidnapped you last night to ask some questions, not the other way around. Do you understand that?"

"I am a prisoner," Serov said with a jerk of the wrist restraints. "Why? I don't know anything."

She was in a chair beside the bed, helping him sip some water through a straw. Then she sat back and placed a writing tablet in her lap. "You are participating in that big Russian military exercise, are you not, Valentin? It must be very difficult for you out in the wild weather."

Serov knew that he should not answer, but she was so nice, and it was no great leap of knowledge for her to assume that he had been part of an exercise that had involved thousands of men and was being watched by the world media. "I stay indoors most of the time," he responded with a grin. "I'm a clerk for the quartermaster. Others do the marching."

Anneli made a tick on the pad, checking off the item. "Yes. That was on your ID card. Good for you. Have you been in the service long, Valentin?"

For the first time, Serov noticed that the two men had stayed in the room, but were seated and in nonthreatening positions. He ignored them to focus on Anneli. "For more than two years now. I either had to join or be conscripted, so I enlisted. Since I had some good schooling and knew how to type from using my computer so much, I was assigned to the headquarters company."

"When did you transfer to the Narva area? Do you like it here?"

He decided to try a trade. "I will tell you that only if you tell me your name." He smiled.

She gave a look she would show a naughty child. "Oh, you want to make a deal? Very well. My name is Darya and I am Estonian."

The soldier brightened. "Well, Darya, can you undo these restraints? I won't try to escape. I promise."

"Not yet, Valentin. Maybe in a little while if you continue being helpful."

"I came in about six months ago, and it is just another routine job. I am no hero."

Kyle Swanson glanced over at his fellow CIA agent. The man nodded in acknowledgment. She had the young soldier singing like a bird and was playing the good cop/bad cop routine all by herself. Swanson scribbled some notes of questions he wanted Anneli to ask after she finished the warm-up pitches. A quartermaster's clerk was a much better catch than some common infantryman or cannon-cocking artillery shooter. This guy actually could see beyond the brim of his helmet because he filed and shuffled papers, wrote reports, hung around bulletin boards, transmitted instructions and received orders. Without realizing it, a clerk becomes a sponge for information, and this one would not need torture or waterboarding. Kyle made a note and passed it over.

Anneli read it and asked, "Valentin, you must be hungry. If I bring you some food and tea, can I trust you not to get violent when I undo the restraints?"

Serov looked at the two men over by the wall. He couldn't escape anyway, so why bother? He didn't even really want to go. "Yes, Darya," he said, ready to agree to almost anything that would keep her nearby. It was a much better morning than being in that soggy barracks near the castle. The corporal was in love, but with a woman who coldly hated him and everything he represented, and was willing to eviscerate him on the spot. Anneli set about killing Corporal Valentin Serov with kindness and finding out about the Black Train that took away the only man she ever loved.

## BRUSSELS, BELGIUM

General Sir Frederick Ravensdale of Great Britain was what his American colleagues called a "warfighter." The small and skinny lad who had started his boarding school education at Culford had matured into military heroism, and some thirty years later was the respected deputy supreme allied commander of NATO in Europe.

When he finished Exeter College at Oxford, Ravensdale entered the military and earned the sand-colored beret of the elite commando unit known as the 22 Special Air Services. The freshly minted lieutenant was part of D Squadron's raid on Pebble Island during the Falklands War with Argentina in 1982. He was later wounded by a bomb in Northern Ireland and served in Germany during the Cold War. The career continued its upward trajectory during duty at the Ministry of Defence, and Ravensdale was a colonel in command of an armored brigade by the time of Kosovo, and later ran the United Kingdom's 3rd Mechanised Division in Iraq. He received the fourth star of a full general upon his appointment to SACEUR. Along with the rank, he was a Knight Commander of the Order of the British Empire, and a Knight Grand Commander of the Order of the Bath, a Companion of the Distinguished Service Order, and held numerous other accolades.

With that perfect pedigree, the easygoing general was popular on the international diplomatic circuit comprising member nations of the North Atlantic Treaty Organization. A respected military historian, he had authored two books on strategy and tactics. He was very tall and still lean and handsome as he neared retirement. His wife had died of ovarian cancer ten years earlier, and his three children were grown and gone. So far, they had blessed him with five grandchildren, all of whom lived back in England. The little tykes did not know their grandfather was a famous and important man, and he enjoyed that leveling experience.

He thought about that during his long morning walk before reporting to his office. For him, retirement should be something to which he could look forward. He had a substantial income and would be paid handsomely on the lecture circuit, so there would be enough money, and his physicians pronounced him to be in excellent health. On the cool April morning, with the winds and rain from the past few days having died down, he was able to stride through the park and consider his options. They were few.

Should he hurry this thing along and keep pushing for Kyle Swanson to ignite the maelstrom? Or should the general try and slow things down, or even prevent the conflict, which would mean his own secret would be revealed? Was the best he could hope for an honorable death on the battlefield, or was that only a distant possibility for a desk-bound general? Would he risk ignominious arrest and a trial for treason, during which he would lose everything? Either way, General Sir Frederick Ravensdale, GCB, GBE, DSO, faced ruin.

## VILNIUS, LITHUANIA

Major Juozas Valteris stared west into the darkness from his perch atop a tracked infantry fighting vehicle of the Iron Wolf Mechanized Battalion, part of the Lithuanian Rapid Reaction Force. The 40mm cannon and coaxial machine gun were loaded and ready. Anti-tank guided missiles bristled from the hull and could go hot in an instant, if necessary. The orders from the joint staff had been clear that this was no training exercise.

The major had served in Afghanistan under NATO command, but this time he was on his homeland, and he had made sure that everyone in the seven-hundred-man battalion understood that basic fact. They were the tripwire against a possible Russian land attack out of Moscow-controlled Kaliningrad, a leftover enclave sandwiched between Lithuania on its east and Poland on its west. Everybody else in NATO was looking the other way, toward Russia itself, but Valteris and his men knew the threat they faced lay in the other direction, to the west. All that was needed was a spark and the Baltic States would be hurled into still another war.

By treaty, Russian military trains could transit Lithuania into Kaliningrad, and for the past months, the rail traffic had increased. The country was also the headquarters for the Russian Baltic Fleet and had been heavily militarized during the Soviet era, when several hundred thousand troops were stationed there. The major didn't know the makeup of forces today, but that surprise exercise that the Russians were running to the north along Estonia and Latvia had spooked the Lithuanian high command enough to get the RBF up and moving.

This was no Ukraine, Major Valteris preached to his troops. They were not going to allow the Russian military to get as much as a toehold in Lithuania, no matter which direction they tried. There would be no victory for Moscow here. The men all knew the small force could not stop a full and determined attack. What they could do, and would do, was hold until their friends in NATO could come swarming in to clean up the mess. A spearhead of several thousand German, Dutch and Norwegian troops was the next line of defense. NATO jets were on call.

There was no movement on the far side of the border, no sounds of war machines clanking about, no maneuvering battalions of Russian soldiers, no thudding, telltale signatures of approaching helicopters, no booming guns from the artillery tubes at Rooster Cap Nowak, the forward Russian base only a few miles across Lake Vištytis. The silence did not translate into peace. He lowered his

binos for a moment to check his personal weapon, a
German-made assault rifle. His boys of the Iron Wolf
hunkered down and prepared for whatever Tuesday
might bring.


TALLINN, ESTONIA

A somber Kyle Swanson and Anneli Kallasti were in
the home of Colonel Thomas Markey of NATO and
his wife, Jan Hollings of the CIA, all of them trying to
read the intelligence tea leaves that might foretell the
future. Each had a slightly different agenda, but a common purpose. The entire Russian border region was so
tense that only a spark was needed to push things over
the brink.

Jan Hollings was furious that Swanson had used
Anneli without permission to snatch a Russian soldier.
Anneli was mad that Corporal Valery Serov knew nothing about the disappearance of Brokk Mihailovich. The
colonel was disturbed that defector Ivan Strakov was
refusing to divulge any cyber-war information, and Kyle
was troubled by his conclusion that Ivan might be telling the truth about a potential invasion. Together, they
understood that the decisions they might make would
reach far beyond the walls of the Markey living room in
a neat Tallinn neighbornood.

"What did you do with the boy?" Colonel Markey
asked.

Swanson took a sip of brandy and coffee, then returned the glass down precisely on the wet circle on the
napkin. "We got him back in uniform, put him to sleep

with drugs again, drove back to Narva and dumped him in a park, stinking of vodka. He was gone less than twenty-four hours, was last seen leaving a bar with a woman, and was found drunk on his ass the next day. Even if he talks, nobody would believe his wild tale of being kidnapped and returning unharmed. Instead of going through the interrogation grinder, the corporal will likely tell a big lie, then accept some punishment for being too drunk to return to his unit on time. He will keep his mouth shut."

"I wanted him dead," Anneli said in a flat voice. "He gave us nothing about the Black Train, or Brokk. Kyle would not let me shoot him."

"You had no authority to do anything," snapped Calico. "I should turn you over to the police. I try to help you and you go off without warning and do this kidnapping with Swanson."

Anneli did not flinch from the sharp comments. "You will not do that, Jan. As you Americans say, we have a bigger tuna fish to fry."

Swanson did not want the two women fighting. "The corporal gave us some good information, Calico. Not a lot of detail, because he was of such low rank, but he was able to confirm that huge amounts of ammunition, supplies, men and matériel have been flowing into the Narva area for months, and hidden in secret. He saw Armata tanks, which confirms what Ivan told us. I wanted a second opinion, and I got it. Don't particularly like it, but that's what we have."

Colonel Markey, in civilian clothes, stood beside the small fire. "The Armatas were already confirmed, Kyle. They came out to play in that Russian military exercise all along the northern border, and it's apparently over now. Just a drill. They seem to be returning to their original positions already."

"So that's a third source. What we didn't know was the Russians have apparently stockpiled enough supplies to support a quick thrust across the border at Narva in another Ukranian-style land grab."

Markey said there had been a blast of cyber-war activity during the Russian exercise, but that NATO had been tipped off when a surveillance plane was temporarily electronically blinded, and had been expecting the bigger hack attempt. "I want to wring Ivan Strakov dry of everything he knows, Kyle. Any land war is going to be supported by their hackers jamming our comm systems. Without computers, we will be in big trouble."

"Do you believe what Strakov says, Tom?" Calico asked her husband.

"No. I know the guy. He's gaming us. That is what he does. I think that he has fed us just enough to keep us interested."

Swanson added, "I feel the same way, Colonel. But I can no longer ignore the bastard. I'm ready to get back in the room with him tomorrow and get him to talk some more. Maybe he is shucking us, but I'll do my best."

"What about me?" asked Anneli.

"You go directly back to the safe house apartment and stay there," instructed Calico. "From what my sources have picked up on the Narva grapevine, Anneli, the police are already looking for you in connection with the murders of two Russian nationals in Narva. You and an unknown male accomplice—that would be you, Swanson—are both on thin ice."

The blond spy then turned her full attention on Kyle.

"And the folks at Langley are tired of you cowboying around on your own, Swanson. You have one more chance, and if you screw it up, the CIA will dump you and screw Excalibur Enterprises for years to come. Got it?"

"Hummph," grunted Swanson. He heard her words, which was not the same as agreeing to obey.

**S**WANSON AND **A**NNELI left together and hailed a cab. They were being pushed along by a tide of momentum, had become the focal point of an international incident, and the unexpected murder investigation changed the entire equation. Now they even had to be wary of ordinary cops on the street. Best to get the hell out of town, and Kyle waved down a Pink Taxi minivan that swung neatly to a stop beside them. Yellow cabs ruled New York, black was the London taxi color, and pink ruled in Tallinn's swarm of taxis.

"Calico said I must go to the safe house," Anneli commented, looking at Kyle with a wry smile. Her eyes had been downcast during the lecture by Calico, but were showing a fresh sparkle. She was getting used to Swanson doing the unexpected.

"The goal is to keep you safe. I know a better place than that little apartment. Tell the driver to take us to the Old City Marina." He slid the side door open and she climbed into the backseat and gave the directions. The taxi driver gave a grunt of understanding, figuring that he would demand five euros for the short trip of about two kilometers. It was a high price, but taxis set their own rates in super free-market Estonia, and these passengers had not bargained in advance.

The harbor was just opening for the season. A number of small yachts and sailboats belonging to more stalwart sailors were already in the water, crowded together at night like a herd of resting swans. People moved about servicing them. The terminal office was closed. Two men in heavy parkas were standing near it when the taxi stopped in front. "Kyle! Over here!" called one.

"Trevor?" He could not make them out fully in the darkness. The inner harbor was protected from big waves, but a stiff wind cut the night, making the men huddle in their heavy-weather coats. Swanson and Anneli felt the cold grip them.

"The very same, mate." The men drew closer.

"Trevor," said Swanson. "Good to see you. And Paul, glad you came along to keep this bugger in line." He introduced Anneli to the captain and the senior mate of the *Vagabond*, the magnificent private yacht of Excalibur Enterprises. "Where's our barge?"

Trevor Dash whipped off his greatcoat and threw it casually around Anneli, almost losing her in its folds, then the four of them walked down a wide, paved pier. He explained, "We moored her on the far side of a cruise ship where there was plenty of space. Lucky for us they are not in full season yet."

The deep voice of Paul Lancaster spoke. "We're ready to pull out as soon as you give the word. The boss sent along a few presents for you."

Anneli was disoriented. This was clearly a pair of British sailors, and they treated Kyle both as a friend and a superior. "What is happening?" she asked. They were moving along the big pier, leaving behind the private boats and sailing craft. Before her loomed the huge bow of a cruise monster that was tied firmly with ropes as large as her arms, and was as empty as a ghost ship. A dome of light bloomed on the far side.

"This is going to be your new home for a while, Anneli," Kyle said gently as a large seagoing yacht with a nose as sharp as a needle came into view. The blinding white *Vagabond* wore its disguise as a pleasure vessel perfectly well, but it was not pirate bait. It was the third yacht to bear the name as Sir Jeff kept upgrading. *Vagabond* was almost three hundred feet in length, had three raked decks with tinted glass all around, plus luxurious spaces below, and was tooled with state-of-the-art electronics and antiair and antiship missiles and other weaponry. It was a pretty thing that could take care of itself in a firefight. Every member of its crew was a veteran of the British armed forces and the *Vagabond* occasionally conducted quiet missions for the intelligence agencies of Great Britain and the United States, snooping deep into harbors where warships could not go. Sir Geoffrey Cornwell had dispatched it to Estonia after talking with Kyle.

Anneli walked up a rubber-mat gangway and was ushered into a salon that seemed like a small club. People were at ease in sofas and chairs, talking among themselves. A large-screen television set was tuned to a chart that was linked to live surface radar sweeps. Every vessel within ten miles was logged electronically. A similar chart painted aerial activity. Not a club; a war room.

Captain Dash made quick introductions, although almost the entire crew already knew Kyle Swanson and gave him a rowdy welcome aboard. Two rugged men turned from a window, both lithe and muscular. "Sir Jeff added these lads for the trip, Kyle. Thought they might be of some future use, eh? May I present Sar'nt Stanley Baldwin and Corporal Grayson Perry."

"SAS snipers, Mister Swanson. Temporary duty on loan to you, compliments of Her Majesty's government." Baldwin shook hands. He was in jeans and a heavy sweatshirt.

"Heard a lot about you, sir. Pleasure." Perry had eyes like a hawk.

"Excellent. Good to have you aboard, guys," Swanson said. "I don't have a project in mind right now, so just hang out and we'll see what happens. Things may get interesting before we're done."

"At your service," said the sergeant, who was checking out the girl beside Kyle. She was a beauty.

Swanson gathered Dash and the senior mate together with the snipers. "There have been some changes ashore. Young Anneli and I are wanted by the Estonian cops for murder."

"Murder? Her?" Sergant Baldwin fought to keep his emotions in check.

"Yes. I had to do away with a couple of Russian spooks who came after her, and they are blowing it up into an incident. She was supposed to go to a CIA safe house tonight, but I want to get her completely off Estonian soil. Nobody will know she is aboard the *Vagabond*. Now you two SAS dudes can be her guards for a while. Don't let anybody take her away from you. And teach her how to shoot."

"We can do that." Corporal Perry was quiet and confident.

"And Captain Dash, I have to leave now and catch a flight to Brussels. You may take the *Vagabond* out of the harbor while I'm gone. Steer clear of the Russian ships, and work toward the general direction of the U.S. carrier strike group in the Baltic."

"Should we anticipate trouble, Kyle?"

"I don't know. Just act like this is some rich man's toy for a few days. Keep your ears up. I'll be in touch."

The captain bobbed his head, then ordered, "Master Samuelson, please make preparations for departure."

"Aye, aye, skipper." The mate left to begin the process of getting the boat under way.

Kyle put one hand on each of Anneli's shoulders and looked her in the eyes. "There are no worries for you, not now. You know that I have to leave to go talk to Ivan."

She leaned close and hugged him. "Calico, I mean Mrs. Markey, will be angry at me again."

"Calico is always mad. I'll deal with her. You stay out of trouble until I get back. And those guys you just met are your new shepherds. They are true warriors. Nothing is going to happen to you with them around."

"What if you need me, Kyle? Aren't I a good partner?"

He gave her a quick kiss on the forehead, like a father kissing a daughter good-bye on a school morning. "Then I will come and get you. This isn't over yet, Anneli. See you soon."

It was not until he trotted down the gangplank that he realized she had not mentioned Brokk.

## MOSCOW

Vladimir Vladimiroch Pushkin wore lifts in his shoes because he stood only five-foot-five-inches tall. In televised appearances, the president of the Russian Federation surrounded himself with short men and usually stood on a platform behind the podium. He was sixty-five years old and physically active in sports, although age had stacked on a few flabby pounds that he could not shed. Despite his physical stature, he was still the biggest man in Russia.

The sky had been a dark blue canopy when he had arisen before dawn on Tuesday morning and did his familiar set of judo exercises to loosen the muscles and tune up for the day. He had been doing judo since he was a child. The mandatory self-control and ability to read the strengths and weaknesses of an opponent had proven to be so useful in many walks of life. On a judo mat or at the United Nations, if a foe left a momentary unguarded opening, Pushkin would attack. Some snow had passed through Moscow while he slept, leaving a small and evaporating white carpet around the Kremlin. After the workout, he walked outside. It was still cold, even for mid-April, and the hardy weather pulled at his flesh and linked him with his ancestors who had prowled the Steppes. He ate a light breakfast, dressed and was in the office by seven o'clock.

After the usual round of global and domestic situation and security briefings, his first official visitor of the day was an old friend, General of the Army Pavel Sergeyev, the chief of the general staff. Pushkin remained in the big chair behind the desk while the general, wearing a civilian suit, angled his body into one of the gold-fabric high-backs diagonally across from the president. They exchanged greetings. Both were from the Leningrad region, and while Sergeyev had been rising to the top job in the military, Pushkin had clawed his way up through the old KGB intelligence service. The partnership worked and they did many favors along the way as they adapted to become new Russians with old dreams.

"What is on your mind, Pavel, that could not have been handled by telephone? I have a full schedule." Pushkin held up a fan of papers and a flash of impatience crossed his face.

"Volodya," said the general, using the president's nickname to calm him. "We may have to make a change in the western military district."

"The west? Why? I thought the commander in St. Petersburg was one of our best."

"Colonel General Levchenko has disobeyed our orders, Mister President. You instructed all of the commanders to remain cautious and undertake no provocative actions while we analyze the impact of the defection of the bastard traitor, Strakov. You remember that."

Pushkin removed his glasses and rubbed his nose in thought. "Yes. Yes, of course. No sudden moves."

General Sergeyev came out of his chair and clasped his hands behind his back, taking a few steps around the carpet. His voice carried a taste of venom. "Instead of obeying that simple directive, Levchenko chose to launch Operation Hermitage on his own. By doing so, he unveiled the new Armata systems for our enemies to see and record. Stupid man! Plus he authorized unnecessary overflights in the Baltic and along the Estonia border. NATO is probably ready to pull the trigger."

"Was there any shooting?" asked the president.

"Fortunately, no. Not this time."

"What do you want to do?"

"We must discipline him severely, Volodya, my old friend. Colonel General Levchenko has become blinded by ambition. He is running his own kingdom out there in the western district while living like a tsar in St. Petersburg. He needs to be brought to heel."

"What do you suggest?" The president calmly wrote a note on a yellow pad.

"I want to replace him with someone more reliable. We should bring Levchenko back to Moscow and make him work for a living at headquarters before he gets totally out of hand."

President Pushin adjusted his glasses and returned his attention to the papers before him.

"No, I will not replace him, my friend. We will need a fighting commander out there in the coming tense times. Levchenko is impetuous, I grant you that, but he is an excellent field officer, which is why we gave him the job in the first place. I agree, however, that he probably needs to be reminded of his proper slot in the chain of command. I definitely do not like that he disobeyed our instructions. Pavel, I want you to order him back here so I can have a private word with him and clarify any misunderstandings he might have about his role."

The chief of the general staff smiled at that direct order. His reckless subordinate, Colonel General Levchenko, was about to have his ass chewed personally by President Vladimir Vladimiroch Pushkin.

BRUSSELS, BELGIUM

The telephone in his pocket burped as soon as Kyle Swanson landed. The directory showed that DSS Agent Lem James up in Helsinki had called several times. Flying on the commercial aircraft meant Kyle could not use his cell phone while in the air, which had left him out of contact. Every other passenger also seemed to have phones in their ears as soon as the plane touched the earth.

"Hey, Lem," Swanson said in greeting. "What's happening?"

The agent's voice was clear and calm, although the words were carefully chosen for the open circuit. "I talked to our Finny friend about that thing you wanted to know."

"And? Did she give it up?"

"Between colleagues and good friends, she told me to blow it out my ass. She would not budge."

Inspector Rikka Aura of the Finland Security Intelligence Service was not cutting them a break. She would not give up her source for knowing exactly when and how Swanson had entered her country.

"Do we have any leverage?"

"None," replied James. "She is stone. I'll keep my ear to the ground up here."

"Roger that, Lem. Thanks for trying." He dropped the phone back into his pocket, continued toward the exit and thought: *Bitch!*

A small crowd was clustered at the arrivals hall to welcome friends, family and business associates. Corporate drivers in traditional black suits held name signs for incoming VIP passengers. Kids shouldered heavy backpacks, as if soldiers going off to war. Porters rolled luggage carts. Adults wrestled with suitcases.

Out of the crowd of well-wishers sailed Jan Hollings, sparks of fire in her sea-blue eyes and her blond hair almost standing on end with her fury. She pointed to an isolated area and he followed. "Where the fuck is Anneli?" Calico demanded. "She never showed up at the safe house."

"Relax. She is perfectly fine. When you told us that we were wanted for murder, I made another plan. She is safe and secure and satisfied."

"Without telling me! I'm the one responsible for that girl. I demand that you tell me, right now!"

Swanson's implacable mask slipped and let his own anger show. "That's not going to happen, Jan. There are hundreds of thousands of people in the intelligence chain of our country, and I know there is a leak. Probably dozens, maybe hundreds of leaks, and that doesn't even get into the local police forces, where any secret is for sale. The fewer people that know her location, the safer she is. You just have to trust me on this one. I'm not going to let anything happen to her."

"Trust you? That's a laugh. I don't trust you. Nobody trusts you."

"And I don't trust you, either, Calico, but it's the nature of the job. You just push ahead to get those new identification papers for Anneli. When she is really needed, I will produce her. Not until then."

She gave him a look that could wither a cornfield, then caught a breath and changed gears. "You had better be right, you arrogant son of a bitch. If anything happens to her, I will scalp you. Now let's get you back into that room with Ivan Strakov, where you were supposed to be all along."

"Yeah. That's why I'm here."

## KOEKELBERG, BELGIUM

**T**HIS TIME, **SWANSON** recognized the Basilica of the Sacred Heart, the landmark of the Brussels neighborhood, and the nearby brick-and-plaster building that was unchanged since he had last been there. Calico drove into the underground garage and Kyle went through the chutes-and-ladders identification routine to reach the interrogation room on the second floor. Colonel Ivan Strakov was already there in his chair, drinking a soda, no more nervous than a midlevel banking nerd figuring out how to best foreclose on a widow.

Gone was the common orange jumpsuit, and instead he was in khaki pants and a soft brown sweater, with unscuffed Italian loafers on his feet. He was spending his first million, and planning on more. Swanson reached the table in a few steps, trading silent stares with the Russian. The man's hair was newly trimmed and his nails were buffed and polished. On his left wrist bulged a large new watch with silver sweep hands on a black face and a little window that clocked the days. Overall, this was a man enjoying his special treatment.

Strakov's snake eyes flickered over Swanson, then he said, "Finally, my hero returns. I knew you would be back." He sipped a Diet Coke.

Swanson cleared his throat. "You are not the only thing happening in the world, Strakov. I had to talk to somebody else, somewhere else, about something else. Now it's your turn again." He would not give Ivan the satisfaction of an explanation, nothing that the Russian could use to play him. It was like walking through a mental minefield.

"Good. Good." Ivan scratched an ear. "I spent some of the downtime watching television. They let me do that now that I have proven myself, so I binge-watched all of *Breaking Bad* and I want to start *Game of Thrones* tonight. Hollywood is a wonderful dream factory." He held up his left wrist to show the timepiece. "And I even went shopping."

"I noticed the new threads and kicks. Hell of a watch." *They had let him leave the house?*

"Of course. I am a guest here, not a prisoner."

Kyle crossed his arms and did not pursue the pampering issue. He had to trust that the CIA minders knew what they were doing; probably just fattening the cow to keep it happy before the butchering. "Whatever. Tell me something I don't know."

"And the news shows, Kyle! I watch a lot of news," Strakov said with a sharp look. "Things seem to be getting a bit tense out there."

Kyle thought, *Damn it all!* Going out into public and open television viewing? Outside information should not be allowed to reach this man. He remembered the crossword puzzle from last time. Newspapers, too? "Don't believe the media, Ivan."

The colonel frowned. "Among the things I watched with interest were reports of a rather large Russian military exercise along the NATO border. Had you not run out on me, I would have warned you that it was coming."

"Sure you would." He dodged the accusation. "You have been so forthcoming on everything. Anyway, the exercise was no big deal. The rabbits ran around for a while, and even now are scooting back into their holes, but not before we took pictures of your hotshot Armata tanks and battle platforms. Yesterday's astonishing secret is old news now."

The defector remained infuriatingly smug. "Of course it is, Kyle. It was called Operation Hermitage, by the way, and it was a practice for defending St. Petersburg. The last tsar had his Winter Palace there, the Hermitage, which is now a magnificent museum. Hence the name. I really wanted to explain the exercise so NATO would not have been taken by surprise. You took off before I had the chance."

Swanson coughed into his fist. "You think that we are unaware that Moscow has forces lined up all the way down the border from Estonia, through Latvia and Lituania? There is no news there, buddy. Your President Pushkin would love to snatch those little countries back for his dream of rebuilding the Soviet empire."

Strakov glanced around the bare room to gather his thoughts before continuing. He smiled. "Consider it this way, Kyle. Suppose Louisiana or Texas broke away from the United States in some ill-considered revolution, but the overwhelming majority in those states wanted to stay allied with Washington. Would Washington want to help those unhappy former Americans rejoin the fold? Same thing."

"No, it's not." Swanson placed both hands flat on the table. "Let's not waste time arguing hypotheticals. It's like when you spout off with poetry. You say words, but nothing comes out. President Pushkin might want to take a bite out of the Baltics, but NATO and the United States will never allow that to happen."

Ivan Strakov let that stupid grin break through again. "And you think that is what Operation Hermitage was about: practice to invade the Baltics?"

Kyle felt as unsteady as if he was standing on a cliff edge. "Yes."

Strakov slowly moved his head back and forth and exhaled heavily, a teacher disappointed in a student. "It was all a misdirection play, Kyle. Your people concentrated on the exciting Armata hardware and the movement and flights along that border, looking for the Red Horde to ransack some beleaguered town so your brave air cavalry could dash in to save the day, all to be reported by your vapid television people. You swung and missed again, Kyle. Strike two."

"What the hell are you talking about?"

"While you people scrambled to meet the nonexistent threat of Operation Hermitage, Moscow slipped forty-five hundred more men—an entire motorized rifle brigade—into the Murmansk region, far to the north. The war game had nothing to do with the Baltics, Kyle. Those three little dominoes will fall back to the Motherland on their own, in due time. Instead, the operation had everything to do with the Arctic Circle." He leaned back and crossed his legs. "Further details will cost another million or so."

Swanson remained outwardly unruffled. "Stop stalling with the bullshit, Ivan. Our satellites and submarines watch and listen to Pushkin's every move up there." At least he hoped they did. "A fur seal can't belch on an iceberg without us hearing it, so let's get back to the real world, which is you and me in this room."

The Russian bobbed his head. "Fine. Did you know that the media is now carrying my name and picture and a story about how important I may be to allied intelligence? I believe it is time to renegotiate the terms."

"I don't handle press relations. I am not a lawyer. The clock is still ticking, Ivan, and I am cold out of patience with this game. To me, you are just a big puddle of useless noise. Your value lies in supposed cyber warfare, not troop movements."

"You are wrong, Swanson. Overall intelligence has always been my game. Computers are but a component, just like the Armatas."

"Give me something," Swanson pressed him. "Convince my higher-ups that you're still worth the trouble, or you may be visiting Guantánamo."

Strakov considered that and stared at Kyle for a few moments. "All right. Do you remember last time, when I said that you were dealing with a madman?"

"Right. Personally, I do not think President Pushkin is mad, in the clinical sense. Crazy like a fox, yes, and much too brutal and aggressive, but he seems to know what he is doing."

"There. You jump to the wrong conclusion once again, Swanson. I should start worrying about your own value to this interrogation progress. I was not referring to Pushkin at all. The maniac behind all of these sudden military moves is General of the Army Pavel Sergeyev, the chief of the general staff."

Swanson thumbed through his memory bank. "Ser-

geyev? He's just another paper-pushing Kremlin bureaucrat, too old to fight and getting ready to retire."

"He is much more than that, Kyle. General Sergeyev
maintains, shall we say, large dreams. He needs to be
locked away in a place that treats the mentally ill before he triggers a nuclear war." Strakov checked his new
watch. "That's enough for now. I need a nap. Check out
Sergeyev. Send in a company lawyer next to discuss my
contract."

## BRUSSELS, BELGIUM

Freddie Ravensdale dined alone that Tuesday evening,
unfit for company while merciless tendrils of memory
squeezed his heart. Really, was there any way out for
him? He didn't think so. The general took a deep breath,
drank off the remainder of his brandy in a single swallow and closed his eyes while he excavated his life as
some anthropologist of a future generation might study
his bones. Beside his right hand lay a Glock 17, a beck-
oning 9mm solution that would end his pain, but not
the problem.

His mind became a time machine that dialed him
back to Berlin in the mid-1980s and the fateful ballet
performance at the Deutsche Staatsoper on the Unter
den Linden. He was a young captain at the time and
looked splendid in the dress black uniform of a British
officer, his bemedaled chest crossed with a brilliantly
shining Sam Browne belt as he drove out of the British
Zone and was waved through Checkpoint Charlie after
a purely routine stop, then entered the Russian Zone.
Berlin was a divided city, but certain courtesies were

extended. As usual, a little Russian car fell in behind to follow, just as the allies trailed any Russians coming out of their sector. It was the Cold War and all that, but a man could still have a good time in Berlin.

At intermission, the British officers stood by themselves in a group, drinking inexpensive champagne, and the crowd around them gave them plenty of space. In postwar Germany, civilians who did not recognize the uniforms were wary of any officers who wore black, once the color of the hated SS.

Lorette had appeared at his elbow out of nowhere, and asked the cheerful group with open curiosity, "Who *are* you men?" Lorette with the fair hair and sky eyes, tall and full-figured; God had made all German women beautiful and had spent extra time creating this one, who was touching his arm.

Ravensdale took a bite of the tempting apple. The ballet and his friends were forgotten and the two began a courtship filled with ecstasy. His little auto bearing the BZ license tag was soon making almost nightly trips to her flat and they went to the theater, for long walks, to new restaurants and always ended up back at her flat. He never missed a day of work, never shirked his duty. Lorette understood. She did not pry. His professional life was full, and now she was giving his personal life meaning, too. It was not an unusual event. A large number of British and Americans had German girlfriends and many were eventually taken back home as wives; glistening, living, beautiful, spirited war trophies.

He did not see Lorette die. She was already dead when he arrived at the flat that night, dead on the bed, her long arms and legs spread and tied with ropes to the bedposts. The neck was purple with bruises as were her face and rib cage. A silk tie was tight around her neck. Several East Berlin policemen were standing in the room, talking calmly, waiting for him. The dreaded Stasi, the Ministry for State Security, made him identify her corpse, then pounced on him like wolves on a lamb, and gnawed on him with questions while Lorette's naked body cooled on the mattress nearby.

About an hour into the questioning, a Russian intelligence agent appeared and spread the bad news before the stunned British captain. They had fingerprints, they had pictures, they had eyewitnesses, and they even had reports that Lorette had written about him. Long pages in her beautiful script traced their relationship from their first meeting at the ballet, how lust turned to romance, almost his every word, and finally her concerns that he was a violent man trained as a British commando, and that she feared him. Their sex play had turned increasingly rough, she lied. By midnight, Ravensdale was informed that he was going to be charged with murdering a civilian in East Berlin.

He had fallen headlong into a honey trap. Lorette was an agent of Moscow. By morning, he had agreed to the offered deal. It had seemed so easy at the time for the naïve, frightened, embarrassed, saddened British officer: He could be wrecked, or he could cooperate. All the Russians wanted was a single favor to be granted by him at some unknown time in the future, a debt that might never even be collected, for who could tell what fortunes life would deal a combat officer? Agree and the evidence and the dead girl would disappear. Otherwise, something quite different would happen. He accepted the offer, and made it back to his duty station on time the following morning.

The happiest days of his life came in 1989, when the Berlin wall fell and the Soviet Union disintegrated. Freddie Ravensdale had risen quite far in rank by then, his career was soaring, and as the bricks toppled, he believed the sword that had hung over his head for so long was gone. The Stasi was dismantled, the Soviets collapsed and even the mighty KGB disappeared as the Cold War ended. Decades passed.

Then two weeks ago, his private cell phone rang and General Sir Frederick Ravensdale, the deputy supreme allied commander of NATO in Europe, answered it.

"Do you remember Lorette?" asked a smooth female voice he had never heard before.

## ABOVE LAPLAND

The Russian MiG-29 fighter jet, an aerodynamic dream, whisked all alone through the darkening sky above Lapland, teasing the Finnish air defense radars that tracked it. The pilot, Captain Ildus Polnykov, knew they were watching him zip across the vast emptiness of the northwestern border. With Operation Hermitage still in progress, everybody was watching everybody.

One of his two assignments tonight was to force the Finns to scramble some F-18 Hornets up on an intercept course so the response could be timed. Once they arrived, Polnykov would peel away and fly back to Murmansk, where technicians would analyze the data collected by his electronics package. That they would come was never in doubt. He would make it happen with his second task, that of sparking a real confrontation.

He was about thirty miles across the international

border into Finland and had come in so fast that no interceptors had yet shown up on his own radar. Normally, that was what these test flights were all about, he thought. To probe. See how far he could push it. See if he could pick a fight. This mission was going to be a lot different. He let the powerful MiG-29, known to NATO as the "Fulcrum," slide down several thousand feet in altitude and bled off some speed to become an even bigger target.

At times like this, Polnykov felt a strange sense of peace, alone in a place of beautiful fantasy. The sky was purpling as the last ridge of the late-setting sun went down before him, while below were untracked snowy miles and great primeval forests. The only sounds were his own breathing into his oxygen mask and the periodic low voice of a controller far back in Russia. He would love to mix it up with a Hornet tonight, to dance in the heavens in playful menace, but that was not the main job. True air-to-air combat was something he had never experienced, and that absence was a hollow place inside of him. He checked his full load of armaments. Pure power lay right at his fingertips

Suddenly Captain Polnykov was snapped back into reality. The sensors were screaming warnings that he was being painted by radar, and the pinging was loud and strong, showing the threat was nearby. They had just turned it on, and it caught him by surprise.

Finland had put some new mobile antiaircraft missile batteries into the field, and the vehicles were secluded in the thick forests and hard to pinpoint because they changed position every day. In the past few weeks, the batteries appeared to be snuggling closer to the Russian border. Captain Polnykov and other pilots had been ordered to find and destroy one and show the Finns the cost of such folly.

Ah. He had done it. A missile radar truck was on line. *Good. Make the run.* He slid down to an even lower altitude, went to full throttle and the Klimov turbofan engines kicked into afterburner. The pilot was pushed back in his seat by that mighty thrust. Destroying the site would surely be enough provocation to draw a few F-18s up to play. He was so low that trees bent beneath the disturbed air of his passing over them.

The captain clicked on his ground-lock radar and let it sweep the evening. The radar instantly pointed out the radiating target below and identified it as an Advanced Surface-to-Air Missile System. He listened to its frantic *beep-beep-beep* and considered what the perplexed Finnish Defense Force soldiers below were thinking as the Russian fighter-bomber roared toward them, eating up the miles only a few hundred feet off the deck and with a full rack of bombs. They would never fire first, and after he set his weapons free, they would not have adequate reaction time to shoot back because he was coming in too low and fast. This was a good find, and Polnykov rode in knowing that even without any Hornets to fight, he could return to Murmansk after this run and be cheered and rewarded. He began his final portion of the attack run.

Just as he sent three air-to-surface missiles sliding from the wing racks to ride down the radiating beam toward the Finns, he saw a brilliant flash against the bleak landscape below, and then the smoking trail of a missile erupting up out of the forest. Even as the avionics warnings shouted in his ears, he knew it was too late. The Finns had actually fired back! Two AMRAAM antiaircraft missiles had thundered out of the Finns' launcher at point-blank range.

The Finnish missiles and the Russian plane collided with an incredible closing speed and the eighty-eight-pound high-explosive warheads blasted the MiG apart. Falling and spinning and the burning fragments gouging deep furrows where the pieces hit the frozen ground.

It crashed not far from the mobile launcher site, which itself was torn to shreds and left as a flaming pyre when the trio of Hermes missiles fired by Captain Polnykov smashed into it.

**18**

WASHINGTON, D.C.

**W**E HAVE A situation, sir."

President of the United States Christopher Thompson was finishing off a small tuna salad lunch at his cluttered desk in the Oval Office when National Security Adviser Dean Thomas entered. Thompson looked up from a thick book of budget numbers. "What is it, Dean?"

"An intruding Russian fighter jet has attacked and destroyed a Finnish missile battery deep on Finland's side of the international border. The plane was shot down during the attack."

The president pressed his thumb hard against the pen in his hand, almost to the breaking point, then shoved aside the briefing book. The numbers from Congress would wait a while. "Dammit! I have warned Pushkin again and again that those overflights risked a confrontation. Do we have any details?"

Dean Thomas dropped a single piece of paper on the desk. It was only two paragraphs. "Not many," said the NSA adviser. "It happened about an hour ago, right at sundown on their local time. A MiG-29, one of the better Russian aircraft, appeared out of nowhere on what appeared to be an attack run and an officer of the Finnish Defense Forces pushed the button in response and missiles flew in both directions."

"What about hard evidence?"

"Yes, sir. Survivors of the missile battery found the plane wreckage and it's clearly Russian. Radar records back them up. No question there."

"Has there been any response from Moscow? Military or otherwise?" President Thompson was out of his chair and leading his national security adviser out the door, heading for the Situation Room underground.

"Nothing yet, Mister President."

"Okay. Let's get the staff together and see if we can get ahead of this thing to keep it from escalating. I want the vice president in on this, and get the chairman of the Joint Chiefs over here from the Pentagon. A video link with our new guy, the supreme allied commander in Europe?"

"General David Lincoln. He has been in the job for less than month. I doubt if he knows anything that he hasn't passed to the Pentagon at this point."

"Right. I remember him now. Hold on that video for the time being. I'm sure NATO is all over this."

Thomas matched the president's big strides as they fell in with a phalanx of Secret Service agents. "Keep in mind, sir, that Finland is beyond the NATO umbrella. Our options there are very limited unless they ask for help."

"I know. I know. But that country is a proven and dependable ally, Dean, and I have no intention of letting Pushkin plant his flag there."

"Like they did under the North Pole."

"Exactly. Remember the new information from the Russian defector about them secretly pushing more troops into the north during that military exercise? Pushkin has some fantasy about owning the whole Arctic Circle." The president was viewing a map in his mind. Russia was pressing in from the Ukraine in the south, the Baltics were a tinderbox, and the big bear was now apparently reaching more boldly into the northernmost territories. "After this meeting is over, arrange something quiet so I can meet with the leaders of the House and Senate. I need them fully informed so we don't get bushwhacked politically if this thing blows up. If there must be a military reaction by our side, I want their fingerprints to be on any document I sign."

"Got it." The national security adviser was working his cell phone speed dial. "Who else?"

"The Central Intelligence Agency. Pushkin went too far with this blatant violation of Finland. I think it is time for some payback, Dean. I'm sick and tired of backing down every time this bully makes another demand."

CIA HEADQUARTERS,
LANGLEY, VIRGINIA

Marty Atkins, the deputy director for clandestine operations for the CIA, considered his options after hearing from the White House. President Thompson had authorized a tit-for-tat operation to retaliate against the Russians for the MiG strike. Atkins was glad the Russky son of a bitch got blown out of the sky. The state department would handle the formal protest, but the big guy in the Oval Office wanted to underscore the message with a dark world dirty-tricks move. That was what Atkins did for a living.

Had Marty been at a poker player, he would have been a smooth-dealing card mechanic with aces up both sleeves, in his pants and even in his shoes. For him, it was only a matter of which to play. He first had to consider the region—a retaliation op in El Salvador or Liberia would be next to meaningless. The men in Moscow might not even connect the dots. The Finland incident was clearly part of Russia's long-range strategy for militarizing the Arctic Circle and grabbing its strategic basins of natural resources. The northern site required something in that general region. Not within Finland itself, which was still maddeningly neutral, but close enough to make the point to the Kremlin.

He ran his fingers along a huge wall map of the world while his top two assistants discussed the problem. They were good tricksters, both former field agents who had earned entry into his room of secrets.

"What about Afghanistan?" suggested Stew Willenson, a burly middle-aged man who once had ridden mules on dangerous missions in those unforgiving mountains. Atkins shook him off. "None of the 'Stans," he ruled. The Russians would laugh. They had left nothing of interest behind after their own ill-fated Afghan adventure back in the 1980s. Moscow was pleased that the U.S. remained bogged down there.

Agatha Brice, an expert in European affairs, spoke, her glasses low on her nose. "Maybe give some TV time to that Russian defector, like Moscow did with Edward Snowden. Embarrass them in public?"

"That's not a bad idea, Aggie. Something we should plan on doing at some point. Not strong enough for this. The problem was military in nature, so we need something military as a response. A small but painful reminder that we're watching them." Atkins's eyes scrolled across the map. Finland was just above Estonia, and the Russians were making those same kinds of pesky overflights along the borders throughout that region, only without any direct attacks. To the south, Lithuania and Latvia were tantalizing plums for Russia. He sat down at his desk and steepled his fingers and was soon lost in thought.

Agatha's comment about the defector formed the nugget of an idea. Calico and Kyle Swanson were in Brussels doing the interviews with Colonel Strakov, which were not yielding the ground-shaking revelations that everyone had hoped. They could change gears on the Russian without a problem, slow that down long enough for his two valuable agents to do the sort of work they did best. Calico knew Estonia like the back of her hand, and Swanson knew the military. Plus, Atkins thought, Swanson was perhaps the most dangerous man on a payroll filled with talented operatives.

"OK, people, I've got it." Marty Atkins smiled like a wolf. "We're going to send Kyle Swanson out on a hunt. He's sitting around Brussels right now with the defector."

"Swanson? Sir, that man is a bull in a china shop!" protested Agatha Brice. "You've seen his report? He thinks Strakov is worthless. "

"Kyle is a clumsy bull only when he wants to be, Aggie. Most times, he is a snake in the weeds. I'll talk to him, and meanwhile, you lot get cracking on a range of options."

Swanson took the video call in a secure communications suite at the safe house, with Jan Hollings crowded next to him at the table. Despite their tendency to grate on one another, Kyle and Calico had settled into a good working team, primarily because she would not be cowed by him, and he would not be pushed around by her. The relationship rotated between stormy and smooth.

They listened seriously as Marty Atkins briefed them over the encrypted link. It was a significant mission change. They were to do an as-yet undefined black op as a balance for a Russian jet that had crossed the Finnish border and destroyed a missile battery.

"What about our defector, Colonel Strakov?" asked Jan. She had been the case officer for the initial interrogation, and was almost as unhappy as Swanson with the early results.

"Don't give me your damned problems, Calico. Give me a solution." Atkins actually had no idea of the next step for Strakov.

Swanson bit back a smile as he saw Hollings flush at the reprimand. "This could be a good break, Marty. I think the asshole is playing us. For someone who wanted to talk to me so badly, we have gotten very little in return. No actionable intelligence at all. Interesting material that we would have found sooner or later anyway."

"I agree," Calico said, almost gritting her teeth, as if

saying those words were difficult. "Suppose we change the rules. I know just the guy to give him a try—my husband, army colonel Tom Markey."

Atkins had to recall that name. "He's a computer wizard or something, right?"

Swanson broke in. "Hell, yeah. Great idea. Markey is the big dog in NATO cyber-warfare and is based over here in Tallinn. He once told me that his and Strakov's careers almost were identical. Let's get me out of the way and put the Russian in the room with someone who actually speaks geek, and he won't be able to dodge the questions. Strakov will understand the logic of us giving it a try."

"Will he clam up because you are absent?"

"He did not like it the first time, so he might bitch a bit when I go away again, Marty. Who cares? Strakov is playing a game. I think the only reason he wanted me was so he could give up the Armatas and establish that he was the real deal."

"Swanson can always go back at him later for more questioning, if necessary." Hollings also had other business that needed her attention. The Narva election was right around the corner, and she had to be there to monitor it.

Atkins approved. "Okay. Done. I will have temporary duty orders cut today that will get Markey in there as soon as possible. Calico, you go back to Tallinn tonight and get your mind back on Narva."

"Wait a minute. If I go back to Tallinn and Tom comes here to Koekelberg, we won't even get to see each other. That isn't fair."

"Sorry, Jan. I wasn't thinking about your personal life. Please take time to share a cup of coffee at the airport, then get your butt back into Estonia. Are we clear on that?" Marty Atkins put an edge to his voice. "Now Kyle, you obviously can't do this thing alone. So while the analysts are finding a target, you go ahead and pick out a strike team, anybody you want, and we'll arrange to have them . . . "

Swanson put up a palm to signal him to stop. "I've already got my team."

"Who?"

"I'm not going to tell you that, Marty. I think there is a leak in this pipeline and this is going to be a high-risk job. Trust me. Keep a really tight need-to-know lid on everything."

"Well, in any case, it is going to take a couple of days to move some operatives into position. . . . "

"We're already here, Marty. I can stage in twenty-four hours."

"You can get the needed hardware from NATO. . . ."

"I have everything we need, except, maybe, for transport. Give us a target and we can roll."


ABOARD THE *VAGABOND*


Brokk was dead. There was not a shred of proof for that conclusion, but Anneli Kallasti knew in her heart that it was true. The Disappeareds never came back, and Brokk's rising stature as an anti-Russian political firebrand had sealed his fate. She was bundled in a heavy coat, and stood alone near the bow of the big yacht, her forearms on the rail as an icy wind flecked her face with spray from the waves, mixing with her tears. He was gone. The municipal election in Narva, on which they had placed so much hope, would be held this Sunday and the pro-Russian candidates would likely win. With Brokk gone, no one had stepped forward to replace him, and there was no organized opposition to the big, heavy claw that pressed down on the city to keep it firmly in line for Moscow. Pushkin's handpicked man would become the mayor, Konstantin Pran of the Workers' Party would take over next week, and the future of her country and home city would be up in the air.

The *Vagabond* had been sailing gently for hours through the swells. It did not matter to her, for her entire life was vanishing. Only a week ago, she had been a waitress, a student, a lover, a political activist and a young woman with a long, bright life ahead of her. Estonia needed her, but she could not return there, for she was a fugitive wanted on a trumped-up murder charge. Her only crime had been the mild and flirty kidnapping of a young Russian soldier for less than a day and setting him free unharmed. He probably had never mentioned it to anyone.

Her only female friend now was Jan Hollings of the CIA, the beautiful and smart but volatile woman who would play a big role from here on. It was too early to determine what that might be, although Anneli had spent a long time trying to guess. On the male side, she was in the magnetic field of Kyle Swanson, which was both a comfortable and frightening place to be. His decisions would have just as large an impact on her as would those of Calico. Anneli felt as though she was being pulled in a dozen different ways. If trust was the final issue, then she would go with Kyle.

She inhaled the salty air. The lights of other ships were in plain view as they sailed through the North Sea beneath the midnight sky. The weather had cleared, but dark clouds still hid the stars. She had never been to sea before and was surprised that the waters were such busy traffic lanes. There were thousands of people around her, separated by a broad apron of water, and yet she had never felt so alone in her life.

Two shadows met on the bridge wing as Sarn't Stan Baldwin relieved Corporal Grayson Perry for the next watch. Except when she was in her cabin, the girl was always within sight of one of the British snipers. "What's happening, Gray?" Baldwin asked in a quiet voice.

"Nothing at all. She has been standing there for two hours now. That story about what happened with her boyfriend would be enough to shake anyone."

"It is a difficult time for her."

"Yes. Any word from Swanson?"

"He will meet us tomorrow. Also coming aboard, flying in from London, is Sir Jeff Cornwell himself. Maybe even a NATO general. Big doings are afoot."

"Sounds interesting. Well, I turn her over to you now, Sar'nt, and I will hit my mattress."

"I have her. Get some sleep." Baldwin brought some binoculars to his eyes. The girl was just standing there at the rail, watching nothing. He wished she would go back inside. He would give her a little more time, then go and fetch her before she caught pneumonia.

**19**

THE KREMLIN
MOSCOW

**C**OLONEL **GENERAL VALERY** Ivanovich Levchenko, the commander of Russia's Western Military District, was ushered into the office of President Vladimir Pushkin at mid-morning on Wednesday, April 13. There were whispers within the upper echelon of Moscow's military hierarchy that the flamboyant Levchenko had finally overstepped his authority and that the president intended to deal harshly with him. Reassignment away from the palatial headquarters in St. Petersburg to some staff assignment was a strong possibility, perhaps even a demotion to some job that would be so insulting that it would force a resignation. Levchenko came across the carpet in his tailored uniform and stood at stiff attention, without a word being said until the door closed.

President Pushkin came around the desk, gave a warm chortle and shook his hand. "How was your flight, Valery?" He moved to a samovar on the credenza and prepared cups of hot tea while his guest collapsed into a chair, all formality gone.

"It was good. I left clouds of doubt in St. Petersburg

by dropping hints that I may not return." Levchenko laughed again and accepted the tea. "I gather that similar rumors are circulating around here. Everyone avoided my eyes on the way in, like I was a leper."

The president took a seat. "Yes. Pavel Sergeyev has done everything but broadcast the news of your imminent demise, so you must look appropriately chastised and saddened when you leave. Now bring me up to date. How goes the Strakov plan?"

Yevchenko drank some tea, put the cup down and opened his hands. "As expected. The man has been almost clairvoyant. NATO intelligence services are hanging on his every word, although he has given them nothing of substance. Meanwhile, the attack by one of the overflights worked out brilliantly. The MiG going down in Finland—being *shot* down, no less—was a statistical guarantee. Sooner or later, it had to happen. Like a clash of swords before a duel. This time, someone was cut. Strakov arranged the attack order before he left."

The president opened a gold cigarette case and offered one to Levchenko, who declined the smoke. Pushkin took his time flicking open a lighter and inhaling, then carefully blowing a smoke ring that hung in the air. "We have received the expected protests, and have denied that the plane was on any hostile mission. The pilot simply did not know where he was because the Finns jammed his communication. When attacked, he defended himself. I have instructed our people to file a protest of our own, claiming the so-called neutral Finns should have helped rather than luring him in and opening fire without cause. The boy will get a nice posthumous medal."

"He did an excellent job. Sacrifices have to be made

at times." The general took out his personal electronic tablet and scanned some sites before speaking again. "Now the Ivanov scheme projects that NATO will retaliate somewhere in the region."

Pushkin agreed. "Yes. From what I know of President Thompson, he will do something. The fact that it happened in Finland was a wonderful touch, because NATO cannot claim that any of its members were attacked."

"The more fog and confusion we sow, the better," the general said. "I expect the response will be something in proportion to the flea bite in Finland. But it will open the door for us to respond even harder. According to Strakov, everything should be ready in time for Sunday's election in Narva."

"Good, good, good." The president was enjoying this. The Western democracies were terrified that a situation similar to the Ukraine would bloom in April like a noxious weed, and Russian troops would once again be on the move. They were right, but didn't yet know it. "How is Ivanov himself?"

"According to our sources in Brussels, he is living very well. They even let him go shopping. American newspapers and television are covering him."

"And he really thinks he will be able to escape when the time comes?"

"Mr. President, the man is a dare-devil and understands the risks. The plan is for the FSB to kidnap a high-ranking American of some sort, maybe a businessman or even a diplomat, this weekend and hold him to create a prisoner-swap scenario for Ivanov's freedom at the proper time."

Pushkin liked that plan. He had used the strategy before. Levchenko continued, "One thing you should also know is that he obtained the presence of the American sniper that he wanted, a psychotic criminal named Kyle Swanson, to begin the interviews. He gave Swanson the Armata systems at bait. Ivanov now has them all dancing to his tune."

"And how go the election preparations? Is that all in place?"

"Under tight control, sir. We will have a mayor and a majority of the council in our pockets after the vote. Democracy will rule in Narva, and we will be permitted to do whatever we wish!" He relished the irony of using the freedom of the vote to lead a revolution.

"That's it, then?"

"Everything is there for now, sir. The plan is on schedule. My army is returning to the barracks after Phase One of Operation Hermitage and getting ready to launch Phase Two right after the election. I should be getting back to St. Petersburg now before they start thinking I've been imprisoned in the Lubyanka or sent off to some corrective colony for my sins. General Pavel Sergeyev will be disappointed that I have not."

President Pushkin rose along with General Levchenko and this time, the two men awkwardly hugged. "Please stay on top of this, Valery Ivanovich. We want Estonia, Latvia and Lithuania back, and the Ivanov plan gives us the best chance to bring them home without starting the incident. For diplomatic reasons, we must not fire the first shot. But once someone else shoots, be ready to strike hard and get across that border in such force as to make NATO think twice about responding. Now, go." He motioned toward the door, and the colonel general departed, masking his satisfaction with a dour look of gloom.

LANGLEY, VIRGINIA

The hardest thing for the CIA's deputy director of clandestine operations to do was nothing. Marty Atkins had set in motion the immense intelligence-gathering resources of the United States government and his main task now was not to meddle. Thousands of the smartest people on the planet were shaking the trees to see what might fall out.

They did not know exactly what they were looking for, but they were specialists. The Russians had screwed up an airspace invasion over Finland and orders had come down to examine anything out of the ordinary in their respective sectors. Not only was NATO fully involved, but so were assets in Asia, Latin America and even the Middle East. It was time to make a statement to Moscow. The messenger had been chosen. All that was needed was an appropriate target.

Every shred they could find was considered, the Internet clouds were combed, the NSA monitoring was scanned, and that harvested mass of human and signals intelligence was then winnowed, either trashed or funneled up to the next level. Step by step, the best of the possibilities crept up the ladder until it was on the CIA desks of Atkins's two top assistants. Stew Willenson, the square-shouldered military veteran, and prim and precise Agatha Brice watched like a pair of hawks, sometimes asking for more information on a topic, but discarding most of it out of hand. Nothing fit.

With his machine humming, Marty Atkins took advantage of a rare opportunity to escort his wife out to dinner at a nice seafood restaurant in Baltimore. They spent Wednesday night enjoying themselves with lobster and white wine and an excellent, romantic hotel. Marty had left orders that he was not to be contacted unless the White House was under direct assault by at least a regiment of enemy ground forces. He would be back on the clock tomorrow morning.

Stew and Aggie labored all night and lashed their troops to get this thing done. There had to be something out there that fit the established parameters. They did not know what it was, but would when they saw it. And they revealed no details to the others who were supporting them, mindful of the final instruction from Atkins that the word "secret" in this case meant exactly that. There was a suspected leak somewhere, and the fewer people who knew what was going on, the better. Within the Central Intelligence Agency, that included only Atkins, Brice and Willenson. The director himself, a political appointee, was not in the loop.

Aggie had gone to the cafeteria for a sugar-and-caffeine fix about dawn, and when she returned to her office, Stew was waiting for her with a big grin on his face. "What?" she said, placing her warm onion bagel smeared with cream cheese on her desk.

"I think our boys and girls have nailed it." He was drumming his fingers on his big knee.

"Where?" She slid into her chair and put on her glasses when he handed her the note.

"It's in Russia, but not the big, real Russia. The target is just across the southwestern border of Lithuania, in the Kaliningrad Oblast." He pushed over a printout of the region. Kaliningrad was a small country of less than a million people, sandwiched in a triangle between Lithuania to the east and Poland to the south. To the north lay the Baltic Sea. "Easier for our team to get in and out."

"What is the target, Stew?"

"Why, Aggie, my dear, we are going to crash a birth-day party."


THURSDAY, APRIL 14
ABOARD THE *VAGABOND*


Kyle Swanson was a firm believer in the six-P sniper mantra that "Prior Planning Prevents Piss-Poor Perfor-mance" and left as little to chance as possible, because something was always going to go wrong on a mis-sion, and usually at the worst possible time. Without good planning, however, you didn't have a prayer. He had been aboard the yacht when Sir Geoffrey Corn-well arrived early on Thursday afternoon. The old man looked good, although still very unsteady on legs that had been smashed during a terrorist attack on his castle in Scotland several years ago. The brilliant mind, though, remained as sharp as ever.

"You should not be here," Kyle scolded the chairman and chief executive officer of Excalibur Enterprises once Jeff was made comfortable in the spacious salon.

"Pat sends her love. She chose to stay at home," said Jeff. Lady Patricia, Sir Jeff and Kyle were the sum of a peculiar process in which three adults who had no one else had decided to create a family amongst themselves. Swanson was the adopted son. "She also told me to re-mind you to stop getting into trouble, get married and present us with scads of lovely grandchildren."

"Yeah, yeah. I've heard it all before." If he lived long enough, Swanson would be the sole heir to what had become a sizable fortune. Cornwell had created a weapons development company after he was forced to retire for medical reasons from the Special Air Services, in which he was a colonel. He broke a leg during a training jump and it did not heal enough for the SAS doctors to risk him doing it again. His little company came of age as the big dollars flowed in the War on Terror, and the springboard to that success was the mighty sniper rifle known as the Excalibur. While recovering from a wound of his own, Swanson had been loaned to Cornwell by the Marine Corps to help develop the state-of-the-art weapon, and the strong relationship with Pat and Jeff grew from there. Once the company became a known quantity in defense contracting circles, Cornwell discovered a genius for business in a variety of fields and the business was now worth billions. Kyle Swanson was executive vice president when he wasn't operating in the dark world as a master sharpshooter for the CIA.

"We have a guest for dinner tonight, Kyle," Cornwell said. "My friend Freddie is flying over to be with us."

Swanson almost choked on his drink. "The same little shit who threatened to blackmail us out of business if I didn't do what he wanted?"

"The very one," Jeff replied genially. "Time to mend some fences, eh? And you will be polite and will not refer to General Sir Frederick Ravensdale, the deputy supreme allied commander of NATO in Europe, as a little shit. At least not to his face."

Swanson lifted his beer. "Gee, Pops, do I *have* to?"

"Yes. Now that I'm settled aboard, please call in the SAS boys and that lovely dark-haired creature that I saw them orbiting about on deck. I assume that is your Miss

Kallasti. Patricia will be quite pleased when I send a photograph, and she may start thinking about wedding gowns again."

"Oh, Jesus, your wife has problems. I suggest we place her in an assisted-living facility."

Sar'nt Stanley Baldwin and Corporal Grayson Perry had known Cornwell only as a legend within their elite unit, and that cemented them as friends from the first handshakes. Anneli stayed close to Kyle, shy in the presence of a man of such obvious wealth and power, but Jeff smashed that barrier within minutes. The waitress from Estonia was soon laughing with the rest of them. Cornwell told a naughty story about a new member of Parliament.

The captain of the *Vagabond*, Trevor Dash, leaned into the cabin and motioned Kyle outside. "You have an urgent contact from Langley," he said.

The private, encrypted call from Marty Atkins did not take very long, since it was just a broad overview. Swanson confirmed that the secure computer was ready to receive a large data dump, and it lofted over the Atlantic Ocean in an incredibly short time, for the yacht's comm suite was totally compatible with the machines in Virginia. Soon, Kyle was calling portions up on the screen while the large printer in the corner spat out page after page. It did not take long to understand that this was a big-league mission that reached far beyond a diplomatic protest note. He liked it, although he knew nothing about the country called Kaliningrad.

A Russian general named Victor Mizon was getting his second star and being bumped up from a deputy chief of the Border Service of Kaliningrad to be a first deputy head of the service. By coincidence, the promotion would become effective next week on his birthday, during a final tour of his field command. A party was being arranged in his honor at a small border camp south of the city of Nesterov, a base where the general had once served as a mere lieutenant.

With bureaucratic efficiency, it was known as FSB Artillery Camp 8351 on Moscow lists, and as Rooster Cap Nowak in NATO, which used computer-generated code names. It lay almost right on the boundary between Kaliningrad and Lithuania, and was only a stone's throw from Poland. That corner emplacement was protected by a battery of 120mm heavy mortars, with a range of sixteen miles, artillery pieces that were capable of lobbing high-explosive rounds into two adjoining countries.

A heavy forest and swamp lay along Lake Vištytis, which stretched toward Lithuania. A road network that fed through the border camp junction showed routes all the way to Poland. Swanson made another note. Doing a sniper hit was one thing; extracting was a different ball game. The entire operation was going to be dicey. Difficult, but he still liked it. It was a straight, sweet and simple retaliation for a Russian attack that had claimed the lives of eight soldiers plus the Russky pilot.

He continued reading, growing more fascinated with each page. Another factor was the quality of the unit there. Once, such a place had been staffed by mere border guards with a couple of machine guns, but in recent years, the duty had been wrapped into the Federal Security Service, the FSB, which indicated an upgraded level of militarized training. The background papers showed it was no isolated independent operation of the state. It now belonged to Russia's huge Western Military

District, which was based in St. Petersburg; in other words, it was part of the Russian army. No FSB general, not even one with personal alumni links, would bother to inspect a mere wide spot in the road where guards checked the papers of truck drivers. There were real soldiers there. It was something else to put in the mix.

When the computer downloads and printouts were finished, he momentarily studied a file photo of the target, then shifted the data to a flash drive, wiped the secured memory and locked everything in a safe. He was astonished to realize that more than two hours had passed since he had entered the room, and also that he needed a shower. The smell of stale sweat might hint that he was under pressure. It was nothing that a bar of soap and some hot water could not cure. Never let 'em see you sweat, he thought, and hurried to his cabin.

His personal warrior ethos did not allow him to quibble with what was, at its root, an assassination order. Marty Atkins had told him that it had been cleared to the top, which Kyle knew meant it had been stamped by the White House. That was enough for him.

**20**

ABOARD THE *VAGABOND*

**G**ENERAL **S**IR **F**REDERICK Ravensdale, GCB, GBE, DSO, had arrived by the time Swanson returned to the great cabin. The famed Briton was immersed in light conversation with his SAS pals—a corporal, a sergeant and a retired colonel—as if they were sitting around a campfire somewhere, telling war stories, instead of at a table set for dinner with fine china and silver. Like other elite services, the SAS did not let rank stand in the way of unit cohesiveness, and everyone was in a good mood. The general was tall, with silvering hair and a perfect smile and impeccable manners. Kyle had last seen him in London, and the man had not lost an inch of gravitas since then. Swanson sized him up and thought, some guys have it all. The welcome was quick and seemed genuine, but Kyle, on close inspection, detected the wary blue eyes had lines in the corners and shadowy bags beneath, not an unusual look for someone under immense pressure in an important job.

Swanson greeted him with courtesy, then sat in the chair that had been kept empty. He took the step needed to bury the hatchet and soothe the general's complaint about Swanson not wanting to interview the Russian defector. "I apologize for the misunderstanding on that other matter, General. That issue is back on track, and I trust any disagreement has been laid to rest."

Ravensdale nodded with solemnity. "Done and done, Kyle. It was never a personal matter. Only that NATO was very concerned with that delicate situation."

"It seems to be getting more delicate by the minute." Kyle had to keep reminding himself that he was now a civilian with money and influence, and did not need to say "sir" to anyone. He changed the subject. "In any case, I am glad you came out tonight. I need your permission to borrow these two SAS boys for a special mission. Maybe we can get them to do something more to earn their keep than babysit Anneli out here on open water."

"Hey, I don't mind this assignment at all!" Baldwin protested with a chuckle. "It may be hard duty, but someone has to do it."

Anneli had been charmed by the suave General Ravensdale and was between the general and Sir Jeff at the table. She followed the banter, but did not understand some of the English old-chap and military idioms. She liked strong men.

"Is it something that we should discuss in private, then?" the general asked, glancing at Anneli.

Swanson rubbed his hands together, shook his head. "Not at all. She is part of it, so she might as well hear it now. Jeff is cleared for everything, so I can read in all of you at the same time." For the next few minutes, he sketched the idea for the job that lay ahead, in very broad terms. The others listened without interruption. In retaliation for the Russian strike against the Finnish missile battery, Kyle had been tasked to raid an isolated Russian fire base in Kaliningrad and take out a senior military officer. The place bore the awkward code name of Rooster Cap Nowak.

Ravensdale kept his face rigid throughout the briefing, but was about to explode inside. "I had not been informed of any of this, Kyle. NATO has not been informed." The voice remained soft, but was suddenly icy, and the jaw was clenched. "I find that to be most disturbing."

Swanson calmly picked up a fork and speared a tiny tomato. "It was decided at the very highest levels, General Ravensdale. My assignment arrived about two hours ago, and I was instructed to inform you verbally. So far, the only people who know about it beyond the six of us in this cabin are the president of the United States, your prime minister in the UK, a handpicked few of their closest aides, my direct boss in the CIA, his target-choosing team, and the head of MI6 in London. The circle could not be tighter."

Ravensdale eased a bit. "Very top secret. I certainly understand that, but the need for such an extreme measure escapes me. I trust every member of my staff implicitly."

Swanson responded, "Of course you do. But a mole exists somewhere in our huge allied intelligence-gathering world. That disturbs me. I want this kept as tight as possible, since four of us at this table are going to be on the ground."

Jeff spoke almost with a laugh. "It is *too* tight, Kyle! Hopelessly so! Many others will have to be involved. The logistics requirements alone will be horrendous. This cannot remain a close secret for very long."

"You are absolutely right, so we do it with the highest possible need-to-know priority and hold all instructions until the last moment. Then we push everything through as fast as possible. Secrecy and speed are our best weapons and greatest protection."

Ravensdale could accept that. "Very well. This is going to be dangerous. I certainly authorize that our SAS lads go with you, but why take Ms. Kallasti?"

Kyle looked over at her and recognized the excitement growing on her face. "She speaks about nine hundred languages and we need a linguist. Also, I think she will want to come anyway. She has a dog in the fight."

Anneli spoke fast, the words gushing from her. "I will go. Of course I will! Are we telling Calico in advance this time?"

Kyle scowled. "She also will be informed when appropriate." He was going to have to give Anneli a serious lecture on security. The people in this cabin could be trusted, but she had to understand that she must never mention CIA operatives in the open, even by code names. Ever.

Ravensdale apparently had taken no notice. He had a sip of wine, and said, "So this border firebase sits close to the point where the Kaliningrad-Polish-Lithuanian borders intersect, Kyle? I must say that it sounds quite dicey. How are you going to get in?"

"Good question," echoed Sergeant Baldwin.

"I have no idea. As I say, I just received the orders and have been reading the briefing papers. We'll figure out something. At worst, we could do a HALO."

Baldwin laughed. "Anneli, HALO means a high-altitude, low-opening parachute jump from an airplane from about twenty thousand feet, into the middle of the night. We free fall forever before opening the canopy."

She paled at the thought.

"Here is a better question," said Jeff. "How are you going to get out?"

"Dunno. A big lake separates it from Lithuania, but there are plenty of roads heading toward Poland, and the Poles are always willing to twist the Russians' tail. I don't have an egress plan right now." He sat back and opened his hands. "In fact, at this point, I do not even know if this thing is doable at all. I have to give the boss my final decision after finishing the planning. I will not lead a suicide mission."

"When do you plan to hit this strange little place?" General Ravenscroft showed his skepticism. "Granted, Kaliningrad is surrounded by NATO territory, but it will be difficult to reach."

Kyle returned the steady gaze. "I'm sorry, General, but I don't know that, either. The shop back at Langley is going to send some maps and overhead satellite surveillance. Obviously, there are going to be a lot of moving parts. It will take some time to assemble everything. The logistics, as Jeff says, are horrendous."

"And do you have the name of the target? Any history on him?"

"No, General. It does not matter. Whichever senior officer is walking around when we get there."

"There are a lot of gaps, Kyle. Having so many unknown factors makes me uncomfortable."

Corporal Perry finished his bottle of beer. "Oh, hell's bells, sir. It will be a walk in the park, hey, mates? I like it."

*Run with it.* A life in the Marine Corps had taught Swanson the importance of keeping control, pushing the momentum envelope, but making decisions based on fact. The longer it took, the more people would become involved. The more people, the more risk. He fell silent while eating a dinner of fresh seafood and vegetables, for his brain was busy processing what was to come. Only one ear was tuned to snippets of conversation that might require a reply.

General Ravensdale made his polite excuses and left right after the meal. Splendid dinner and all that. Delighted to see you all. Have to be back at work first thing in the morning. Good hunting and don't hesitate to call if I can do anything. His ride back to shore was provided by the Excalibur Enterprises helicopter.

As soon as the bird whirred into the darkening sky, the *Vagabond* leapt forward at full speed and made a sharp course change. Kyle went belowdecks and brought the briefing materials as the others gathered in a conference room that almost floated in security. Once the door bolt was sealed, no sound escaped and the comfortable cabin was immune to electronic spying. He spread on the table the paper squares that had been transmitted and they taped them together to form a single map of the region. An electronic image of the area was projected on the wall screen. The men liked hard maps when the going got hairy and the electronics might blip and start giving directions to the nearest McDonald's.

"Here's what we are going to do," he started.

"I thought you didn't have a plan." The corporal coughed.

"That was bullshit for anybody hanging around the dining area," Kyle said as he stabbed his finger onto a neat layout of buildings. "I got it all. Our target will be at this fire base, this Rooster Cap Nowak, just inside the very tip of Kaliningrad. It's about two miles from

the Lithuanian border and about the same from Poland."
His finger moved east to the border area with Lithuania, which was dominated by a large body of water.
"There is a low-lying beach area just on the edge of this
big lake; you can see it here. I'll blow it up on the screen."

Swanson worked the computer keyboard and the
screen narrowed to a satellite view of the lake, and magnified it to show a strip of cleared land that jutted from
a thick forest. He flicked on a red pointer and put the
laser dot on the beach. "Apparently, soldiers at the camp
use this little place to go swimming and relax. Nobody
should be there when we arrive in the dark, and besides,
the weather and the water are still too cold in April. We
insert and extract right there by helo."

The sergeant looked over at Anneli and arched an
eyebrow. "Do we fast rope or land?"

"Ropes. We hook her onto one of us with some
D-rings on a harness and get down quickly. It should be
only about thirty feet."

She was standing with her hands on her hips. "You
want me to jump out of a helicopter?"

"Consider it a very short circus ride, Anneli, but it
will be over in a few seconds. The only alternative would
be a HALO, trying to parachute in between a forest and
a lake. Very bad things could happen," said Baldwin.

"Oh. Okay." She recalled with a shudder the idea of
falling thousands of feet. "Helicopter, then." The SAS
guys laughed with her.

"Later," snapped Kyle, keeping their minds on the
job. "Once we are on site, we spend the day in our hides.
The Russians are planning a little party right after dark
for a visiting general, and when we acquire our targets,
we all fire at the same time on a countdown. I call the

bird to come get us, we exfiltrate back to the lake and the helo zooms in, we get aboard and are gone."

"Where do we stage?"

"I'm setting up something out of Lithuania."

"There are a lot of questions," said Jeff in a pleading voice. "Are you really thinking this through?"

Swanson clicked off the pointer and studied the table map a little while longer in silence. "We can do it, Jeff, with a little luck."

"What's my job?" Anneli wrinkled her brow. "I'm not a sniper."

"You will have a directional microphone that will allow you to listen and translate everything they say in the camp. That's a pretty big intelligence edge for our side."

"When do we go?"

"Two hours. I have to make some final arrangements, but you people go ahead and get ready. I want to be boots-on-ground by sunrise."

The Excalibur helo, a gleaming white machine with the company's gold logo, was radioed instructions to stay overnight in Belgium after dropping off the general. That left the helipad empty as the *Vagabond* pounded hard out of the North Sea and into the Baltic. At 2200 hours the aft deck lights were doused and the yacht nosed into the wind when a large MH-60R Seahawk helicopter, the Sikorsky workhorse of the U.S. Navy, arrived unseen in the blackness. It touched down only long enough for Swanson, the SAS team and Anneli to scramble aboard. The arrival, pickup and departure took only thirty seconds. The yacht peeled away to return to the popular pleasure cruising routes along the shoreline.

The helicopter crew chief slid the door closed and resumed his seat in the rear of the cabin, chewing gum and looking with interest at the four black-clad operators. One was a woman whose figure and face could not be disguised by the flight suit and smeared black and green face paint. All three of the men were strapped up with weapons, including long rifles in protective sheaths, while she wore a square backpack. Swanson was offered a helmet and a microphone, but did not want to communicate. His plan was in motion. The crew had been instructed not to ask questions, just to make the pickup from the *Vagabond* and fly directly back to the nuclear-powered aircraft carrier CVN-73, the USS *George Washington*, the centerpiece of the Baltic Sea Battle Group.

Anneli had never ridden on a helicopter before, much less one this large and noisy. Her friends rode as if they were on a familiar trolley car. Kyle was silent, running over the plan again and again. Baldwin read a novel on a back-lighted video screen. Gray Perry fell asleep. She could see only night through the small windows on the bulkhead and her entire being was tight with excitement. The helicopter clattered away and they were all enveloped by the dome of gloomy sky overhead and the dark waters beneath.

## BRUSSELS, BELGIUM

There was a new woman in the staid life of General Ravensdale. She had the green eyes of a jaguar and was as sleek as the jungle cat. Her chestnut hair was as stylish as her clothes. It was all very prim and proper.

There was no outward change in his behavior, but everyone just *knew* because he was seeing her frequently in his off hours, or for lunch at some bistro or for an evening theater performance. The female staff members thought it quite romantic that the aging hero had finally discovered his Guinivere after mourning so long for his late wife. The men thought the general had landed a winner, for she was rich and beautiful and of an appropriate age, a better match for the boss than some sexy little Euro hard-body.

Arial Printas was about ten years younger than the general, the widow of a German industrialist who had left her a fortune, and she lived in a suite at a fine hotel. It was to that hotel that the general drove in his own car after being deposited ashore following the dinner aboard the *Vagabond*.

Arial met him at the door and gave him a peck on the cheek. "Hello, Frederick," she said, drawing him inside by the hand and thinking how the NATO deputy supreme allied commander in Europe at times looked like a lost boy. She was barefoot and wore sky-blue silk pajamas beneath a light wrap. "You have something for me?"

Ravensdale stalked across the thick carpet and poured a stiff drink, no ice, at the bar in the long living room. "I hate myself."

Arial settled into a big chair and tucked her feet beneath her. "Oh, stop the pity. Quit feeling sorry for yourself. It's unbecoming."

"I am nothing; a traitor."

Arial made a show of yawning and pretending boredom. "We are not going through another of your emotional scenes, Frederick. You stamped your ticket many years ago with your fling with little Lorette. We rescued you from the Stasi and have left you alone for decades. In a few more weeks, we will disappear again and you will go back to whatever you want to do."

"You people will always come back."

"Probably not." Her voice was smooth and disinterested. "Frederick, you are important to us right now only because of your job. I doubt that we could find much use for you after you retire unless you are foolish enough to go into politics. Now, why did you awaken me?"

The general took another full glass and sat on the dark maroon sofa. "NATO is planning a military response for the MiG attack in Finland," he said. "Snipers are going to attack a fire base in Kaliningrad and kill a senior officer there."

Arial spread her palms and rolled her eyes. "Is that all? When? Who?"

Ravensdale stared at the Russian intelligence operative. "The place is called FSB Artillery Camp 8351 and is located at the point where Kaliningrad meets Lithuania and Poland. I do not know the name of the target, and I do not know when, except that it will happen in no more than a few days. The information is just too fresh for all of the details. My guess is they will come in from Poland and egress the same way."

"Frederick, my darling, this is nothing. Certainly it is not worth putting our private and personal contact at risk. One dead officer in Kaliningrad? Who cares?"

The general drank off half the glass, furious with himself for giving up an operation involving four people with whom he had just dined, and stung by her rebuke and rejection of the information. "You interpret it any way you wish, Arial. I see this raid as a strong reprisal, and therefore it is both militarily and politically important. Your superiors will want to stop it."

She smirked, barely lifting the curved eyebrows. "Oh, very well. I will pass it along first thing tomorrow. But I warn you, Frederick. Stick to what we instruct you to do, and let these little matters go. We are not interested in every little scrap of soldier stuff that passes across your fancy desk. You are to help Ivan Strakov and legitimize his information."

Ravensdale finished his drink and left the woman sitting there. He did have something better, but wanted to keep it as an ace that he could play later. The girl at dinner, Anneli, had mentioned the name "Calico," and had asked Swanson if she would be angry about them leaving. Swanson had silenced her. So Calico was a woman, and a code name, probably CIA. The general would set his NATO intel dogs sniffing around to pin down that identification by claiming she might be an allied spy who was feeding information to Moscow.

**A**N HOUR LATER, the crew chief touched Kyle on the shoulder and held up two fingers: two minutes. Baldwin put away his book; Perry detected the movement, awoke and got ready without saying a word. Baldwin tapped a gloved finger on Anneli's knee and gave her a thumbs-up sign of encouragement just as the bottom seemed to fall out of her world. The helo dumped power, bucked into a descent, nosed up and settled to the deck of the aircraft carrier as easily as an elevator. The chief pulled the door open, pointed outside and threw them all a quick salute.

A carrier never sleeps while at sea, so the time of day means little, and a helicopter coming aboard was a routine piece of business. Anneli was almost overwhelmed by the smell of fuel and oil, the rumble of machinery and the activity of crew members in vests of various colors who rushed about in choreographed chaos. The wind came across the deck from a sea that was surging near gale force.

A young woman officer collected them, tugging a

gold-braided blue baseball cap over her brown hair, the gold leaf of a naval lieutenant commander glinting on her jacket collar. "Which one is Bounty Hunter?" she asked in a loud voice that could barely be heard over the wild wind and the shipboard noise. When Kyle acknowledged his code name, she said, "Follow me." She led them across the wide deck to where a long silver aircraft was tied down by cables of braided steel, with its big wings folded back against its sides like a big butterfly at rest.

The turboprop Grumman C-2A Greyhound was a carrier onboard delivery plane, better known by its initials: COD. The rear hatch was open and the officer led them into the passenger bay where pairs of empty blue seats awaited in twos. She saluted and left without another word, not knowing the mission or the names, but having done her assigned job.

Now, under the watchful eye of still another crew chief, the group buckled into over-the-shoulder harnesses before it dawned upon Anneli that they were all facing backward, toward the rear hatch that was already being sealed shut. They were the only passengers. The flight crew had completed the preflight checks before they arrived. The wings folded out, the *GW* deck people performed their tasks flawlessly and the COD trundled into launch position and hooked to a catapult. The carrier was making twenty knots straight into a ten-knot wind, for a combined speed of almost thirty-five miles per hour that maximized the air flow to help the plane get more lift off the deck.

"Hold tight," Swanson said to her, reaching over to place his hand on hers as the twin engines went from a comfortable whine to a howling roar, and the aircraft vibrated like a juice mixer. "This is going to be a kick."

An enormous jerk threw them against the straps as the steam catapult hurled the plane straight and hard off the bow, and they accelerated from standing still to better than 160 miles per hour in two gut-churning seconds. Kyle gave Anneli a single absentminded pat. "That's all there is to it," he said when it was done, then settled into his seat. Anneli fought to remain as quiet as everyone else and tried not to throw up.

Kyle mentally ticked off another point on his checklist and looked at his watch. It was just after 0100. *So far, so good.* This aircrew also knew the destination, but not the reason for the trip, or the identities of the passengers. The awkward COD climbed higher and moved onto a westerly course toward a small airbase located southeast of Riga, in Latvia, near the town of Lielvārde. The pilot jacked the speed up, as fast as the old bucket could safely fly.

The transfer routine was repeated when the COD touched down in Latvia, deposited its passengers, made a quick visit to the refueling barn and then took off back for the carrier. The quartet of special operators was on NATO turf now, which gave Swanson confidence that the secrecy level was holding. They swapped into a fast little Gulfstream passenger jet that was the property of the Central Intelligence Agency. The plane wore no markings and was painted in a flat black. It had flown in earlier to provide for the next leg of the trip. They were soon back in the sky, this time for the quicker jump down to Lithuania. There was no crew chief this time, just a couple of CIA pilots in their front cabin, and rations were stored in a small galley. Swanson bit into a turkey and cheese sandwich, still thinking about the timetable. They were racing the dawn, and everyone felt the tension, which built by the mile. He had no options at this point: either his hasty plan worked, or it didn't. Step by step. Brick by brick. Outrun the rumor mill, gossips and informants.

Darkness was still as thick as ink when the Gulf-stream sliced down and made an easy landing on a narrow military airstrip. It rolled to a halt at a hangar that sat off by itself some distance from the tower. Armed guards were alert along the perimeter. Inside the hangar was still another helicopter, a unique, angular bird that was one of only a handful of its type in existence. One more ride, Swanson told his team. Not long now. They climbed aboard the stealth helicopter.

Thirty minutes later, Major Juozas Valteris heard a big presence pass overhead as he stood on an armored car near the Kaliningrad border, but the sound was much softer than he had expected. He was the only member of the Iron Wolf Mechanized Battalion who had been briefed in advance about what was happening, and he had the men on alert, but with their fingers away from their triggers, under a firm order not to fire. The soldiers looked up when they heard muffled thuds in the sky, but saw nothing. Whatever it was had come and gone so low and fast that it was invisible.

The stealth UH-60 helicopter was flown by an American crew from the 160th Special Operations Aviation Regiment (Airborne), the highly trained Nightstalkers, and it almost skimmed the big lake as it flew across the water. The aircraft, although rare, was a distant and customized cousin of the old Sikorsky on which Swanson, Anneli and the SAS snipers had begun their trip hours earlier.

This new crew chief also eventually held up two fingers for the two-minute warning, and then prepared to throw out long coils of heavy rope that were attached inside the cabin. Swanson and Baldwin watched the looming ground before them through night-vision scopes, and Anneli held her arms wide while Gray Perry, the strongest member of the group, snapped on four heavy D-rings to secure her harness to his own. The helicopter flared to a stop and the ropes went out.

The four made their way through the forest on soft feet. Baldwin, on point, moved like a bug with his enhanced night-vision goggles painting the way. Kyle was next so he could control the operation, and watched both flanks. Anneli was right behind, concentrating on stepping precisely where Swanson had stepped and not saying a word. Corporal Perry was Tail-End Charlie, guarding the rear. They avoided the matted path that had been worn into the forest floor over the years by the passage of many Russian soldiers and vehicles visiting the beach. The trees offered protection and safety.

The slope up from the lake was gradual, and the ascent was no problem for the physically fit men, but Anneli felt the burn in her thighs and lungs, and was breathing harder. Instead of being afraid, she was fascinated by the strange world and the three snipers who were moving so slowly and smoothly through it. They disturbed as little dirt and as few leaves as possible, and even the nocturnal animals gave them space without panic, somehow understanding that these new beings in the habitat were not threats to them. This was a different sort of predator, after some other species.

The snipers smelled the smoke before they saw the orange glow of a cigarette being enjoyed by a sentry at an outpost shack beside the trail. They stopped and watched for a minute, logging away the information that it was just one man, and the position would have to be dealt with on the way out. They could do nothing immediately because the man probably was due for relief within a few hours and any new sentry finding the corpse would raise an alarm. Baldwin led them deeper into the woods and they bypassed the guard without being noticed.

Onward they moved, taking one careful step at a time and keeping their weapons ready beneath old growth trees that blocked the stars and held the moisture in a mist of damp, chill air. Baldwin suddenly went to one knee and raised a fist, bringing everyone to a halt. Having become accustomed to the night and the wooded labyrinth, they felt the presence of other humans. For a full minute, they remained silent and still, then Baldwin whispered into the small microphone on the radio that linked the team members, and while the others went flat, he snaked away in a low crawl and disappeared into the muck.

He told them a few minutes later that they were there: They had reached the final firing position.

By the time the new sun began to brighten the sky at their backs, the snipers had built a pair of hides among the thick bushes and tangled roots at the crest of a ridge overlooking Rooster Cap Nowak. Many years ago, when the camp was first built, bulldozers had pushed the forest back, but the need for total vigilance had been slight during decades of no wars in this tiny part of Russia that was not even in Russia, and the woodland vines had marched back in their own time.

Hide sites had been easy to find in the remarkably thick undergrowth, and they had used entrenching tools to dig in from below and behind the old foliage, and swept away their tracks. The resulting spaces were like the burrows of large animals. Through openings between the leaves and branches, each had a clear view of the artillery base, although they remained invisible to any naked eye from below. Before settling in, they took turns cautiously emptying their bladders in the undergrowth and covering the scent with dirt, and then began the long and arduous day of waiting and watching, lasering ranges and sketching the target area. Waiting. Waiting.

The camp guards stirred to life with a morning formation at 0630 in a small central square and ran the Russian flag up a pole. Around the open area were a number of buildings that were standard for any such site—supply sheds, barracks, garages and mess halls. The nearby roads had been closed at midnight, and the first shift of soldiers carrying AK-47s opened the yellow barrier gates to serve the few early-bird trucks waiting to be checked through. The snipers estimated that about seventy-five men were in the camp, all going about routine duties and indicating no unusual level of alertness. "Just another day in paradise," Sergeant Baldwin quipped over the radio net as he studied faces through his scope.

Swanson examined the firepower at the camp's three strongpoints—all of them .50-caliber machine guns mounted behind sandbag parapets and interlocking the road junction, not facing the surrounding area as they should. The crews were running normal checks, cleaning and loading the weapons. Each guard post also had a protected pit holding a 120mm mortar, real man-eaters that could reach up to sixteen miles with an explosive charge that had a kill radius of some seventy yards. Now he knew which monsters would be chasing them back to Lake Vištytis.

Anneli wore a set of headphones attached to the man-pack acoustical surveillance device that she had hauled in. The simple device designed for field use emitted an invisible and narrow laser beam that bounced back to a small parabolic dish and delivered signals so clear that she could pick up individual voices. During the formation, an officer addressed the men, and she listened carefully, her face scrunched in concentration as she simultaneously translated word for word. It was all routine housekeeping assignments until the end.

"This evening at eighteen hundred hours, Lieutenant General Victor Mizon will arrive by helicopter. He has been our commander as deputy chief of the Border Service here, and has recently been promoted. The general is making a farewell inspection of all Kaliningrad facilities before his reassignment to Moscow. Our camp is on the agenda because he once was posted here when he was just a lieutenant." When the briefing officer paused, so did Anneli. When he continued, so did she.

"This is also the general's birthday and we will honor him with a celebration." She added as an aside that some of the men in ranks quietly cheered that news.

The briefer continued. "Most of today will be devoted to preparing for this inspection. We want our camp to be immaculate by the time his helicopter arrives. At his request, there will be a reception line at eighteen thirty hours so he can personally greet each soldier and officer here. Afterward, General Mizon will have dinner in the officers' mess, and our cooks will prepare special dishes for everyone. The men on duty will eat on a rotation schedule. He will spend the night here. His departure is scheduled for ten hundred hours tomorrow morning. Look sharp, men. One of our own is ascending to high rank!"

Anneli removed the headset and rubbed her ears. "Was that okay?" she asked Kyle.

"Finest kind," he said, astonished at her literal and immediate translation. "You boys hear all that?"

"Oh, yes," said Corporal Perry. "We have him right down to the minute. He is coming in right at six o'clock. No guesswork. Good job, Anneli."

22

KOEKELBERG, BELGIUM

**IVAN STRAKOV SHOWED** no surprise when the door of the private conference room opened at nine o'clock on Friday morning and a tall colonel of the U.S. Army entered. There was instant recognition of the long face with the brown eyes and brown wavy hair, and it was confirmed by the man's name tag. The Russian stood and offered a hand. "Tom Markey. Good to see you again," he said with a touch of respect. "I haven't seen you since that conference down in Istanbul. About two years, right?"

"Something like that. The world has changed a lot since then, Ivan." Markey shook the hand, then they both sat down.

"A lot of change, Tom," agreed the Russian. "We have slaved away our best years on government salaries, doing cutting-edge research and development, only to see young techies came along and use our discoveries to become filthy rich."

"I hear you're becoming a bit on the wealthy side

yourself, Ivan." He loathed the man with whom he was having this quiet conversation. Strakov was a dangerous genius and could not be taken for granted. If this was a game, it was a very serious one.

Strakov shrugged. "I should have left the army long ago. So how are tricks over at the Cooperative Cyber Defence Centre of Excellence? Who thought up that name anyway?"

"We have developed a nuclear death-ray wrist-watch app for our soldiers. Let's get down to business, shall we?"

The Russian did not waver. "Fine. However, my rule is that I talk only with Kyle Swanson about the good stuff. No exceptions, I fear, not even for you, Tom."

Colonel Tom Markey's voice remained soft but was emphatic. "Swanson thinks you are a fake and a fraud, so there is no use having him in the conversation any longer. I was given the job because nobody—nobody, Ivan—is more familiar with your work than me."

"So where is Kyle?"

"Gone. Totally in the wind as far as you are concerned."

"Humph. After I gave up the Armata, he bails on me? And the troop movements? What an ungrateful asshole." His face screwed up and he bent forward for a moment, then straightened. "Sorry," he said. "Stomach problem last night. Now, about Kyle. He does not get to decide whether to do the interview. I do."

"He had a good reason to stop. I told to him about your playacting back when you were pretending to be a sniper to infiltrate his course and make your bones as an intelligence officer. He was not very happy about that."

Strakov did not react. He actually had expected Colonel Markey to intervene at some point. It was logical. "I still want Swanson."

"Here's the deal," Markey continued. "I am going to give you until noon today to think things over. If you choose not to cooperate, then your entire lucrative CIA deal falls off the table. You lose your celebrity status, your money and your freedom. From this moment, you are to be treated as a common criminal who might very well spend the rest of your life in a maximum-security prison."

Ivan Strakov did not blink. "That's a pretty harsh deal, Tom."

"It is the only bargain in town, Ivan. You are cold out of options. I will be back at noon."

"Could you please send me a couple of Tylenol in the meantime? I have a headache coming on."

When Markey left, two muscular men in blue suits took his place. He had never seen them before. "Stand up," the bigger one snapped. When Strakov did as he was told, the second agent clamped on the handcuffs.

BRUSSELS

The unexpected visit from Freddie Ravensdale had played hob with her sleep, and Arial Printas had not found slumber until she resorted to a little white pill washed down with a taste of champagne. The dark curtains in the bedroom shielded her from the morning light, and she slept until almost eleven o'clock. She lay still when her eyes finally opened and she remembered that it was a special day.

Since Arial had been at university, her passions had been art and architecture and, as an adult, she had traveled the world to visit the lasting treasures made by artists with oil, canvas, stone and iron. Her husband happily paid the bills. Now, being a wealthy and attractive widow allowed her advantages unavailable to ordinary tourists. Arial liked that. Today was her long-anticipated art nouveau walking tour of nearby Sint-Gillis, then, after returning to the city, a private visit to the *Amerikastraat* studio and home of architect Victor Horta, the master of stained glass.

With a burst of enthusiasm, she threw off the soft white duvet, was out of the big bed and into the tiled bathroom, which she considered rather plain and utilitarian. She shed the pajamas, did a quick body check in the mirrors, approved of herself, then luxuriated beneath a steamy hot shower. Skirt or pants? Walking would be tiring, so she opted for designer jeans, a Parisian top and a light jacket. Comfortable white tennis shoes for the hard streets and sidewalks.

Breakfast was just tea, fresh fruit slices and a scone while she skimmed through two newspapers and studied a map of the coming walk. Finally, she pulled out her tablet and linked to the hotel Wi-Fi for a couple of laps around the Internet. It was important to hit a number of IP addresses, whether or not they were needed, for she was wary of possible surveillance and the extra IPs were good cover.

She logged onto Facebook and her mail and responded to a few posts. Buried deep in the electronic addresses was a dead drop that she shared with another Russian operative. One could draft a message but not transmit it, and the other could log on to the same account to read and erase it. Since it was never actually filed, it would not show up to electronic snoopers.

This morning's information was somewhat silly, she knew, but she had been instructed to pass along whatever Ravensdale told her. Since she had not taken notes, and knew nothing of artillery, she recollected what she could, did a basic letter-and-number transposition code and wrote:

### FIRE BASE 8351 KALININGRAD DANGER RAID EX POLAND TO KILL OFFICER.

The recipient would take care of whatever was necessary. She didn't know who it was, nor the location, nor did she care. She looked at the time and was shocked to see that her tour was scheduled to start in fifteen minutes. Arial scribbled her name on the restaurant bill and hurried out to catch a taxi.

## ROOSTER CAP NOWAK, KALININGRAD

Kyle Swanson jotted a midday status report in his sniper notebook: temperature 72 degrees F, sporadic breeze from north reading less than one mile an hour. The flags in the Russian camp hung like rags, and Kyle and the SAS guys had zeroed their weapons on the central pole. All guns were ready.

They took turns watching the camp through the strong telescopes in thirty-minute rotations to lessen eyestrain. Anneli lay on her side, resting her head on the soft earpiece of the listening probe and filtering out most of what was being said. It was routine soldier talk, with no sense of urgency. At the checkpoint, cars and trucks came, stopped, papers were checked and the vehicles were sent along their way.

"Baldwin. You read?" Swanson broke the silence. He had been thinking about the next steps.

Stanley Baldwin clicked his microphone twice in acknowledgment. He was only thirty feet away, but whisper-level noise, not normal conversation, was the rule in enemy territory.

"One of you guys take off in about an hour and set up on that guard shack we passed. That vehicle that went out at oh-eight-hundred was probably his relief, because two men went down and two came back. A new shift will start this afternoon if they are pulling eight-hour posts. We most likely will execute at about eighteen thirty during the reception line. When you hear that, take the guard down and clear the position. We will rendezvous there as soon as possible. Be ready to lay down suppressive fire for us."

Baldwin and Perry exchanged looks, and Perry pointed at himself. The sergeant nodded. "Affirmative," he told Swanson.

"I'm getting hungry," said Anneli.

Swanson reached into a pocket and handed her a package of peanut butter crackers.

"That's it?"

"That's all." He did not mention that the snack would help gum up her intestinal tract to prevent bathroom breaks. She had already had to go twice, sneaking back to a thick grove for privacy and scared to death that she would be jumped by a Russian soldier while dropping her suit.

She bit the cracker, following it with a sip of water.

Her directional surveillance ears had allowed her to become familiar with some voices and start identifying specific people. One enlisted man down there really hated his lieutenant, and sounded off frequently to his buddies about the officer's shortcomings. A guard at the checkpoint was a friendly guy who joked with the motorists. She hated them both equally.

MOSCOW

### *FIRE BASE 8351 DANGER RAID EX POLAND TO KILL OFFICER.*

The message from Arial Printas dumped into the system of Russia's Foreign Intelligence Service, the SVR, and was pulled up by a clerk in a large room of men and women located in individual cubicles and monitoring computer terminals. The room was busy all day long and the clerks were the first to receive messages that poured in from agents around the world. There was a lot of traffic. This one came from Brussels.

The man called it up and read it a few times to decide where to send it next. It contained no supporting details. Was that a coding or translation problem? He had no idea of the location of any Fire Base 8351, but that was military, so he would forward it to the GRU. The mention of "Poland" meant he should also get it over to the Foreign Ministry. The phrase that an attack was coming did not earn it a higher priority, for the very idea that Poland was about to attack Russia was ludicrous, and the bureaucrat decided that the agent who gathered the information was exaggerating.

He punched the appropriate keys and sent the message on its way, then secured his terminal and took a break.

## KOEKELBERG, BELGIUM

Ivan Strakov spent his alone time in the CIA cells preparing for the next meeting. He had to waste a little more time. He scrubbed some dirt in his eyes to make them red and watery. Then he stuck his finger down his throat and vomited.

When the beefy guards came to collect him, they noticed the vile puddle on the floor and radioed the information ahead: the prisoner looked sick. With handcuffs in place, they marched him to a different room in the building. The new location was larger than the usual little conference room, and there were several other people around a long table. Normally, the space was used for meetings by groups of lawyers and diplomats, but this afternoon, the spooks had taken over, and they looked grim.

The Russian had anticipated that there would be an escalation in the questioning as time wore on after the defection. Kyle Swanson had been just his opening move, to show that he possessed information the allies wanted and needed. In fact, they had allowed Strakov to go much longer than he would have if the situation had been reversed. Defectors were supposed to talk and he was never above using force or blackmail: whatever worked.

Well-placed leaks had led the media to discover his existence, and requests for interviews had arrived at the

CIA. All were denied. The burst of notoriety meant all of the men and women at the table were under stress, feeling public and private pressure to pull more sensitive intel from him. Again, he had expected that, just as he had anticipated a meeting with Tom Markey. Strakov had already turned over some interesting tidbits, and these people needed to get even more to make their superiors happy. He rubbed his wrists in a show of exasperation, restoring blood circulation, and thinking that he still held the upper hand, and had a lot of leverage in the negotiations.

"Decision time, Ivan," said Colonel Markey, at the far end of the table. He noticed that the defector did not look well.

"Who are all of these people, Tom? Can we speak freely before them?"

Markey folded his hands on some papers. He was tired of playing mind chess with this guy. "Stop it, Ivan. Don't even think of stalling any longer. What is your decision?"

"Change is the light at the end of the tunnel," Ivan quoted from memory. "That's from a Welsh poet named Jack Harris." In contrast to the rigidity of everyone else, Strakov slouched a bit into his chair. "I have decided that Kyle Swanson is no longer necessary for further conversations. Does that mean that our earlier agreements remain in place?"

Markey shot a look at a pudgy woman in a gray suit halfway down the table. She looked over the top of her half-rim glasses and said, "We agree."

Ivan thought to himself: lawyer. Everything stayed the same, including his freedom to go outside when accompanied by security. "So who will be my primary contact now, Tom. You?"

"I will be it for a while. After that, various others will be chosen according to their expertise, to tackle specific subjects. You know a lot about many things, Ivan. No one questioner could get it all." Markey felt good about this. He wanted to turn this guy over to the CIA as soon as possible and go back home.

"So we have a deal. That's good," said Ivan. "For now, I ask to be excused for the rest of the day, Tom. I need to go back to my room and rest, and be examined by a doctor. My stomach is raging and this headache is pounding. I suggest that we pick this up again in the morning, when I promise to be ready to do some real work."

MOSCOW

A woman left her one child, a six-year-old boy, with her mother and took the purple metro train out to the Polezhaevskaya station at the Khodynka Airfield. She was running a little late for work, and looked up with weary eyes at a massive, ill-maintained building that contained so many windows that it was known as "the Aquarium." She hurried to her desk and checked in with her supervisor, who scowled and reminded her that she was fifteen minutes overdue. She apologized, promised that it would not happen again, and settled in for her long evening shift as one of hundreds of cipher clerks in the Main Intelligence Directorate of the General Staff of the Armed Forces of the Russian Federation, which was better known by its acronym, the GRU.

One item waiting in her queue was from an agent in Belgium, who gave bare details that Fire Base 8531 in Kaliningrad had been targeted for an enemy military raid out of Poland. It disturbed her enough that she summoned her supervisor, who was still upset about her tardiness.

He read it carefully, and they agreed that the agent perhaps had filed erroneous information. Some unreliable field people on government expense accounts drank too much with their sources and produced cow dung. Any chance that Poland was poised to attack Russia seemed remote in the extreme.

"Kaliningrad is in the Western Military District," said the supervisor, who was tempted to delete the message entirely, but the idea of taking on such responsibility frightened him. "Send it over to St. Petersburg for headquarters attention, low priority," he told the clerk.

## ROOSTER CAP NOWAK

**ANNELI THOUGHT IT** odd that she was not frightened at all. She was wearing commando garb, was illegally inside of Russia and was about to be part of a deadly attack on a military base. A normal person should be scared to death, while she lay almost at ease in the sniper hide listening to the voices coming over her powerful electronic ears. The three men who would do the actual fighting had fallen silent except for an occasional swap of information about changing conditions. She trusted them all. Anneli had seen Kyle Swanson work before and was totally confident in him. Sergeant Baldwin was a very polite Englishman who carried the same dangerous aura as Swanson. And Gray Perry had slithered out of the other sniper hide some time ago with such stealth that she did not even know he was gone until he called in from his new position overlooking the guard shack on the trail.

She was picking up increased activity down at the base and noted the time on the thick olive-green wristwatch she had been given. It was fifteen minutes before six o'clock in the evening. She added twelve to that to figure the military equivalent. It was almost 1800, and the early spring sky had dimmed from bright blue to an overcast slate as the sun set beyond the huge trees in the west, below strings of low clouds. It had glared into their eyes late in the afternoon, then slowly fell out of sight and was replaced by the early shades of darkness. The camp lights had been on for an hour, for the general's helicopter was due soon. Things were getting busy down there.

"Heads up, Bushman Two," Swanson warned in a soft voice. "There's a Goat heading your way." It was the same dirty green UAZ-469 utility vehicle that had been used for the earlier shift change at the guard post. Looking very much like an old American Jeep, the rough-terrain four-wheel-drive car was called a Goat, the English word for the Russian *kozlik*.

"Driver plus one," Kyle said, watching through his scope. "Seems to be in a hurry but it is staying on the road. "Maybe just another shift change."

Gray Perry clicked his own mike twice in affirmative response and remained perfectly still in the underbrush on a slight rise some sixty meters from the shack. The single soldier was still inside. Perry heard the coming vehicle long before he saw it, then the Goat arrived chewing dirt and made a sliding halt. The guard was suddenly alert as another soldier vaulted from the vehicle and a sergeant stepped from behind the steering wheel. The SAS sniper could not make out what they were saying, but their actions were obvious enough.

"Bushman Two to Bounty Hunter," he reported on the radio when the sergeant finished giving orders, got

back into the car and left by himself. "They just doubled the guard out here." He heard two clicks.

Swanson did not consider the move unusual with the
arrival of a VIP who was expected at any moment. Perry
would be able to take down two men as easily as one.
"Are they doing anything?" he asked.

"Nope. As soon as the sergeant drove off, both of
these blokes relaxed. Rifles leaning against the building and the smoking lamp is lit."

Anneli had clapped her palms over the pads to keep
them close to her ears. "Kyle, I'm picking up a lot of noise
in the camp. Something about moving the mortars."

Kyle chewed his lip in concentration, analyzing the
changing situation. Again, by itself, such a reorientation
was not alarming. Maybe the general was going to inspect the individual firing pits, and the officers wanted
everything shipshape. The soldiers would appear to be
more efficient, active and professional if they were doing something more than just standing at attention. Each
of the big 120mm weapons needed a five-man crew,
because the weapon weighed about 500 pounds and
rested on a bipod and a huge metal baseplate shaped like
a saucer. It was more powerful than a U.S. 105mm how-
itzer and just as difficult to move from one place to another. To manhandle the mortars to face a different
direction would require a lot of work and give the look
of a busy base.

"Bushman One to Bounty Hunter." It was Baldwin.
"Any instruction?"

"Negative, Bushman One."

Kyle glanced over to the border crossing. It was closing early tonight, and he watched as an eight-wheeled

BTR-80 armored personnel carrier arrived at the gate after a short trip from the motor pool. The thirty-ton fighting machine with multiple machine guns and cannon was a serious addition to the overnight watch. The rumbling amphibious vehicle had a bit of trouble getting situated on the road before it settled down with its slanted nose facing south. *More showing off for the general . . . or something else?* Swanson was satisfied, at least for the moment, that it was pointed away from the snipers.

At five minutes after six o'clock, the distinctive thump of spinning rotor blades clattered in the sky and a Mi-17 helicopter began its descent into Fire Base 8351. The chopper had a camouflage green paint pattern that blended its silhouette against the darkness, but the landing lights glowed brightly, so it was easily spotted long before it actually lowered onto the concrete pad and cut power. The few officers in the welcoming party held their hats and turned their faces away from the brief storm of rotor wash.

The snipers were rocks as the moment of truth approached. All emotion had been put aside, and their bodies were draped into prone positions, with their big rifles now part of them, extensions of their physical being. They were back far enough in the hides so that their weapons did not extend beyond the foliage, and squares of camo cloth were beneath the barrels to suppress telltale blossoms of dirt when the shots were fired. The two shooters breathed easily and watched. Kyle clicked on the computerized scope of Excalibur and was instantly rewarded with adjusting lists of numbers that told him everything from the temperature and humidity to the effects of gravity and the rifling spin on the .50-caliber bullet at that precise distance. He read the figures and adjusted slightly, then turned it off again. Too much information could be a distraction.

The chopper blades slowed and swirled to a halt, leaving a gap of silence around the base, almost as if a curtain was being raised at a theater to start the performance. A side hatch opened outward and fell to become a staircase as crewmen in flight suits jumped out and chocked the wheels, locked the stairs into place and raised a collapsible handrail, then hustled away. Next out was a military photographer with cameras strapped around his neck. He moved a short distance away to record the moment, as if this purely routine visit had some historical significance. Such pictures would be autographed and sent back to the officers and men as souvenirs.

A skinny aide with a briefcase scooted down the stairs, followed by a grim-faced, corpulent colonel whose bulk almost filled the open hatchway. He was obviously in charge of security, and nodded to the welcoming committee while taking his time to look around the illuminated area. The lights blinded him to anything in the gloom beyond. The gathered officers waited at attention until he was satisfied.

This was not part of the plan. The snipers' scheme was to wait until the general was standing almost immobile in the receiving line, an estimated thirty minutes from now, glad-handing and saying hello to his troops. At that moment, General Mizov would be a steady target. However, Kyle Swanson knew a good thing when he saw it.

"Bushman One. I'm going to take the shot when the

general steps into the hatchway. You do the fat guy. Anneli, get your ears packed and be ready to move. Bushman Two, get ready."

In the next hide, Baldwin wiped everything but the
face of the arrogant security chief from his mind. The
florid skin filled his scope so much that the SAS sergeant could have counted the blackheads on the man's
nose. He adjusted down to the body. The British sniper
had been thinking exactly as Swanson; there would
never be a better target picture. Situations change. His
heartbeat was slow and the finger eased about a pound
of pressure onto the trigger and held it as the colonel
turned to the open hatch and called inside. All was clear.
It was safe.

Victor Mizon, wearing the new gold-braid shoulder
boards that proclaimed him to be a two-star general,
poked his head forward, then came to his full height of
five-feet-eleven. The face was identical to the file photograph that Kyle had received. Unlike his security officer, the general was in excellent physical condition, and
smiled broadly at the committee that was obviously ea-
ger to greet him. After all, it was his fiftieth birthday. He
deserved spotlights and salutes tonight, for Mizon had
advanced a long way since the miserable days when he
was a common lieutenant at this sorry little post isolated in the middle of nowhere. Tomorrow, he would
enter Moscow and be installed as a first-deputy head of
the entire Border Service. For an instant, it was as if the
general was standing in a picture frame, unmoving and
stark in the bright light against the darkness inside the
helicopter. Standing still, fully erect, holding the handrail, looking out over the fire base.

Swanson shot him dead so fast that the general did

not even feel the big bullet tear into his heart, nor hear
the loud roar of Excalibur shake the forest like a giant's
bellow. The handrail helped support his weight for a moment, and just as he took the fatal bullet, Baldwin fired
the second one, and the big colonel jerked, staggered
backward and fell hard against a wheel of the helicopter with blood pumping from his ruptured belly.

The troops at the fire base remained frozen in position,
their arms still cocked in salutes, unwilling to believe
what their eyes told them was true. General Mizon lay
crumpled at the top of the stairs and the fat colonel was
bowled over beneath the chopper and the double-thunder
blasts from two big rifles raped the orderly parade
formation. Moving simultaneously, everyone scattered
for cover.

Swanson, Anneli and Baldwin were already sliding
backward out of the hides and pulling things together.
Kyle brought up a portable satellite radio from his web
gear and hit the transmit button to the helicopter waiting on the far side of the lake. "Bounty Hunter to Vampire. Bounty Hunter to Vampire."

"Vampire to Bounty Hunter. Send your traffic."

"Bounty Hunter to Vampire. Turn and burn."

"Roger that, Bounty Hunter."

From down the hillock, Anneli heard an explosive
round of shouts, almost panicky commands from officers and sergeants. She said, "They are ordering the men
to get up and get to their guns."

"Yeah," said Swanson. "We're out of here."

As soon as he heard the shots, Grayson Perry erupted
from the darkness and hit the two guards at the shack,

both of whom had turned to face the camp, wondering what was happening. Perry slid the long blade of his old Fairburn-Sykes fighting knife into the neck of the first guard, pushing it easily all the way to the hilt in a single motion. Perry knew the knife was old school, almost an antique, but why change a good thing? He pushed on right across the dying man and clobbered the other guard on the head with a rock the size of a cantaloupe. The sentry fell with a crushed skull and Perry finished them both off with a few well-placed strokes of the FS knife. He dragged the bodies into the woods and dumped them, then lay beside the shack and again became invisible in his Ghillie suit of rags and leaves, gripping his submachine gun. The attack had taken less than thirty seconds, and the disposal time was about the same.

The Nightstalkers had been on alert and close to the UH-60 stealth helicopter almost since they had inserted the sniper squad into Indian country early that morning. The special-operations aviators understood how things could go bad in a hurry on any mission and stood ready to react.

They had stayed near or inside of their bird as it rested on a small, bare landing zone near the Kaliningrad border, and other than refueling, getting some hot food and taking shithouse breaks, they had little interaction with the stern Lithuanian soldiers of the Iron Wolf Mechanized Battalion who had clamped a tight, protective perimeter around the skinny, hard-edged helicopter that was impervious to radar. The battalion commander, Major Juozas Valteris, roamed nearby. The pilot had warned him that a target was to be struck at about 1800 hours.

At five o'clock the chopper crew had begun their pre-flight checks, and a half-hour later they strapped in. The mini-guns on each side were loaded and locked, and the strange bird code-named Vampire was ready to fly.

The pilot received the call from Bounty Hunter just before six o'clock, and waved for Major Valteris to come over even as the twin General Electric T700 engines were given life and the four long major blades began to rotate. The major jumped into the deck and put on a pair of earphones connecting him to the internal network.

"We are leaving now, Major, and we thank you for the hospitality. I am authorized to tell you that the team has hit a border firebase called Rooster Cap Nowak this evening, and there is likely to be some return fire coming this way soon. That's all I know. We will be heading out via a different route unless there is an emergency that requires us to return here."

The Lithuanian officer gave the pilot a thumbs-up, removed the headset, jumped back to the ground and sprinted away. The helicopter blades were spinning faster as the engine ate more power, and in seconds, the Black Hawk was airborne, nose down and speeding into the darkness with a methodical *hush-hush-hush* instead of the normal helo roar.

Valteris snapped his men to full alert and ordered an immediate change of position for his whole unit. The Russians had probably pretargeted their current location. The soldiers knew this was no drill. They buttoned up their vehicles and sped away.

**A**UTOMATIC RIFLE FIRE erupted from the first Russian soldiers who came out of their fugue state and opened up with long rips of AK-47s that shredded the night in every direction, laying down a 360-degree mad minute of suppressive fire. Simply pulling the trigger was the easiest thing to do. An unlucky civilian truck driver went down in the wild salvo, his penalty for deciding to stay overnight at the border crossing so he could be first in line at dawn tomorrow. He had been watching the arrival ceremony from beside his truck, making him a stranger in the wrong place at the wrong time and perceived as a possible threat by panicky soldiers.

Kyle, Anneli and Stanley Baldwin were galloping along the single trail to the east when the shooting began. They stopped a few times to catch their breath and plant some Claymore mines with trip wires as booby-trap surprises for anyone who might give chase. That initial gunfire back at the base meant little—harmless noise with no danger. Snipers throughout the ages have stayed alive by sowing confusion among their enemies, and the men at the base were reacting to a frightening, new situation. The extraordinarily loud booms of the .50-caliber sniper rifles had echoed back to the inexperienced border guards from the deep forests. None had seen any muzzle flashes. The attack could have come from anywhere, so the answering fire spewed everywhere. Every moment that the Russians spent trying to sort things out meant that the American, the Briton and the girl from Estonia would be that much farther away.

About fifteen seconds after the ineffective shooting started, it trailed off, then ceased as officers and sergeants got control of the situation. Kyle could hear orders being shouted. Beneath the ruckus, he heard the giant diesel engine of the BTR-80 armored personnel carrier grunt to life. It was the one thing at the camp that Swanson considered to be a truly dangerous wild card. Should the amphibious vehicle come roaring down this narrow road, things would get interesting in a hurry. It could even follow them right into the water. "Run," he told his mates, and they abandoned stealth in favor of distance.

Heavy machine guns opened up next, the big ones on the corners of the camp, and although the firing became more methodical, it was still combing the tangled foliage that had been allowed to grow wild around the base. The gunners were still shooting at things they could not see, and followed the sweep of searchlights that were sliding around the borders. They were confident that any frontal charge from the bush would fail against the reaping bullets. To the retreating snipers, however, it was a sign that the counterfire was still in a defensive mode. The soldiers were hunkered down inside the base, waiting for another shot from the unseen enemy.

"Bushman Two! Bushman Two!" Swanson breathed heavily as he called for Gray Perry on the net. "Coming up on you in about two minutes."

"Clear here," came the immediate answer. "Come on in." Perry lifted out of the undergrowth and assumed a kneeling position to give suppression fire if necessary. Like Swanson and Baldwin, he knew what was on the next page of the battle. Panic in the camp was evaporating and people were beginning to think. Patrols would be organized and those big damned mortars would start coughing out shells the size of small dogs.

The team reassembled at the guard shack, but they were still some distance from the designated pickup point beside the lake. Anneli was panting with the exertion, bending beneath the square pack that held the listening device and weighed better than twenty pounds. She gasped for breath.

"Give me that pack," Swanson snapped.

She looked up, hands on knees and gulped, "I can handle it."

"The extra weight is slowing you down and we can only move as fast as our slowest person. Give me the damned pack." He shrugged out of his own gear and slid his arms into the electronic unit's straps and adjusted the straps tight. Then he pulled his own ruck over his right shoulder. Stan Baldwin took both sniper rifles. "You are point, Sarn't Baldwin. Move out."

Swanson came next with Anneli at his side, and Perry was once again rearguard. They all heard the new sound in the fight, the distinctive grunt of the 120mm mortars, and cocked their ears for the expected whistle of incoming rounds. Instead, the shells went the other way and impacted far to the south, where the machine-gun fire seemed to be also growing in volume. Before long, the large mortars were rhythmically thumping out round after round, plastering the road network that led toward Poland with high explosives. A flare went up and glared over trees in that direction as it drifted down on a small parachute and made shadows dance in the woods.

The sniper group was feeling the stress and the pressure, not knowing how long the Russian mortars would ignore them. The guards at the camp had a dead general and a dead colonel on their hands, but no idea who had killed them. It had to be snipers. But where were they?

The base commander had received a strange and rather cryptic message shortly before General Mizon was due to arrive, an alert from St. Petersburg that some attack against the camp might soon be coming from the direction of Poland. It contained no specifics; not a time, nor even a date. He had taken the precaution of re-adjusting the mortars to face south, never expecting that the attack would come so soon, or if it would come at all. Nevertheless, he had distributed his firepower to best answer the situation, doubled the guard and called out a BTR-80. Now he walked a concentrated mortar barrage up the roads to Poland, blast after blast after blast.

The infantry troops following the shells reported by radio that there was no return fire and no opposition to their advance. No bodies were discovered along the roads, nor in the woodlands, which would be more carefully searched after daylight. The BTR-80 had prowled the area close to the camp and also failed to find anything of interest.

The commanding officer paused. He knew the layout of the area from having studied the maps so many times in the continuing efforts to interdict smugglers.

There were numerous little trails and small ravines and natural hiding places to the west, but all were within Russian territory, and therefore unlikely routes for any attack force. He sent a squad to probe the area. Same thing to the north, but with limited manpower, he had to make careful choices. Then there was the road from the camp to the lake, but he had already increased the guard manpower there, and had received no call of alarm from them.

In fact, he had not received anything at all from those two men. The commander had an aide call the guard shack, and there was no answer. After a low, private curse, the officer remembered that message had been very clear about the threat from Poland, and had not mentioned Lithuania at all. While he had been throwing everything to the south, were the snipers escaping to the east? He summoned the BTR-80 to get down to the guard post for a look. As insurance, he also instructed one of the 120mm mortar crews to turn and start laying rounds along the track from the shack all the way to the beach.

"Bounty Hunter to Vampire," Kyle called as he jogged along with Anneli right behind. "Bounty Hunter to Vampire."

"Vampire to Bounty Hunter. Send your traffic." The voice of the stealth Black Hawk pilot sounded as cool as an airline captain flying over Montana. But in the distance, he could see the bright flashes of deadly fireworks coloring the sky.

"Vampire, we are about ten minutes from the LZ. So far, it not hot." The action was still happening far behind the fleeing team.

"Our ETA is about the same. I can see detonations from up here."

"Nothing coming at us so far. That may change."

"See you in ten. Vampire out." The aircraft commander checked his dials and tried to squeeze a little more thrust out of his big engines. He did not want any dials in the red, because if this bird went down, there was none other around to take up the mission. Usually, there was a spare in the neighborhood, for helicopters could fall out of the sky for a myriad of reasons. That hard lesson had been learned on other raids over the years, from the ill-fated Iranian hostage rescue mission through the assault on Osama bin Laden's house in Pakistan. This mission had been thrown together so fast to keep security tight that it had become an all-or-nothing play, which suited the cocky attitude of a Nightstalker crew just fine.

Swanson called out the good news to his jogging friends. Ten more minutes and they would be gone. The snipers kept their personal weapons at the ready and their minds alert. During combat, ten minutes could pass in the blink of an eye, or last a century. The fact that they had not yet been detected had been a pleasant surprise, one of which they intended to take full advantage, because it would not last forever.

Anneli Kallasti loped along better without being burdened by the comm pack. Her eyes were on the dark shape of Kyle right in front of her, with the moving shadow of Stan Baldwin beyond him. Gray Perry was behind somewhere. She had never felt more excited, and believed that she had done well on this dangerous job. She would now really have something to tell her grandchildren.

*WHAM!* The unexpected explosion behind them jarred the air with a passing sweep of wind and made her look back. Corporal Perry pushed to keep her going and explained in a calm, unhurried voice, "That was somebody or something tripping our Claymores. It's a mine packed with about seven hundred little ball bearings and an explosive package big enough to choke a cow. I guarantee it just ruined their entire day. Move along, girl."

The driver of the BTR-80 was using night-vision sights, which were not good for seeing details like the steel wire stretched a few inches above the familiar pathway to the beach. He was also being guided by the vehicle's commander riding up top beside the large machine gun and calling down directions. The explosion wrapped the vehicle in a momentary balloon of fire and steel balls that flew from the Claymore. The commander was killed instantly and six of the eight tires were punctured, making the machine slow to a halt. The driver had been rocked by the jolt, he was temporarily deaf, the night-vision device was damaged and unusable, and the headless corpse of his commander slouched down the hatch directly behind him. He didn't know the fate of the rest of the crew.

The base commander also heard the detonation. The soldiers at the guard shack still had not reported in and now the BTR was incommunicado and probably had struck a mine down there. The silence of the troops and the savage booby-trap helped him decide that the attackers were using the beach path for their egress. He snatched his radio operator by a shoulder strap and yelled, "Tell that BTR to keep moving! Have the northeast mortar turn and saturate the area near the lake. That's where they are!"

The BTR driver heard the instructions, ignored the dead commander in the hull, and put the big armored troop carrier back into motion, rocking it to and fro to escape the tangle of vines and trees into which he had run. Some other crew member tossed out the body and took his place, but buttoned the hatch tightly. Some of the tires might be shredded, but the BTR could still ride on the rims, and he had fresh orders to keep going. The damaged machine would be slower and more awkward, but it was still able to move. It jerked free of the brambles and roots with screeches of protesting metal, only to run over a second Claymore after struggling only fifty feet. This time the explosive charge penetrated the gas tank, and the entire BTR brewed up in a ball of flame.

The action was speaking to Kyle Swanson. In his mind's eye, he had been able to picture the response back at the camp by the sounds and direction of the gunfire. That was all a puddle of harmless noise, and he had filtered each sound as they moved ever closer to the lake. Not a single shot had come near them. The BTR's loud engine had been distinctive enough for him to picture it grinding up the path on which they were running, then the familiar explosions of Claymores—sharp and jolting— meant that the armored vehicle had taken two in its guts, for he no longer heard the engine. The most immediate threat was off the board.

"Spread out!" he called. "Anneli, stay behind me."

Baldwin went off the path for about ten yards to the right and Perry angled out to the left, while Kyle hugged the path with Anneli. The snipers knew that mortar fire would be incoming, and by fanning out, no one round could take down all of them. A few more minutes were all they needed. They could actually smell the fresh water of Lake Vištytis.

They did not stop when the first 120mm round nosed over at the top of its trajectory and fell to earth with a shrill whisper. It was far behind and to the right, just ranging fire with no true aim. The problem for such indirect fire was that it required a spotter to give the gunners accurate coordinates. This mortar crew had to be working from a grid map showing preregistered points. Swanson heard a second distant cough and, within seconds, picked up the sound as the rocket round tipped over and started down. It came in off to the right and still behind them, tearing into the forest with a ferocious roar.

"They are going to give us a rolling barrage up the path!" yelled Gray Perry. "Going to get closer."

"I got water straight ahead!" called out Baldwin.

The downward whine of another mortar shell signaled for all of them to hit the ground, and Kyle pulled Anneli down hard. The blast was still in the woods, on the left, and while the trees ate the metal shrapnel, they also loosed a storm of wooden splinters. As soon as the explosion was over, the four were on their feet again and running as hard as they could.

"I see the helo coming," said Stan Baldwin. He broke open a green glowstick and waved it toward the big shadow approaching low on the water.

Another ominous whistle in the sky gave warning of more incoming, and everyone hit the dirt again. "Hang on, Anneli. We're almost home." She cuddled close to his back, almost spooning with her arms around him. For her, safety meant being as close to Kyle as she could get.

The incoming mortar round struck the tops of the trees just above them and detonated with a lethal airburst that forced the cone of destruction straight down on the path and a mini-hurricane of metal shards and jagged wood swept the area as entire branches cracked off.

"They're hit, Stan! Kyle and Anneli are down!" Gray Perry sprinted from his position and started pulling debris from atop his mates. Baldwin dropped his guiding luminescent wand as the helo settled into a hover just inches above the sandy beach, and ran back up the path to rescue his friends. They heard Kyle groaning.

A crew member of the Nightstalker team hustled up to help, and they flung away the junk until they reached the two people trapped beneath. There was a lot of blood, and Anneli lay still. "I got her! You guys bring Kyle," Perry shouted and lifted the girl as easily as picking up a pillow. "I got you, Anneli. Don't you worry, girl. Old Grayson has you."

Another mortar blast whizzed in to punish the forest again, off to the right, and the concussion shook the Black Hawk chopper that fought to maintain its midair balance. Gray Perry laid Anneli flat on the deck, and a medic moved in to examine her. She made not a sound.

Swanson was regaining his senses by the time he reached the helicopter and was helped aboard, then the other two men jumped on, the crew chief told the pilot that all were accounted for, and the stealth bird immediately put on power and eased up and turned north, clawing for altitude and invisibility. Swanson, from a height of a hundred feet, saw two more mortar rounds explode simultaneously and harmlessly along the beach. He turned to Anneli, but when he reached for her, Baldwin stopped him hard.

"You stay still, Kyle. The others are tending to our girl. You've been hit, too." The SAS sergeant began cutting away the sniper's trouser legs, which were soaked in blood.

**25**

IT TOOK **STAN** Baldwin a while to determine that Swanson was fine, other than being knocked silly by the blast. A cut on the left thigh would need a few stitches and the Brit slapped a sterile bandage around the leg. There was a neat puncture wound in the right forearm from a sharp splinter. Baldwin pulled the wood free and patched the hole with gauze pad and tape. Most of the blood that drenched the American was not his. Anneli had absorbed the full force of the blast while clinging to Kyle's back when they dove for cover. She, plus the extra protection of the backpack and his ruck, had shielded him.

When Baldwin finally sat back on his heels and turned Kyle loose, Swanson scrambled over to Anneli. She lay on her stomach and her lacerated back was fully exposed, as was a massive head wound. Perry and the medic were already pulling a green plastic sheet over her body. The Estonian girl had died at the moment of impact; aboard the helicopter, the medic had found no signs of life. Kyle had one last look at the pretty face, which was turned sideways, with black hair still trailing over her forehead to the sightless eyes, then Perry finished covering her with the sheet.

The medic packed up his gear, and the three snipers sat stunned on the vibrating deck of the helicopter, all watching the sheet as if willing it to move aside so that Anneli could spring up and bathe them with a smile. The death of a comrade always hits close to home, but this was especially tough. She had been their friend, their ward, almost a pet in many ways because she was so different from them. She was just a kid, a fascinating and brave kid, small in stature but strong in everything important. Her political activism in her hometown of Narva had helped start what was fast becoming a global showdown between great powers.

"Don't mean nothin' " was a normal refrain among troops when a soldier was killed, for soldiers often died. It was part of the job description, part of the warrior creed. If you did not know the name of the unlucky guy, then it was easier to accept. "Don't mean nothin' at all." Such bravado help shut out the nightmares that were sure to come, and for special operators like themselves, it was a peculiar armor that protected their souls against the monsters. Everyone had to die sometime. "Don't mean a thing." Such mutterings did not apply in this case, not where Anneli Kallasti was concerned. The snipers knew they would be seeing her face in dreams forever. Her death really did mean something. They took it personally.

Kyle Swanson tore his eyes away from the grim scene only by turning his entire body around until he faced out into the infinite darkness and the harsh, hammering wind chilled him. *It was my goddam fault. Why did I bring her along? We didn't really need her, but her incredible translation pinpointed the target and kept them informed in real time on what was happening in the camp. Like when the officer was bullshitting the men about making things perfect, and the men were criticizing the officer behind his back, and the advance knowledge of the exact time that the general would arrive, and that they had swiveled the mortars to point south. Everything she had done had added value to the overall mission. But she was my responsibility and I might as well have murdered her back on the boat or at the Narva castle. Stupid decision. Stupid. What a dumb fuck I am.*

The helicopter whirred on low, fast and unseen by radar, and landed once again at the secret air strip in Lithuania, where it rolled to the hangar shared by NATO special operations. The CIA Gulfstream was waiting inside, engines shut down. On the return trip, time was not the important factor it had been when it had delivered the sniper team en route from Latvia.

Swanson, Baldwin and Perry climbed out, weary to the bone and mentally exhausted as well. They were at a loss for what to do. Leaving the body of Anneli behind was unthinkable. Swanson leaned against the side of the helo, with the Englishmen facing him, as the Nightstalker crew unbuckled and exited the aircraft. The pilot, Major Rick Allen, took off his helmet and left it on the seat, then joined them. The pilot of the waiting CIA jet walked over and was shocked at the condition of the men, who seemed drained of energy and on the point of utter collapse. Allen headed him off before he could speak, took him back to the Gulfstream and explained things. One of the team members, the woman, had been killed and her body was still on board.

Then the army flier went back to the group of operators. He had been through this before on other special missions. Their sense of loss had set in during the ride and the battered operators felt they could only communicate to those who had endured exactly the same experience. "Hey, guys. I'm sorry about your friend. Rough one."

Perry lifted his gaze. "Yeah. Well, thanks for coming to get us." Swanson and Baldwin also muttered appreciation.

Allen took over. "Look. I know this is a dirty thing to do, but you three men have to get on that airplane over there and get the hell out of here."

Swanson's eyes glittered like green crystal in the harsh fluorescent lights of the big building. "Not leaving her behind."

"Yes, you are going to do exactly that, sir. She was not left on the battlefield, so the conditions are different. Give her to us now, and we will take her back to our own base, our own people. We will render every possible consideration, as if she was a Nightstalker herself. My entire crew and I personally promise that."

Sergeant Baldwin and Corporal Perry watched their leader. Swanson was still swathed in dark, dried blood and shaky on his feet. "The major is right, Kyle," Gray Perry said. "To keep this story secret, we have to get back to the *Vagabond*."

"So it will be like we had never been anywhere else at all," Baldwin agreed. "That's important."

The pilot added, "Honest to God, Mister Swanson.

It will be an honor for our team to take care of this operator. You've got to go."

Kyle knew they were right. The end of the mission was as important as the start. He had planned it to the minute, and it was best to stick to the schedule. Had it been from anyone else, he probably would have refused. Major Allen was one of them, and had flown unflinchingly into a mortar barrage to bring them out. He deserved to be heard. Swanson inhaled a deep breath and blew it out. Get back on the horse. Deal with the shakes later.

He reached back into the helo and wrapped his hand around one of Anneli's small boots and squeezed. He didn't have the proper good-bye words, and this wasn't the time. "It's better to die young and have truly lived, than to grow old merely to exist," he said, louder than intended.

"What's that, Kyle?" asked Perry.

"Something she told me the first day we met, when I asked if she understood the risks she was taking by being such a rebel." Then he picked up his weapons and his pack and walked away, followed by the two British shooters.

KOEKELBERG, BELGIUM

Ivan Strakov ripped open a pink packet of artificial sugar and dumped it into his morning coffee, and then used his fingernails to open three small plastic tubs of creamer. It was 0900 on Saturday morning, April 16. The election in Narva was tomorrow.

"You seem to be feeling better this morning," said Colonel Tom Markey, sipping his own coffee.

"It was just a nasty bug of some sort. I thought I would shit myself to death." Strakov gulped the hot brew. "This nectar of the gods will finish the cure. I saw on the morning TV news that Russia and Lithuania are trading accusations about provocation. Some general got shot? What's that all about?"

"Not my monkeys; not my circus," Markey said. "I'm just a NATO nerd, so let's talk about why we are here."

Strakov wandered over to a window, cup in hand, its heat warm to his palm. The morning was bright and the outside temperature was warming. All was well in the world. "Blaise Pascal started it all, don't you think? The Frenchman who built the first mechanical calculator to help out his tax-collector father?"

Markey played along. "Pascal gets the credit, but Gottfried Leibnez in Germany and Charles Babbage in England were just as important. The history of computers is hazy, going back to Arab and Chinese merchants using beads on a string or an abacus to count. Don't fuck around with history, Ivan. You are just wasting time again."

The Russian came back to the table and fingered a triangle of toast, then bit off a corner. "Let me continue in this vein, Tom. You'll see my point in a minute. Anyway, after the manual age, like the beads on the string, the mechanical devices moved in, with inventors such as Pascal, Babbage and Leibnez. Handcrafted metal and wood counting machines could do basic computations."

"Uh-huh. Then electricity comes along and, presto, we are into punch cards and rudimentary computers as big as warehouses." Markey drank from his cup, waiting.

"Follow that trail into war and the space age and

computer science really surges forward." Ivan seemed more animated than usual.

Markey enjoyed the history of computers. You couldn't understand today without knowing about yesterday. "Silicon chips and miniaturization, and now automobiles that possess more computing power than the early rockets that went into space. Almost everybody has a desktop computer."

Ivan was back in his chair with a fresh cup of coffee, his eyes almost sparking. "And it all goes to prove that computer science is not static. What comes next? That is where you and I come in, Tom, about halfway through the play. We specialize in cyberwarfare and are always looking for the next shiny thing so we can kill each other better and faster. A new and improved space race; both sides have to have it first!"

Markey was puzzled by this new direction. "What are you talking about, Colonel?"

"We, I mean the Russians, are, I estimate, about a year ahead of you guys."

"We are all working on optical systems. Everybody in the world is trying to figure it out."

Strakov leaned back and cupped both hands around his coffee. "Once again, Russia was first. The Z-seed protocol was the key, Tom. We already have a fully operational optical computer system. I watched it at work, and it is about a thousand times faster than today's best digital systems."

Markey tried to keep his emotions in check and his face neutral. If Strakov was telling the truth, then everything NATO had on line was obsolete. "Bullshit. We would have known."

"Right. Remember that you didn't know about the

Armata weapons systems being in the field until I told you? Same story again, Tom. The first militarized optical computers are ready—think of it; computing with accelerated lasers through the air instead of electricity through circuit boards, using photons instead of electrons. We call it the *Nehche,* which means 'Eyeglasses.' This is good information."

Markey recognized it as another game-changer. The frustrating Ivan Strakov was once again proving his worth. Markey and others in the cyber-war field believed that such a gizmo was barely in the theoretical stages at the Skolkovo Innovation Center, the Moscow version of Silicon Valley. "Where is it?"

"Not an *it*, Tom . . . *them*! Plural. I helped install the first Nehche myself."

"Where?"

"Up north. Actually, it is not too far from where the MiG tangled with that Finn missile. This is all part of the Arctic Circle strategy. Moscow chose to put the first optical lens up there because there is no place more important for President Pushkin's climb to regain superpower status."

Colonel Markey unconsciously looked up at the camera recording the session. He hoped other people were hearing this news, too. "Actually, we have that iceberg territory under pretty tight control," he said, feeling somewhat defensive. He could not comprehend NATO and the United States having fallen behind in optics.

It was as if Strakov was not even listening to his comments. The Russian was on a roll. "When Moscow controls the Arctic, it can control the world, and it's there for the taking. You Americans and NATO are so militarily scattered, from Afghanistan and the Middle East to Ukraine to the Baltics and all over Europe that you are virtually naked in the region. A couple of submarines, some airplanes and some soldiers on skis? Why, President Pushkin could take that frozen frontier in no more than two weeks of fighting. It would be over before it started, unless you went nuclear."

"If all that he has is an untested computer system that may not even work under stress in extremely cold weather, we will be all right." Markey did not believe his own words.

Strakov was totally calm. "The Nehche system was more than a peaceful breakthrough. It opened the door, Tom, for improved laser weaponry. Where you use missiles, we will use beams of light. Mounted in a long-range Tupolev bomber, for instance, a high-energy laser system with Nehche guidance is a fearsome weapon."

It was another blow to Colonel Markey. The U.S. Air Force had tried to build that very type of airborne laser with the YAL-1 system but eventually scrapped it. Years ago, the Boeing 747 that carried the experimental device had been taken to the USAF boneyard in Arizona and turned into scrap metal.

Markey put down his coffee and leaned forward. "Are you telling me that Russia has an operational airborne-laser system?"

"We have a lot of things, Tom. Which is why I came over to tell you about all of them." The Russian stood and stretched, ready for a mid-morning nap.

"I'm no American general, Tom. But if I was, I would start looking more at the sophisticated enemy in the north and less at the deserts of the ragtag Muslims. Your country and NATO are pledged to defend these little nothings like Estonia, Latvia and Lithuania. Pushkin counts on that, which is why he is pushing these minor military diversions such as overflights. So while you are tied down in the Middle East, and locked here in the Baltics defending the indefensible, things are going to get pretty hot in the world of the polar bears, who are not members of NATO. You are totally out of position."

ABOARD THE *VAGABOND*

After a shower and clean underwear and a heavy robe, and then some chow, Kyle Swanson disappeared into the communication suite and set up a secure link to Marty Atkins at CIA headquarters in Virginia. "It is done," he said.

"Yeah, I heard. Any damage to our team?" Atkins knew the risk factor had been high.

"One KIA," Swanson replied, tired and expressionless. The emotions were under steel bands. "Our translator. The girl we pulled out of Estonia."

"Does Calico know that?"

"Not yet. When she finds out, be ready for some blowback."

"Tough."

"Yeah. Did her death really make any difference, Marty?"

The CIA's deputy director for clandestine operations chose his words carefully. "We may never know, Kyle. That's not unusual in our world. But it definitely has created a stir. The Russkies are all bent out of shape because their general got popped. The Lithuanians are denying that any of their troops were involved except for ducking incoming Russian mortar shells."

"Okay. Watch out for Calico. She will be on the warpath. Now I'm going to sleep. Appreciate it if you contact the One Sixtieth SOAR concerning the body."

"Talk to you later, then. Good job."

Swanson terminated the call and sat motionless for a few minutes. He had brought both Sir Jeff on the yacht and Marty at Langley up to date. Nothing more important left to do. Then he made his way back to the infirmary to get a few stitches and sterile bandages for minor scratches. A pain pill would help get him to sleep, although he knew as soon as he was in dreamland, the nightmarish but familiar Boatman probably would come to visit with a boatload of guilt. Anneli had crossed over. She would be a passenger.

**C**OLONEL **G**ENERAL **V**ALERY Levchenko of the Western Military District was amused by the worry in the voice of his superior officer, Pavel Sergeyev, chief of the general staff of the Russian Federation. Pavel was scared.

Levchenko lit a cigarette and carefully blew out a ring of smoke that went almost to the ceiling of his office before being shredded by the air-conditioning drafts. "We cannot say that something like this attack was unexpected," he told the man in Moscow. "Some snipers took out Victor Mizon and his security chief and got away. It was a very professional operation. I admire professionalism."

"Is it true that we were warned in advance? Why wasn't something done? Why wasn't I told?" Sergeyev hardly knew Mizon, but that was beside the point.

"Yes," replied Levchenko. "My people received and passed along a very vague warning that had taken its own sweet time coming through the security service pipeline. You should ask the FSB why you were not copied on the message." He decided to dig at his superior a bit more. "If Moscow had been more alert, that message could have made a difference."

General of the Army Sergeyev was provoked by the haughty attitude of General Levchenko in St. Petersburg. "Never mind that. A Russian general has been murdered!"

"He was only a fucking border cop, Pavel. You can promote another deserving soldier to fill that empty desk in Moscow."

Sergeyev huffed, "I remind you that this happened in the Western District, not in Moscow. Your territory and your responsibility, General Levchenko."

If that was a threat, it failed. Levchenko actually laughed, and the sound rattled in the ear of Sergeyev. "Actually, I do wish they had picked some other general, but the snipers did not ask for my choice of targets. We all knew that something was coming because of the MiG attack on Finland. This was it. Now it's our turn again. Time to move on."

"I shall confer with President Pushkin this afternoon about overall strategy along the border." In his mind, Sergeyev remembered how his arrogant subordinate had only recently been raked over the coals personally by the president. This incident would further undermine the man's reputation.

"Do not bother yourself with that, General Sergeyev. My staff is already taking the steps necessary and will suggest an appropriate response to President Pushkin. And forget about young General Mizov, sir. Let it go. Think of it as if he died in battle, and give him a medal if it will make you feel better. I have this matter under control." He hung up before the old man could respond.

Levchenko thought that Russia could use a few more dead generals.

## ABOARD THE *VAGABOND*

Swanson slept as hard as a flop-eared hound, snoring on his back. Occasionally, he scratched at the leg bandage. Someone looking at the slender warrior would have thought this was a man at peace, although the closed eyelids twitched with the rapid eye movement going on. His brain was firing in overdrive.

One and one always equal two, he thought, while sound asleep. Always. No. In some computer languages, one and one equal only another one, because twos do not exist in those codes that open and close microscopic electronic gates. Therefore, nothing is truly absolute. Something did not add up.

Kyle had been anticipating an ugly dream visit by the Boatman, for those brief unconscious confrontations were his way of dealing with his post-traumatic stress. He had killed a man today, and had lost a good friend who had traded her life for his. Swanson had been on too many battlefields not to know that shit happens out there. A rise in terrain, a slip on a rock, the turn of a head can make all the difference between getting hit and being safe once the shooting starts. That was what happened with Anneli. She zigged when she should have zagged. It could just as easily have been Kyle in a body bag tonight.

So he was making peace with her passing from this life, for it was not his fault. It was the fault of some anonymous Russian soldier who dropped the mortar shell into its tube and sent it zooming off to explode above the trail. In that linear sense, one and one still made two. Swanson ground through the entire mission, start to finish, over and over, and the answer was always the same. Something was not right about it. He did not know the answer, and that nagging, unanswered question itched worse than the stitches on his leg.

BRUSSELS, BELGIUM

The general's mistress was not doing her job, in the opinion of several staff members and office workers. General Ravensdale was moody and waspish when he should have been bright and cheerful. There was trouble in paradise, they gossiped, but it was probably nothing that could not be cured by some little blue pills. Erectile dysfunction was a serious issue for a couple in that age bracket. The staff fervently hoped things would improve over the weekend.

Senior members knew that Ravensdale had a lot more on his mind than romping with rich widow Arial Printas. They had been briefing him throughout the day about the new border incident in Kaliningrad, and with updates on the interrogation of Colonel Ivan Strakov. That was being transcribed almost as fast as the Russian spoke, and the comments were distributed with top-secret classification among the NATO member nations. The general had every right to be concerned.

As bothersome as the dire predictions was the total absence of information about who killed the Russian general. The *why* was pretty plain, although unspoken. Ravensdale knew the name of the shooter, but pretended he did not. The intelligence community trying to track the event got very little help from London or Washington. The NATO deputy commander was impressed and surprised that the secret had held because Swanson had struck in Kaliningrad only hours after the dinner aboard the yacht. The sniper escaped without a trace.

By the time the cobalt sky faded into drifting and heavy clouds that edged toward the city like a soggy warning, the general had vigorously pursued his official functions. Through private meetings and encrypted telephone communication, Ravensdale insisted that the startling new data being revealed by the Russian defector required immediate action, almost radical. NATO troops, insisted the British general, had simply been caught too far out of position and too engaged in other places when the true threat was growing in the north.

The Russians were being totally bellicose up there, and had even threatened to point nuclear missiles at Danish warships if Denmark became a part of the NATO antimissile shield. Article V of the NATO charter clearly stated that an attack on one member would be considered an attack on all twenty-eight nations. Ravensdale was forceful and eloquent as he pointed out that Sweden and Finland were non-members and could not be counted as full allies. They might even open the gates to the troops of Moscow rather than try to repel them. The prudent thing to do, he argued, would be to immediately start shifting NATO forces into the region. Prove to Moscow, Helsinki and Stockholm that the North Atlantic Treaty Organization would do whatever was necessary to protect its northeastern flank.

He finally left the office at ten o'clock Saturday night

for a late dinner with Arial Printas at Aux Armes de Bruxelles. The tall man looked tired, but his companion was radiant. She had mussels and he nibbled at a medium-rare steak, with wines both red and white. There was little conversation. Afterward, they took a stroll along the Beenhouwersstraat.

"I tried to warn you about that attack," he said quietly. "Why didn't you stop it?"

Arial rolled her eyes. "Oh, that. It was sent through the usual channels, Frederick. We did all we could from this end."

"A general was killed."

"General. Sergeant. Lieutenant. What does it matter? Forget it." She slid her arm into his. "Why did you call me tonight? I thought you were angry."

Ravensdale took his time before answering. "We have a problem, and I have a solution."

"Tell me," she said. She gave his arm an affectionate squeeze and he did not recoil. Something had him excited.

"I was informed this afternoon that Colonel Thomas Markey, the American who is interviewing Ivan Strakov, is drafting a report that will cast doubt on the defector's story. Markey does not believe the scary scenario that Strakov is painting."

"When will this report go out?"

"Probably not until Monday. They were interviewing all day, and then Markey flew back to his home in Tallinn for the weekend."

"Will his report have an impact?"

"Yes. It could block everything, for Markey is well respected in the cyberwar field. For instance, he will challenge Strakov's claim that Russia has fielded an advanced computer system known as 'Eyeglasses' that could alter the balance of power."

"I know nothing about computers."

"Well, Strakov describes it as a secret optical system that is superfast. Faster than anything the West has operational. Markey calls it bullshit and doesn't believe any such thing has been developed. He plans to show that the Eyeglass system, even if it exists, has been rendered obsolete by the research being done into neurocomputers and artificial intelligence."

"Hmmm." Noncommittal. She bumped his hip slightly. Again, he did not pull away.

"Those new machines—ours—are being designed to think more like a human brain, and to actually learn from themselves as they go along."

"Never mind. I understand the point. This Markey person therefore presents a danger, and that is the problem. You said you had a solution for it, too." She brought them to a halt in the shadow of a wall, pulled him close and gave him a kiss.

"I want a deal first," he said, his voice hoarse. "I have persuaded the allies to start pulling forces away from the Baltics and into the Arctic, which is what you really wanted. I will continue to support Strakov, although he is getting too cocky and careless. So in exchange for this solution, I want your people to leave me alone in the future. If I pursue things any harder, I will draw unwanted attention. Let me finish this and retire in peace."

She wrapped her arms around his waist and leaned against the stone wall. "I agree, Sweetheart."

Ravensdale's heart jumped when he heard the soft endearment.

"You advanced the cause nicely. After tonight, we can be done. If you wish. What is this solution?"

"We give Colonel Markey something more important to worry about than Ivan Strakov. I have learned that his wife, Janice, is the CIA station chief in Estonia. If something unfortunate should befall her this weekend, the colonel will forget all about writing his report."

"Hah." Arial Printas laughed aloud and crinkled her nose as soft raindrops began to sprinkle. "I love the way you analyze things so brilliantly, Freddie. Let's get a taxi."

The general was going to have a good night. Arial would make a private call and pass along the information as soon as they reached the hotel. This time, the message would rocket along to the intended recipients. Even clerks would understand its importance. Instead of wanting to kill her, Ravensdale now just wanted her.


Combined Task Force 10 was created with great urgency within the Pentagon and its British military equivalent located at Northwood, in a suburb of London. With not a moment to waste, CTF 10 was hammered into shape, only on paper for the moment, but those papers would kick-start a massive movement of men and machines. It was a huge organization that would draw naval power from ships from the U.S. Sixth Fleet in the Mediterranean, the Second Fleet in the Atlantic and the Royal Navy in the North Sea. The initial land force, with the power of a full corps, would be provided by the 1st Marine Expeditionary Force and their brethren in the Royal Marines. Land-based NATO units from around the region would redeploy to Denmark.

With the U.S. Army Central Command tied down in

the Middle East, a new command headquarters would be opened at the Northwood facilities in Eastbury, Hertfordshire. The major problem as seen by both Washington and London was that there would be inevitable friction between the United States military establishment, NATO and the civilian governments of non-members Finland and Sweden. An overall commander with great experience and a diplomatic touch was needed, and it should not be an American.

While he slept peacefully beside Arial Printas in her hotel suite after enjoying the best sex he had had in ten years, General Sir Frederick Ravensdale, GCB, GBE, DSO, the deputy supreme allied commander of NATO in Europe, was promoted to lead the new military force being created to counter the threatening Russian moves in the Arctic.

**27**

NARVA, ESTONIA

**E**LECTION **D**AY WAS on Sunday, April 17, and it was more like a fair than a civic crisis in the troubled border city. Despite pittering rain in the early morning, the weather quickly warmed to pleasant temperatures. The old cobblestones rang with traffic, business was brisk and kids capered among the banners and streamers that urged voters to favor specific candidates. Turnout was high to decide the makeup of the new council and elect a new mayor. Everyone was aware that the election was really about much more than that.

Not so long ago, the charismatic lawyer Brokk Mihailovich and his nationalist followers had been favored to win it all. Then he had vanished, and his fragile coalition of supporters who also wanted Narva to distance itself from Russia collapsed into their own feuding camps. Old Guard politicians who wanted even stronger ties with Moscow were confident.

CIA special agent Janice Hollings watched the vote unfold from a table at a street-side café. Another woman, a legitimate supplier of material for Hollings's cover business in Tallinn, was chatting away and paging through sample books of colored cloth. Calico listened with appropriate interest, although her thoughts were elsewhere. The election was on her mind, as was the death of Anneli.

She was absolutely going to *kill* Kyle Swanson when she got back! Ruin him! Hurt him! She had never been as furious with a single human being as she was with that damned unfeeling robot sniper. He had no emotion, no decency, no sense of right and wrong. He had killed Anneli Kallasti as surely as if he had put a knife to her throat. When this voting was done, she would deal with him face-to-face and crush him beneath the wrath of the CIA. Put the bastard in prison and throw away the key!

Calico had embraced Anneli, whom she saw as a refugee child in dire need of help, love and guidance. She saw her as well as a potential valuable asset for the Company in this strange land. Her language skills, daring and eagerness were a perfect blend for a CIA recruit.

Without even the courtesy of informing Janice in advance of what was going on, Swanson had taken he girl on a secret mission. Now she was dead. Jan had gotten the news directly from Marty Atkins, her big boss at Langley, who told her to quiet down. They could straighten things out when the election was over. Calico was ordered to keep her head in the damned game. As a seasoned professional, she had only been able to speak obliquely about the situation when she had called her husband last night. Tom said he missed her. She missed him. After being on the road all across Estonia for the past few days, she wanted to go home. And then she wanted to kill Kyle Swanson, damn his eyes.

The other woman at the table displayed some printed

cotton designs, and Janice ran her fingers over the soft fabric to maintain her cover story, the reason for a blond American woman being in Narva at such a time. They talked for some time about the colorfast Turkey Reds, and the patterns drawn from native costumes in the region. It was good material, and the product always sold fast, so Jan would place an order after some obligatory bargaining.

The electioneering was in full swing all around them. The carnival atmosphere only intensified as the day wore on. She did not like the way it seemed to be going, for the former communists who anchored the status quo seemed too happy instead of being their usual gruff selves. The younger crowd was somber. Beer and wine started to flow early in the afternoon, and although there was little violence, mostly bar fights, it became obvious that the hardliners and ethnic Russians would win. In the afternoon, she toured a few more voting areas, listened to the gossip, and knew it was over except for the victory celebrations.

The count was quick and by eight o'clock on Sunday night, it was all done. Calico drove to the edge of the city in search of a quiet spot from which she could report her conclusions: Narva had chosen to move closer to Russia, just across the river, than it was to the rest of bustling Estonia. Langley was awaiting her analysis. Then she could go home.

## ABOARD THE *VAGABOND*

It was time to go home. The three exhausted snipers slept through most of Saturday as the gleaming yacht moved with the rhythm of the easternmost sector of the Mediterranean. Sir Jeff and Trevor Dash, the captain of the boat, were both former special-operator types and they threw a protective web of quiet around those three cabins. The death of young Anneli Kallasti had saddened everyone on board.

The SAS men Baldwin and Perry left just before dark after a final round of fist bumps, the understated equivalent of a bear hug for snipers, who did not like big shows of emotion about anything. *See you around, buddy. Right you are, mate.*

Swanson saw them off, had something to eat, talked awhile with Sir Jeff and went back to bed to get back on a normal day-night schedule. He was surprised at how easily he fell asleep on Saturday night, but the pressure was off him and that felt good. By Sunday morning, after a good breakfast of eggs and bacon and strong coffee, he felt almost human again.

Sir Jeff was also at the table, watching the seagulls scour the shipping lanes of the Med for discarded garbage or pouncing on a hapless fish too close to the surface. Kyle was in baggy Boston Celtics basketball shorts and a T-shirt, having discarded all bandages except a three-inch-square pad taped over the nick in his leg and a Band-Aid on the arm. The mood was good.

"Here's a piece of news," Jeff said. "Our good friend Freddie Ravensdale got a nice promotion. He is to command a new Anglo-American-NATO task force that will counter the Russians up in the north. Farewell, Brussels; hello, London."

Kyle poured some more coffee from a warmer. "I thought he was getting ready to retire."

"So did I, but I never thought of Freddie as someone who would drift off into obscurity after his service years. This new post will provide him public visibility, and perhaps he will pursue politics. I shall ask him out for another dinner with us before he heads to his new headquarters."

"Fine. Whatever," Swanson said. He had read the morning traffic on the secure computer. "His new outfit, this Joint Task Force Ten, is going to suck up a lot of resources."

"Admittedly it will thin the wall elsewhere, particularly in the Baltic region until all of the shifts can be made. NATO members will have to man the borders on their own for a little while. Quite a capable bunch, from what I have seen."

He pushed aside the breakfast plates. "It has been thrown together too fast, Jeff. That asshole Ivan Strakov is playing us for suckers. We can't trust him."

"Don't forget that he gave up the Armata systems, Kyle," Jeff reminded. "This new computer technology he unveiled sounds rather fascinating, too. Maybe Excalibur Enterprises needs to look into it."

Swanson glanced at Cornwell and saw that the bushy gray brows were drawn together, the expression he usually wore when making Kyle go deeper into available information. "Just because he was right about the new tanks does not mean he won't lie about something else. He was a top Russian intelligence agent. His job is to tell and sell lies."

Cornwell leaned back in the comfortable deck chair, feeling the sun bright on his face. "I agree. There has been too much reaction, and much too fast. You don't trust Strakov and I don't trust President Pushkin. That evil man is up to something."

Kyle agreed. "Not our problem, Jeff. You and I have

to get off this boat and back to work. Some routine in our lives would be good about now. Let the guys with the big paychecks solve the world's problems."

The older man laughed. "You have a big paycheck yourself."

"So I need to get back to earning my keep."

The rest of Sunday was uneventful at sea. By dinner, they had learned that arrangements had been made to give Anneli an honored final resting place, in Section 60 of Arlington National Cemetery. The girl who had never been to the United States would be treated as a fallen hero. True to the promise made to Kyle, the Nightstalkers had made her one of their own. Kyle would be able to visit her often.

When the sun set in a glorious blaze on Sunday night, Swanson stared into the golden glow in the west and had a feeling of inner peace that he had not known for some time. Things had a way of working out.

KOEKELBERG, BELGIUM

It was time to go home. Colonel Ivan Strakov of the FSB waited for his big wristwatch to show midnight, and as the second hand swept across the "12," the day changed from Sunday to Monday in the tiny window. He rolled from the soft bed in the CIA apartment and cleaned up.

If Arial Printas had Ravensdale under control, and Valery Levchenko over in St. Petersburg had played his role properly, and the Narva election had gotten the desired result, his task was complete. The president of Russia, Valery Pushkin, would soon add Estonia—perhaps the entire Balkan region—to his bag of puppet countries. The starting point, Narva, will fall in a masterful "soft grab," with hardly a shot being fired.

Threats, manipulations, dodges and misdirection, lies stirred with drops of truth, and the fear of a looming war in the north had been his tools. Pushkin would get Estonia, Valery would take command of the army in a bloodless coup over that senile old coward Pavel Sergeyev, and Arial would get even wealthier. And as if in a fairy tale, Ivan Strakov would get anything he wanted. He smiled into the mirror, saluted his image and quietly said, "Well played, sir."

Strakov ambled over to the door. He was in no hurry because this was going to take some time. He knocked once, and waited. A CIA guard was always awake near the door. The swipe of an electronic card unlocked it, and Strakov took a few steps back and folded his hands on his head.

"Yes, Colonel?" asked the guard. Strakov knew his first name was Chester, but his friends called him Chet. Strakov had become friendly with the man over the past week and never had given him a moment of trouble. Chet was from Little Rock, Arkansas. "Do you need something?"

"Indeed, if you please, Chet, you fucking moron. Go wake up somebody important and tell them that I have decided not to defect after all."


ABOARD THE *VAGABOND*


Swanson was asleep again as Sunday night gave way to Monday morning. Lulled by the rocking of the yacht, he tried to ignore the persistent knocking on his cabin door. The pounding increased in tempo and volume, a big hand making a lot of noise and a voice yelling, "Kyle! Wake up!"

He awoke, staring at the ceiling in the dark. "What?" he called out.

"Urgent call in the comm center. Washington."

A pause while he collected his wits. *Now what?* "Be right there."

Swanson kicked off the sheets, rolled from the bed, flipped on a light and slid into the underwear, baggy shorts and T-shirt he had discarded only a few hours earlier. A fresh set of clothing, from shoes and slacks to a tailored wool sports coat had been laid out for his scheduled ten o'clock departure in the morning and he saw no reason to wrinkle them unnecessarily. He went out on deck barefoot. Stars shone overhead around a crescent moon, and the briny smell of the Med was carried by a light wind.

The communication center hatch was open, and a deckhand waved him in. "CIA from Langley. Deputy Director Atkins." The man closed the hatch and Kyle engaged a security-jamming device to cloak the conversation. Atkins was on the screen. "Marty? What's up? Sorry for the wait, but I was asleep."

"When was your last contact with Jan Hollings?"

That's what this was about? "Before the mission. I guess she's pretty angry, huh? I expected her to call you and holler for a while. Losing the girl was tough for everybody."

"Nothing all day Sunday? You sure?"

"Absolutely," Swanson replied. "Wasn't she on that election thing over in Narva?"

There was an uncomfortable silence as Atkins stared into the camera. "Calico is missing, Kyle. She has missed two mandatory check-ins and does not respond to our prompts. Colonel Markey hasn't seen her either, and he expected her home in Tallinn by midnight at the latest. She didn't show. He's worried."

"How about the cops?"

"They report no major road accident between Narva and Tallinn in the past twenty-four hours."

Swanson was wide awake now. Despite their differences, he admired Jan Hollings as a bright intelligence agent who had entrenched herself into the country that was her responsibility. "Quick question, Marty. How did those elections turn out?"

"It was a clean sweep for the pro-Russians, the Workers' Party. Narva might as well be a Moscow neighborhood. Jan was supposed to give us a full analysis, but her call never came through." Atkins cleared his throat. "When a CIA agent goes missing, we pull out all the stops, Kyle. Consider yourself back on duty."

"Yeah. Okay. What's my assignment?"

"Go find her," said the clandestine operations boss. "Go find Calico."

## 28

BRUSSELS, BELGIUM

**G**ENERAL **R**AVENSDALE **ASKED** Arial Printas if she might want to live in London, and received a quick rejection of that idea. He was getting dressed in the hotel bedroom where a high ceiling vaulted above them. She was still curled abed on Monday morning, a long bare leg exposed over the wrinkled white sheet. Ravensdale had been awakened by the insistent chirp of his official cell phone and an aide informed him of the new assignment to be commander of Combined JTF 10. He flipped his tie into a Windsor knot, then sat beside her. Smiled down.

"Does this mean you will get yet another star on your shoulder?" she asked.

"No. I already have four. In fact, this could be seen as a demotion of sorts because my NATO position is very near the top of the mountain." He slid his hand along the soft exposed skin. *Exquisite*. She was absolutely lovely, especially in the predawn light after a breathtaking bout of making love.

"Well, I am very happy for you, Freddie. It is a most deserving honor."

"Unexpected, to be sure. Sudden transfer and all. Such is the life of a military man."

"Our weekend was special, wasn't it?" She coyly bit her lip. "Are you going to toss me aside now; the soldier seducing the local girl and moving on without a thought?"

"Oh, no, my dear. Not at all. No. As far as what has happened between us, yes, it was quite special. I didn't know I had the strength in me."

She reached out and pulled his head to her for another kiss. "I knew it all along. From the minute I first met you, I knew that you were an extraordinary man, General Ravensdale."

His eyes showed a flash of inner confusion. "Still, you turned me into a traitor."

Arial threw the sheet aside and lay there naked. "I did nothing of the kind, Freddie. I was sent to collect a debt that you incurred a long time ago. You have not been asked to do anything other than support events that were inevitable."

"I told you about the CIA spy, Calico. I should not have done so."

She laughed brightly. "And that is a minor point, darling. First, Mrs. Hollings is not British, so you did not betray your country. Second, the FSB seemed to know her identity already. They did not act at all surprised, nor follow up with any questions for me."

"What will be done to her?"

"Why, nothing! Why should it? Calico is much too valuable to hurt." Arial's deep eyes searched for weaknesses. "That's not really why you are worried, is it?"

"You believed Moscow would leave me alone in exchange for the information about Calico. Now, with this promotion, I will be squarely in the middle of the Arctic offensive. Will they still pressure me?"

Arial rose from the bed and slid her arms through a creamy silk kimono, then stood directly before him, between his knees. She did not close the robe. "I will see to it that they live up to the bargain, Freddie. Anyway, Moscow would only want you to command aggressively, as you have always done. Do not start feeling guilty again, or I shall have to punish you severely." Her breasts were soft against his cheeks.

"If you will not move to London, will you at least come to visit?" He peered up at her, breathing her fragrance. Something long forgotten had awakened within Ravensdale. It could not be love, for he had hated her, and such strong, opposite emotions were impossible. Or were they?

"I often get over to the UK. It's right across the channel by air, train or automobile, you know."

"You will come and see me, then. Promise me that. We shall remain discreet."

"Of course. Now you go home, get into that pretty uniform and go do your duty, whatever it is that you generals do. I am so happy for you."

A final kiss and he was out the door. Arial poured a drink of whiskey and padded barefoot to the tall window and gazed out at the city, the robe still open and her not caring if anyone was watching. It was early in the morning, and the morning chill made her nipples stiffen, so she closed the curtains. Smiling to herself, the heiress went to the entertainment cabinet that dominated the far side of the bedroom and was stacked with video and audio gear below a large flat television screen. It was so obvious that Ravensdale had never even questioned its presence. It was just a stereo and a TV. The setup actually did provide cable television, entertainment and music on demand, but it also worked in the opposite direction by recording everything that happened in the room. She snapped it off and proceeded to the bathroom to fill the hexagonal Jacuzzi tub and added a full packet of bubble bath crystals. As she sank into the warm foam, she congratulated herself.

She had told him Moscow would have no interest in him if he became a lowly goose farmer or beekeeper, but now the general was assuming an even more important post. There was no plan behind that; it was an unexpected bonus. Of course she would meet him in London, and just as surely, she would be carrying new orders.

A little kindness, a lot of flattery and an energetic roll in the bed were invisible hooks that had sunk deeply into the man. She owned him now more than ever before. The same formula that had left him befuddled so many years ago with the agent known as Lorette had been duplicated, and he did not even realize it was happening. Some men, whether government officials, prelates, money men, athletes . . . or generals . . . never learn.

## TALLINN, ESTONIA

Colonel Thomas Markey, for one of the few times in his exceptionally organized life, was totally at a loss for what to do by the time Kyle Swanson arrived at his home. Several other people were already there, including a woman who was stacking fresh groceries in the cupboard. The somber look and awkward silence reminded Swanson of a funeral. There was coffee on a side table, alongside a stack of gooey pastries. He expected a green bean casserole might soon be brought over by a sympathetic neighbor.

That would not be the case, because this was no ordinary mourning. The report that Jan Hollings Markey had vanished without a trace was a tightly held matter. Everyone in the neat house was either NATO or CIA, and agents were posted around the neighborhood to keep watch beneath the overcast sky. Swanson had been admitted by a guard just inside the front door only after showing his credentials. The house was cold.

Markey nervously toyed with a rubber band wrapped around his fingers. His face was lined with worry and his eyes were damp. He looked pale and listless, but got up when Kyle came into the room. "Anything yet?"

"No, Tom. I'm sure these guys will keep you up to date as soon as they hear. You probably know more than I do at this point."

The colonel wore old jeans and a tattered gray sweatshirt with WEST POINT across the chest. He absently picked at the rubber band. Swanson took him by the elbow and guided him to a corner so they could speak quietly.

"Let me cut to the chase, Tom. The Agency has assigned me to find her. Gloves are off. Do whatever is necessary to bring her back. Do you know anything that might help me?"

Markey shook his head, staring into the dark fireplace where only a few charred sticks remained. "No, dammit. I have gone over and over this thing in my head. We were going to meet here last night, after she finished in Narva and before I had to get back to Brussels. There was no earlier indication that anything was wrong. Did you hear that the asshole Strakov wants to undefect?"

"Fuck him," Swanson said in a low voice. "He's somebody else's problem now. You concentrate on Jan."

"I've got to finish my report on the interview." The man was jittery, perhaps just looking for something to keep his mind busy and to make him think about anything other than his missing bride. That was impossible, and awful scenarios marched through his mind.

"Get hold of yourself, Tom. Stay strong, and if you think of, or hear, anything that might help me, tell these people to contact me immediately. The official investigation is going to kick in soon and you will be swamped with investigators. I want to stay ahead of all of that. Do not tell anyone what I am up to. Should they ask, just say we're old friends and I came by to see how you were doing."

A smile crept across the colonel's haggard face. "Kyle, you work for the CIA. They know what you're up to, what you are capable of doing."

"Not really," Swanson said with a return grin.

NARVA, ESTONIA

The new mayor of Narva was a pudgy, well-mannered man with a full head of silver hair and a Hero of the Soviet Union medal pinned to the pocket of his neat blue suit. He had spent his teenage years fighting the fascists in the Great Patriotic War, and became a superior communist in the process. During his middle years, he continued the struggle against the imperialists of the West, and as he entered the second half of his life, watched in dismay as the Soviet Union fell apart. He understood economics and how the combined Western nations had crippled the socialist countries with ruinous sanctions. They accumulated wealth while making certain that the poorer East, ravaged by war like no other region, remained that way.

So it was with a satisfying sense of revenge that Konstantin Pran stepped up to take his oath of office at one o'clock in the afternoon on Monday, April 18. He was a common workingman who had earned success in business, unpolished but smart, and considered himself totally unlike that elitist lawyer Brokk Mihailovich, who wanted to turn Estonia into California. Pran was not sad that Mihailovich had vanished, for he always thought the man to be weak and untested on the battlefield, and a quitter. Pran had a different dream.

The citizens had turned out for his speech, and he made it short. He announced that Narva would adhere to the traditions that had made Estonia great, and that this victory would lead to new success for the Workers' Party across the country—in Tartu, Viljandi, Pärnu and even in the capital, Tallinn. Estonia would remain beneath the protective wing of Mother Russia while meeting the challenges of the twenty-first century.

NATO, he promised, would eventually be forced to leave the country on the path chosen by its residents. NATO had to go! He offered as proof that the organization of Western nations was duplicitous and dangerous as shown by the fact that the United States Central Intelligence Agency had attempted to interfere with the city's free and open elections. He let that charge linger for a moment. The mayor slowly announced this was not just political bombast: A CIA spy named Janice Hollings had been arrested by Narva police while she was trying to escape, as per an instruction from Russian intelligence officers. She was in custody at this very moment at the Town Hall and would be turned over to appropriate authorities, but not to the Americans or the nationalist Estonians. No, he said, the spy would be surrendered only to representatives who would arrive from Moscow tomorrow.

Kyle Swanson was by now familiar with the road to Narva and he charged over it aboard a matte-black Kawasaki KX450F, a mean little rice-burner of a dirt bike. Not much to look at, but with its 449cc four-stroke engine, the damned thing could climb a wall. He had paid $8,700 cash at a dealer in Tallinn and drove it off the showroom floor and onto the highway, and not long thereafter, rolled into Narva with a backpack full of tricks and the deadeyed look of someone who is beyond caring about what he does, as if life itself was a fuzzy and meaningless mirage. By the time he reached the traffic circle, a plan had formed.

The last time he was in the city, he had the luxury of Anneli as a guide and translator. Since he still had no idea of what the people were saying, he needed language help but did not want to be obvious about getting it. With the Kawasaki parked and locked, he drifted into St. Peter's Square, where a big political rally was under way. He looked around, saw the TV cameras, and made his way to the press area. Flashing his false press pass as freelancer Simon Brown from Toronto, he was allowed into the cordoned-off media section.

Four cameras were on tripods and pointing at a fat little old man with white hair up on a stage.

"Excuse me," he said to a woman writing in a notebook. "I'm Simon Brown, Canada, and I just got here. Who's that?" He smiled at her, but she was concentrating. The credentials around her neck stated in bold letters that she was with Sky News. Obviously an English-speaker.

"That's the mayor," she said, somewhat waspishly, not really wanting to share information with a competitor. "Konstantin Pran."

Then she looked up and saw a rugged, handsome guy with gray-green eyes smiling at her. Obviously a print guy, so no real competition. "I'm Marian Mansfield, Sky."

"Mind if I hang out with you guys for a little while? This guy saying anything interesting?"

"Damned if I know. Who understands this language?" She pointed to a young man nearby. "That's our translator. He feeds me tidbits while making a transcript that I can review later."

"Maybe you can do your review over a drink at the German Pub?"

Marian unconsciously brushed at her dark hair. She was interested. "Sure." The press liked to huddle together in foreign lands, particularly when they flew in for a single story like this border town voting in a bunch of antiquated hard-line old commies. Simon Brown looked more interesting than the mayor.

"Oh, shit!" The translator burst out, "Marian! He says they caught a CIA spy who was messing with the elections! She's being held in a cell at the Town Hall."

The reporter's eyes lit up as if jolted by a burst of

electricity, and she drew her telephone from her pocket like a six-shooter. "Well, that changed things in a hurry," she said. "I'll go on the air with this as soon as they can set it up. Raincheck on that beer? Simon, is it?"

"Yeah, you gotta work. The pub is on Malmi Street if you get a chance later on. Good luck." Around them, the other camera crews had also sprung to alert. Kyle backed away and was immediately dismissed from the thoughts of Marian Mansfield. He went back to his motorcycle and threaded carefully to a new vantage point. He had gotten what he needed.

NARVA

**J**AN **HOLLINGS SQUINTED** up at the single bare bulb that had burned all night long. It was annoying. Putting her palm across her eyes did little to ease the glare, for when she took her hand away, the bright light was still there, staring at her. During her training to become a CIA agent, she had gone through a program of what to do in the unlikely event that she was ever captured, so this was not startling. Bright lights were a painless torture, for it robbed a prisoner of sleep and left them weary and with lowered defenses and ruined the sense of time. Soon, they could not remember if it was day or night.

Her capture had happened so quickly that she barely remembered it. She had been ready to leave Narva, and was walking to her car, her mind not tuned to her surroundings while she mentally composed her report. Then there was a sudden large shadow and a small popping sound, followed by a pinprick on her left arm and a paralyzing electrical shock. Taser, she eventually decided. Little prongs had delivered a charge that knocked her on her butt. Calico was thankful that she did not remember the severe neuro-muscular contractions that would have left her writhing on the dirt like a broken puppet.

She had awakened in captivity. Searching her memory, she was positive that she had not made some grievous tradecraft error on Sunday, for she was an established professional with an iron-clad cover; a well-known fashion dealer throughout Estonia. But Calico, well, Calico was a very different person, and her captors had known exactly who she was. They took her because she was an agent, for capturing a rag merchant made absolutely no sense. She rolled to her side to avoid some of the light, remembering Swanson's suspicion that there was a mole, a leak, somewhere in the system. He was right, but he was still a bastard. *Poor Anneli.*

She counted it a small blessing that she was not in the Middle East, where fanatics cut off heads and/or inflicted other medieval tortures. Here, wherever *here* was, meant at worst that she faced spending the rest of her life in some rotten prison. That was unlikely. There was more of a purpose in play.

Jan got off the cot and walked the room, measuring it. About twelve feet by twelve, and maybe ten high, with rough and unfinished concrete walls. That one damned bare bulb, a hundred watts at least, hung in the middle, caged to protect the bulb and too high to reach. A small utilitarian bathroom to one side contained a metal toilet and a sink. No windows. She tried the door. Metal. Locked. She pounded. No response. It was a basement, chill and damp. On a little table was a pitcher of water and fruit, bread and cheese. A small kindness that indicated she was in a special category of imprisonment.

Her captors had something specific in mind. The "something" she did not know. It would all be revealed in time.

And she did not know who had taken her. She really did not know much at all.

Jan returned to the cot and sat on it stiffly, as if her spine was iron, and pulled a threadbare white blanket around her shoulders. There had to be a camera and audio device recording her every move, although she could not see them. Pinholes. Then she closed her eyes because her thoughts turned to the unthinkable. If the Russians had her, then their security services this very minute were combing through her history, her client lists and eventually would find the people who comprised her intelligence network throughout Estonia. A few tears fell as she prayed silently for them to run for their lives.

WASHINGTON, D.C.

The CIA brain trust did not panic upon receiving the news that the station chief in Estonia had vanished. Calico was not even the only crisis they would face today. Crisis was their game.

"So this new puppet mayor of Narva has announced to the world that they captured her." Marty Atkins was summing it all up during a meeting of section chiefs. "We have received nothing through official channels. Then, over in Brussels, this jerk Strakov suddenly decides that he does not want to defect after all. Am I the only one here that smells a Russian rat?"

A general muttering of agreement rumbled around

the room. Nobody in the meeting believed in coincidence.

"I agree," said National Security Adviser Dean Thomas, who had come over from the White House. "What have you done so far?"

Atkins took off his reading glasses and studied his old friend. "Nothing much. We have to let it play out for a while. State Department is enlisting our embassy people in Tallinn to get the Estonian government to help. She is apparently being held in the Town Hall, probably a special cell. The Estonians will stomp all over the mayor to let him know that kidnapping Jan Hollings was a pretty dumb move that will backfire."

"Are the Russians really involved?" asked Royals.

"Not a peep from them yet, Dean. You can bet they are somewhere in the woodwork, and the mayor says he will turn Calico over to them at some point. "

"Okay. President Thompson wants her back safe, sound and soon. The State Department will make that very clear to both Tallinn and Moscow. Are you doing anything specific that I can tell him?"

Marty Atkins leaned back and spun an ink pen around in his fingers. "On the clandestine side, yes. I sent one of our operatives, Kyle Swanson, into Estonia."

"Swanson. The sniper?"

"Yep."

Royals thought about that for a moment. "He is a very dangerous man, Marty. Maybe you should have Swanson back off until we get a clearer picture."

"I'm afraid it is too late for that," said Atkins. "He has dropped off the grid. No idea what the boy is up to. He likes to work alone."

"Boy?" snorted Dean Thomas. "Swanson's a damned frothing Rottweiler with a gun."

"But he is *our* Rottweiler, Dean, and I did not let him off the leash just to do a half-assed job of locating our missing agent. We wait and see."


MOSCOW

President Vladimir Pushkin and his Western Military District commander, Colonel General Valery Levchenko, walked side by side on a secluded gravel path in the Neskuchny Gardens. Security police fanned out in a distant circle around them, shooing away tourists and Muscovites alike. April was being kind to the gardens, which had braved another Russian winter and were springing to life earlier than usual, and both men were in good spirits. The heart of Moscow was turning green.

"It is as if someone handed me a diamond of great value," the president declared with a chuckle and a grim smile. "I confess that I had many doubts about these grandiose plans of Colonel Strakov. He seems to have accomplished the impossible."

Levchenko kept his hands behind his back and matched the president's stride. He had flown over from St. Petersburg again, beginning to feel like a commuter, as soon as he heard about the CIA woman. The colors of the park were remarkable, and new leaves nosed out of healthy limbs. Flowers that had been frozen seeds for months were erupting into shades and varieties that had not yet made it up to St. Petersburg. "He seems to have been damned near clairvoyant."

Pushkin looked up as a noisy pair of ducks lumbered overhead, aiming for the nearby Moscow River. "None of us counted on having the CIA's Estonian chief of station in custody. Strakov just wanted us to snatch some prominent American like a businessman or a tourist or a reporter, and accuse them of spying. This is so much better."

"She fell into our laps, sir. But with her in our grasp, we also secure our hold on this weak-chinned General Ravensdale, who is forcing NATO to weaken its forces throughout the region. In addition, we dissolve the troublesome Calico intelligence network. Then we put Narva in our pocket as the springboard into Estonia. We also get Colonel Strakov back with a prisoner swap. It is a great coup. All I need right now is your final permission to wrap up Operation Hermitage when the moment comes. Phase One accomplished its mission of screwing up the NATO defenses, and our men and equipment are all back in place. Phase Two is ready to launch, and I will be in Narva tomorrow morning to personally command the movement. No weaklings will be allowed to back out at the last minute."

The ducks came to a splashy landing out on the river, joining a paddling of several dozen others floating about and discussing the warm weather.

President Pushkin watched them while he considered the entire situation. "You have my authority. I will put that in writing. Keep me informed, Valery. Bring this all together and I will see that you replace Sergeyev as chief of the general staff."

The general from St. Petersburg promised that he

would. The president was tempted to remind him that history was littered with the bones of generals who had grown too ambitious.


KOEKELBERG, BELGIUM

Ivan Strakov had dealt the game from a stacked deck, played the hand, made the bets and won. It was sweet. The CIA people were unhappy with him for reneging on the agreement. So what? The first outburst had been to threaten to send him to a supermax or the Guantánamo prison or turn him over to some banana-republic dictator who would do their bidding. That was a bluff. Ivan knew that a prisoner swap eventually would be arranged because some important American should have been arrested by this time. Better than a fortune-teller, he had already written the future. A prisoner exchange was certain.

They had become petulant, and moaned and taken away his privileges, which bothered him not at all. Everything would work out. About now, NATO would be holding emergency meetings and urgently shifting units toward the North Pole, war-gaming worst-case scenarios and trying to envision what would result from a nuclear exchange at the top of the world. Those non-NATO nations like Finland and Sweden would be shitting their pants. And on the Russian side, Valery Levchenko would be orchestrating everything. Phase Two of Operation Hermitage should be ready to begin.

There were always unknowns, but nothing was perfect. Strakov was confident that his meticulous scheme would overwhelm any obstacles. He shook out a cigarette and lit it, blowing smoke toward the camera mounted in a corner.

## NARVA, ESTONIA

Mayor Konstantin Pran was one of thirty-one members of the City Council, but his Worker's Party had won all but five seats from the upstart Social Democrats. The decisive political victory gave him a huge majority, and the five minor-party members were not even invited to the first meeting of the new government. If they showed up, they would have been barred from the room under the claim that the meeting was a not a public meeting, but a private caucus of the Worker's Party.

Russian was the only language spoken that afternoon in the upper corridors of the Town Hall, for the Old Guard had already made its authoritarian presence known. Pran and his henchmen had worked hard to craft their majority and saw no reason to waste time now. The mayor had been handpicked for the position by friends in both Moscow and St. Petersburg, and was the acknowledged leader of his party. His voice was the only one that really counted.

In public during the campaign, the party's candidates spoke of corruption within the Social Democrats, promised higher wages for all, an improved standard of living, a severe crackdown on criminals, a fight against greedy capitalists in Tallinn, lower taxes and strong security. In private, after hours, they always remembered when the city tried to secede from Estonia and reunite with Russia a number of years ago. Some 97 percent of voters had approved, but the federal government in Tallinn ignored the election and forced Narva back into line. Mayor Pran and his friends believed the time was ripe to try again; no, not to try, but to do it. Back then, Narva had no army standing by to guard its decision. This time would be much different. The entire police force was made up of tough Russians; active-duty soldiers in mufti. An entire protective armored force was poised in the town next door, separated by just a river. The council's first and only piece of business that afternoon was to vote to secede.

With that accomplished, the new council members cheered and congratulated one another and drank toasts of vodka from little glasses. Food carts were wheeled in for a party, and families and friends joined them. Konstantin walked out hours later, filled to bursting with pride, and also a little drunk. He decided to make one final stop before going home. He had never seen an American spy.

The basement of the Town Hall smelled of decay and mildew. Over the years, it had primarily become the resting place for things that were unwanted elsewhere in the government building. During the Cold War, the space had been expanded to be deeper and wider to create several special rooms that would be bomb shelters when the Western powers attacked. These small rooms had been furnished, had stores of food and water, waste facilities and ventilation, and were expected to last for up to two weeks. The doors were of steel. When Russia pulled out, Estonia could not afford such useless hidey-holes, and all but one had been turned into giant storage closets for boxes and crates. The final room was used to hold special prisoners until the Russians could come and pick them up.

A young policeman with close-cropped dark hair was on sentry duty, seated in a wooden chair and reading. He put aside the magazine when he heard someone coming down the stairs, and snapped to ramrod-straight attention when the mayor appeared. Mayor Pran paused and inspected the guard. A sharp Spetsnaz commando. "Good man. You remain alert in this dreary place. I shall mention that to your chief. Now, please open the door. I need to speak to our prisoner."

The tall cop did as he was told, and Pran knocked quietly on the steel panel three times before opening the door. The prisoner was a woman and he did not wish to find her in a compromising situation. Then he went inside.

Jan Hollings was on her feet, waiting, tense but not weeping. She was tall and had piercing blue eyes that made Pran think for a moment that she was Swedish or Norwegian and not American at all. A lightweight blanket was around her shoulders.

"Mrs. Hollings, I am Konstantin Pran, the mayor of Narva," he said in good English.

"I know who you are. Why have I been taken prisoner?"

"Because you are a spy of the CIA, my dear." He seemed amused, and looked at the little table with the wilting flowers and leftover food. "You have been treated well?"

"A spy? Mayor Pran, I am just a housewife who also runs a clothing company in Tallinn."

"Yes, of course. You were here to spy on our election and report back to your masters." He giggled girlishly. "This is the conversation of a thriller movie, is it not?"

"I want to go home."

"And you shall. You shall be reunited with your important U.S. Army colonel husband very soon."

Hollings felt a surge of hope. The man was tipsy. "Well, that will be very good, but I am no spy. You have made a mistake."

Konstantin Pran smiled, his cheeks pulling aside to show capped white teeth. Such dentistry required money, Calico thought. She sat on the cot and crossed her legs, noticing when his small eyes checked her. He continued to stand, hands clasped before him.

"I watched you speak at the square this afternoon. Congratulations on your election."

"I thank you for that, madame. It is quite an honor for me. My city is at the most important juncture in its history."

Jan was looking directly at him, unafraid. She had just established that it was still the same day. She smiled shyly. "Narva has been around for many, many years, sir. Why is this time more important than all that has gone before?"

Again came the giggle and he waved one hand to dismiss this. "Ah, you are playing the spy with me again. It is no matter, for you will know everything by this time tomorrow. By then, Narva will once again be part of Russia."

"You know that the Estonian federal government will never permit that," she said, her eyes narrowing.

The mayor shifted his weight and his ego was boosted by the alcohol he had consumed. "There will be another rally in St. Peter's Square tomorrow morning and I will formally issue a declaration of secession. At precisely nine o'clock on Tuesday, I shall walk across the bridge and invite Russian troops to come over from Ivanogrod to defend us. Colonel General Levchenko himself, the powerful district commandant, will personally lead the force into town."

Calico was stunned. "NATO will consider that an act of war."

The mayor spoke faster. "NATO is in disarray because of the new threats in the Arctic, so our move will meet little resistance. Russian troops will be in defensive positions before you Yankees and your NATO helpers can react in any significant manner. Afterward, things will only bog down in endless negotiations. The final piece will take place when you, Mrs. Hollings, are exchanged for a very important person."

"Who?"

The mayor laughed aloud. "Probably, I have said too much already, but as I mentioned earlier, it will make no difference. By the time you can get back tomorrow night, this will all be over. A fait accompli, with no options but war or negotiation, and NATO will not fight for Narva."

"You're wrong, Mr. Mayor. Sadly, so very wrong. You know that if the Russians take Narva, they won't stop until they have all of Estonia, and then they will move to make the rest of the Baltic dominoes fall. We will definitely fight to prevent that from happening. Without question. You are putting the world on the brink of a new war, and your city, Narva, will be ground zero. Your city will be utterly destroyed. Thousands will die."

He shook his head, bid her a pleasant night, gave a slight bow and left. The door locked behind him, leaving Calico sitting there trying to absorb the enormity of what would happen. She wanted to shout the news, but no one would hear her.

The mayor stepped into the night and felt the moist air cool his cheeks. He got into a small car driven by an old friend, a retired policeman and who had become chief of the mayor's security team, all ethnic Russians. Not that Pran thought he needed protection, because on this day, everyone loved him.

Moscow, always skeptical, insisted. There might be a few Social Democrat thugs who wanted to protest. Most of the dissidents had been disappeared over the past months, but a handful of activists were still around. In a way, he regretted helping make some of his countrymen leave aboard the Black Trains, never to return, but the dream of reunification was more important than a few lives.

The mayor and the guard shared a few laughs as the car drove away from the middle of the city and threaded through traffic to reach Pran's suburban home, a modest detached building with a garage. He had raised his family there and knew every stone. Pran danced merrily up the steps and through the front door, calling for his wife. The guard parked the car at the curb, adjusted the seat and made himself comfortable. His twelve-hour shift lasted until dawn.

Neither the guard nor the mayor had noticed a black motorcycle that had followed them, staying about a block or so behind, ducking out of sight briefly now and then, only to appear again in some blind spot. When the car stopped and the mayor went inside, the small dirt bike roared past the house and evaporated into the failing light.

**30**

HELSINKI, FINLAND

EM JAMES WAS wrapping up a long day. The special
agent of the U.S. Diplomatic Security Service had
been up to his elbows in work for the past forty-
eight hours as tensions increased throughout Finland.
The Russians were on the move on one side and NATO
was awakening on the other, and Finland was in the
middle. Diplomats in the laid-back city had been as busy
as honeybees in the bright spring weather, and that
meant that Lem and his fellow agents were working
around the clock to protect them. Late-night meetings
were becoming the norm, but maybe tonight he could
get home to his wife and son in time for dinner.

He had locked his safe and his desk and was putting on his jacket when the cell phone began a little
bebop tune that meant a call was coming in. He was
tempted to let it go until he saw the picture and name of
Inspector Rikka Aura of the Finland Security Intelligence Service.

"I told you never to call me here," he answered in

a teasing voice. "My other mistresses will get suspicious."

"I have no time to be a mistress for anybody," Aura said. She sounded tired. "Sorry to call you so late."

"I always have time for you, Rikka. You know that."

The woman paused, as if gathering courage. "This is way off the record, Lem. You remember that friend of yours with whom I had a disagreement a while back?"

"Yeah. You threw him out of the country."

"Meet me at Molly Malone's as soon as you can."

Ten minutes later, they each had a foam-topped beer before them at a table in the rear of the pub, their heads almost touching so they could talk above the racket of a local band trying to play Irish music. Lem had rarely seen his friend so concerned, but understood that her neutral country was caught in a tightening vice because of its ardent neutrality. Failing to stand up to a bully never works—not on a playground and not in a global showdown.

"My source for the information about when and how Kyle Swanson was coming to Finland was General Sir Frederick Ravensdale of Great Britain. He called me personally from Brussels. I assumed at the time that he was acting in his role as NATO deputy commander."

Lem pulled back, took a slug of beer, and said, "No shit? The guy who just got named to head the special northern task force? Why would he do that?"

"I thought it was an unofficial favor. You know how that works, Lem. Now I'm no longer certain. The general did not want Swanson to linger in Finland a moment longer than necessary. Having me expel him forced your friend to act immediately and not make other arrangements. It forced him along a certain path. Does that make sense?"

"No, but I'm not very smart. I will pass this along to my people. Thanks, Rikka. I know this was a difficult decision for you."

"It was, Lem. It could get me fired or imprisoned if it gets out, but Helsinki is in the crosshairs of whatever is about to happen and I think this might have something to do with it. You go home now and say hello to the family for me. Tomorrow may be hell." She got up, touched his shoulder lightly and left the bar while he ordered another beer to help him digest the news.

NARVA, ESTONIA

The guard parked in front of the home of Mayor Konstantin Pran had a problem common to most men his age. As the time passed, and darkness fell like a shade across the neighborhood, boredom set in and his attention drifted to the edge of sleep. He jerked himself awake and checked the time. Too many more hours. He decided to get out, stretch his legs, bend his back a few times and go to the trees and pee. Tomorrow, he would pack a plastic jug in the trunk so he could do his business in the car, just as he had on stakeouts when he was a young cop.

The night air was cool and welcoming. He could smoke out in the open, but not in the car. Silly rule. The neighborhood had settled down like a snoozing dog. The guard had done a pee break an hour before without incident. A jug would be better than getting a complaint from some neighbor who might see him urinating on the flowers. This time, the shadows were longer and the shade was deeper. As he unzipped his pants, a double garrote of fine piano wire was slipped over his head and bit into his neck.

Kyle Swanson had waited patiently, knowing that it was likely the guard would repeat his earlier behavior to empty his bladder. He snapped the wire loops into place, crossed his hands to tighten it and pulled hard with a knee in the man's back to force a bend. The garrotte cut through the flesh as fast as a spinning butcher's saw, and went hard and deep completely around the neck. Kyle kept pulling through pharynx, larynx, trachea, esophagus, pharyngeal muscles and a field of blood veins. In a few seconds, the thin wire was sawing on the top of the spine. The guard had automatically reached up to pull on the wire, but Swanson was using the French Foreign Legion method. By using a very long wire, he was able to wrap it twice around the neck, so even as the victim clawed at one loop of the collar, the other was made tighter. Once snared, there was no way out. The man went down and Kyle straddled him until it was over. The corpse had been almost decapitated.

Swanson unwound the wire, having to pull a bit to free it from the muscles and flesh, and stuffed the metal weapon in the backpack. He grabbed the dead guard by his shoulders and hauled him deeper into the trees. Peeling off a black raincoat that was smeared with blood, he spread it over the corpse.

Then he pulled down the knitted balaclava mask, drew his .45-caliber Colt, slung on the backpack and headed toward the front door. An ankle holster held the 9mm Beretta Px4 Storm Compact. There was a light on the small porch. He unscrewed it and rapped lightly, four times.

The mayor was at the dining table. His wife, Ivi, had come home right after the swearing-in ceremony and devoted herself to building a spectacular meal of roast chicken, fresh vegetables, potatoes and a salad mixture of her own design. A thick, sweet *kissel* with ice cream waited as dessert. She was very pleased both with the meal and with her husband, and the tapping at the door annoyed her.

"You stay and enjoy the food, Konstantin. I will get it. Maybe the guard has to use the bathroom." Ivi put aside her folded napkin.

The mayor watched her go with a private smile. They had been married more than thirty years and he still loved her spirit and admired her grace. He called, "Whoever it is, send them away, Ivi. The workday is over. This is our time."

She pulled the dead-bolt free and undid the thin brass chain. Just as she realized the light was not working, Kyle Swanson kicked in the door and sent her spinning across the hall, bouncing off of the wall. By the time she hit the floor, he had closed the door, was wrapping strips of duct tape around her hands and over her mouth like a cowboy roping a calf.

Three and a half seconds after the door had opened, Swanson was down the hall, across the living room and descending on Konstantin Pram like an indoor hurricane. The mayor had managed to drop his silverware and begin rising from the chair when Kyle hit him with a body-tackle, feeling the weakness of the old man. In a few more seconds, the mayor was also hog-tied.

Swanson stood and took a few deep breaths, then put them both in facing chairs in the living room. He had holstered his Colt, but now took it out and pointed the barrel directly at the top of Ivi's head. In conversations with Anneli and Brokk about their election opponents, Kyle had been told that the mayor spoke English. In fact, the mayor bragged about his ability to bring in foreign investment because he could negotiate face-to-face. "You speak English?"

Both of them nodded in the affirmative, and he put the gun away, went out and locked the door.

Swanson shrugged out of the backpack and opened a side pocket to withdraw a block of gray plastic, which he placed on a table. He rolled the mass with his palms in easy strokes until the malleable material was a long, thick string. Moving to the wife, he roped it around her neck, gently pulling her hair free, and then connected the awkward necklace at the front of her throat.

Ivi Pran tried to struggle, but Kyle whispered for her to be still. Her husband could not hear the promise that she would not be hurt. Her eyes remained wide in fright as the man in the black mask stood back and studied his work.

Satisfied, he went into the backpack again and found a pencil-like device that he held for them both to see. "Mr. Mayor, that material around your wife's neck is a powerful plastic explosive called C-four," he said, then wiggled the pencil. "This is a detonator. I am setting it to go off in exactly one hour." He adjusted the detonator and showed the mayor a little screen that said 60:00, then pushed it into the plastic necklace on his wife.

"There is only one way to stop this from blowing up." He moved to the mayor and knelt before him. "You will get in your car and drive to wherever you are keeping Jan Hollings, the American. You will bring her back here to me. Understand?"

Konstantin shook his head, thinking, *If I can only get out, I will get the police.*

Swanson knew what he was thinking, because it was natural. He walked slowly around the room and gathered the framed photos of children and adults. Christmas, beach scenes, new babies, teenagers and friends. "You should know that I am not the only one working tonight. Friends of mine are tracking all of these people even as we speak. Do you understand me?"

The mayor was horrified and jerked at his bindings. His children and grandchildren were being threatened.

"You have crossed a mark. You have begun toying with war, little man, and that is not allowed." Swanson dumped all of the pictures at the feet of the man, and then he ruthlessly crushed the glass and frames beneath a thick black boot. "Not only is your wife at risk now, but if Hollings is not standing here within the hour, all of these other loved ones of yours will be murdered tonight or tomorrow. I will burn this house. We will kill your brothers, sisters, parents, friends and in-laws. Your line will come to an end. If you try to bring in the cops and the military, I will not be able to call it off. Still understand me? It will be wholesale slaughter. Just like you guys did to the Disappeareds."

The mayor was pleading with his eyes. He flinched when Swanson jerked the duct tape off his mouth. "Wait, sir. Please," he gasped.

Swanson casually reached for the detonator and started it, so the mayor could see the little numbers begin to count down . . . 60:00 became 59:59, then 59:58.

"I suggest you leave now, Mayor. You will have to drive yourself because your guard outside is dead. Go, you fat bastard. Bring me my friend."

Konstantin Pran drove as a man possessed, barely noticing other cars or people, pushing his old green Volvo hard as he retraced the route back to the town hall while counting seconds in his head. So much was at stake that nothing mattered but retrieving that woman spy from the basement cell. There was no time to call out the guard, or summon any other kind of help, because he believed in his soul that the madman back at the house would carry out his threat and not give it a second thought. Pran would worry about possible repercussions to his career later, but right now the only way to save his entire family was to do as he had been told.

When he reached the Raekoja Plats, light were shining from the spire of the Town Hall, which had been closed for the night. It had taken almost ten minutes to drive there and he looked at his watch in panic. Less than fifty minutes left. He stopped directly in front and leaped from the car with his chest pounding so hard he thought for a moment that he might be having a heart attack. That slowed him. Dying meant the deadline would be missed. He did not stop, but slowed and swallowed big bites of air as he went up the stairs. The place, so familiar to him, now seemed like an evil castle.

The double door was locked, which forced him to ring a bell and shout and pound and wave at the security camera to get the attention of the night watchman. No one else was in the entire plaza and the sounds he made stirred only sleeping pigeons. Seconds of waiting stretched to minutes. *He is asleep! The watchman is asleep!* He was about to leave and try to break through a window when a voice whined out from the intercom speaker on the wall.

"Who is it? The town hall is closed." The voice was accusatory as the night watchman showed his authority.

"It's Mayor Pran! Let me in immediately!" Konstantin demanded, sounding as mean as he could.

"Why?"

The mayor thundered, "*Why?* You don't question me, you fool! Open up now or I will have you fired and arrested. I am on official business that is of no concern to the likes of you."

There was a bit of silence before the man thought it over, then replied, "Yes, sir. Right away." He moved slowly because of the way he was being treated. Reluctantly, he obeyed, and left his post.

Two more minutes were wasted for the mayor, who was huffing air and leaning against the wall while his feet moved in a nervous dance. The locks clicked and the door swung open. The night watchman, in a sloppy uniform, stood back as Konstantin Pran sailed past him. "You asshole," the mayor said, and dashed for the marble stairs. *Tick, tick, tick* went his mental clock.

Kyle Swanson went to the woman and laid a hand on a shoulder. "Now that he is gone, ma'am, I can tell you not to worry about that thing around your neck. It is not a bomb, just some ordinary children's clay, and there is no charge in the detonator. You are going to be fine, and your family is safe. I apologize for frightening you and damaging the pictures, but I had to scare your husband into doing what I wanted."

He saw her close her eyes in relief. She murmured

something impossible to understand from behind the tape.

"I have to leave you taped up for a while longer to be sure that you don't scream or try to escape. You have no reason to trust me, but you can relax. He will be back soon, then I will leave. You will be fine. OK?"

Ivi Pran stared at him, then visibly eased her posture. It was impossible for her to fight against this man.

Kyle turned to the dining table, drawn by the aroma, and he gave the other rooms a quick search as he went. He rolled his mask up far enough to allow him to eat some chicken and potatoes while he waited, and it was delicious. He kept his big pistol on the table.

At the Town Hall, the guard in the basement was the same patrol officer as before and he once again snapped to attention when he recognized Mayor Pran. "Good evening, sir."

"Good evening." The mayor's voice was a gravelly rumble in the echoing basement. "I have come to collect the prisoner."

"Sir?"

"Open the door for me, Comrade Officer," he said, falling back into the communist jargon. "I don't have time to explain."

The policeman said, "I should check in with my sergeant first, sir. My orders were that after the building closed for the day, she became my personal responsibility."

Pran was short on patience and even shorter on time. "This is for a high-level and confidential meeting, young man. Officials from Moscow have arrived to interview this spy in a private place that has the proper equipment.

Also, I am the one now giving you an order, and I out-rank your sergeant."

"Nevertheless, she remains my responsibility, Mayor Pran."

That was the sticking point. Pran said, "Then you will accompany us. She will be in your presence except while being interviewed concerning sensitive informa-tion, then you and I will return her back here in a few hours. We will not awaken your sergeant. If any ques-tion arises, I will take full responsibility. I want no trace of her being with the Russians before the official trans-fer tomorrow. It might worsen an already delicate inter-national problem, do you understand?"

The policeman was satisfied. It was a thoroughly Russian operation. He was covered. "Just one moment, sir." He reached for his keys.

Inside the bomb shelter cell, Jan Hollings heard the scrape of metal on metal as the door was unlocked. She dropped the blanket and awaited the unknown, willing herself to remain strong, no matter what.

31

**T**HE SNIPER HAD to make certain he did not eat too much. A taste of the creamy dessert and a sip of water to finish. This was the way to work, Kyle thought. All the comforts of home. It was much better than slumming around in a hole in the ground, dirty, hungry and uncomfortable, as was the case just a few days ago in Kaliningrad. Unbidden, the memories flooded back and he was running for the chopper, Anneli at his heels, while high-explosive mortar shells slammed down.

Damn! The niggling feeling that had been itching in his brain ever since the fight, that something was off-kilter, came around again and he still could not put a finger on it.

The sound of an automobile pulling up outside brought him back to the job at hand, and Swanson readjusted his mask, picked up the gun and checked his watch. Forty minutes had passed since the mayor had left. Moving to the wife, he tied a napkin around her eyes for a blindfold. "This is almost over," he said.

Swanson heard one car door close, and a few seconds later, another was shut, and then a third, which was one too many. He put away his Colt because any shooting inside would be loud enough to draw attention from neighbors. Instead, he slid a broad-bladed KA-BAR knife into his hand. He backed against the wall beside the door and waited. Footfalls on the steps, then the porch, and the door opened. Mayor Pran came inside first, calling out desperately for his wife, "Ivi!"

Calico was next in line, handcuffed. She stepped tentatively inside, guided by the hand of the uniformed policeman who was last in line. Swanson jerked the cop off balance and jammed seven inches of razor sharp carbon steel into the neck twice, and ruthlessly gouged through muscles, tissue and arteries. Another thrust went into the chest and sliced through a chunk of heart before the point stopped against the spine. The cop exhaled a long, final bubble of breath. While Swanson closed the door, blood poured from the cop's severed carotid artery and hosed everything near it, painting the floor and the furniture crimson.

The mayor had thought about his next move during the drive home, betting that the man in the black mask would attack the policeman. Ignoring his wife's scream, Pran yanked open the top drawer of a small and polished table to grab a Makarov PM pistol stored inside. He stopped cold when he saw the drawer was empty. He turned with his hands in the air, and saw the invader watching him, holding a long knife that dripped blood on the carpet. "No. Please don't kill me," he mumbled.

Kyle waved him to the chair across from his wife and lightly touched the arm of Jan Hollings, who had rolled away from the fighting. "You OK?" he asked softly, never taking his eyes off the mayor. Calico knew it was Swanson. She bobbed her head.

Konstantin Pran was roughly bound with tape again until he was completely immobilized, except for his mouth.

"I warned you not to bring the police," Swanson hissed at him.

"I tried. The man insisted, but we were wasting time. I knew you could handle him." Pran's eyes were huge in fear. He looked at the dead policeman and the quarts of red blood that were still spilling from the body.

"Well, you made it with eleven minutes to spare."

"The bomb," said the mayor, his eye catching the red numbers of the detonator of his wife's clay necklace. They were still blinking. *9:36 . . . 9:35.* "Stop the bomb. Don't blow us up."

Kyle ignored him. A quick search of the mayor gave up the car keys, and the key to the handcuffs was on the belt of the dead cop. Swanson freed Calico. "Don't say a word until we're in the car. Walk normally. Let's go!"

The mayor shouted as they left, no longer pleading for his life, but a bellowing, defiant challenge. "You cannot stop it! Even if you kill us tonight, you cannot stop it!"

That made no sense to Swanson, but as he opened the door, he felt Jan Hollings hesitate and look back over her shoulder. The mayor was wobbling in the chair, trying to escape. He was trussed like a trapped hog, and his screams were matched by the muffled cries of his terrified wife. "Oh, shit," Swanson muttered, and dashed over long enough to slap strips of tape over Pran's mouth.

Calico was still in the doorway, with tears running

down her face. She also moved to the mayor and slapped him hard across the cheek. "Yes, we can, and we will!" she hissed, then slapped again with the other hand.

Swanson pulled her back. "Stop that. We've got to go, and right now! Get to the car." He gave her a push and followed her out. Something he did not understand had just happened right in front of him, and Calico seemed to be on fire.

In less than two minutes, the Volvo was on the move. Kyle rolled his mask off and tossed it in the back. Jan knew the roads better, but she was bent over in the passenger seat, her head between her knees and her hands threading in her hair as she hauled in great gulps of air. "Are you sick? What's wrong, Calico? Talk to me."

She turned to look at him. There was effort and fright in her gaze that he had never seen before. "Kyle, do you have comms? Anything at all we can use to get in touch with somebody?"

"No. I don't do this sort of thing with a phone on me. No tracking allowed. What's the fastest way out of here, back to Tallinn?" He took a corner and drove down a darkened street.

She peeked up over the dash and got her bearings. "Take a right in two blocks. That leads to the traffic circle, then straight west on the E-20." She still seemed on the edge of panic.

"Calm down now. We're safe. Comms aren't necessary because we are only a couple of hours from Tallinn. You will be back home. Tom is worried sick about you."

She squirmed around to face him directly, gathering her strength. "I can't wait to get there and be with him,

Kyle, but that's not why we need immediate communications."

"Then what the hell are you talking about? Don't play games."

"World War Three, Kyle. World War Fuckin' Three!" She looked at the digital clock on the dashboard. "Almost midnight. We have only got nine hours!"

Swanson struggled to stay steady on the wheel and not stomp the accelerator. Getting stopped for a traffic violation would be a disaster. The egress on a mission was critical. He kept his eyes on the road. Thankfully, there was not much traffic and in a moment, the Volvo was leaning through the traffic circle. "What happens at nine o'clock?"

"This new city council of Narva is seceding from the rest of Estonia. At nine, that crazy mayor will go to the bridge and invite Russian troops to come over and occupy the city."

He couldn't believe that. It was insanity. Such a move would mean war. "That was probably booze talking. He was almost drunk when I first found him at his house. He told you that and you believed him?"

"The man was drinking and bragging, yes. But, Kyle, we cannot afford not to believe him."

Swanson pushed the button and lowered his window to allow some night air to wash through the car. She was right. "Well, we can't use a regular cell phone for this kind of stuff anyway. If we tried a pay phone, it would take fifteen minutes, when instead we could be fifteen miles closer to Tallinn. The CIA is all set up at your house, so we can get direct links to Langley. So let's see how fast we can drive a hundred and twenty miles," he said as they plunged onto the E-20. Traffic cops be damned.

Twenty minutes went by before they spoke again.

"Thanks for coming so quickly. You are very good at your job, but despite the rescue, you and I still have an unsettled debt."

"You're welcome, and whatever," Kyle responded. "We will straighten up sometime in the future. There's something more important at hand right now, wouldn't you agree?"

"What bomb did the old man want to stop?"

"Nothing. He believes I put a necklace of C-four around his wife's neck, but it was just a roll of Play-Doh with a dud detonator. It will not go off. Even so, it will be several hours before they wiggle out of the tape, and then the mayor is going to have to explain how he lost two cops and his prized CIA spook."

"You have a cold, dead heart," she said.

"Warm and fuzzy doesn't get the job done in this line of work."

They lapsed back into silence for another ten miles, letting the cool night air rush through the open windows. "Do you know anything about the status of my network?" she finally asked.

"No. I doubt if it exists any longer. The Agency probably pulled the plug and warned them all to take off as soon as you went missing. You can ask the people at Langley." He leaned his head back, adjusted the seat down and to the rear. The Volvo went on cruise control at eighty.

Ten more minutes of quiet, and few cars passed in the

night. No headlights loomed in the mirrors. "Tell me about Anneli." This time her voice was softer. "What happened?"

"You sure we need to do this right now?"

"I know you did not personally kill her," said Hollings. "We still have an hour on the road. Help me understand. I really, really liked that girl."

Without emotion, Kyle told her the story and when he was done, Calico said, "She wanted to go?"

"Yes, it was her choice. I am glad she went because she proved to be a valuable asset. Just like when we snatched that prisoner during the war games. I really liked her, too."

"And she was not just another tool for you to use? I know how you are, how you put mission before everything. And your rep with women stinks."

"Anneli saved my life by giving her own, Calico. Do you think that I can ever forget that? When she died, something inside me went away, too. So whatever you want to do to me, go ahead and take your best shot. I don't give a shit. Enough of that for now."

It was almost one o'clock, the beginning of Tuesday morning. In eight hours, Russian tanks would be on the Narva Bridge.

## IVANGOROD, RUSSIA

A lone figure stalked the ancient battlements of the Ivangorod Fortress, looking to the west and planning the future. Valery Levchenko had arrived about midnight, and after reviewing plans with the local staff, he gave in to temptation. Like generations of generals before him, he climbed up to the highest point and peered with lust at the rich panorama right across the Narva River. The night chill invigorated the man from St. Petersburg, and his obvious confidence inspired his soldiers. It was an impure dark, with a fog hanging on the river like a gray beast, and clouds cut off the moonlight. If he couldn't see over there, the enemy couldn't see over here, even if they had been looking.

The colonel general could not make out the Narva end of the big, wide bridge in such decimated visibility. Turning around, he also saw thick darkness coating his side of the river, where strict light and noise discipline had been imposed. What could not be totally suppressed was the grumble of dozens of vehicles being guided into position: Armata tanks and armored personnel carriers and missile batteries and trucks of every sort clattered and ground their gears and squeaked. The stirring of troops rose as a hushed shuffle.

He took a final look at the bulk of the Hermann Castle on the Narva side and thought briefly about how useless such things had become. Instead of months of bombardment by cannonballs and a starvation siege, the big castle would fall to him tomorrow morning with a simple handshake with the mayor, whose name Levchenko could not recall at the moment.

Months had been spent planning this thrust, now everything was being shifted into final positions through these vital last hours of darkness. When nine o'clock came, his force would uncoil like a powerful snake. As they moved over the 530-foot-long major bridge, they would also seize the pedestrian bridge near Kreenholm

Island and the important railroad span that connected the two countries. Trains loaded with gear and supplies waited on sidings deeper in Russia.

By the end of the day, he would have about two hundred vehicles and five thousand men across the river. They would be guarded by artillery tubes set deep behind Ivanogrod, thickets of antiaircraft missiles, squadrons of helicopter gunships and stacks of fighter-bombers.

Once it began, Levchenko had no intention of stopping at the Narva city limits. The Estonians probably would be in action by then, and the general could order a full assault all along the border. The battle for the Baltics could begin in earnest. He took a final sniff of the wet air, and it had the smell of glory. He then left the rugged stone wall and walked back to his headquarters. The staff was hard at work, and a big clock was just striking two o'clock in the morning.

**S**WANSON AND CALICO made the trip in about two hours, each minute clanging like a church bell marking a funeral. The closer they got to Tallinn, the more she demanded that he hurry. He refused. *Slow is smooth; smooth is fast.* No room for error this close to home. He pulled to the curb in front of the house at two fifteen a.m., and slumped over the wheel that he had been gripping so hard that his fingers hurt. Jan Hollings flung open her door and dashed for the stairs, where an astonished CIA agent recognized her and yelled inside, "She's here!"

She hurried past the entranceway and hurled herself at her husband, Tom Markey, who grabbed her like she was the essence of life itself, and they rocked together in the unison of a slow dance while hugging and murmuring and weeping.

Swanson came in more slowly, moved around the embracing couple, and barked, "Clear this house of all unauthorized essential personnel. Get a full guard detail outside, call some local cops for backup, and fuck if the neighbors complain. We have a full emergency on our hands, people."

Everything stopped for a confused moment. "Who the hell are you?" asked a startled army captain, one of Markey's staff members.

"Kyle Swanson with the CIA." He brushed past the officer and into the dining room, where a table and sideboard were laden with radio and satellite communication gear. "Whoever works this rig get me a direct link to Langley right now. I want Marty Atkins, the deputy director of clandestine operations, on the other end. The operator, I and Colonel and Mrs. Markey will be the only ones in the room. Close it off."

"You can't—" the captain started to say, following him into the room.

Kyle effortlessly punched him in the gut. "Yes I can, and I just did. We are *NOT* playing around tonight, people. Consider yourselves, as of now, on a war footing. Get off your asses and do what I say and we will work on the details later."

"I'm the comms officer. War?" sputtered the captain, who had fallen onto a chair and was trying to catch a breath. He felt that an anvil had been dropped on him.

Swanson helped him to his feet. "Now you're getting the hang of this. Crank up your stuff."

From behind them came the soft voice of Colonel Markey: "Do as he says."

Estonia was seven hours ahead of Washington, so while it was 2:30 on Tuesday morning in Tallinn, it was still Monday evening in Virginia. Marty Atkins was about to adjourn a group situational briefing when an aide rushed in with a note. The time stamp was 1935, or 7:35 p.m., Eastern Daylight Time. He read it, broke into a smile and clapped his hand on the conference table. "Calico is out!" he shouted. "She's free and safe. I've got a call waiting from Estonia. You folks stick here until I get back with the details. Somebody pass the word over to Dean Thomas at the White House."

## MOSCOW

Sleep would not come to President Vladimir Pushkin. He had done everything he could and, as much as he hated it, he was at the point at which he had to trust his subordinates to carry out his orders. He was not strong on trust.

Pushkin tried not to disturb his wife when he climbed out of bed and headed for the bathroom, and she only turned over and changed the tone of her breathing momentarily, then resumed a normal rhythm. The Russian leader found his slippers and his robe and after doing his business at the toilet, went to a full-length window that opened onto a patio, and pushed it wide.

He had spent other nights like this, when his nerves jangled with excitement, but he had never lost courage. One by one, his targets and opponents had fallen, because he stayed firm in his belief that he could restore Russia to its rightful place as a global superpower. Keep pushing the West, ever so gently, but always pushing. The United States, badly bloodied in the Middle East, had lost its taste for foreign wars. Europe still remembered two world wars, the Cold War and innumerable conflicts between themselves of the past hundred years or so, and hid behind the shadow of NATO. Their combined power seemed formidable on paper, but that unity was about to be severely tested. Would France abandon her flighty lifestyle to send soldiers to die for Estonia? Would the selfish Italians lay it all on the line for Latvia? Would little Portugal really commit the lives of its troops for Lithuania?

The official declaration sounded good; twenty-eight nations guaranteeing mutual defense. But would Iceland really join the fight, and if it did, who cared? The country had less than four hundred troops, including reserves. Albania? Slovenia?

Pushkin's conclusion had been that NATO had become a paper tiger. In Ukraine and Georgia and Chechnya, they had done little more than chant protests. Never back down, he reminded himself.

The tabletop digital clock flashed its scarlet numbers as he climbed back into bed and pulled up the coverlet and snuggled against his wife. Three o'clock in the morning, the same as in Estonia. Six hours. Time would tell.

WASHINGTON, D.C.

The president and his first lady had been hosting a formal state dinner at the White House for the prime minister of Japan, starting with a receiving line at eight o'clock. He was in a great mood after receiving the news that still another problem had been resolved: the CIA agent in Estonia had been rescued and was safe at home.

She and her husband would be flying to Washington tomorrow, and he looked forward to their private meeting. She had done a wonderful job over there for eight
years.

The grip-and-grin receiving line gave way to cock-
tails for a hundred VIP guests, and since it was so warm
outside, the dinner was held on the South Lawn beneath
a trellis of little lights. His national security adviser,
Dean Thomas, also wearing a tuxedo, came up, trying
not to look worried. He whispered in the president's
ear that an emergency meeting was being called in the
Situation Room. President Thompson glanced at him
and saw the seriousness in his friend's eyes. "Start it
without me. I will be there right after the speech," he
said.

The president carried on with smooth, practiced normality, for there were members of the media present
and the nearby press room guaranteed that anything he
said out of the ordinary would be instantly turned into
a news story. Jumping up and running to the basement
was out of the question. He and the Japanese PM toasted
with *sake* and both gave brief statements about the
importance of the Pacific Rim while never mention-
ing the trade imbalance. While the dinner had been
a marvelous concoction, the words were very standard
fare. Then he told the guests to enjoy the musical portion of the program, and apologized for having to
tend to a few things. He would rejoin them later, he
promised.

As soon as he was in the Situation Room, he knew
that he would not be listening to the concert at all. Instead, he was listening to Kyle Swanson, in Estonia, talk

about a possible war with Russia that could commence in only six hours. The Pentagon generals recommended getting ready for anything, and President Thompson agreed. He ordered DefCon Four.

The orders flashed to the isolated bomber bases at Diego Garcia in the Indian Ocean, to the Marine Corps at Twentynine Palms in California, to every naval battle group afloat, and to Army units based in Korea. Everybody wearing a United States military uniform was to be put on alert and every light in the Pentagon would soon be on.

The United States military establishment snapped to Defense Condition Four at the order of President Christopher Thompson. Normally, things operated at DefCon Two in most theaters, which was just a bit above normal readiness conditions. The unending threat of terrorism had done that. This was much more serious. DefCon Four meant that all American armed forces throughout the world were to be ready to deploy and begin combat within six hours. The only step higher, DefCon Five, meant that nukes were flying. The nations of NATO were warned to prepare to repel an invasion. He placed a personal call to the president of the Republic of Estonia. America, he promised, would stand with them.

## BRUSSELS, BELGIUM

General Frederick Ravensdale was asleep, alone, in his quarters when he was awakened by his aide. He automatically reached out to touch Arial Printas, only to find empty space and realize where he was. "Yes, I'm awake. What is it?" He was grumpy. Middle of the bloody night!

"Sah!" A full colonel was beside his bed and someone else was turning on lights. "The U.S. has gone to DefCon Four and all NATO commanders are needed for an emergency meeting at oh-five-hundred hours. That is in thirty minutes, sir."

"What is this ruckus, Colonel?" Ravensdale rubbed his eyes against the sudden brightness.

"I don't know, sir. Our chums the Russians seem to be up to something over there in Estonia. A video conference is being set up and you are needed at our headquarters."

Ravensdale's gut churned. Narva, he thought. They are going for Narva.

"Your car will be waiting as soon as you are ready, sir. Staff is being gathered." The colonel started to leave, but had one more thing. "Bit of good news, sir. That American spy who was captured has been freed. Stroke of luck there, eh? We will have hot tea and biscuits waiting at the office, sir."

The general looked up blankly. "Very well," he said, and the visitors left the room so he could dress. He went to the bathroom and almost puked before getting himself under control. The change of command to CJTF 10 had not yet occurred, so he still had a hand in shaping the NATO response. He knew what Arial would advise.


TALLINN, ESTONIA

"I can stop this," Kyle Swanson declared with his usual absolute certainty. He was on the screen with Marty

Atkins. Jan Hollings was absent, having been taken to her upstairs bedroom. As feisty as she might be, Calico had been through an emotional ordeal and desperately needed rest. A doctor gave her a sedative and she was sound asleep. Colonel Markey had stayed with her until she was down for the count then came downstairs for the video conference.

Kyle saw him enter the room and turned from the screen momentarily to inform him about the jump to DefCon Four. That meant the colonel would have to report to his office immediately to handle the cyberwarfare front. His team probably was already on the way. The doctor said Jan would be asleep for about eight hours solid, so he could leave her with the nurse.

"How?" Atkins asked Swanson. "What can you do that the rest of us can't?"

"I can go back to Narva by helicopter with a squad of Estonian troopers for protection, and take a ground-laser designator up into that big castle that overlooks the river. Then give me an F-18 with some Paveway smart bombs overhead and I will paint that bridge for them. Blow it to hell and back. Piece of cake, Marty."

"No," Atkins answered firmly. "You've been constantly on the go. Get some rest."

"I can sleep when I'm dead, Marty. I'm the best person available for this job and I'm almost next door to the place. I can do it."

"Kyle, you are at least two hours away, using a helicopter or not. Things are moving too fast for you to pull another Lone Ranger mission. So. No. Anyway, we are discussing something else for you to do later today."

"Damn it!" He looked ferocious.

Tom Markey broke into the conversation. "Kyle

sometimes forgets that he is smack in the middle of Europe's Silicon Valley, Marty. Electrons move faster than men around here. I have an idea."


NARVA, ESTONIA


The mayor was found a little after six o'clock on Tuesday morning, still tied to his chair. The relief guard had arrived, found no Volvo outside and no guard. He rang and knocked and called out, but all of that went unanswered. He walked around back and peered in. Nothing but a mudroom with a door closed. Going back the other way, he spied a lumpy black plastic raincoat between two trees, and a foot sticking out beneath it. The cop drew his gun, ran to the front and kicked in the door. Konstantin Pran and his wife were safe, but locked down. And another policeman, quite dead, was drenched in blood.

Mayor Pran was livid with rage, but the single officer was in no position to do anything else alone. He radioed for help and police cars flooded into the neighborhood. Despite his loud demonstrations, complaints, demands and threats, the new mayor had some serious issues that needed to be explained. Two dead guards and an escaped American spy required a thorough investigation. The mayor protested that he had to get to his office immediately, and could reveal what happened later.

The chief of police refused to let him leave the house until Pran went over everything in detail, including why the alleged raider in the black mask had not killed him. Another question was the clay necklace and dud detonator worn by his wife. The chief thought the mayor might be in on this so-called escape, so he called across the river to ask Colonel General Levchenko for instructions.


WASHINGTON, D.C.


Almost midnight. It was time for the presidents to talk. Both knew their words would be studied by future generations, particularly if things went bad. Special phones carried the conversation so it would be heard by hand-wringing aides in the Situation Room and in the Kremlin in Moscow. Once the courteous pleasantries were observed, they got directly to business.

"It is my duty as president of the United States to make it plain, President Pushkin, that we will stand beside our NATO ally, Estonia, should hostilities begin there." Thompson had removed his tuxedo jacket but still wore the starched shirt, unable to break away from the crisis even long enough to go up to the executive quarters and change clothes.

"And I, President Thompson, emphasize that we have no designs on Estonia."

"Sir, your country has gathered a very large military presence at the border, particularly at the Narva bridge. That is an aggressive posture and one that we must take most seriously."

"President Thompson, the troops you mention are merely preparing for the second phase of a war game named Operation Hermitage. Your people observed the first part only a few days ago. It is designed to repel any attack on St. Petersburg. Meanwhile, the United

States has elevated its readiness status to DefCon Four? We find that quite troubling."

"That was our reaction to the entire situation that has developed during the past week, President Pushkin. NATO has no intention of harming St. Petersburg, or any other place in Russia. You know that. Please forgive me, but it is a ridiculous scenario."

"As is your assertion that Russia plans to storm into the Baltic States."

Chris Thompson looked around the room. Nobody believed the Russian president, but the conversation was in danger of falling into a he-said, he-said exchange. It was better to remain subtle. While Pushkin was waffling words, the clock was ticking and history was watching.

"We both desire the continuing peace between our nations, Mr. President," said Thompson. "Nothing must jeopardize it."

"On that we are in absolute agreement, Mr. President," replied Pushkin. "I can pledge that Russia will not be the first to fire in any Estonian border skirmish that develops because of your DefCon Four. I ask for your restraint. Good day, sir."

Vladimir Pushkin was still relaxed, although he had not expected the DefCon-Four development. However, he had gambled with fate many times, and usually won. There was still time left, so he decided to let the dice roll a while longer.

In Washington, Thompson said "Good-bye" and the U.S. Army Signal Corps operator terminated the call. The president stuffed his hands in his pockets and let his eyes go around the room, then said, "Pushkin is blowing smoke and leaving himself a lot of wiggle room. My opinion is that they're going to do it. Let me hear some final alternatives and go over that SSGN thing, the submarine-launched cruise missile, again."

A marine lieutenant-general in one of the chairs that were not placed in the top echelon of importance raised his hand, as if wanting the attention of the teacher in school. Brad Middleton, the deputy national-security adviser, had been listening closely to the Russian, as had everyone else. Instead of parsing the real meanings, he had noticed something odd.

President Thompson looked at him, nodded. "What is it, General Middleton?"

"Nothing about what he said, sir, but something he did not say." Middleton once had been the head of a secret and elite group of special operators known as Task Force Trident, whose triggerman had been Kyle Swanson. Although Swanson was now a CIA operative, Middleton stayed in close touch with him as a back-channel contact. "Pushkin made no mention of the CIA agent who has been rescued. She was likely going to be a bargaining chip to be swapped at the Narva bridge, probably for Colonel Strakov. Having her was an important part of their overall plan, a vital piece of propaganda, and now she's not there anymore."

"Go on," said Thompson. He had not mentioned the agent called Calico either.

"This whole thing has been running like a finely tuned engine, sir. But with her safely back in our hands, they have lost important leverage, she has spilled the beans on their intention, and Russia is suddenly off balance. They had claimed she was meddling in the election over there, so it would have been very easy for Push-

kin to throw her in your face as the reason for them being on high alert. He may still be planning to do that."

"Your conclusion?"

"Pushkin does not know that she is gone. Nobody
told him. The president of Russia is out of the loop. Moscow is not running the show."

**C**OLONEL **T**OM **M**ARKEY ushered Kyle Swanson into a chilly and dim room at the NATO Cooperative Cyber-Defence Centre of Excellence. This was his domain, a never-never land of computer hackers, programmers, nerds, theoreticians and developers who pulled strings of electrical DNA from the air and wove secret computer projects that ordinary mortals probably would never see. Parts of the work would eventually leach into the public domain, but the Centre was primarily Europe's electronic war room. "Welcome to my world," Markey said with pride.

"We're running out of time, Tom." Swanson was not in the mood for a show-and-tell computer seminar.

"In real-world time, you are right, but within these walls, the clock is not really much of a factor. Have a seat over there." Markey pointed to a row of chairs positioned around a silvery table. The colonel took the chair at the head of the display board, flanked by two military assistants, one each from Latvia and France.

"Now, Kyle, what did you tell Atkins about your personal preference for handling the situation at the bridge? Do you recall?"

"Of course. I wanted to point a laser at the bridge and blow it up with a load of smart bombs. The answer was negative because I probably couldn't get down there in time with the needed manpower support and equipment."

"Right." Markey said. "We conquer time and distance in here on a regular basis, so let's first get you in place. Captain Vauban? Captain Augulis? Please build the Narva bridge."

The shiny tabletop began to hum with a low vibration, and light blue lines rose from the edges and divided into squares that shimmered with flashes of energy and formed a visible plate that floated a foot above the surface of the table. "That is our canvas, Kyle. Now we paint," Markey said.

A column of blue numbers scrolled in the air, and a blizzard of photographs slashed along one side. It reminded Swanson of the calibrations he saw in the scope of his Excalibur sniper rifle. The computer was thinking.

"We are creating a hologram. With unimaginably exact measurements and images gathered over the years, we have every inch of the Narva bridge on file, almost from every possible angle. Other bridges, other things, other places, too, of course."

"I thought you guys just hacked e-mails."

"Cyberwarfare can take many forms, my friend. Snooping on e-traffic is not our purpose."

The floating image took shape, squares and rectangles flashed into being, found position and shrank to pixels, which then were sharpened until finally the image of the Narva bridge hung before Swanson, correct in every detail. "Amazing. Nice picture, but so what?"

"Wait for it. Captain Vauban, proceed to real time, if you please."

"Yes, sir," replied the French officer. He slid his fingers across a flat-surface pad that took the place of a normal keyboard and directed new instructions into the holographic interface.

There was more shimmering and the image smoothed out even more until Kyle realized with a start that he was seeing it exactly as it was, with such clarity that even the water beneath was rippling. Two men in police uniforms walked along an edge.

"The Russians closed it this morning, Colonel," said the Latvian. "That's why there is no traffic."

Markey nodded. "Very well. Now, Kyle, take that pen from the holder before you. Click it on and a laser will fire up that is slaved through our system to the image."

Swanson pushed his thumb down on a small bulge on the titanium-encased laser. A bright, emerald beam popped to life from the end. He danced it across the bridge, a bright green lance of light with a small circle as a pointer. "Are you saying that I can paint the bridge from right here?"

The colonel laughed. "Exactly. Wherever you rest the point, the bombs will strike with precision. I suggest that we now call NATO and tell them we are ready on this end. All they have to do is scramble a plane suited up with a package of GBU-12s."

"Son of a bitch," Kyle muttered.

IVANOGROD, RUSSIA

Levchenko was back outside, having found his headquarters a claustrophobic hive of busy people, while out
in the open, he felt the energy of his mighty force pulling at its leash. The night had been short and gloomy,
but had provided the needed cover to move the pieces
into their final jump-off positions. The fog and haze had
cleared to give him a better view of the city of Narva
sitting there, waiting for him to come and take it.

As always, the situation demanded late changes. That
damned fool mayor had let the American spy escape and
gotten himself captured in the process! The chief of police had personally called Levchenko several hours ago
with that news and for instructions about what to do
with him. For months, the Russians had been inserting
Spetsnaz soldiers into the security forces across the
river, and the chief was a Russian by birth and on the
payroll.

How much did the spy know? The police chief reported that she had been isolated in a holding cell prior
to the escape. The mayor then came on the phone and
promised she knew nothing of the morning's plan. He
had been forced by a mysterious and murderous agent
to fetch her. Two officers were dead. Levchenko detected
the lie in the nervous voice, but he had to analyze the
situation as it stood at the moment.

It didn't really matter. The mayor should still come
across the bridge at nine o'clock. One hour from now.
The idiot could be dealt with later.

As the Russian watched from the rampart of the fortress on his side of the border, he saw some dots appear
above the western horizon. He grabbed his binoculars

and zoomed in as a flight of four Estonian Army choppers rushed in to land, and soldiers popped out and formed into ranks. He matched that move by ordering a platoon of assault troops to the front of the line to provide support for the advancing tanks. The police chief would try to interfere with the Estonian troops over there, but that was a losing proposition in the long term. No matter, thought the general. His forces would brush that light force aside like wolves going through a family of rabbits.

The biggest decision he had made that morning was to keep all of this new information to himself. Spreading it to higher levels might cause fear in Moscow, and he did not want any interference from afar. He was the commander on the ground, and he would command.

## THE SPIRIT OF KANSAS

Lizzie Borden and Calamity Jane had been in the air for hours after taking off from Royal Air Force Fairford base in Gloucestershire, England, and were loitering in a racetrack pattern at forty thousand feet before getting their final instructions. They were the chosen ones. "Fuck, yeah," exclaimed U.S. Air Force Major Elizabeth "Lizzie" Sullivan, the thirty-four-year-old command pilot of the huge B-2 bomber named the *Spirit of Kansas.*

"Watch your language, bitch. There are ladies present," shot back the only other member of the crew, copilot Captain Janie "Jane" Dean, as she started punching in the target coordinates and other data.

This would be a relatively short hop. Two days ago,

they had been at the home base of the 509th Bomb Wing in Whiteman Air Force Base outside of Knob Noster, Missouri. Despite their notorious nicknames, the two officers were among the best in the squadron. Sullivan, who held a graduate mathematics degree from the Massachusetts Institute of Technology, lived alone following a divorce and had no problem preparing for the flight to England. Dean, a Georgia Tech graduate with a master's degree in electrical engineering, had to line up a babysitter for her kids because her husband was also a B-2 pilot and was off somewhere else in the world for the entire week. Reaching the RAF Fairford forward-operating location had been little more than a long, easy glide for the two friends. Being smaller than men, they had more space in the tight cockpit, and the plane had carried no ordnance; it was simply moving closer to a potential battlefield.

That changed overnight in England, and by the time Sullivan and Dean strapped in early that morning, the old stealth bird was toting a load of eighty precision-guided bombs that weighed five hundred pounds apiece. Each could be used for a different target on the same mission and they'd fall before enemy radar even knew the B-2 was there. There had been jokes back in Missouri about this unique girl's-night-out mission.

When she smoothly carved the B-2 toward Estonia, Sullivan recited the old singsong verse on the private intercom, as she did on every attack run: "Lizzie Borden took an axe . . . "

Dean picked it up as she ran the numbers, ". . . And gave the Russians forty whacks."

"And when she saw what she had done . . . " Sullivan

eased the throttle forward and the bat-winged aircraft rose easily upstairs to a higher altitude and flowed to a speed of over six hundred miles per hour.

Calamity Jane studied her full-color flight instrumentation system to adjust for the go-to-war mode, and finished, ". . . She gave the Russians forty-one."


## NARVA, ESTONIA

Gunfire. Levchenko was at the Russian edge of the bridge when sporadic shots cracked like whip-snaps on the other side. Excellent, he thought. Excellent! Ivan Strakov had predicted that federal troops of Estonia would come in and clash with the Narva cops whose real loyalty lay with Moscow. That would only legitimize the official position in the future propaganda blitz that the other side, the Estonians, had fired first. All the Russians did was to answer the plea of the city's legitimately elected mayor to stop the attempted military takeover of Narva by the Estonian troops. Levchenko could explain at any future hearing that he moved in to declare martial law in the embattled zone so as to protect civilian lives while cooler heads settled the results of the city's free and fair vote.

He turned and saw the first Armata tank was only twenty-five yards behind him, with the assault commandoes in position on both sides of the road, ready to dash across. Radar was showing nothing but the mothlike dots of helicopters in the sky, but the antiaircraft missiles became hot and ready. All he needed now was the invitation, the final spark.

Mayor Konstantin Pran was now in sight, scurrying

behind a phalanx of Narva cops. The shooting was over by the Town Hall area, and the police had spirited him out through a rear corridor. He was breathing hard from the physical exertion, but could see Colonel General Levchenko standing at the other end of the bridge, watching through binoculars, waiting for him. Pran waved with a white envelope that contained a letter on official city stationery, in which he sought the protection of his Russian comrades, along with a copy of the Worker's Party resolution for Narva to secede from Estonia and rejoin the beloved Motherland. He was sweating and wiped his brow and face with a handkerchief as he hurried along.

"Bounty Hunter to Shady Lady," Kyle Swanson said in Tallinn, where he was watching the hologram. He had no microphone nor headset, but simply conversed with empty air that was alive with communications. Swanson recognized the tubby man approaching the Estonian edge of the bridge as the mayor. Russian men and armor were waiting, but still not moving from the other end. "Bounty Hunter to Shady Lady."

"Shady Lady to Bounty Hunter." The controlled voice of Captain Janie Dean came back crisp and sharp through the cyberwarfare network.

Swanson took his green laser and put the little circle right on the shiny head of Mayor Konstantin Pran, easily tracking him as he came to a stop and adjusted his suit, and then resumed his travel in a slow walk. "Bounty Hunter to Shady Lady. Execute! Execute!"

Calamity Jane locked her weapons to the computer data feed that was flooding up from Tallinn and looked over to Lizzie Borden, who nodded her approval with a bob of her black helmet. The B-2 released four GBU-30 bombs that dropped like anvils for a second, then flexed their fins as the internal navigation and the global-positioning guidance system took control. At that point, the weapons began a highly accurate and irreversible power dive that lasted almost a full minute.

Swanson had a fleeting thought that this was the ultimate sniper hit. He could see the target, but the target did not even know he was in the crosshairs. And while Kyle worshiped his .50-caliber Excalibur sniper rifle, a B-2 stealth was a no-brainer upgrade. Even if those four bombs missed, it had another seventy-six ready to go with the flip of a switch. At present, each of the extra bombs was being electronically locked onto individual Russian tanks and vehicles arranged so neatly at the eastern end. But that was not Swanson's job nor his decision. His green circle remained right atop Mayor Pran, who was a quarter-way out on the span.

The mayor tugged again at his vest and straightened his tie. He was making history with each stride. The sporadic gunfire in Narva had become irrelevant to him. In about a minute, his dream would become a reality. Levchenko put aside his binoculars and stood at parade rest, waiting for the civilian to make the last bit of distance and formally ask for his help.

In Tallinn's cyberwar center, Colonel Markey counted down from five . . . four . . .

The floating hologram shook in a storm of static as all four bombs hit with eyeblink simultaneous detonations. On the ground, the joint cities of Narva and Ivanogrod jumped with the dramatic force of the shock and concussions. Old stones flew in every direction as flames flashed, spooling clouds of smoke enveloped the area, and a giant spout of water erupted from the river. The computers more than a hundred miles away soon regained their satellite video feed, ironed it through the programs and solidified the real-time image again.

Through the debris and smoke, Kyle saw that the entire western half of the bridge had disappeared. A gaping hole was being filled by the river with a powerful whirlpool of water. There was no trace of Mayor Konstantin Pran. Swanson moved the laser across the bridge to the Russian side and saw that men were down and vehicles, even tanks, had been pushed around like toys. The officer who had been standing out in front had taken the full force of the sudden explosions and had disappeared. But the Russian half of the bridge remained intact, untouched by the precise tornado of bombs. The planned attack died in its cradle.

"Bounty Hunter to Shady Lady."

"Shady Lady to Bounty Hunter," responded Calamity Jane.

"You may depart your station. Many thanks."

"Anytime," replied Lizzy Borden, and headed her B-2 back to England.

## ABOARD THE *VAGABOND*

I**T TOOK A** week for normality to return. There had been no war, although it had been a very close call. Kyle Swanson had experienced a new side of combat that seemed to have come straight out of a Hollywood special-effects studio. Drones and cameras and robots and gigantic computing power were the tools of future combat. Even the stealth B-2 was so obsolete that only twenty of them were left on active service. The best bomber in the sky was little more than a flying dinosaur. Eventually gadgets would replace pilots in the heavens and grunts down on the dirt. Creepy-crawlies would roam the battleground. Hadn't he himself just blown up a bridge and killed the bad guy, or guys, while being nowhere near the actual combat? He looked out over the sharp bow of the *Vagabond* and took another gulp of cold beer. Lethal collections of wires and transistors would replace the guy on the ground with a gun. Nah. Not going to happen.

Everybody on the planet was cocked and locked after the bridge incident until President Vladimir Pushkin blinked, called President Christopher Thompson and lied like a thief. The man who headed the Russian government offered that he had not been kept accurately informed of what was happening in Narva because a previously trusted general had gone rogue. Pushkin insisted that after the earlier presidential telephone conversation, he had sought out the true facts and learned how Colonel General Valery Levchenko, acting without authorization from the general staff or the Kremlin, had decided to turn the routine Operation Hermitage war game into an invasion of Estonia. General Levchenko had, by some miracle, survived the bombing of the bridge and was now under arrest, although he was in grave condition from wounds. Doctors were pessimistic about whether he would survive to face trial.

Thompson responded that his own information had also become more clear. Apparently the mayor of Narva was trying to secede from Estonia. The man's body had been recovered from the rubble of the western half of the bridge and the federal government in Tallinn had invalidated the local council's decision. The rebellious local police had been temporarily replaced by NATO troops.

The Russian president commented that he considered that to be an internal matter for the Estonian government.

Thompson, in response, canceled DefCon Four and resumed DefCon Two.

Pushkin declared that the situation had stabilized all along the border, even in the northern climes of the Arctic Circle. The traitorous Levchenko had been in command of that area, too. Troops were told to stand down.

"One last thing, Vladimir," said President Thompson.

"We have this defector, a colonel Ivan Strakov, who, apparently, had watched the success and celebrity of Edward Snowden and hoped to get the same treatment from us. He was working with Levchenko to take the Baltics . . . against your expressed policy."

"Christopher, are you asking for an exchange: Snowden for Strakov?" The Russian was curious.

"Not at all. You can have Strakov back for free, if you want him."

Pushkin chuckled. "No deal, Mr. President. We have no use for such a worm. Do with him what you wish."

"Then let us get back to work, President Pushkin. I've got an angry Congress to deal with on budget matters."

"Have a good day, President Thompson."

The colorful change of command ceremony in Brussels had gone without a hitch and Fred Ravensdale turned over his keys as deputy supreme allied commander for NATO with proper pomp and ceremony. Afterward, he was helicoptered out to the *Vagabond* for a few days of rest on the way home to England and his new job with CJTF 10. The yacht would cruise leisurely across the Strait of Dover, out into open water, and then up the Thames River to deposit everybody on the piers of London, and take a bit of time doing so.

The *Vagabond* was already swimming in deep water, headed due north, and Swanson joined the small group on the rear sun deck. Jeff and Ravensdale were side by side in high-back chairs at a long table spread with snacks and drinks for afternoon tea. Trevor Dash, the captain, was chewing a cookie and giving his passengers the current schedule. They would continue into the fringes of the North Sea overnight, then head east to London the next morning. Easy seas all the way. Should dock about this time tomorrow, he said. Kyle pulled up a chair on the other side of the table.

"Watch out for icebergs, Trevor." Swanson dug out another beer. Afternoon tea was not his thing.

"Thank you for that vital warning, Kyle. We would never have thought about that on our own. I shall see you gentlemen at dinner." Dash toured a lap around the deck to check details, then went up to the bridge. Privately, he spread the word for all crew members to confine their work for the next hour to the forward decks. No exceptions. If asked why, he told them to keep a sharp watch for icebergs. No one was to even look aft until further orders.

Jeff and Kyle kept the conversation vague for a while, talking about the never-ending and expensive American election cycles and contrasting them to the quick, cheap British voting rules. Cornwell looked over at his guest and asked, "Are you thinking about getting into politics, Freddie? When you retire?"

"Absolutely not," the general replied. "No desire at all."

"Too bad. Government needs good men."

Kyle put his beer on the white tablecloth and leaned back, seeing that the sky was blue forever. "I have a question, General Ravensdale, if you don't mind."

"Ask away," Ravensdale replied. He was in an excellent mood. It was finished. All over. Nothing had happened. His blood pressure was back to normal and last night he had slept a full seven hours. The only aching point was that Arial was not answering her cell phone. But now he was aboard a huge luxurious yacht, dressed in relaxed seagoing whites, from boat shoes to an old pair of cricket slacks and a linen shirt with sleeves rolled up to his elbows. It was nice to just be among friends and have a good time.

"Well, when I got back to the boat a few days ago as things heated up, I had a call from a friend at our Department of State. He says that you called the Finnish Intelligence Service back when all this first began and gave them my arrival date, place and time. That started the ball rolling. Why make that call?"

He saw the lines tighten slightly around the eyes and mouth as Ravensdale coughed a little embarrassed laugh. "We have gone over all of this before, Kyle. I simply was making sure that you met with Strakov as soon as possible. You were the only person to whom he would speak."

Swanson smiled. "Yes. That's right. So I was thrown out of Finland the very next day to be sure I got there in a hurry."

"Just so. And you did!" Sir Jeff took a triangle of cucumber and cream cheese sandwich as he watched the verbal exchange. "Played hardball with us, Freddie."

"Just business." The general shrugged.

"Then a few days later, when my team was down in Kaliningrad, I watched the Russians reposition their big guns until all were pointing south, toward Poland," said Kyle. "No firebase would ever bet all of its firepower on a single azimuth without good reason, and our girl Anneli mentioned there was a rush of last-minute orders that she could not understand. Then the guard was doubled on our escape route and a BTR-80 was activated. At first, I thought they were just showing off for the arriving two-star, but I was wrong." He looked directly at Ravensdale. "They knew we were coming."

The man shifted his position. "We must never under-estimate the Russian's intelligence network. As I recall from our earlier conversation, you worried that there were a lot of unknown parts to that job. They moved quickly, but not fast enough. You still got your man; good for you."

"Thanks. I had help. Then a short time later, the Russians kidnapped our spy, Calico, down in Narva. I got to thinking, which is never good for a jarhead marine like me, and is why I leave that stuff to officers. Anyway, Anneli had accidentally dropped the code name of Calico during the quick briefing I gave aboard this ship. Coincidences add up, General Ravensdale."

"Kyle, are you saying that I am responsible for these situations? Preposterous." The general was feeling an angry heat rising at the base of his neck.

Swanson got up from his chair and drank some beer. "Let me continue before you get too high and mighty. Before coming out to the *Vagabond*, I had a final meeting with Ivan Strakoff."

"Excellent. Did he provide more information on the northern situation? I would be interested in anything he said."

"Not exactly." Kyle smirked. "I told him the decision had been made in both Washington and Moscow that he was a worthless piece of shit, and had no information that we wanted. The man was a master manipulator, and just as he had pretended to be a sniper to infiltrate my sniper course many years ago, he was now flying a false flag to masquerade as a cyberwar expert. He had been trained by computer experts just enough to be dangerous, but Colonel Markey nailed him right away on the technical stuff."

"The man was nothing but a fraud," said Sir Jeff. "He was trying to maneuver us into a full war to take the Baltic States."

"Thank God we stopped that." Ravensdale could not stand up because the table was in the way.

"Anyway, I had the pleasure of telling Ivan that the good news was that he was not going to go rot in Guantánamo. We're a bit overcrowded down there and President Thompson wants to close the place. So I informed Ivan that we were turning him over to Turkey, where he would be kept in a dungeon for the rest of his life."

Ravensdale was fighting to remain calm. "That is a fitting punishment for his kind," he said. "Another good job by you, Kyle."

"But Ivan didn't give up easily. He said that he had something else to trade, something really important. At first, I thought he was just blowing more smoke, but I told him if it was worthwhile, we might still get him into Guantánamo. And guess what? He earned his orange jumpsuit and a ticket to sunny Cuba instead of rotting in Istanbul!"

Ravensdale was very quiet. He politely lifted the china teacup with its saucer and took a sip.

"He gave up *you*, General Ravensdale."

"What poppycock! Cornwell, are you just going to sit there and listen to this man spew insults at an old friend?"

"Actually, he brings up some interesting points," said Sir Jeff. "Kyle, please continue."

Swanson was ready. "So investigators questioned some of your NATO compatriots, who said you continued pushing hard to transfer troops to the north even after the danger to Estonia became obvious to everyone else. Even when your boss ordered everything to remain in place!"

"That was my new job, you fool!"

"The final straw was when your staff members revealed your new German mistress. Even a quick look at her finances and background by the computer boys and girls turned up links to the Russians. Arial Printas was arrested last night and, just like Ivan, made a deal to save her own ass." Swanson paused for a breath. He could hardly believe this trail of facts that showed how a man of impeccable reputation had sold out.

"I barely know the woman!" It was a poor and obvious bluff.

"She had the whole thing on video, General. She handed it over."

Ravensdale finally fell silent, rooted in position by his guilt.

"You were the mole all along, Freddie-boy. You have been in Moscow's pocket for years. God only knows how much damage you have done. I should kill you right where you stand."

Sir Jeff gave a sharp grunt. "No, Kyle. Leave him alone. Freddie has been my friend for many years, and we will deal with this. Leave us for a few minutes. Please?"

Swanson stalked off to the stern, propped against the rail with his back to the dark waters of the North Sea, and watched the two older men still sitting there, drinking fuckin' tea and talking as if nothing unusual had just taken place. He opened a storage box.

"Well, now, Freddie. It does seem that you are in a

bit of jam, doesn't it?" Sir Jeff kept his voice low. "Traitor and all that. I never would have believed it of you. I saw some of the video. Astonishing."

Ravensdale felt some of the tension leave him as Swanson stayed far away. "I never meant for it to happen. They trapped me and I foolishly played along, hoping not to do harm until they went away."

Jeff clapped his hands together once, a sound of finality, then put them in his lap. "Let us resolve this situation, then. You cannot escape from this yacht, and you will embarrass the queen and government if you are publicly exposed. Not to mention smearing the army and especially our beloved SAS. You really are quite a disgrace, old man."

"Does that mean Swanson is going to kill me out here? Just dump my body overboard?"

"That really all depends upon you, Freddie. We can do it that way if you choose, but let me offer an alternative." Jeff lifted up a Glock 17 Gen4 handgun that had been beneath his hip and placed it on the table. The weapon was loaded with a single 9mm round, a close-quarters bullet that would explode on impact and not go through the target.

"Take this and go over by the railing, put it to your head and pull the trigger, Freddie. It ends there. The official story will be that you suffered a heart attack while on the way to London and we buried you at sea. A memorial service with full honors will be held in London."

"Swanson or myself, eh?"

"Yes. Quite. But please, let's just get on with it, shall we?"

"Suppose I shoot you instead?" Ravenscroft had not yet touched the weapon.

"That, I fear, is not possible." Jeff pulled out a second Glock. "This one has a full magazine." He lost his smile and commanded, "Go."

Ravensdale stood and brushed off his trousers and straightened his shirt. One look aft showed him Swanson standing there holding an M-4 rifle. Jeff was pointing his own pistol. The general let out a long sigh, looked around, smelled the ocean, heard the gulls and picked up the gun. It was only four strides to the rail, and he took them, then with a fluid motion, he brought up the pistol and blew his brains out.

Swanson trotted back just as Trevor Dash arrived from the bridge. Together, they picked up the body and hurled it into the passing water. It landed with a big splash, bobbed in the wake, then vanished from sight. Jeff reached for a cookie and Swanson and Dash sat beside him. A crewman came back and flushed away the bloody debris with a high-powered hose before it could stain the deck or the side of the yacht.

"So, are you ready to fly back to Washington? We've got a business to run, you know." Jeff did not seem disturbed, but why should he be? Ravensdale had sold out his country and gotten the fate he had so richly earned.

"I was talking to Marty Atkins about that last night," said Kyle. "My original mission was to take out two jihadi fools, one in Rome and the other in Egypt. I had to postpone the second one when Ivan Strakov popped onto the screen and really screwed things up. Now I want to finish that assignment. It shouldn't take more than a few days."

Jeff Cornwell closed his eyes and rested beneath the warm sky. "I understand. Get back as soon as you can."

"Yeah," Kyle said. "I will."

Read on for an excerpt from the next book by
Gunnery Sgt. Jack Coughlin with Donald A. Davis

# IN THE CROSSHAIRS

Coming soon from St. Martin's Press

## PROLOGUE

**THE CIA SNIPER** team huddled unseen in a shadowy crevice that had been created when an earthquake scrambled the Pamir Mountains of Afghanistan four years earlier. Luke Gibson and Nicky Marks were eyes-on the scruffy home of old Mahfouz al-Rashidi, warlord of the Wakham Corridor.

They had been there for almost twenty-four hours, having been dropped by a helicopter onto a high plateau six kilometers away and then humping the hills beneath a cold and cloudless black sky spangled with bright stars. The terrain was so silvery that the night-vision goggles were not needed. The chopper's racket which had pounded their ears during the flight had given way to silence as their ears adjusted, and all of their senses finally clicked into sharpness. Along their quiet way, the two men dressed in local garb made frequent stops just to look and listen and smell the surroundings. A dog in the nearby village of Girdiwal yelped as if being whipped. The stalk was sweaty work, even on the chilly night, but they had found the predetermined slot without difficulty, converted it into a hide in the scrub bush, did a soft radio check and were burrowed into position and with rifles zeroed and telecoms set before the sun rose. It was no big deal. The pair of seasoned veterans had been in this area before, for a CIA safe house had been set up there many years ago. It could not be used this time so the strike could not be traced back to them. The loose shale covering hard rock on which they lay was as familiar as an old couch.

About 0800, there was a buzz in the heavens and a lightweight AS 550 Fennec scout helicopter belonging to the Pakistani Army popped over the horizon. Nicky heard it first and pointed as the dot brew larger and the bird found a landing spot near the front gate of the home. The snipers had been expecting it, as had Mahfouz al-Rashidi, for this was a regular payday for the master of the Wakham.

"Right on time," Gibson said softly as he watched the camouflaged rotary-wing aircraft shut down, its rotors revolving slower and slower. An officer climbed out and was escorted through the gate while a soldier and the pilot unloaded freight and lugged it in.

Nicky Marks unzipped a satchel that he had brought with him and powered up an electronic array of miniaturized snooper technology, pushing buttons to start recording. "We are green across the board, Luke. The audio is five-by-five and we should be getting a picture any minute."

Al-Rashidi put down his cup of mint tea when heard the sweep of the blades, anticipating the homage that would come to him on this special day. The host welcomed the courier from Islamabad and bade him to sit and visit with the family, the custom concerning strangers.

Outside, Luke Gibson watched the swirling dust settle from the helicopter landing to gauge the wind speed between the hide and the house. He was as still as a sleeping snake. Nothing bothered him.

The warlord had a peculiar relationship with ISI, and it had been fruitful. The Islamabad government provided cash in return for information about what was happening along the long valley in neighboring Afghanistan, particularly at the point where it met the closed Chinese border. The first gift from the officer today was a black nylon suitcase filled with shrink-wrapped bricks of American greenback dollars. The second was a huge new flat-screen television set with a powerful receiving capability that could pick up broadcasts from around the world, almost everything from the Sky Network to Netflix, plus a built-in CD player. The technician, a lowly enlisted man, was ignored as he set up the amazing equipment, burying his real purpose in the maze of wires and controls that only he understood.

The TV set, the receiver and the suitcase also worked the other way, and contained a hive of mini-microphones and sophisticated spyware. Within a few minutes, Nicky Marks and Luke Gibson could see and hear as if they were sitting inside with Mahfouz al-Rashidi and his sons.

The old guy had an unkempt beard and looked comfortable in loose trousers beneath a long tunic. He was totally at ease, feeling quite pleasant, not just about the courier and the gifts, but because all four of his sons had come together for the first time in months to celebrate their father's 70th birthday. He also had two daughters, both devout and placed beneath the veil early in their teens, then married off to worthy men and gone from his life. Soon, the ISI officer, his men and the helicopter were gone, and the warlord turned to the business at hand. The TV set was not even turned on, for it was a mere entertainment trinket and of no true substance, just a gift from an appreciative customer to mark the first day of Muharram, the start of the Islamic new year.

The four young men sat with him in a circle, paying close attention to his words. Together, the family of Mahfouz al-Rashidi comprised a *jihadi* terrorist cell whose five members were known only to each other. As a family, there was no worry of betrayal.

The clan originally came from the Egyptian intelligentsia in long-ago years when Islam existed in the shadows and, in the opinion of the old man, the people strove not to exalt God as was proper, but to be ever more like the infidel Westerners. Had not his own father and uncle earned wealth from an international import-export business created by their own forefathers along the Nile? Mahfouz had been born into a life a privilege just after the war in 1949. But for the grace of the Prophet, praise be unto him, he also would have been lost to the secular temptations available in his formative years.

Instead, he had puzzled out deep meanings of the Koran, befriended radicals mullahs and fell beneath the hypnotic sway of Osama bin Laden, al-Qaeda and the dream of Jihad. It was with Osama's advice that al-Rashidi migrated with his family away from secular Egypt to this forsaken place on what once had been a trade route to China. That heathen nation had closed the border at their end of the Wakham Corridor, making it a dead end for official trade, but creating a thriving black-market haven, a valuable pipeline for information, and a prosperous place for the cultivation of hillside hectares of opium poppies.

It provided priceless isolation in which al-Rashidi raised his own den of lions. His religious mentors and the billionaire bin Laden kept him going as a special project, almost cut off from the world, tediously making ready for a strike at some unknown future date when the tawdry Western world would cower in fear.

"Tell me of our purpose." The old man addressed his eldest son, Mohammed.

"To destroy America," came the answer. Mohammed was a forty-year-old architect who was born in 1965 and now lived in Paris.

"Ali. Our mission?" The watery dark eyes of the old man passed to the second son, a year younger.

"To grind fear into the heart of the United States! To make them eat ashes!" There was no hesitation from the skilled attorney who was a prosecuting lawyer for the Afghan government.

The old man nodded again. Very good. "How do we do that, Kalil?"

"Follow the teachings of Osama bin Laden and make a memorable strike to glorify the Prophet, whose name be praised." Ali rocked back and forth, as he had done as a child while memorizing the Koran. He was employed as a petrochemical engineer by a British company and spent much of the year aboard North Sea rigs.

"And who among us shall do this thing?" He turned to the last of the four.

The youngest spoke with the same certainty of his brothers. "Why, Father, that will be me," replied the smiling and clean-shaven Stephen Rush, who ran a reputable industrial real estate business in Houston, Texas.

The father felt as though he might burst with joy, and rolled his eyes heavenward as he said softly, "Allah be praised." It had been a very long and hard to raise this family beyond the reach of so many enemies, keep them pure, educate them in fine universities and place them in strategic occupations. To sacrifice them all simultaneously was a tragic decision, but it was a promise he had made to Osama. He knew that after the simultaneous attacks were made in Texas, Pakistan, France and London, the honored house of al-Rashidi would be hunted down like rabid dogs and extinguished from the face of the earth. They would reunite as martyrs in paradise. Who could ask for more?

Gibson decided he had heard and seen enough of the Rashidi boys. They had just confirmed the intelligence gathered over the past few years. "Put up our radio link," he said over his shoulder to Nicky Marks without taking he eye from the powerful spotting scope that was poking through the tumbled foliage. When Marks confirmed the encrypted signal was available, Gibson said, "Tell them it's a go on this end." Then he made some final minor scope adjustments to his old-school M24 (SWS) sniper rifle and chambered a $7.62 \times 51$mm NATO cartridge.

The house, five hundred meters distant, loomed large in the magnified image, and Gibson scanned left to right, then up and down. Al-Rashidi should have heeded the Prophet's warning against becoming arrogant, for it had been his undoing. The Egyptian was proud of his relationship with Osama bin Laden, who had left notes about him and the special project in his private files. Unfortunately, when an American commando team killed

Osama and found that information, the careful and loyal Mahfouz al-Rashidi stood exposed. The little warlord in the small house in the no-name wasted valley became a person of interest. He had reached too far.

Then he was groomed as carefully as a teen-aged girl tends her hair and eye makeup. Money began to flow in exchange for information about who was doing what in his valley. He liked the new power and importance and his sons had been happy to get out of the Wakham, with money to spend. Mohammed developed a liking for the whores of Paris. Ali enjoyed the perfumed boys of Islamabad. Kalil was up to his neck in gambling debts to London bookies, and young Stephen Rush, whose real name was Syed, was a cocaine freakazoid. The boys had all gone Western, but told their *jihadi* father what he wanted to hear, not what was necessarily true. All hated having to come back to this crude shack and were about as capable of planning a coordinated attack as a herd of turtles.

No matter, thought Gibson, who knew their backgrounds. It was time to end this game and take all five of them off the map. He slowed his breathing and steadied the rifle. Forty-thousand feet above him, an MQ-9 Reaper drone had been loitering for two hours in sky circles on 66-foot-wings under the control of a pilot and a sensor operator back in the United States. When Nicky passed along the permission from Luke, the drone slid into a straight path over the target and jumped up as it released a pair of GBU-38 Joint Direct Attack Munitions, smart bombs that weighed 500 pounds apiece. The JDAMs rode the laser beam flawlessly directly through the roof of al-Rashidi's home and exploded with a thunderclap that rolled far down the valley.

Gibson had been expecting it, but it was still quite a show. With the thud of detonations, the building actually blew apart in a canopy of debris and dirt. A tower of smoke rolled up and fire flashed horizontally. He kept his eye on the scope as the concussion pushed against the mountains.

He had been doing this kind of thing for a long time, and it still surprised him that anyone could live through such an attack, but invariably someone did. Even Hitler walked away from a bomb blast that killed or wounded almost everybody around him in a closed room. And sure enough, down in the smoking rubble, a figure stirred. An arm was raised, not much more than a claw in Gibson's scope, and then fell, and rose again. A man was digging out. The head emerged. It looked like Kalil, but the sniper couldn't be certain because the face was so badly burned. It really made no difference. The torso wiggled and struggled and emerged from the ruins. It slowly stood, holding onto a torn wooden beam for support, and Luke Gibson shot him through the chest. The target fell and there was no more movement.

Gibson pulled the rifle back. "Tell them mission completed." As Marks passed along the message to send the drone back to its base and bring in the extraction chopper. There was no hurry to get away. No cavalry would be riding to the rescue for the al-Rashidi gang. Luke pulled out a packet of chocolate, took a sweet bite and thought to himself, *Happy New Year, Mahfouz, old buddy.* That thought was followed quickly by, *Damn, I'm good at this.*